D0459384

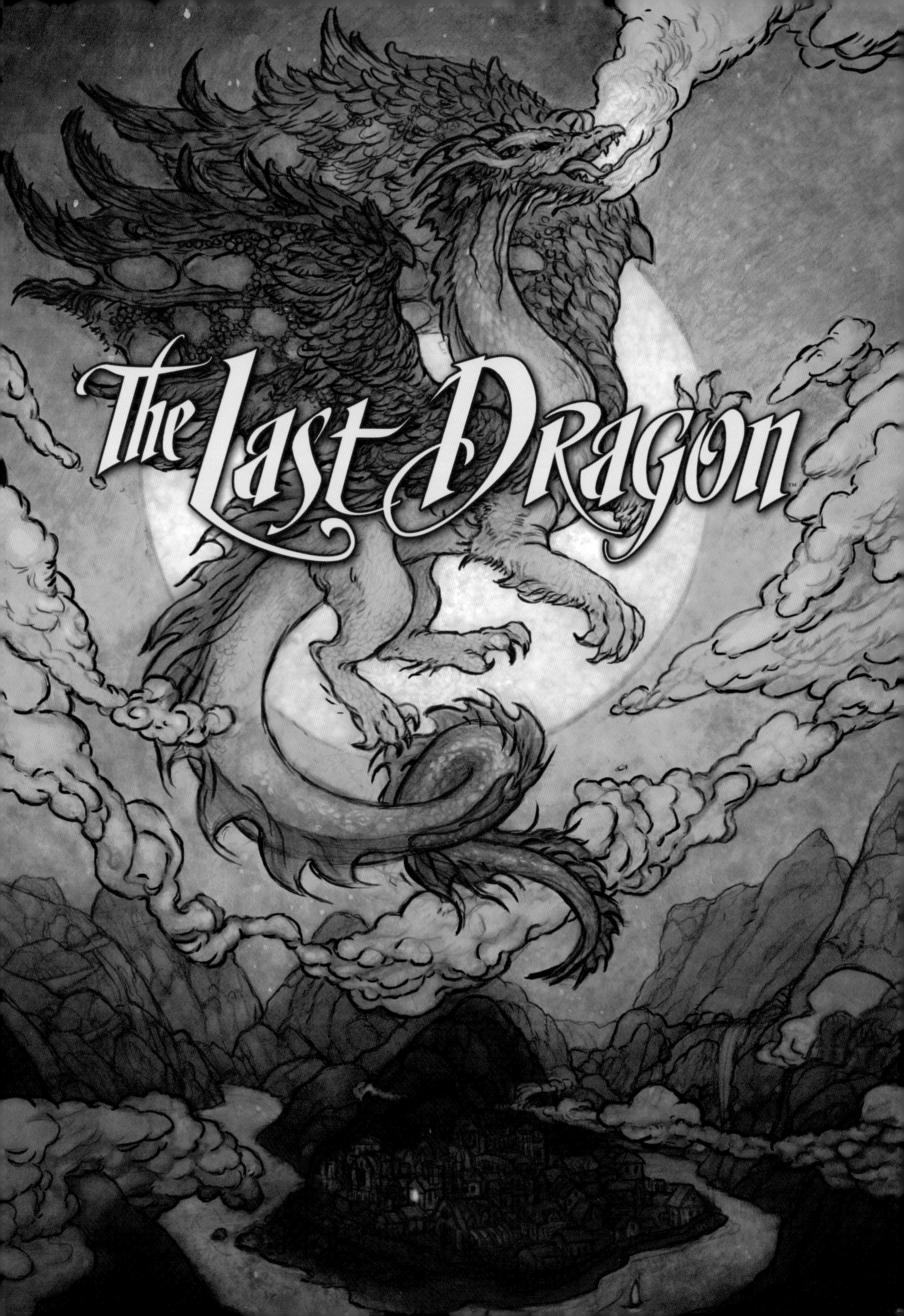
The Last Dragon™

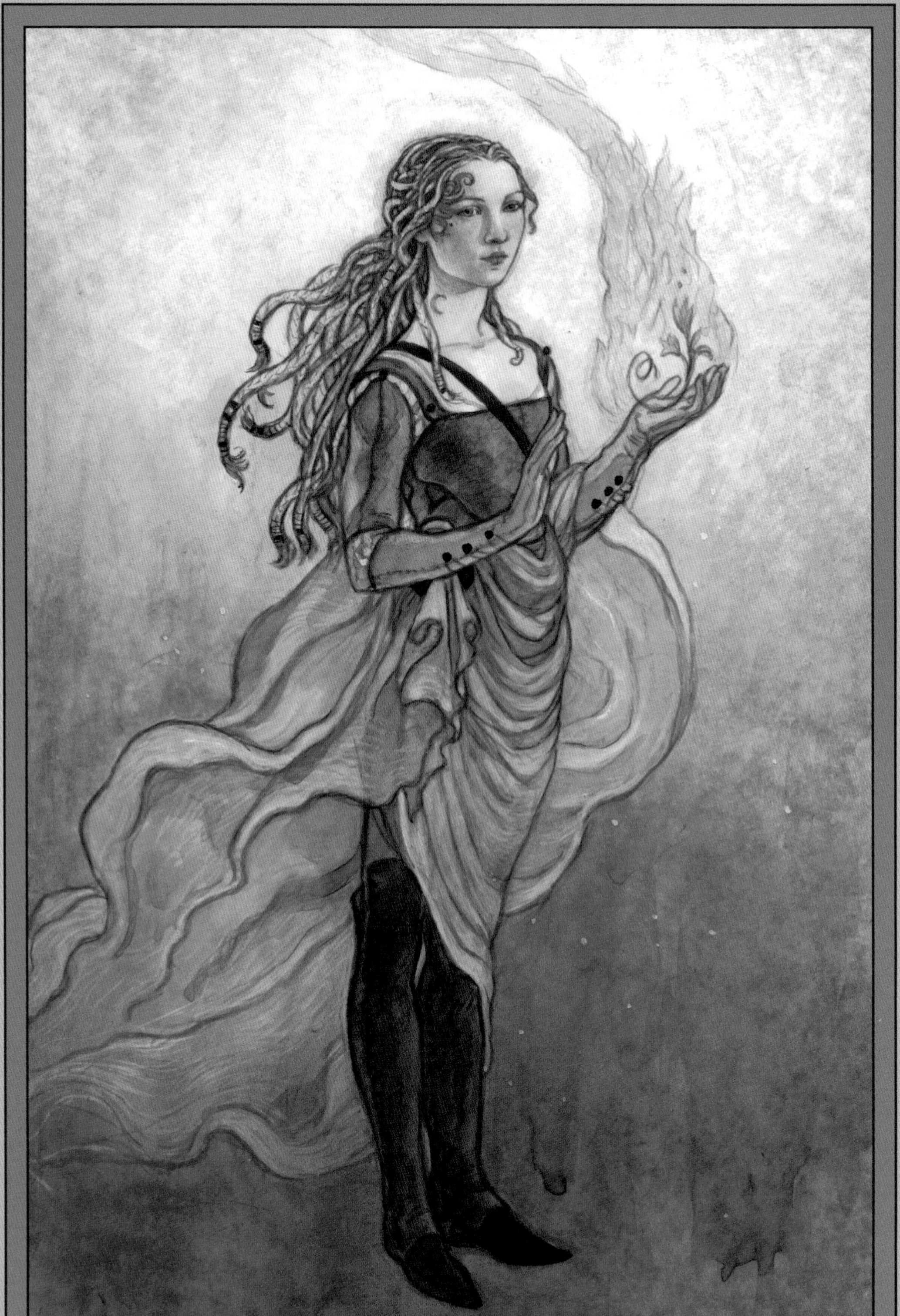
RGM.

The Last Dragon

Created by
Jane Yolen and Rebecca Guay

Story by
Jane Yolen

Art by
Rebecca Guay

Letters by
Clem Robins

Editor
Rachel Edidin

Designer
Kat Larson

Assistant Editor
John Schork

Publisher
Mike Richardson

Special thanks to
Chris Horn and Rob Simpson

DARK HORSE BOOKS®

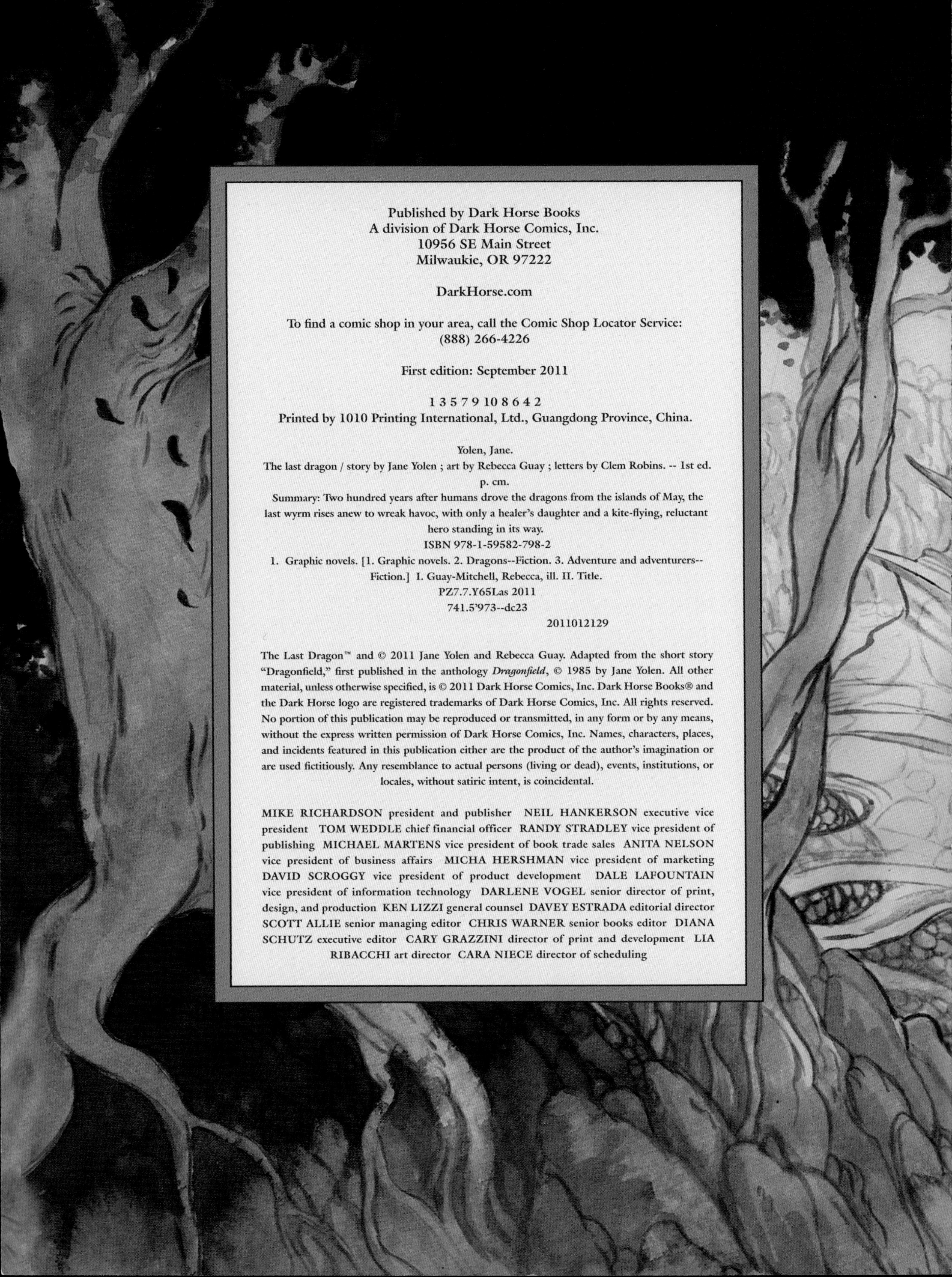

Published by Dark Horse Books
A division of Dark Horse Comics, Inc.
10956 SE Main Street
Milwaukie, OR 97222

DarkHorse.com

To find a comic shop in your area, call the Comic Shop Locator Service:
(888) 266-4226

First edition: September 2011

1 3 5 7 9 10 8 6 4 2
Printed by 1010 Printing International, Ltd., Guangdong Province, China.

Yolen, Jane.
The last dragon / story by Jane Yolen ; art by Rebecca Guay ; letters by Clem Robins. -- 1st ed.
p. cm.
Summary: Two hundred years after humans drove the dragons from the islands of May, the last wyrm rises anew to wreak havoc, with only a healer's daughter and a kite-flying, reluctant hero standing in its way.
ISBN 978-1-59582-798-2
1. Graphic novels. [1. Graphic novels. 2. Dragons--Fiction. 3. Adventure and adventurers--Fiction.] I. Guay-Mitchell, Rebecca, ill. II. Title.
PZ7.7.Y65Las 2011
741.5'973--dc23
2011012129

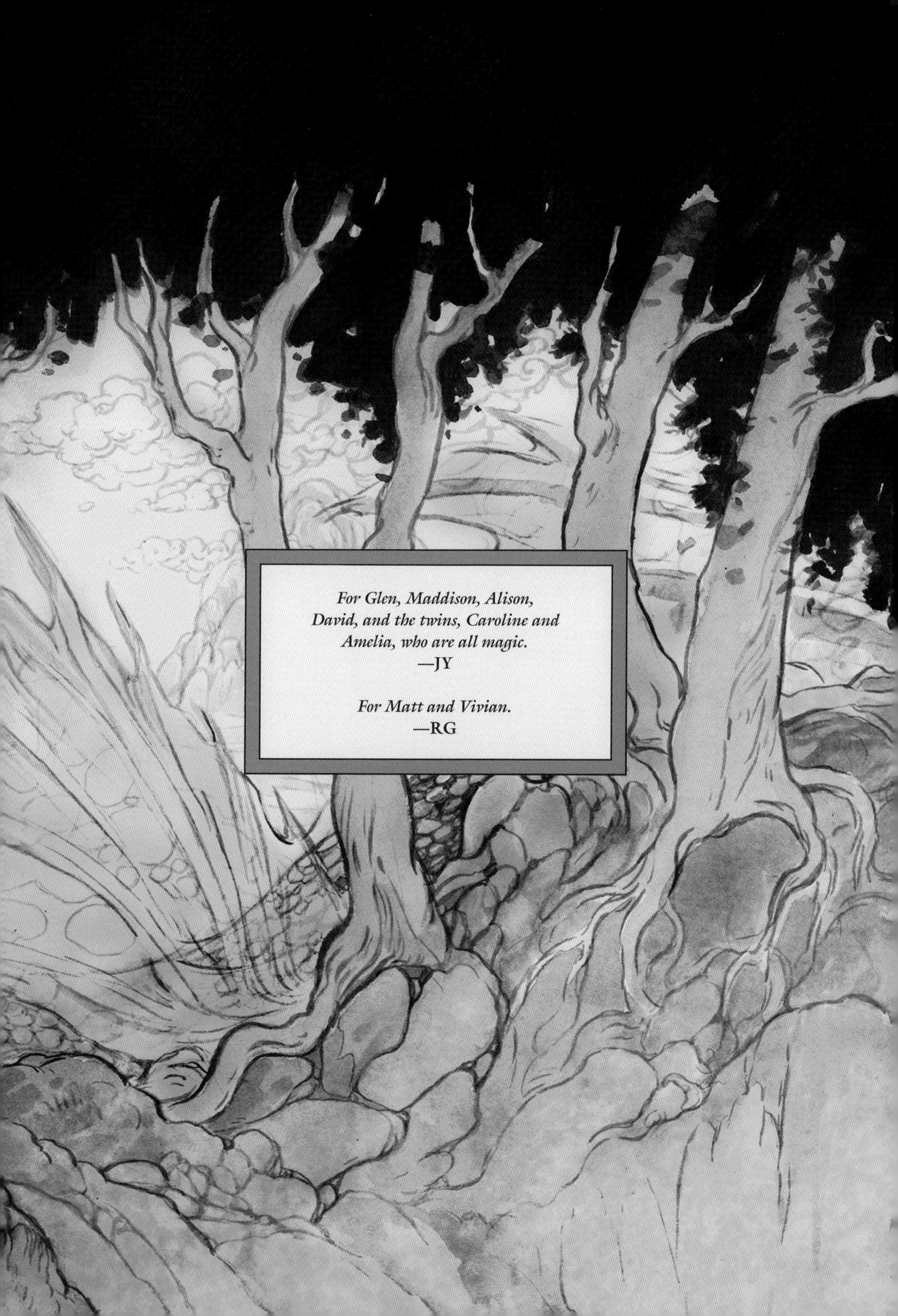

For Glen, Maddison, Alison,
David, and the twins, Caroline and
Amelia, who are all magic.
—JY

For Matt and Vivian.
—RG

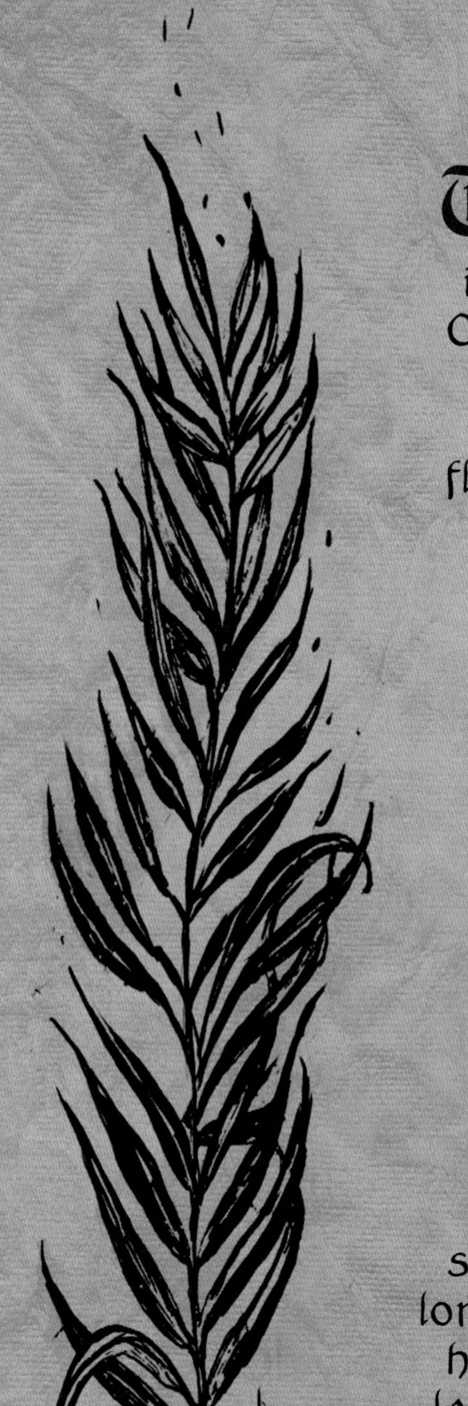

There is a spit of land near the farthest shores of the farthest islands known as Dragonfield. Once dragons dwelt on the isles in great herds, feeding on the dry brush and fueling their flames with the carcasses of small animals and migratory birds.

The dragons slept by the ocean's edge, in the green shade of trees that wept their leaves into the water. The females laid huge clutches of eggs which they buried deep in sand caches between the roots of the trees. Many of the eggs did not hatch, or hatched too early, or much too late.

There are no dragons there now, though the nearer islands are scattered with rocks scored with long furrows, as though giant claws had once been at work. And the land is exceedingly fertile, made so by the flesh and bones of buried behemoths.

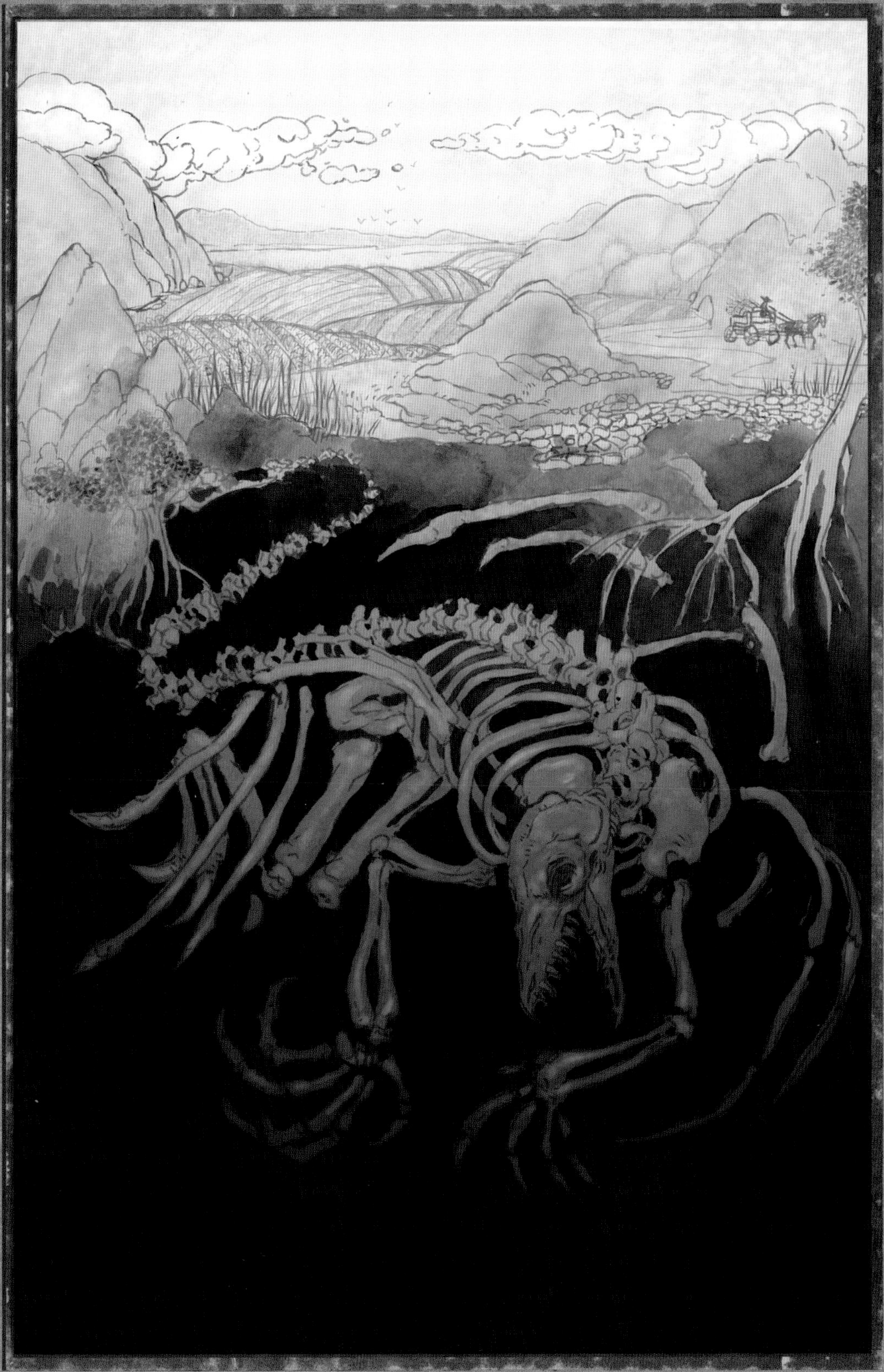

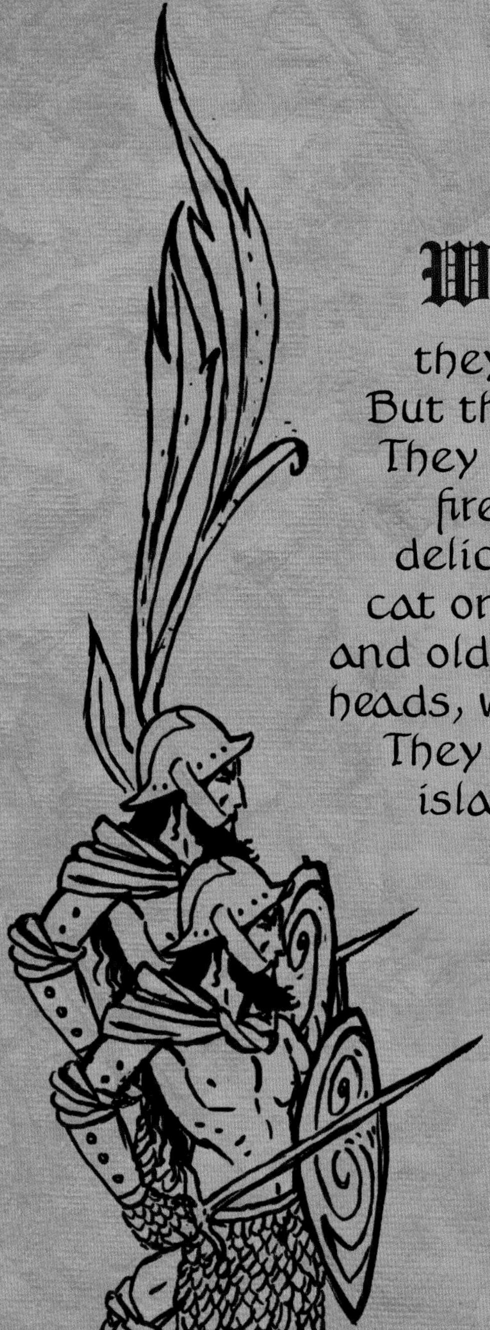

When men and women came to fish and farm those islands, they took them from the dragons. But the dragons did not leave easily. They fought with tooth and claw and fire. They learned that men were delicious to eat, better than pig or cat or hare. They gnawed on babies and old crones alike, starting with the heads, where the sweetest morsels lay. They would not retreat to the lesser islands. Indeed, why should they when this new food was now so abundant?

But in the end, like most wars with the beasts of the world, the humans won. They brought the dragons down with nets and they clubbed them without mercy, remembering their dead children, mothers, wives. The men spitted the wyrms on pikes and lances, slaughtered them with their pitchforks and gaff hooks, cut them to pieces with swords and knives.

The isles
ran red
and dark with
dragon blood
till all of them
were gone.

Or so the
humans
believed.

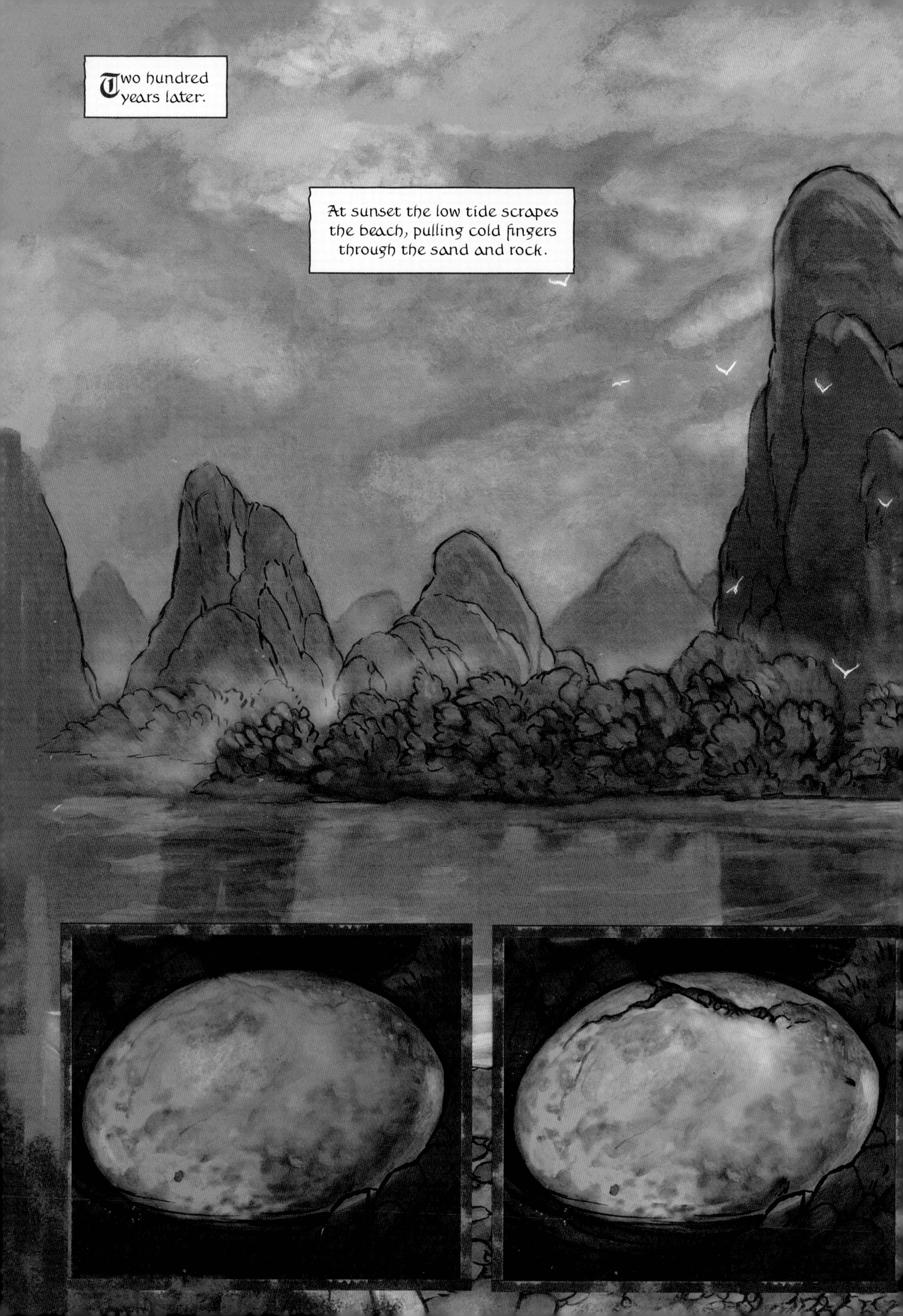
Two hundred years later.
At sunset the low tide scrapes the beach, pulling cold fingers through the sand and rock.

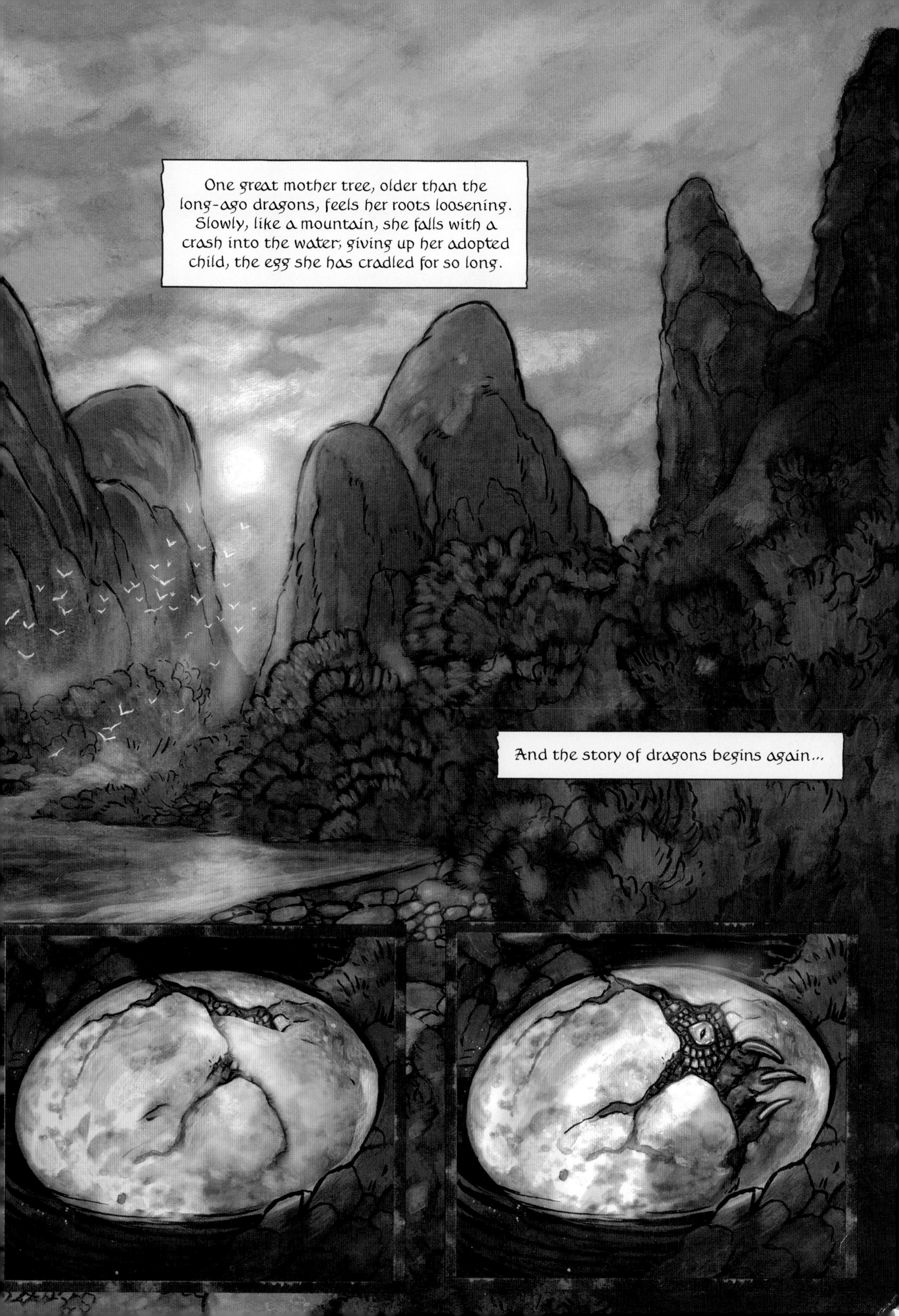
One great mother tree, older than the long-ago dragons, feels her roots loosening. Slowly, like a mountain, she falls with a crash into the water; giving up her adopted child, the egg she has cradled for so long.
And the story of dragons begins again...

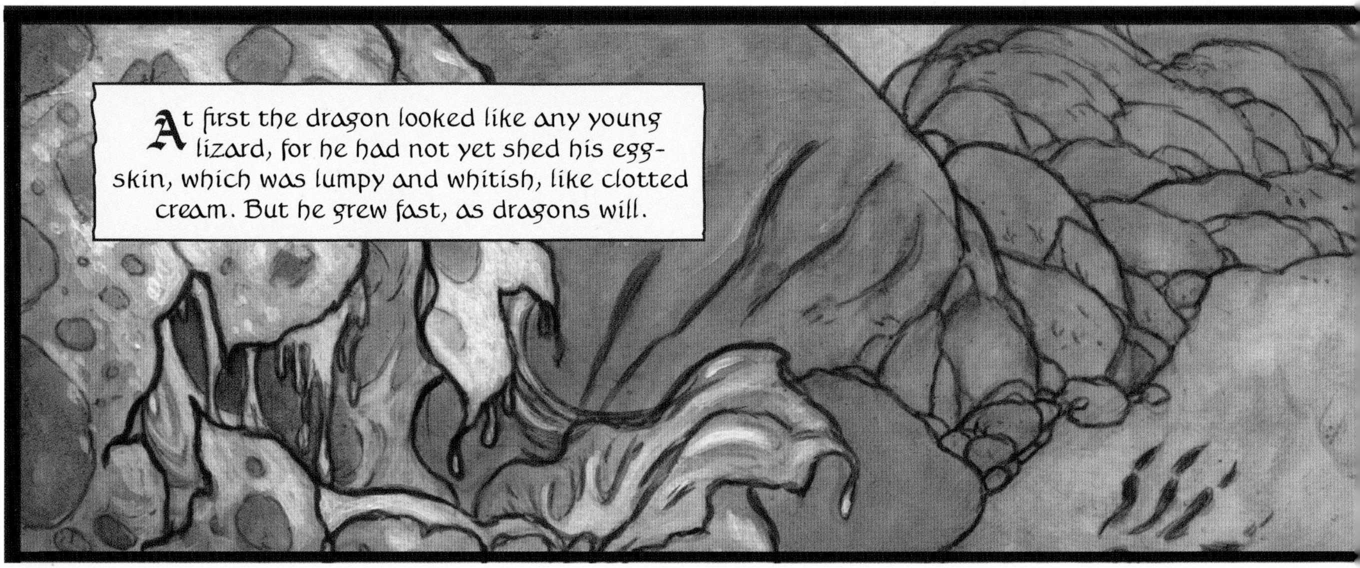
At first the dragon looked like any young lizard, for he had not yet shed his egg-skin, which was lumpy and whitish, like clotted cream. But he grew fast, as dragons will.

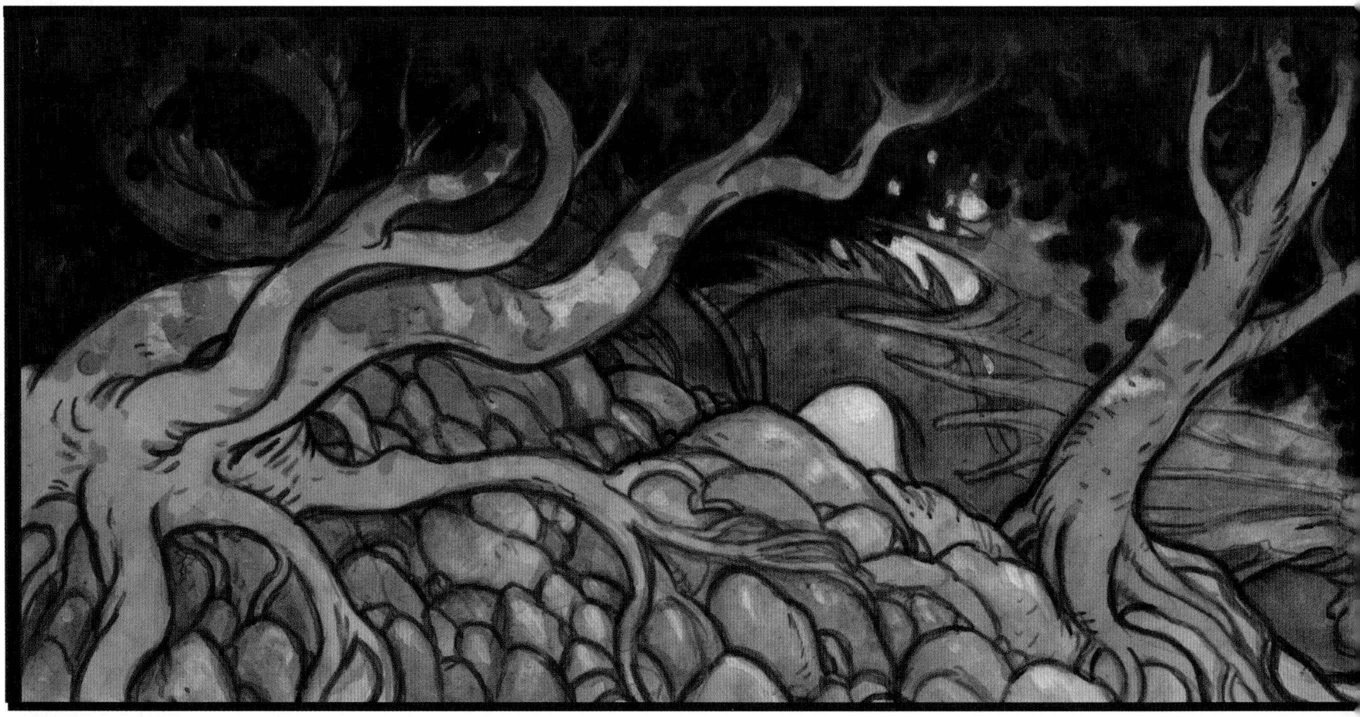

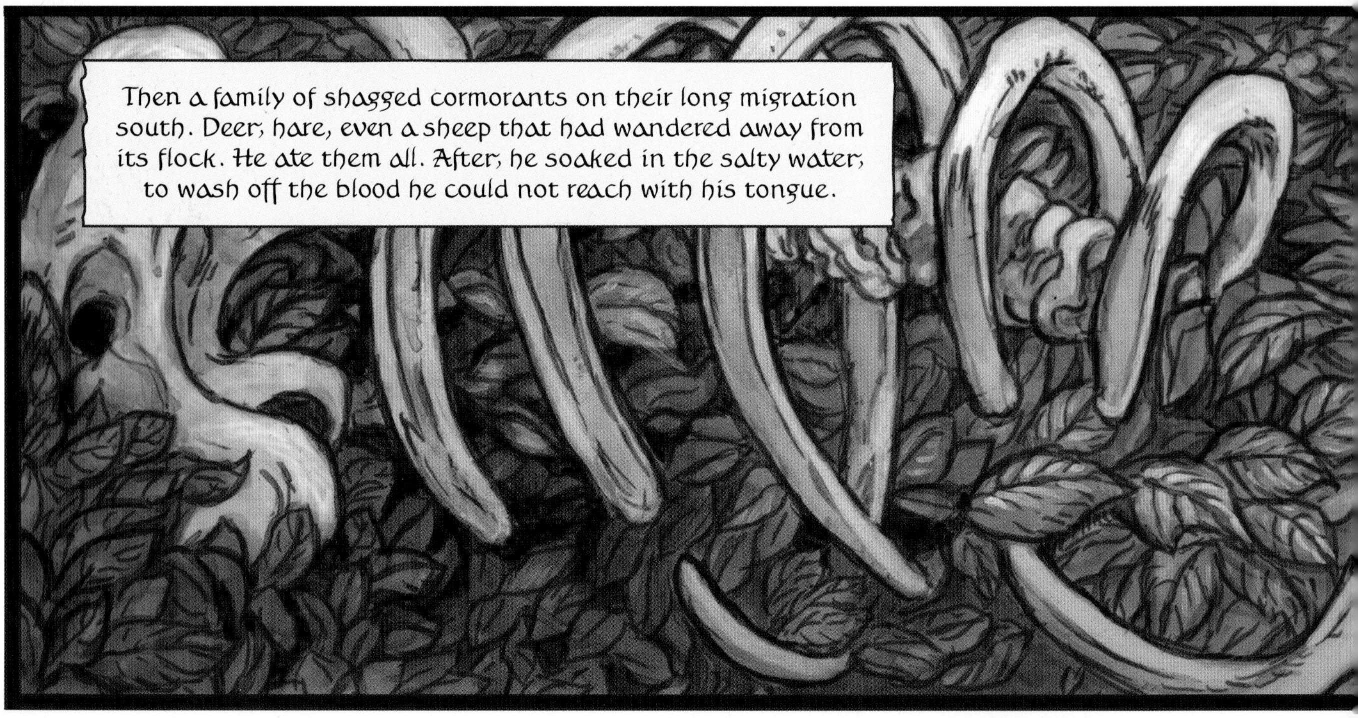
Then a family of shagged cormorants on their long migration south. Deer, hare, even a sheep that had wandered away from its flock. He ate them all. After, he soaked in the salty water, to wash off the blood he could not reach with his tongue.

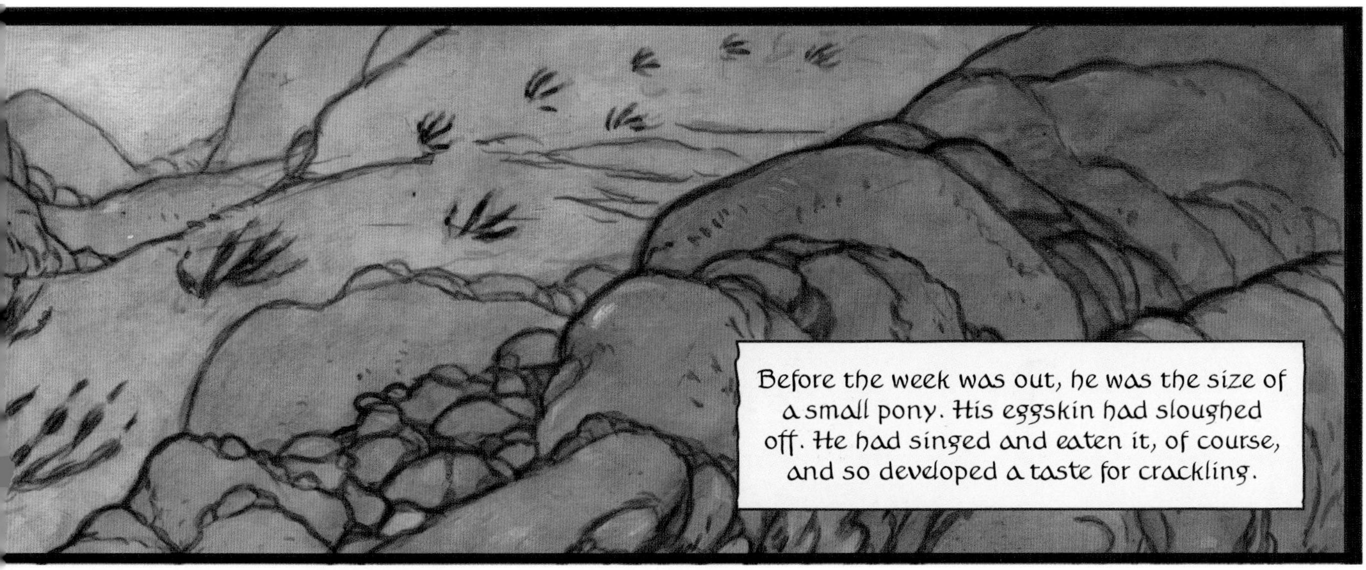
Before the week was out, he was the size of a small pony. His eggskin had sloughed off. He had singed and eaten it, of course, and so developed a taste for crackling.

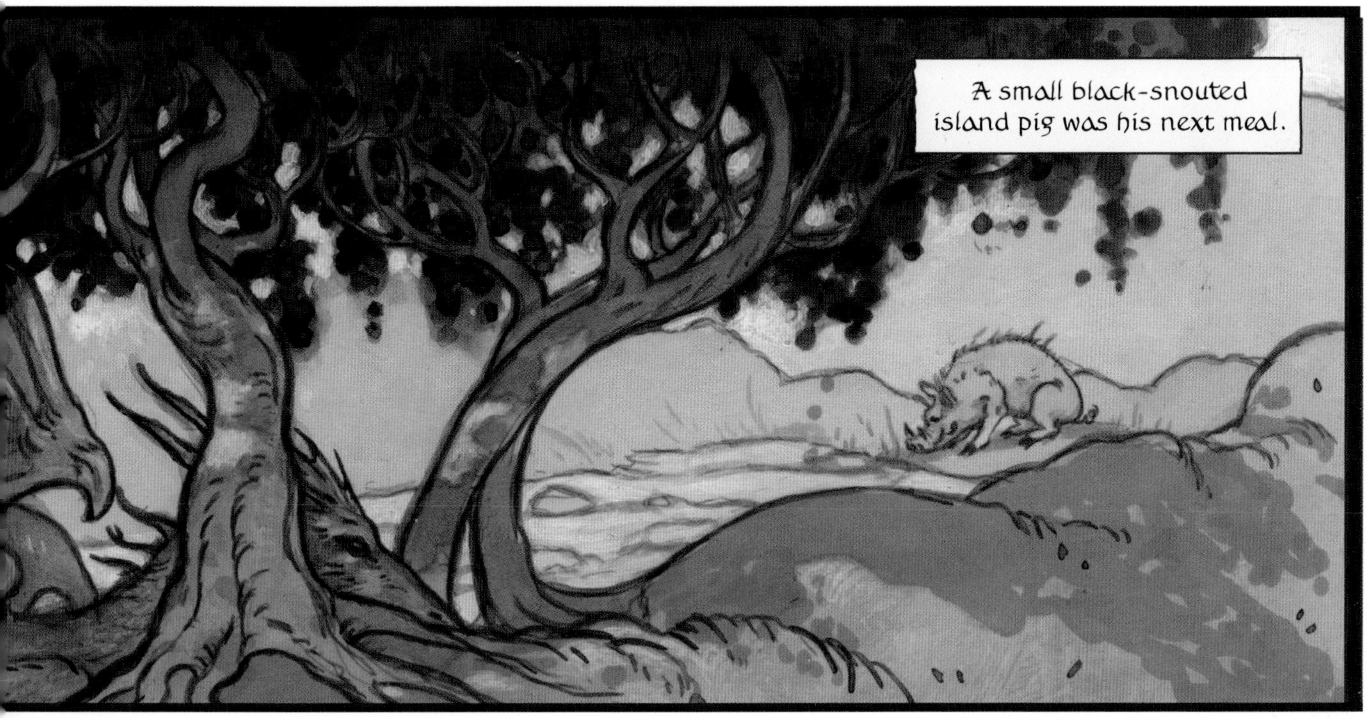
A small black-snouted island pig was his next meal.

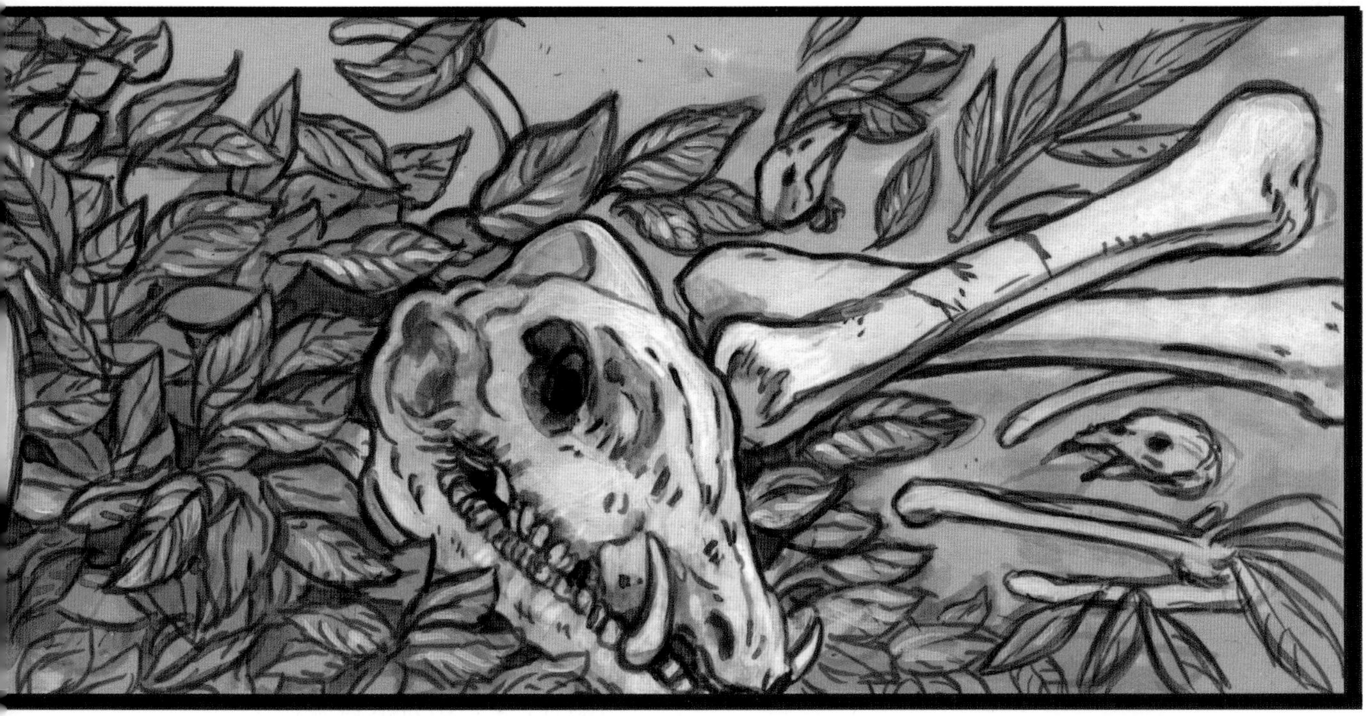

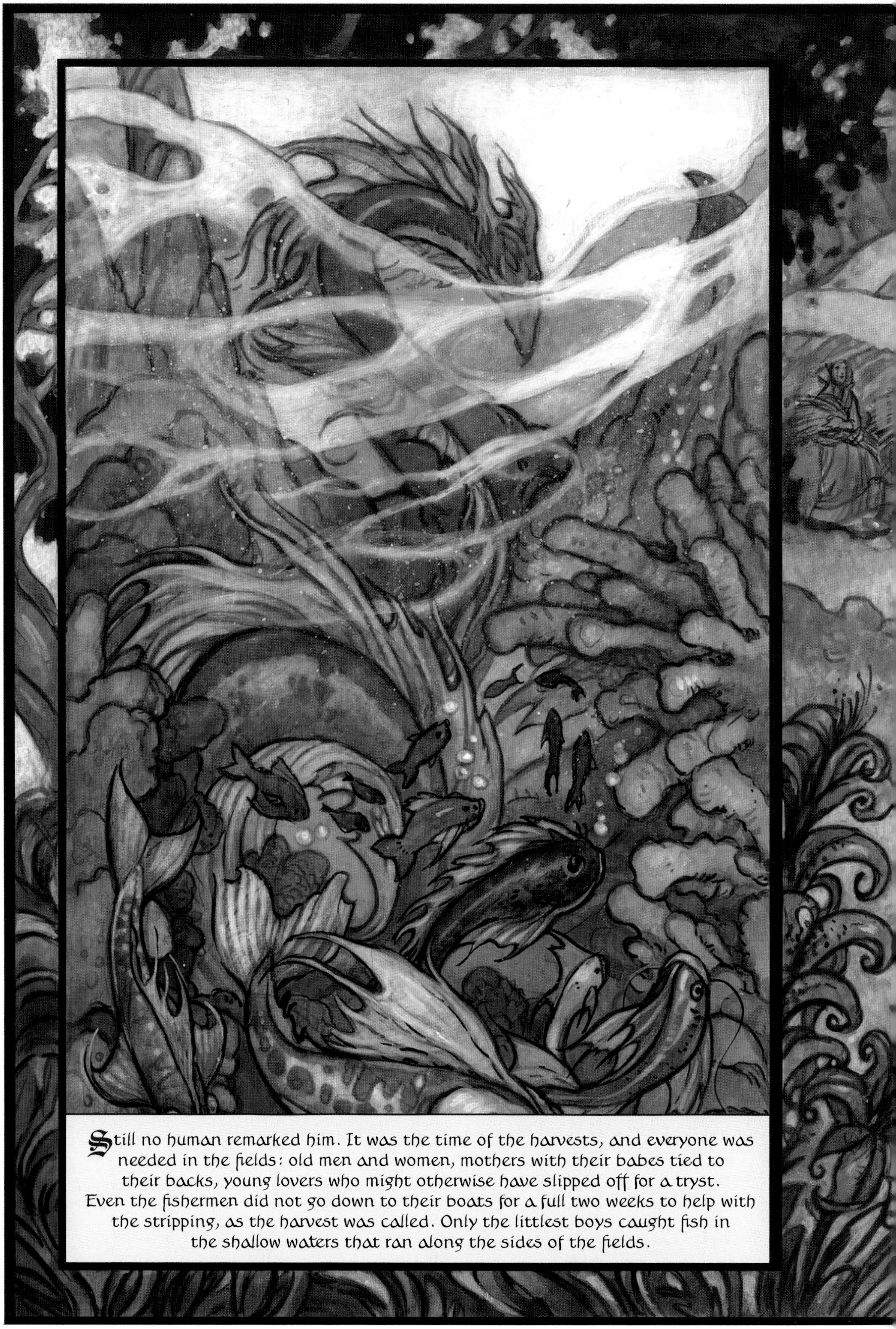

Still no human remarked him. It was the time of the harvests, and everyone was needed in the fields: old men and women, mothers with their babes tied to their backs, young lovers who might otherwise have slipped off for a tryst. Even the fishermen did not go down to their boats for a full two weeks to help with the stripping, as the harvest was called. Only the littlest boys caught fish in the shallow waters that ran along the sides of the fields.

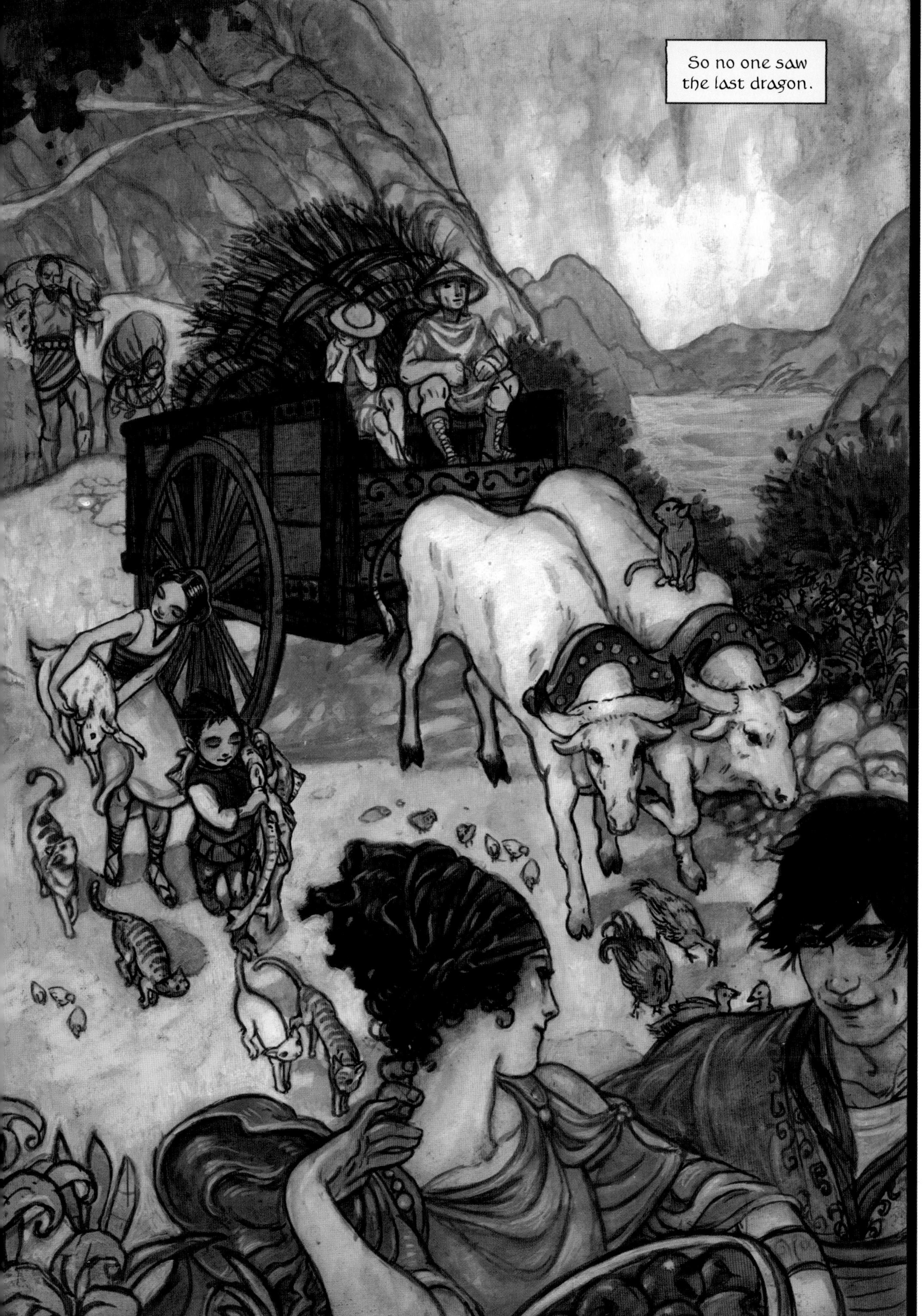
So no one saw
the last dragon.

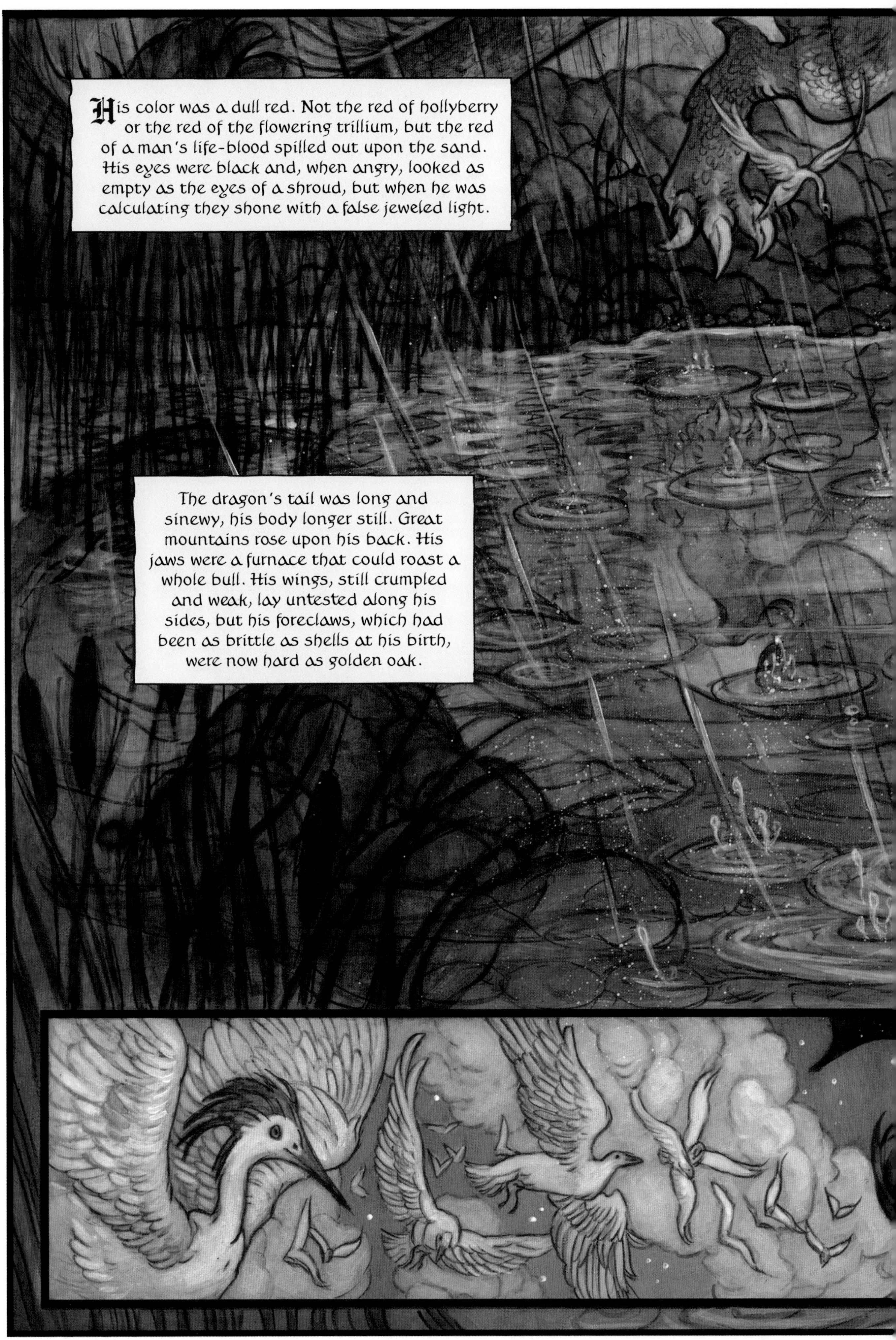
His color was a dull red. Not the red of hollyberry or the red of the flowering trillium, but the red of a man's life-blood spilled out upon the sand. His eyes were black and, when angry, looked as empty as the eyes of a shroud, but when he was calculating they shone with a false jeweled light.
The dragon's tail was long and sinewy, his body longer still. Great mountains rose upon his back. His jaws were a furnace that could roast a whole bull. His wings, still crumpled and weak, lay untested along his sides, but his foreclaws, which had been as brittle as shells at his birth, were now hard as golden oak.

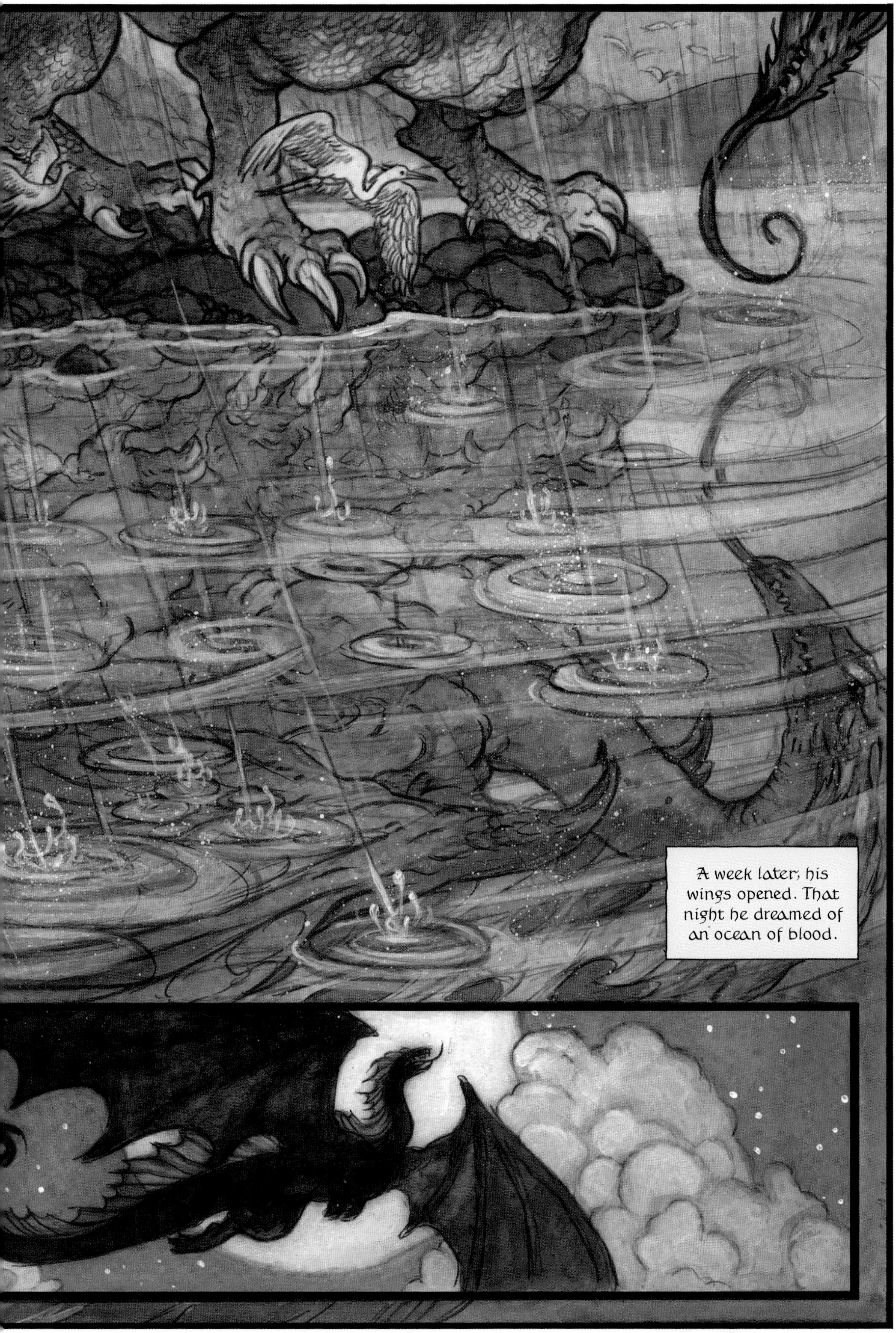
A week later, his wings opened. That night he dreamed of an ocean of blood.

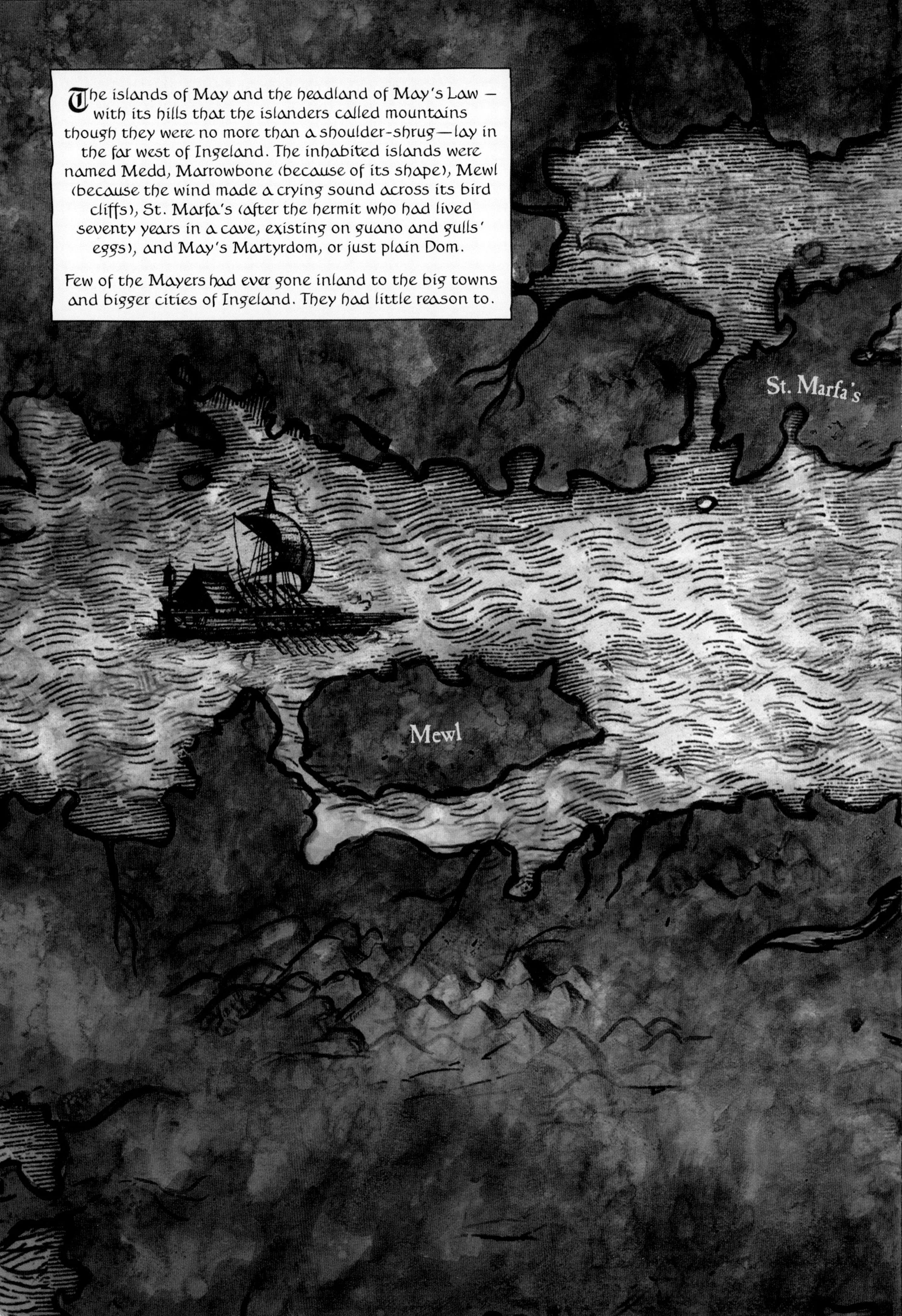
The islands of May and the headland of May's Law — with its hills that the islanders called mountains though they were no more than a shoulder-shrug—lay in the far west of Ingeland. The inhabited islands were named Medd, Marrowbone (because of its shape), Mewl (because the wind made a crying sound across its bird cliffs), St. Marfa's (after the hermit who had lived seventy years in a cave, existing on guano and gulls' eggs), and May's Martyrdom, or just plain Dom.
Few of the Mayers had ever gone inland to the big towns and bigger cities of Ingeland. They had little reason to.
St. Marfa's
Mewl

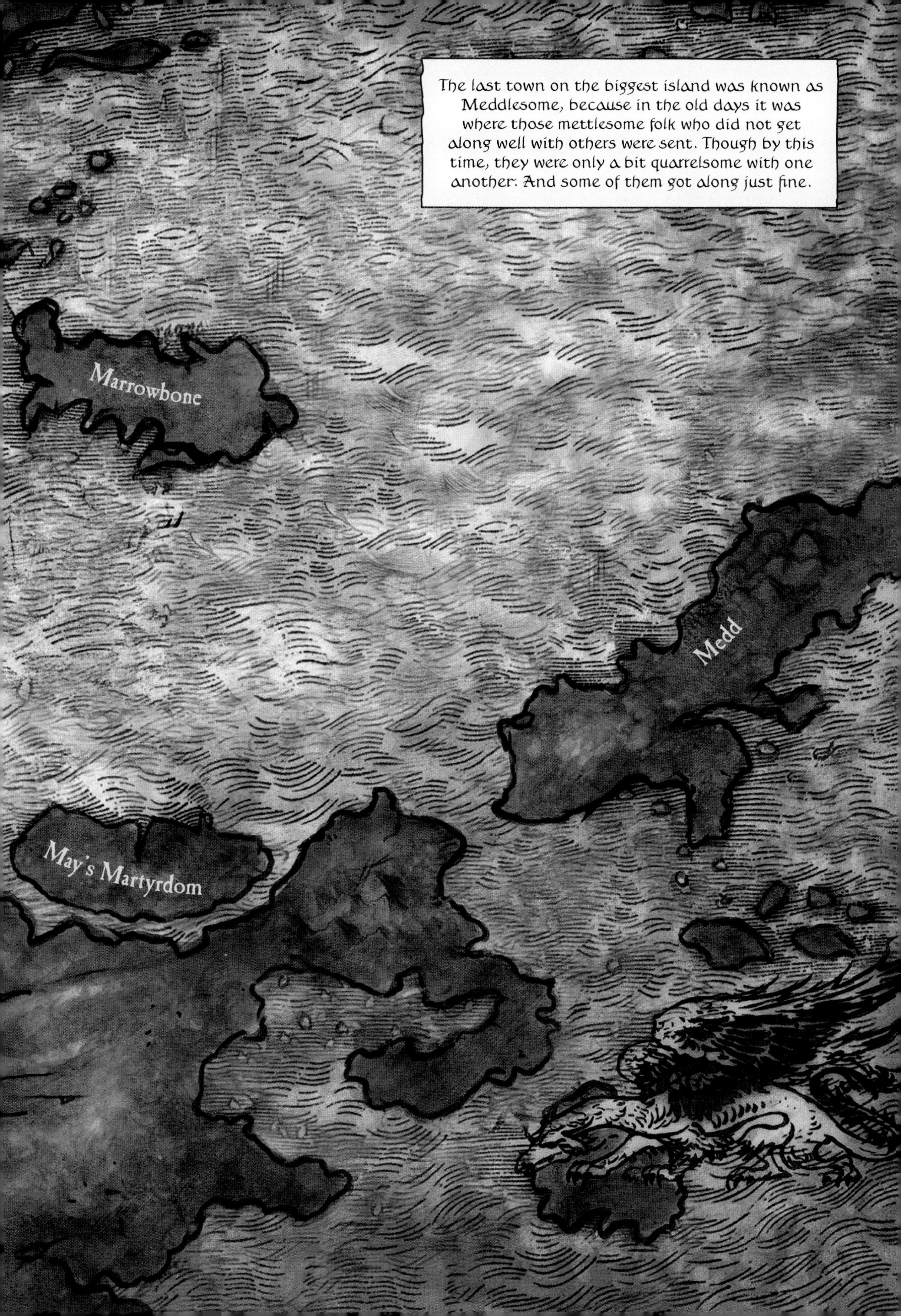
The last town on the biggest island was known as Meddlesome, because in the old days it was where those mettlesome folk who did not get along well with others were sent. Though by this time, they were only a bit quarrelsome with one another. And some of them got along just fine.
Marrowbone
Medd
May's Martyrdom

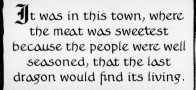

It was in this town, where the meat was sweetest because the people were well seasoned, that the last dragon would find its living.

WHERE *IS* THAT GIRL?

SHE ONLY TAKES THAT TONE WITH TANSY.

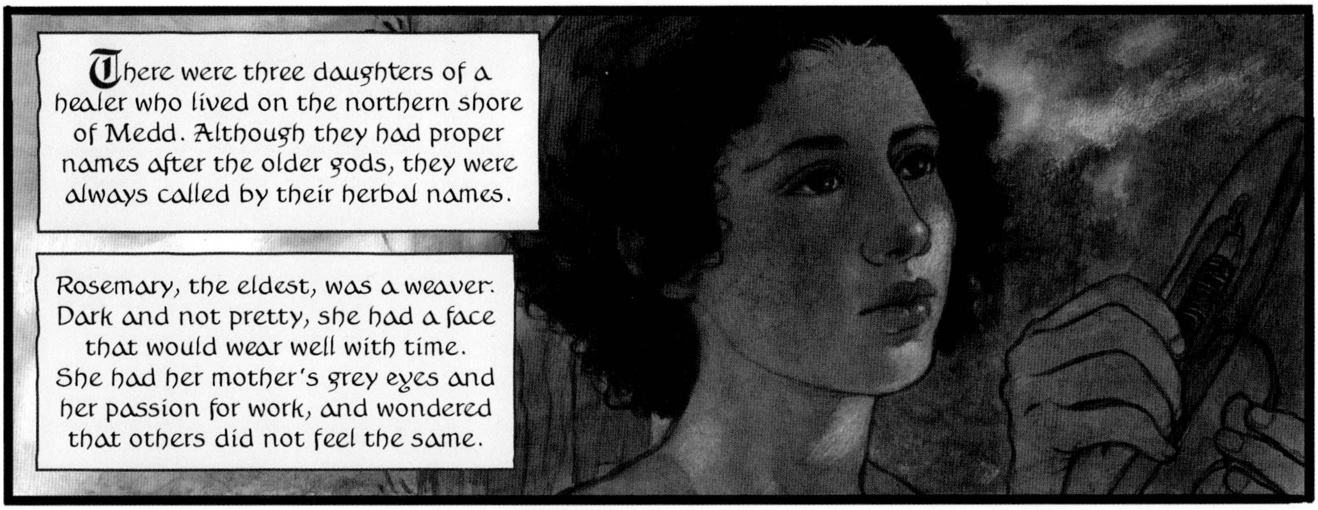
There were three daughters of a healer who lived on the northern shore of Medd. Although they had proper names after the older gods, they were always called by their herbal names.
Rosemary, the eldest, was a weaver. Dark and not pretty, she had a face that would wear well with time. She had her mother's grey eyes and her passion for work, and wondered that others did not feel the same.

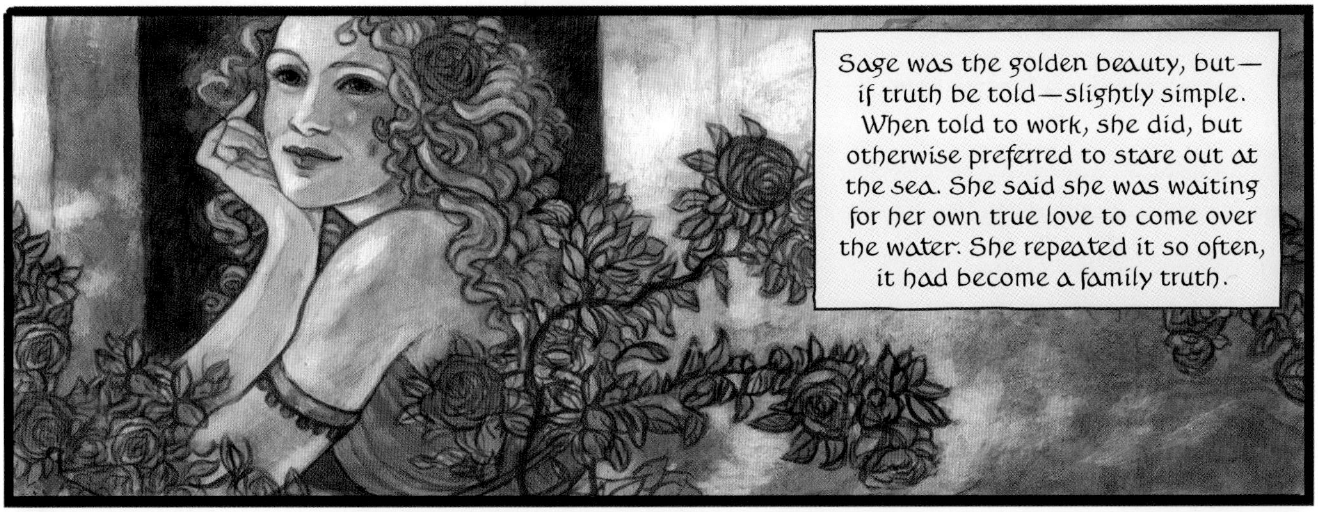
Sage was the golden beauty, but—if truth be told—slightly simple. When told to work, she did, but otherwise preferred to stare out at the sea. She said she was waiting for her own true love to come over the water. She repeated it so often, it had become a family truth.

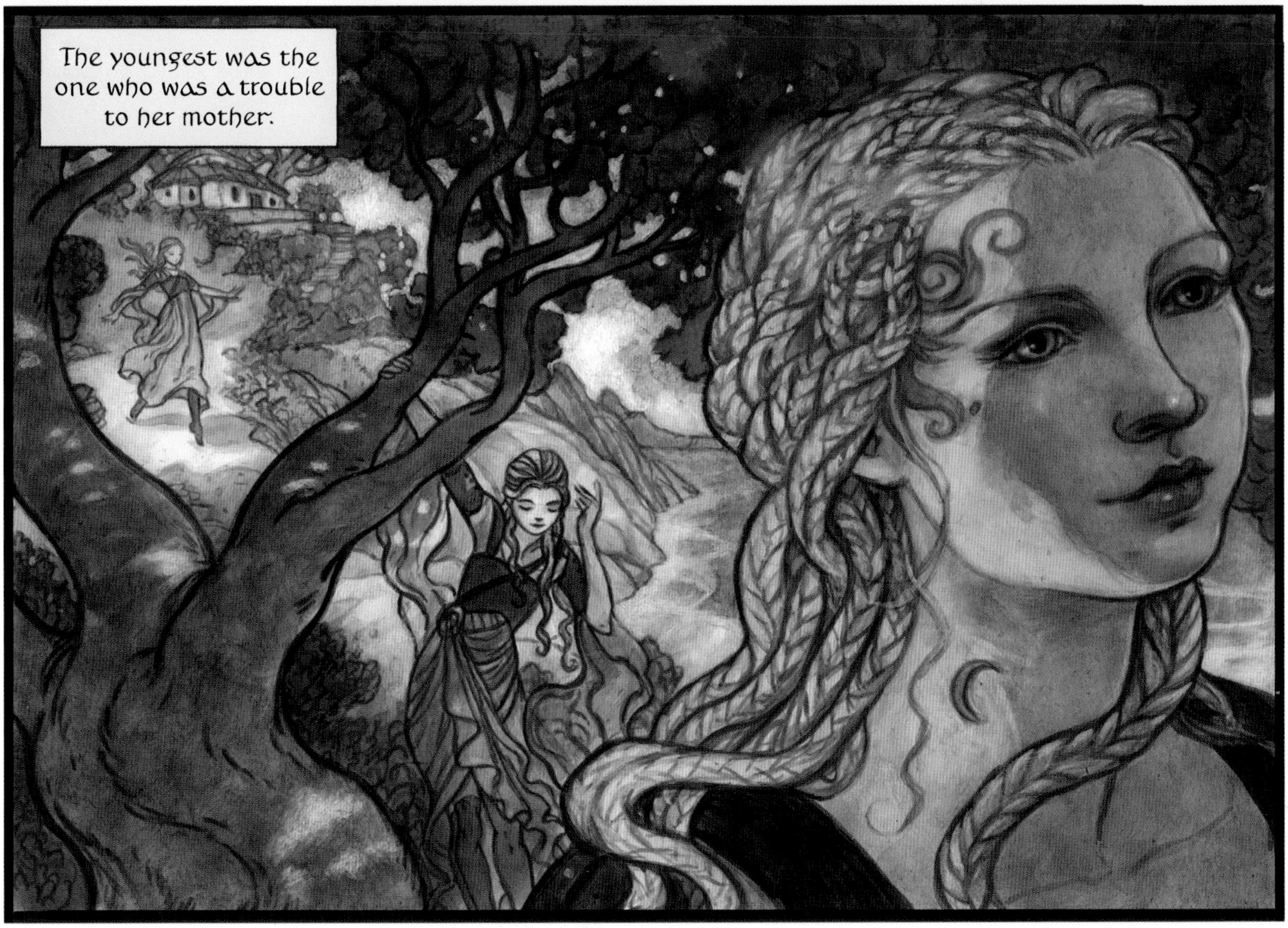
The youngest was the one who was a trouble to her mother.

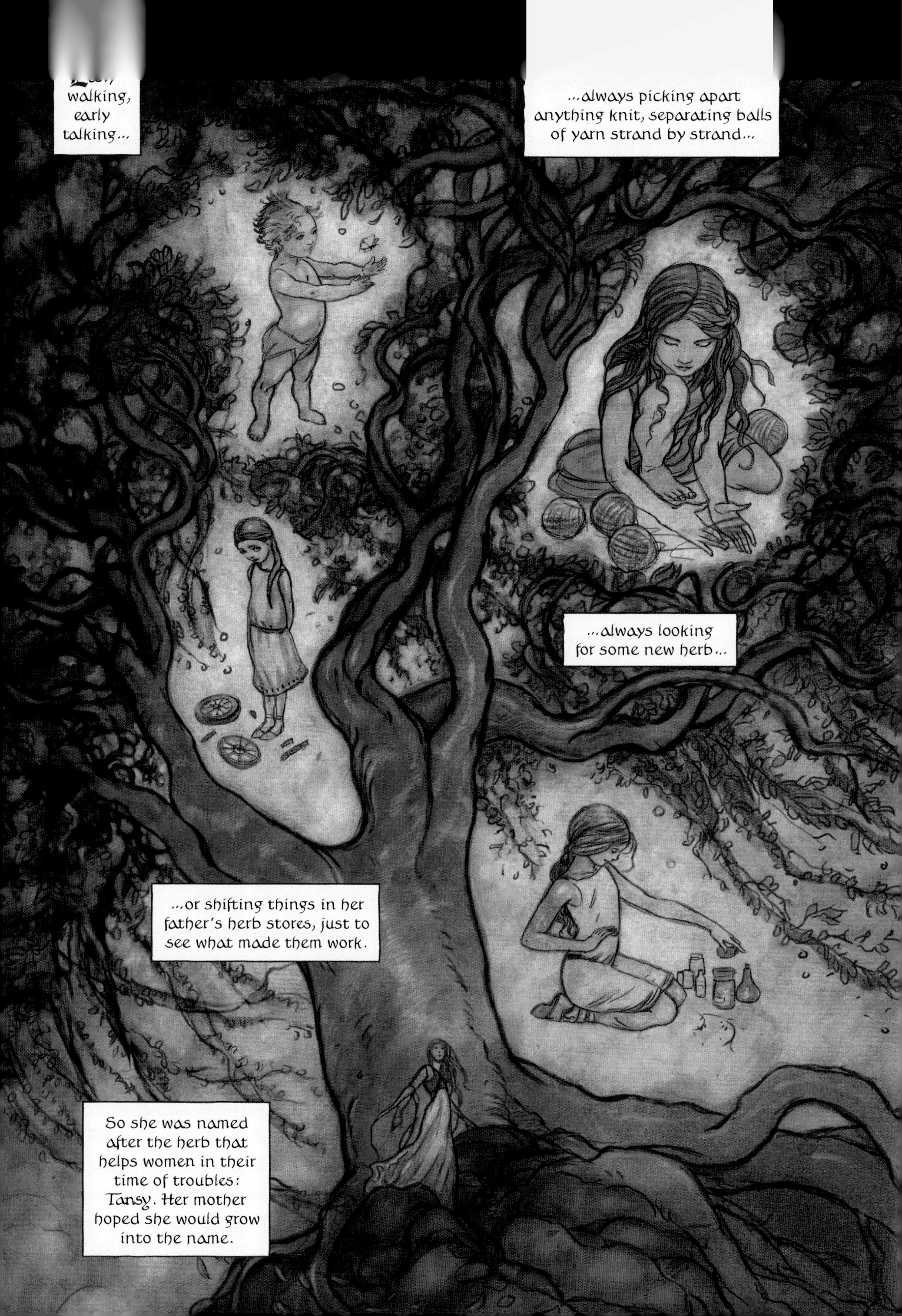
walking, early talking...
...always picking apart anything knit, separating balls of yarn strand by strand...
...always looking for some new herb...
...or shifting things in her father's herb stores, just to see what made them work.
So she was named after the herb that helps women in their time of troubles: Tansy. Her mother hoped she would grow into the name.

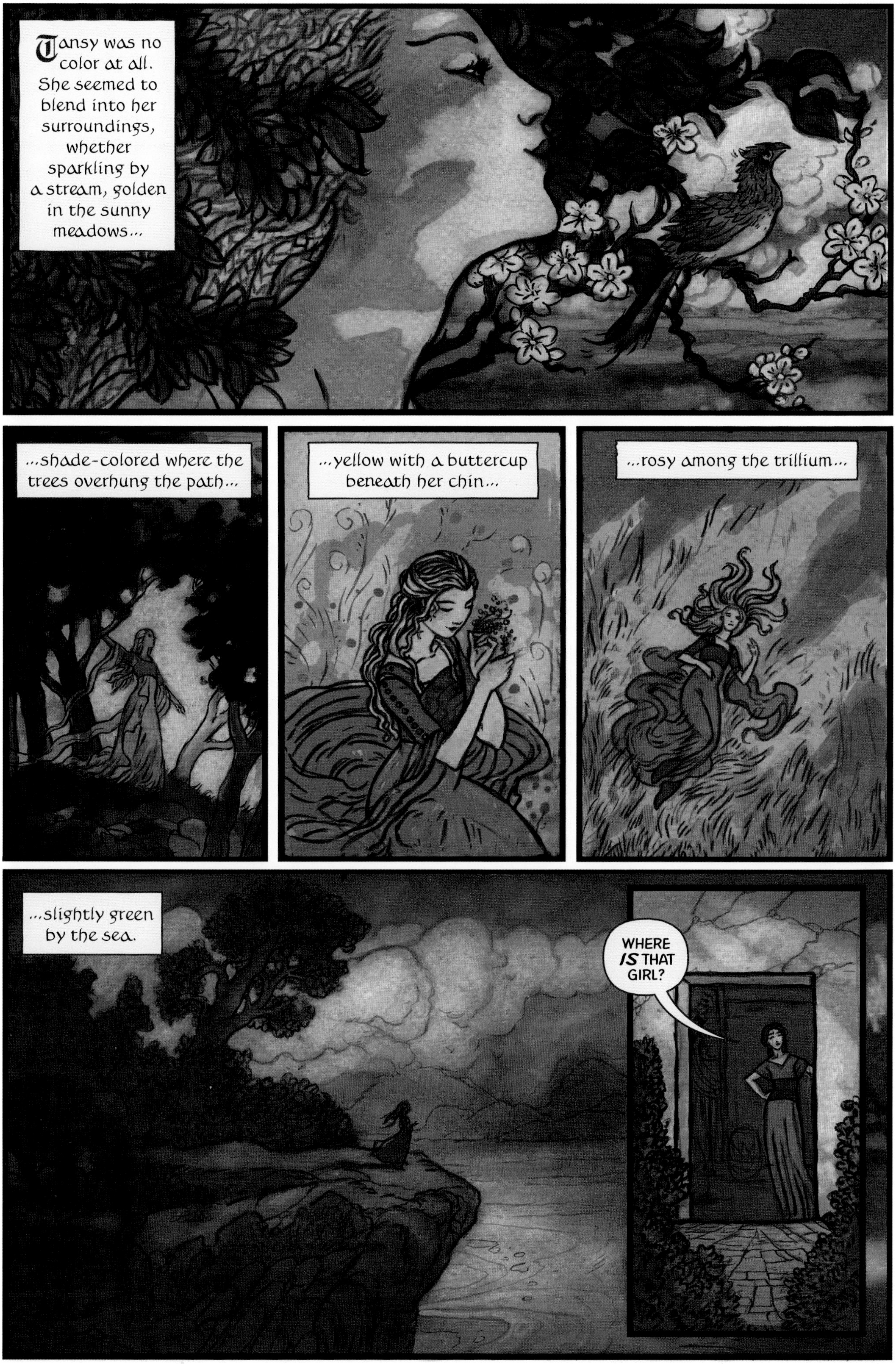
Tansy was no color at all. She seemed to blend into her surroundings, whether sparkling by a stream, golden in the sunny meadows...
...shade-colored where the trees overhung the path...
...yellow with a buttercup beneath her chin...
...rosy among the trillium...
...slightly green by the sea.
WHERE *IS* THAT GIRL?

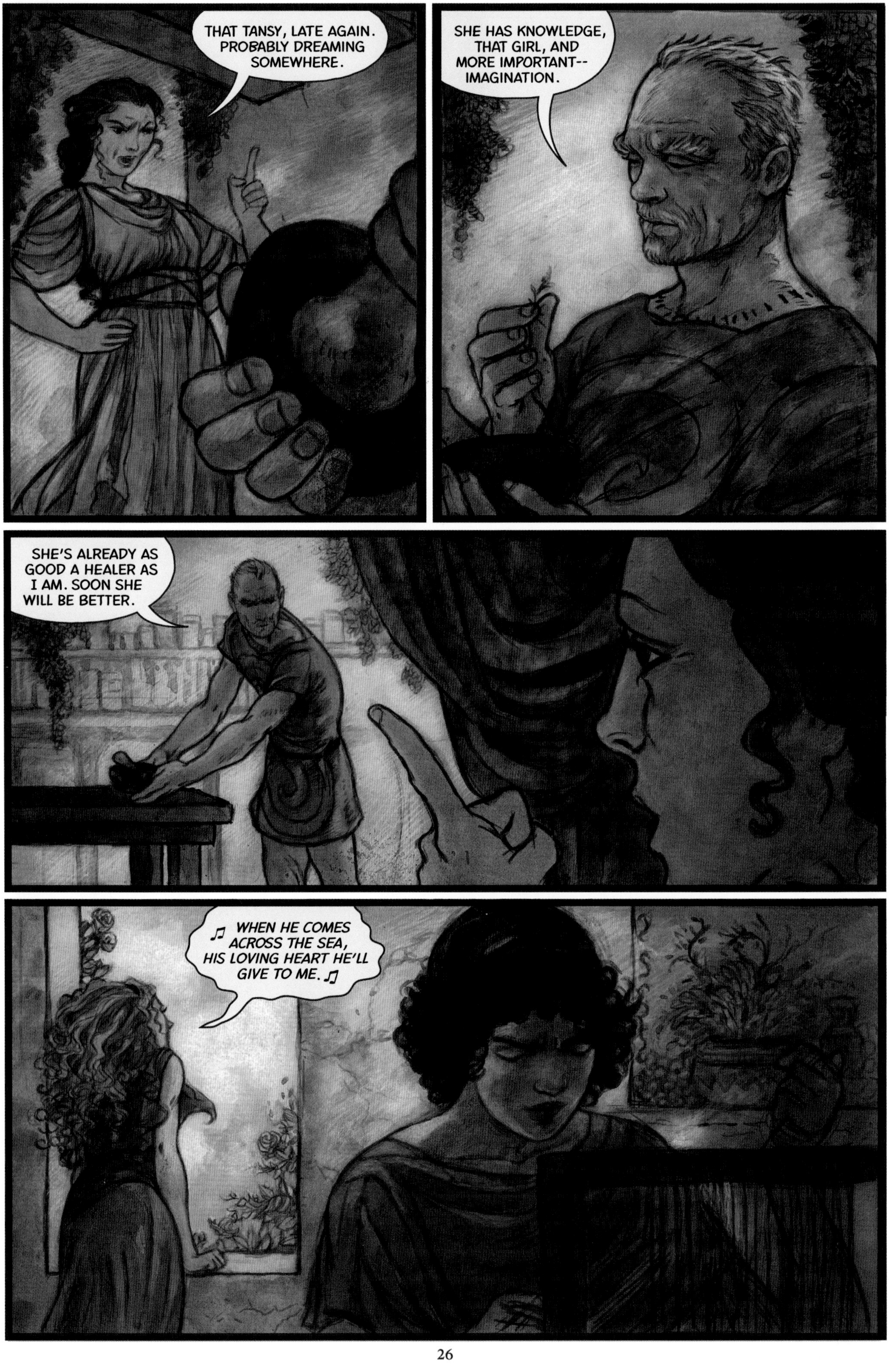
THAT TANSY, LATE AGAIN. PROBABLY DREAMING SOMEWHERE.
SHE HAS KNOWLEDGE, THAT GIRL, AND MORE IMPORTANT-- IMAGINATION.
SHE'S ALREADY AS GOOD A HEALER AS I AM. SOON SHE WILL BE BETTER.
♫ WHEN HE COMES ACROSS THE SEA, HIS LOVING HEART HE'LL GIVE TO ME. ♫

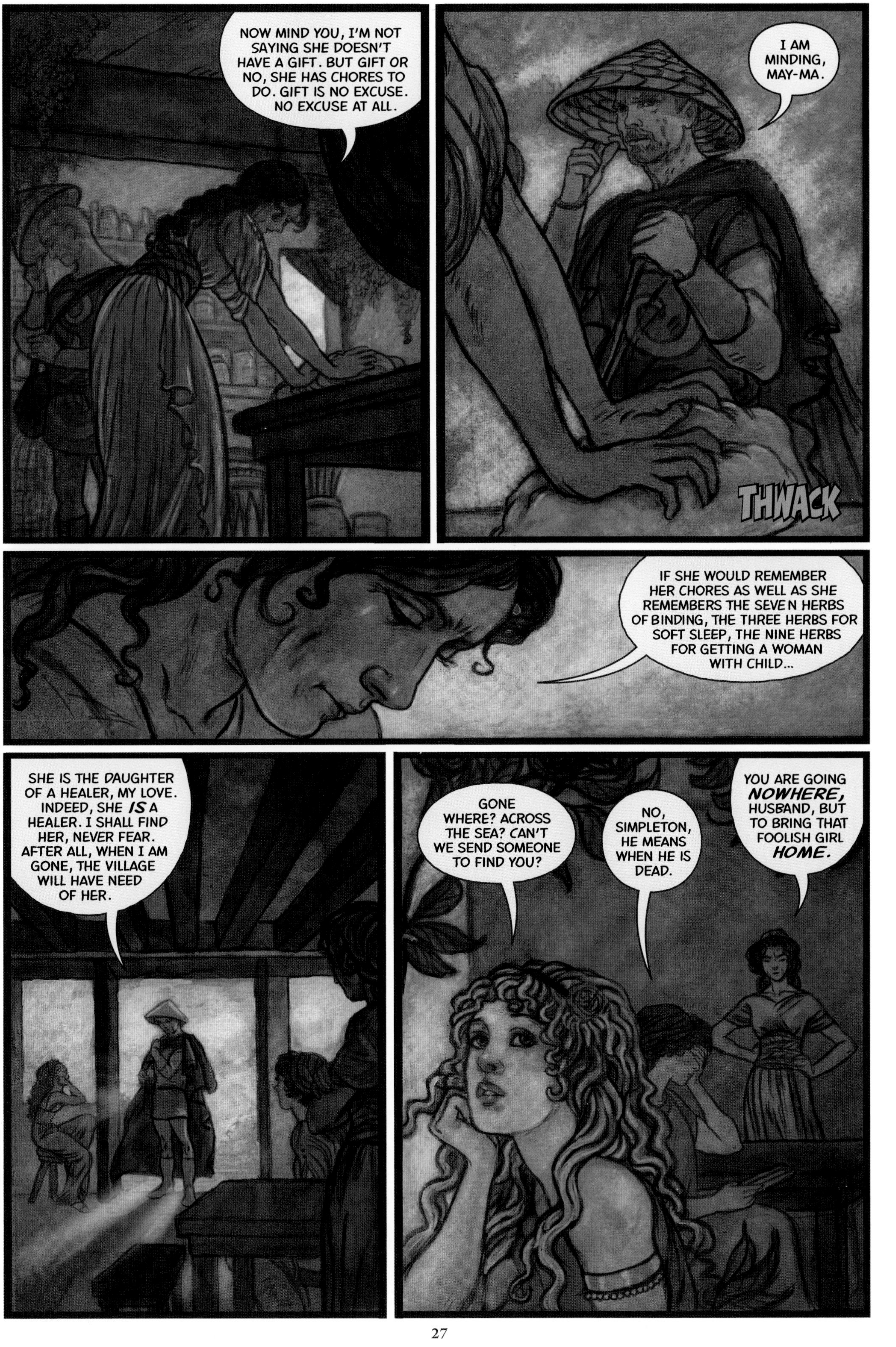
NOW MIND YOU, I'M NOT SAYING SHE DOESN'T HAVE A GIFT. BUT GIFT OR NO, SHE HAS CHORES TO DO. GIFT IS NO EXCUSE. NO EXCUSE AT ALL.
I AM MINDING, MAY-MA.
THWACK
IF SHE WOULD REMEMBER HER CHORES AS WELL AS SHE REMEMBERS THE SEVEN HERBS OF BINDING, THE THREE HERBS FOR SOFT SLEEP, THE NINE HERBS FOR GETTING A WOMAN WITH CHILD...
SHE IS THE DAUGHTER OF A HEALER, MY LOVE. INDEED, SHE *IS* A HEALER. I SHALL FIND HER, NEVER FEAR. AFTER ALL, WHEN I AM GONE, THE VILLAGE WILL HAVE NEED OF HER.
GONE WHERE? ACROSS THE SEA? CAN'T WE SEND SOMEONE TO FIND YOU?
NO, SIMPLETON, HE MEANS WHEN HE IS DEAD.
YOU ARE GOING ***NOWHERE,*** HUSBAND, BUT TO BRING THAT FOOLISH GIRL ***HOME.***

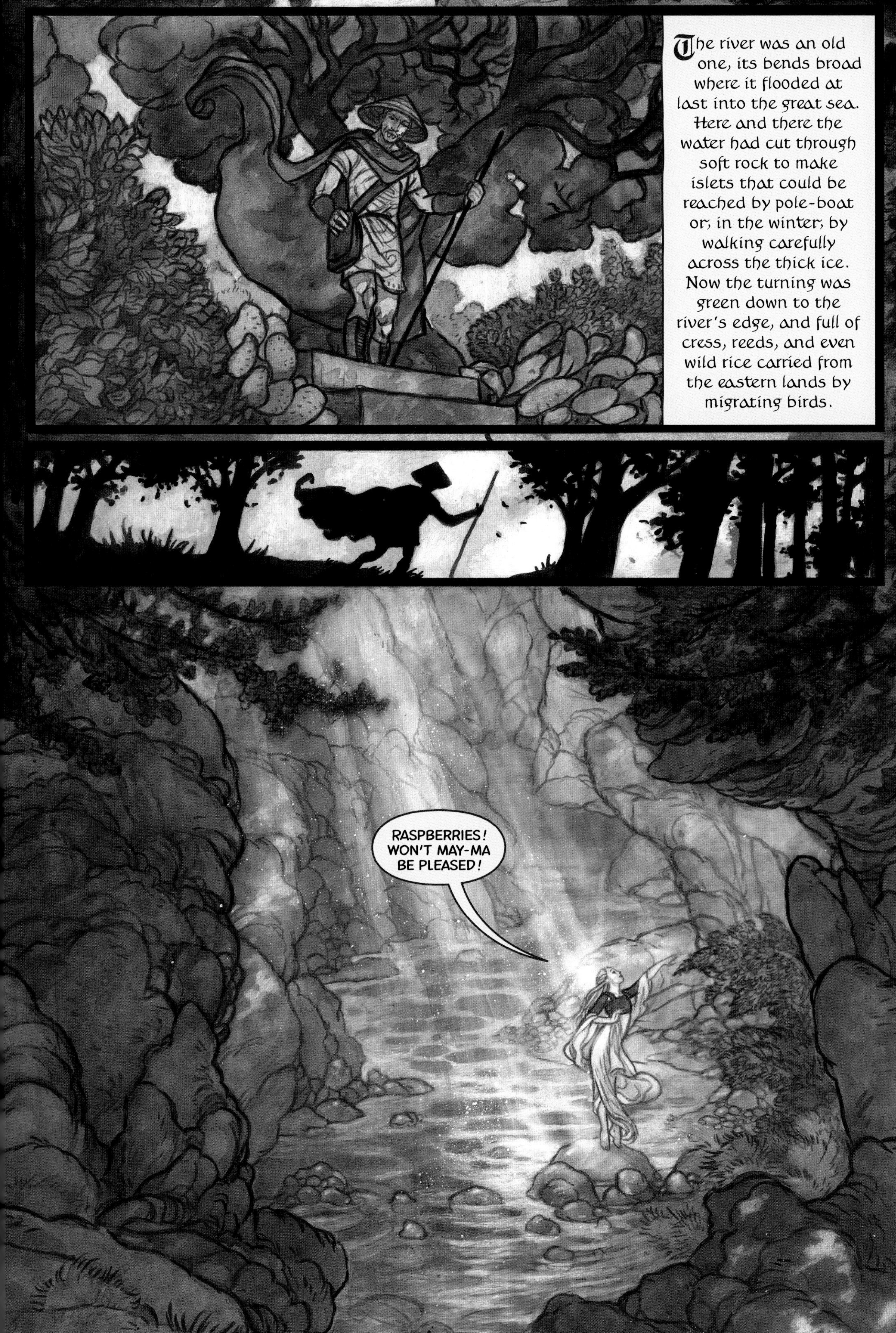
The river was an old one, its bends broad where it flooded at last into the great sea. Here and there the water had cut through soft rock to make islets that could be reached by pole-boat or, in the winter, by walking carefully across the thick ice. Now the turning was green down to the river's edge, and full of cress, reeds, and even wild rice carried from the eastern lands by migrating birds.
RASPBERRIES! WON'T MAY-MA BE PLEASED!

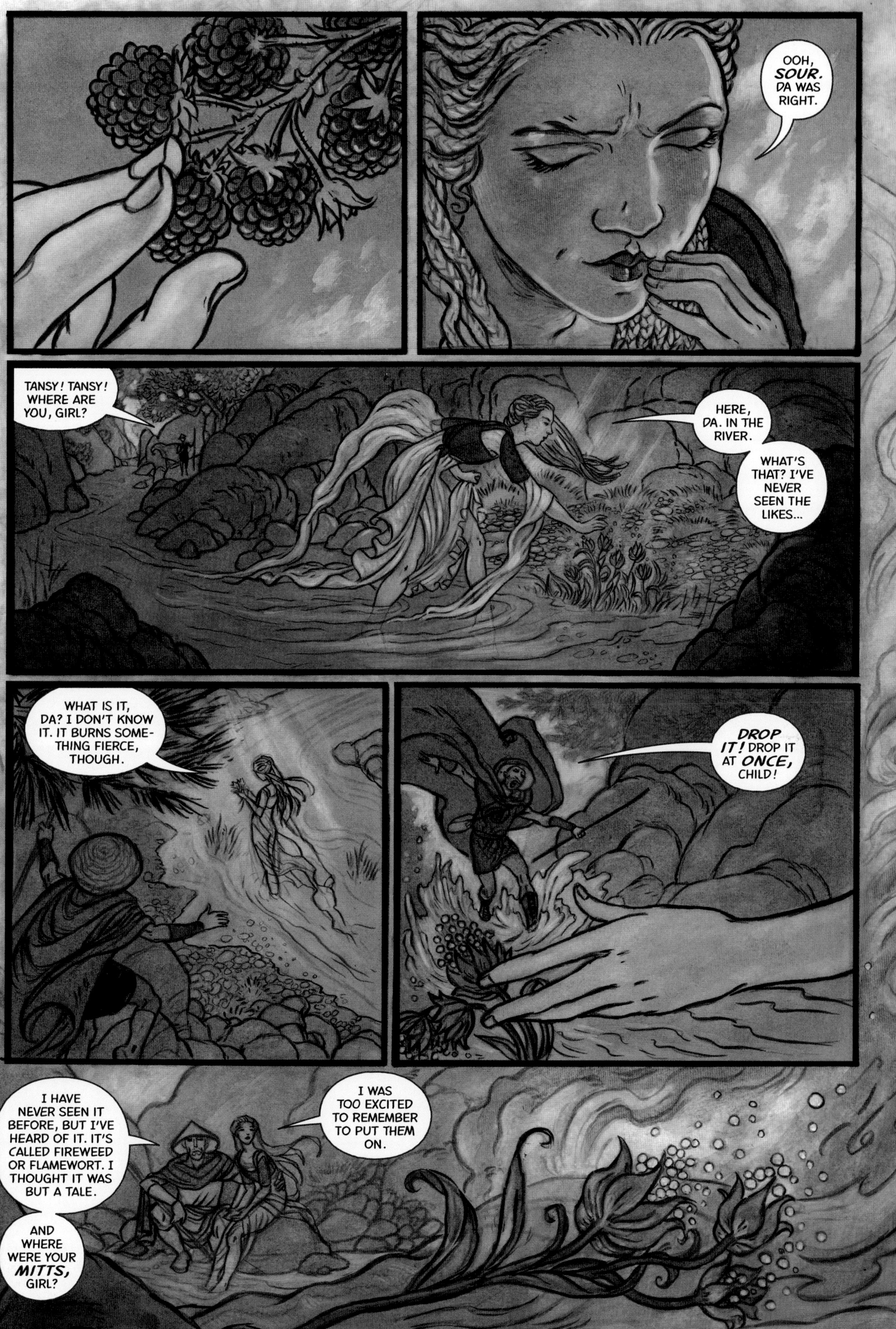
OOH, SOUR. DA WAS RIGHT.
TANSY! TANSY! WHERE ARE YOU, GIRL?
HERE, DA. IN THE RIVER.
WHAT'S THAT? I'VE NEVER SEEN THE LIKES...
WHAT IS IT, DA? I DON'T KNOW IT. IT BURNS SOME-THING FIERCE, THOUGH.
DROP IT! DROP IT AT ONCE, CHILD!
I HAVE NEVER SEEN IT BEFORE, BUT I'VE HEARD OF IT. IT'S CALLED FIREWEED OR FLAMEWORT. I THOUGHT IT WAS BUT A TALE.
AND WHERE WERE YOUR MITTS, GIRL?
I WAS TOO EXCITED TO REMEMBER TO PUT THEM ON.

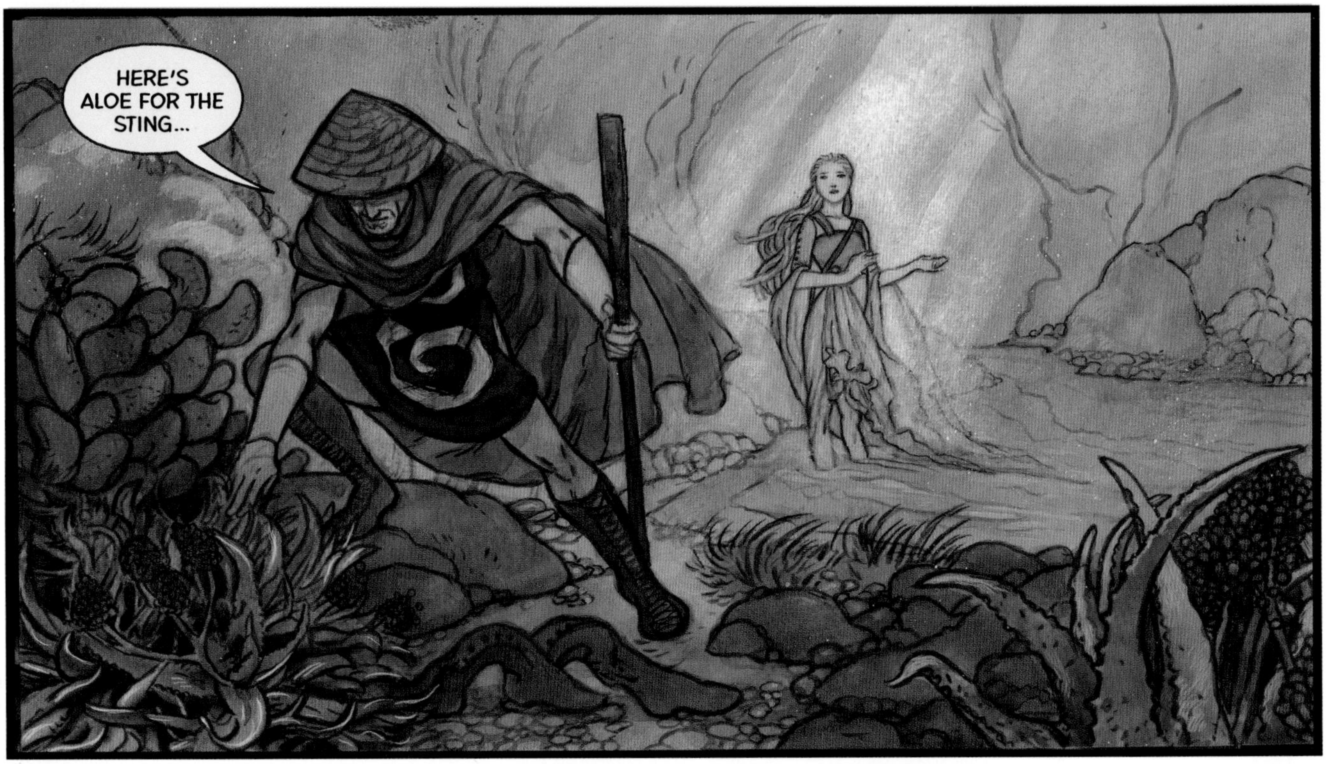
HERE'S ALOE FOR THE STING...

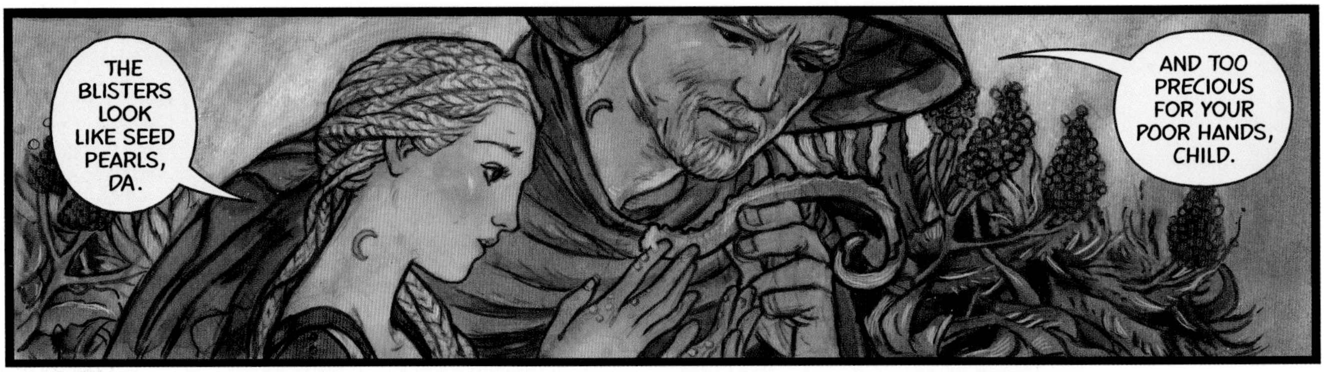
THE BLISTERS LOOK LIKE SEED PEARLS, DA.
AND TOO PRECIOUS FOR YOUR POOR HANDS, CHILD.

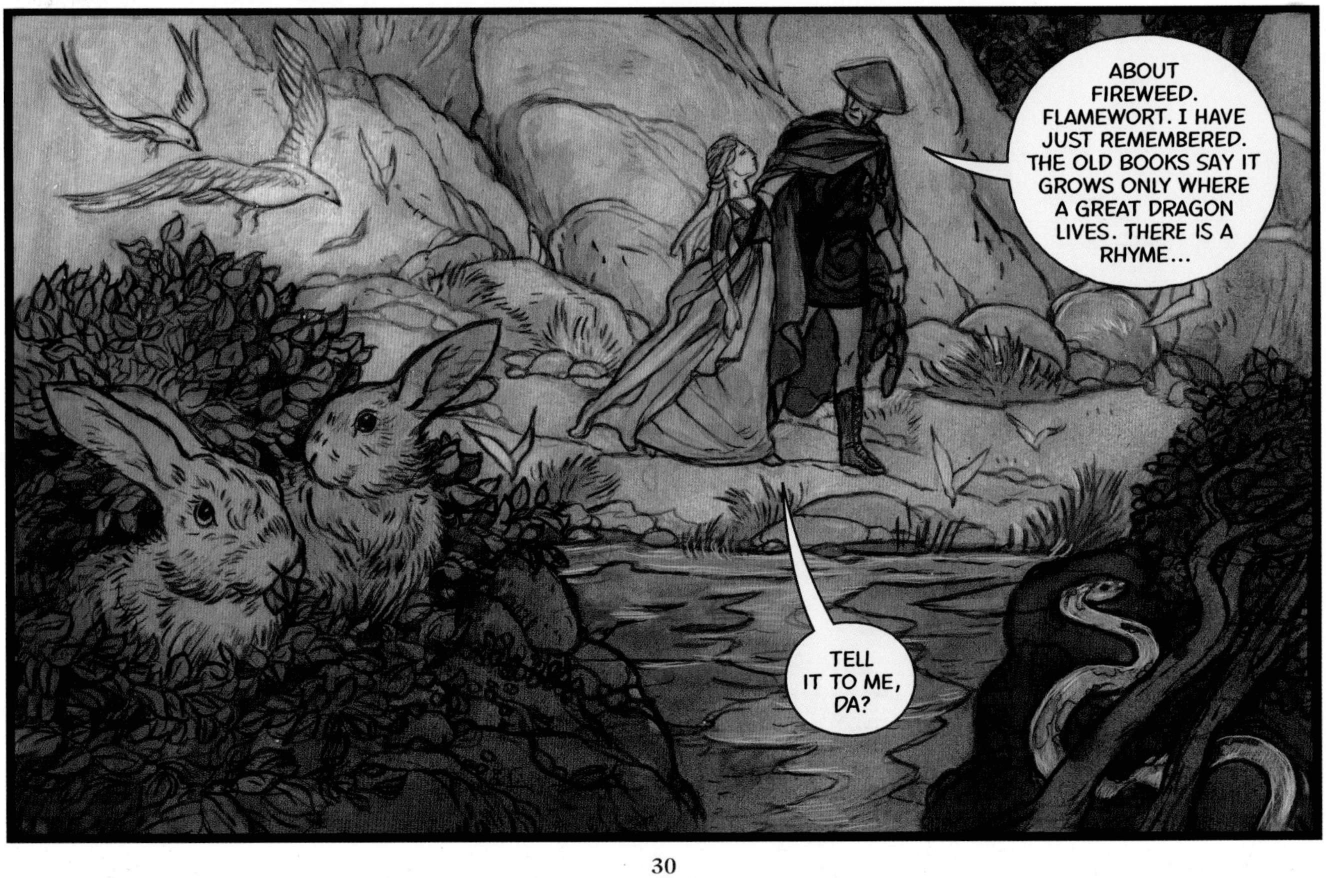
ABOUT FIREWEED. FLAMEWORT. I HAVE JUST REMEMBERED. THE OLD BOOKS SAY IT GROWS ONLY WHERE A GREAT DRAGON LIVES. THERE IS A RHYME...
TELL IT TO ME, DA?

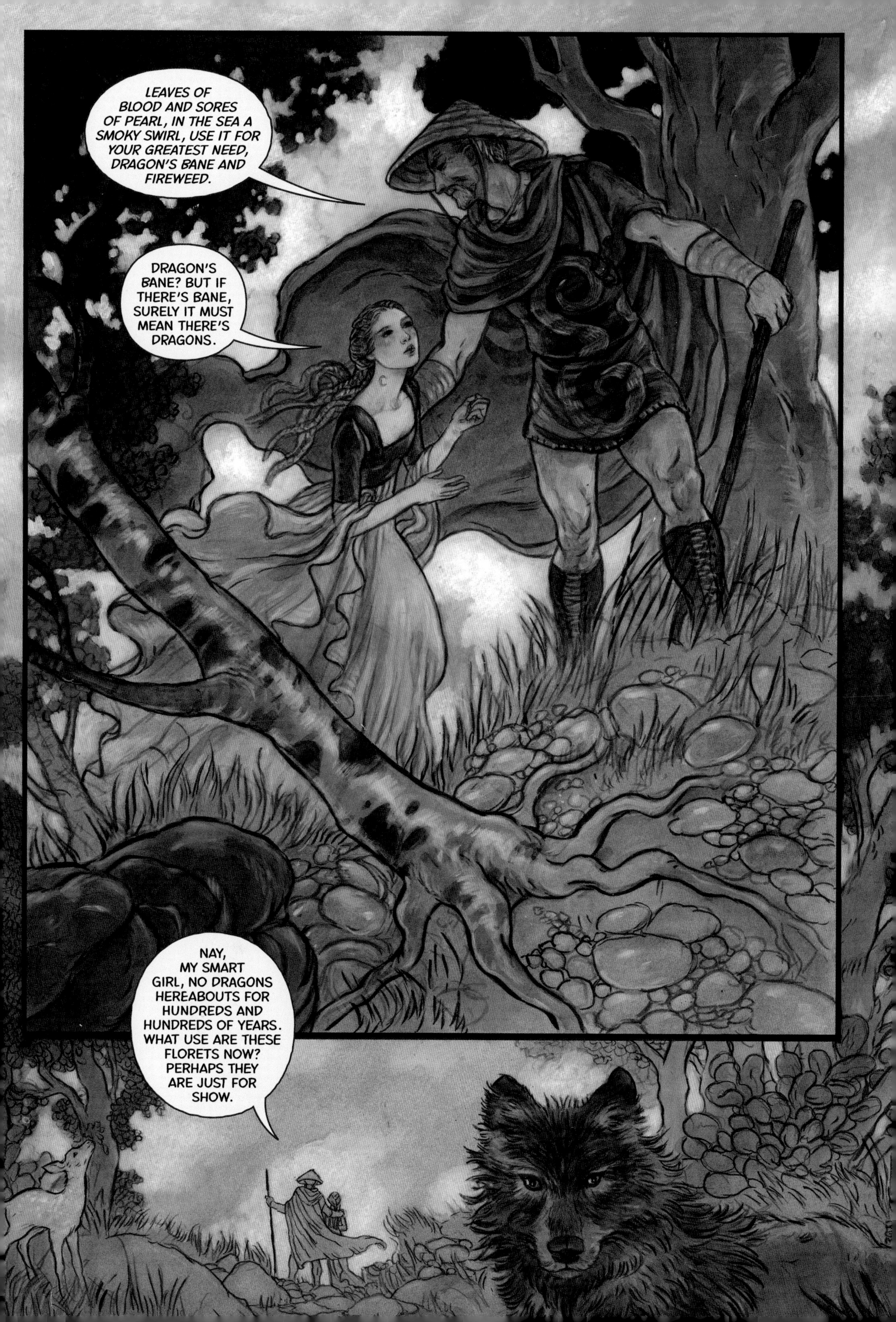
LEAVES OF BLOOD AND SORES OF PEARL, IN THE SEA A SMOKY SWIRL, USE IT FOR YOUR GREATEST NEED, DRAGON'S BANE AND FIREWEED.
DRAGON'S BANE? BUT IF THERE'S BANE, SURELY IT MUST MEAN THERE'S DRAGONS.
NAY, MY SMART GIRL, NO DRAGONS HEREABOUTS FOR HUNDREDS AND HUNDREDS OF YEARS. WHAT USE ARE THESE FLORETS NOW? PERHAPS THEY ARE JUST FOR SHOW.

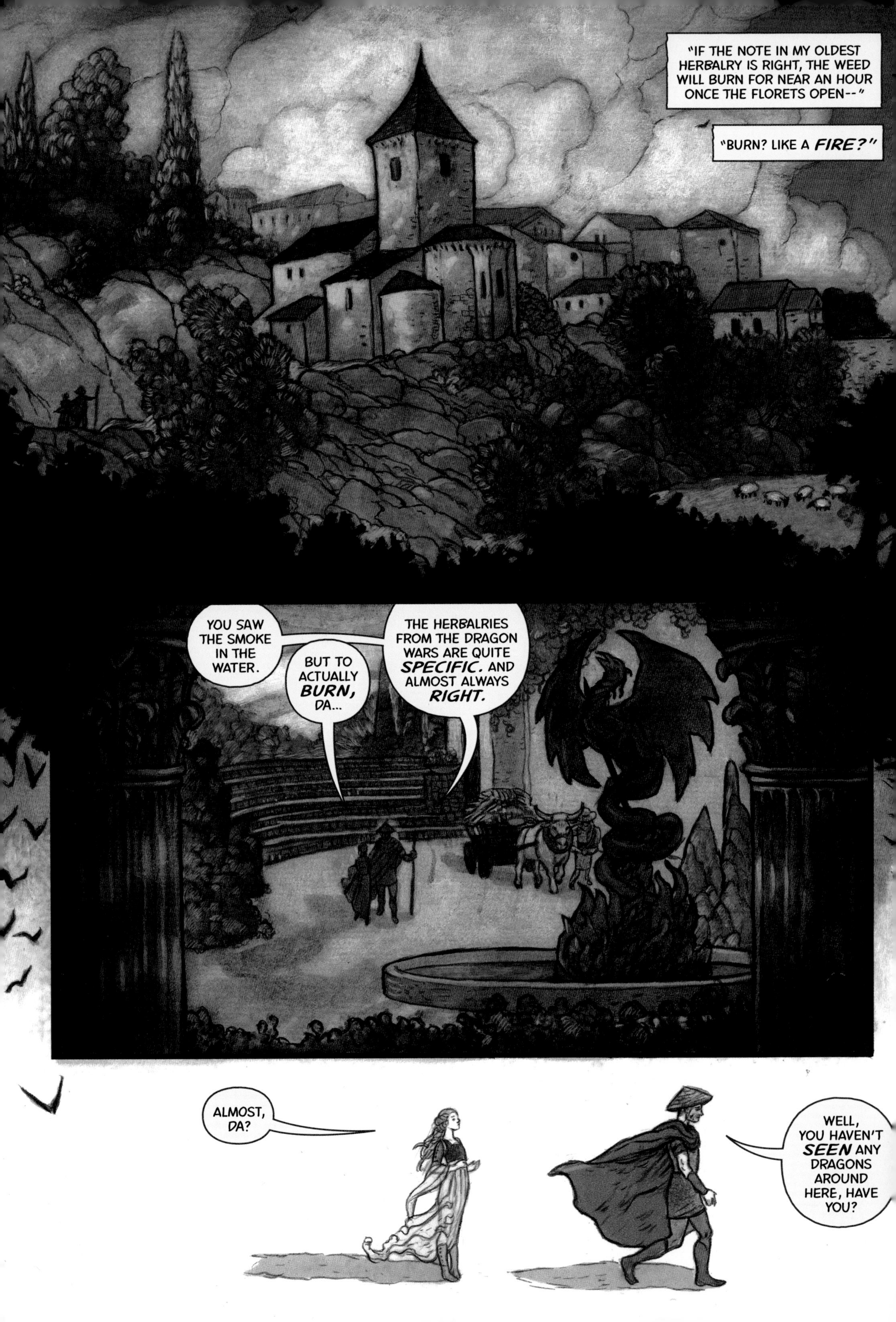
"IF THE NOTE IN MY OLDEST HERBALRY IS RIGHT, THE WEED WILL BURN FOR NEAR AN HOUR ONCE THE FLORETS OPEN--"
"BURN? LIKE A FIRE?"
YOU SAW THE SMOKE IN THE WATER.
THE HERBALRIES FROM THE DRAGON WARS ARE QUITE SPECIFIC. AND ALMOST ALWAYS RIGHT.
BUT TO ACTUALLY BURN, DA...
ALMOST, DA?
WELL, YOU HAVEN'T SEEN ANY DRAGONS AROUND HERE, HAVE YOU?

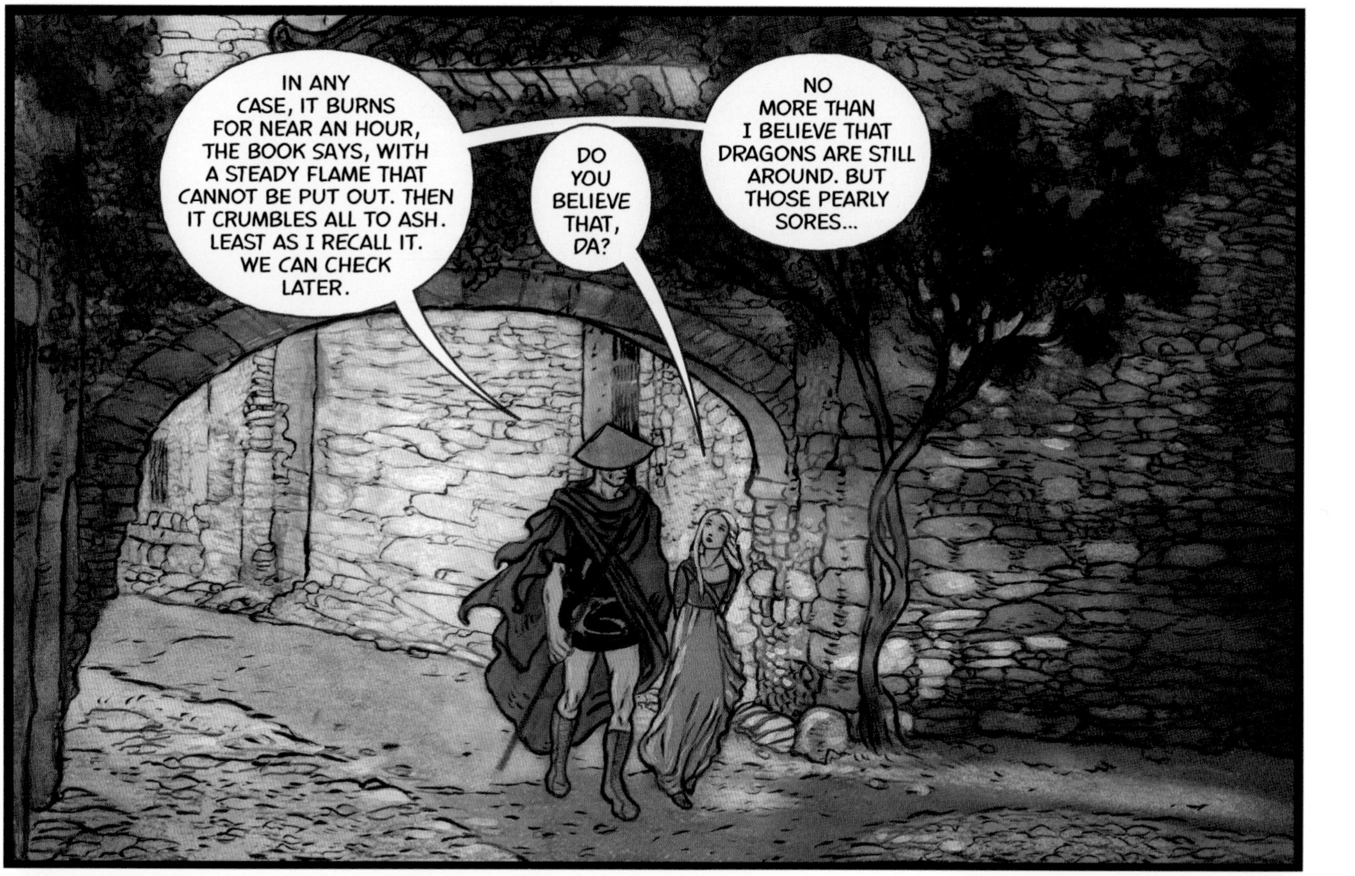
IN ANY CASE, IT BURNS FOR NEAR AN HOUR, THE BOOK SAYS, WITH A STEADY FLAME THAT CANNOT BE PUT OUT. THEN IT CRUMBLES ALL TO ASH. LEAST AS I RECALL IT. WE CAN CHECK LATER.
DO YOU BELIEVE THAT, DA?
NO MORE THAN I BELIEVE THAT DRAGONS ARE STILL AROUND. BUT THOSE PEARLY SORES...

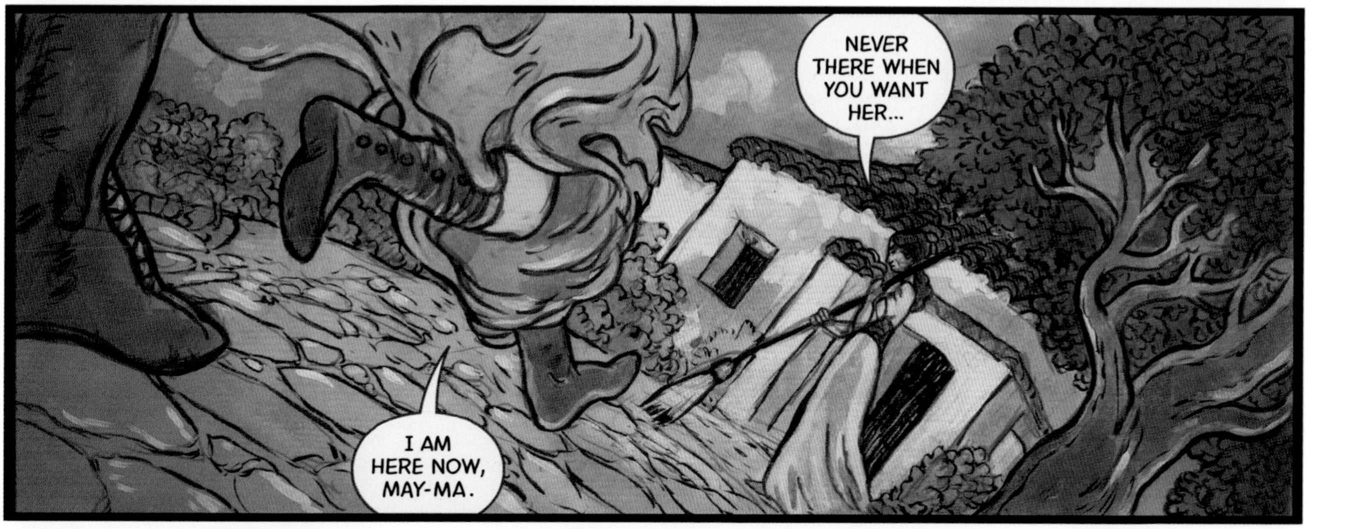
NEVER THERE WHEN YOU WANT HER...
I AM HERE NOW, MAY-MA.

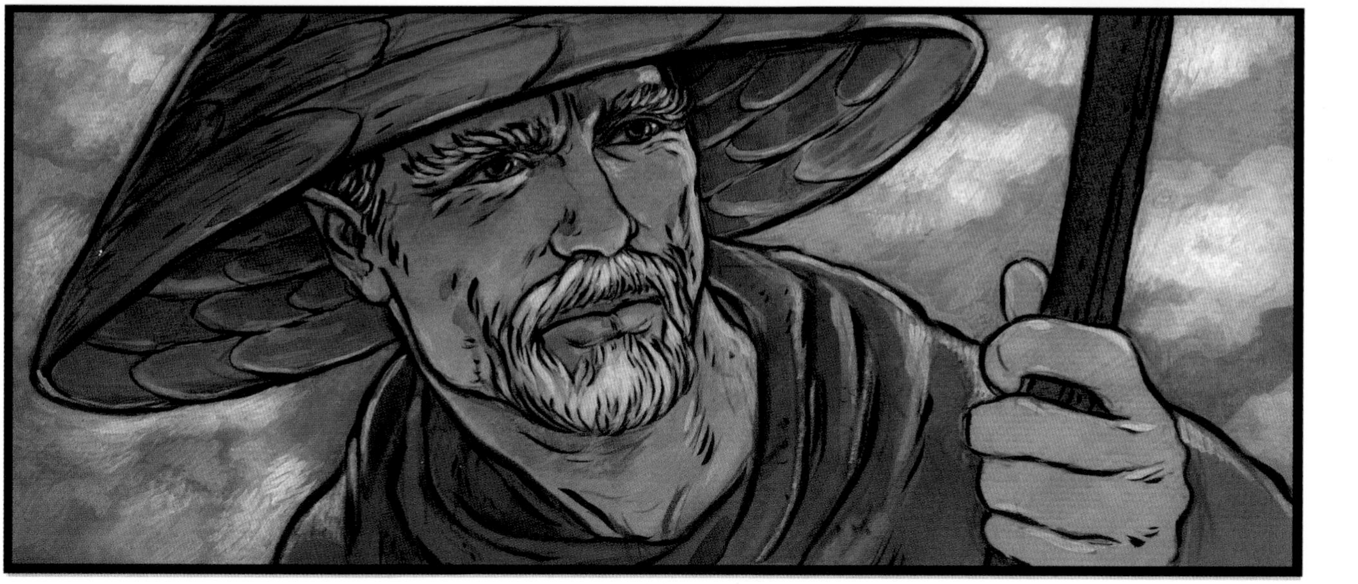

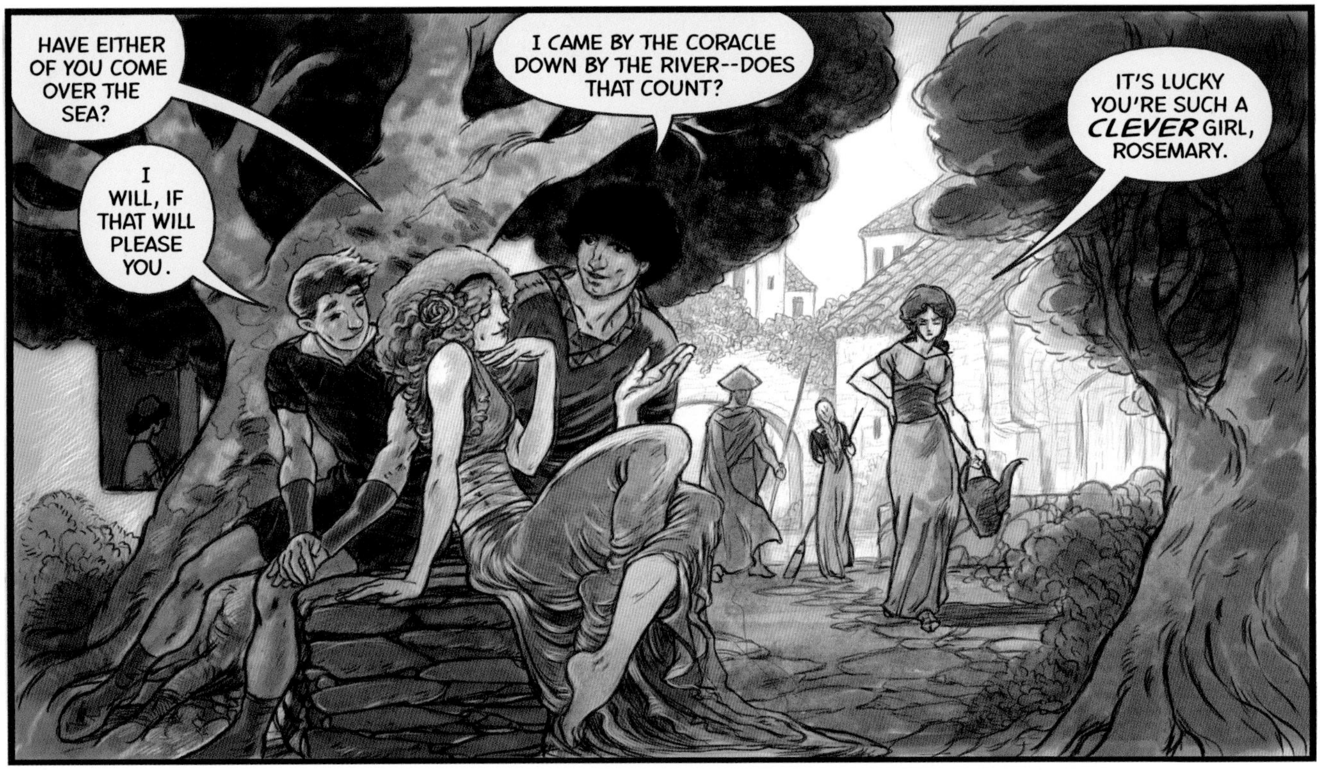
HAVE EITHER OF YOU COME OVER THE SEA?
I WILL, IF THAT WILL PLEASE YOU.
I CAME BY THE CORACLE DOWN BY THE RIVER--DOES THAT COUNT?
IT'S LUCKY YOU'RE SUCH A *CLEVER* GIRL, ROSEMARY.

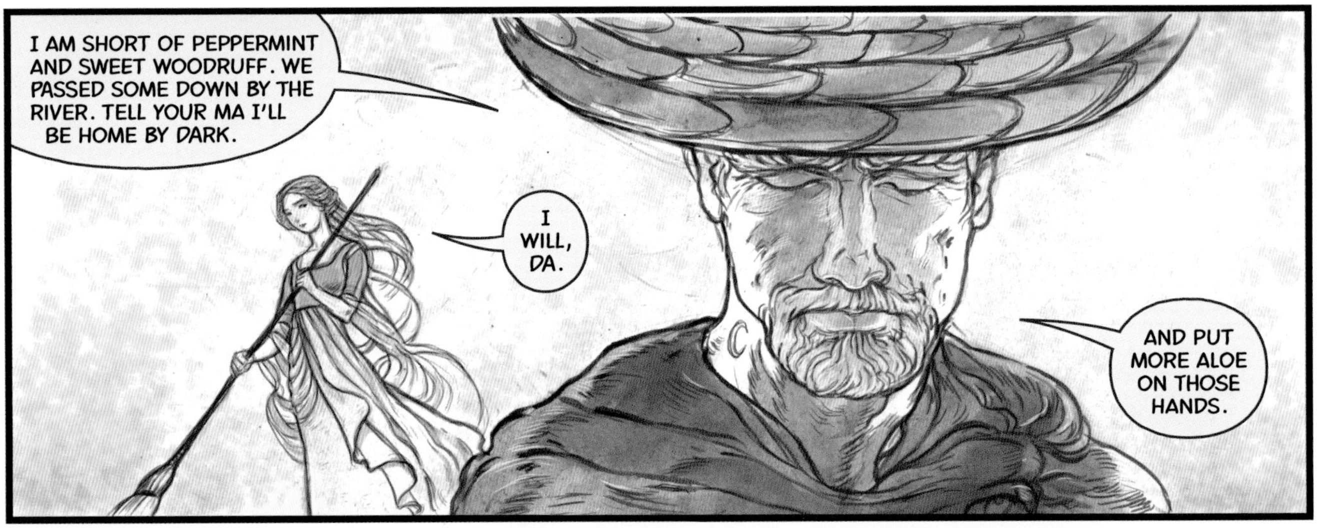
I AM SHORT OF PEPPERMINT AND SWEET WOODRUFF. WE PASSED SOME DOWN BY THE RIVER. TELL YOUR MA I'LL BE HOME BY DARK.
I WILL, DA.
AND PUT MORE ALOE ON THOSE HANDS.

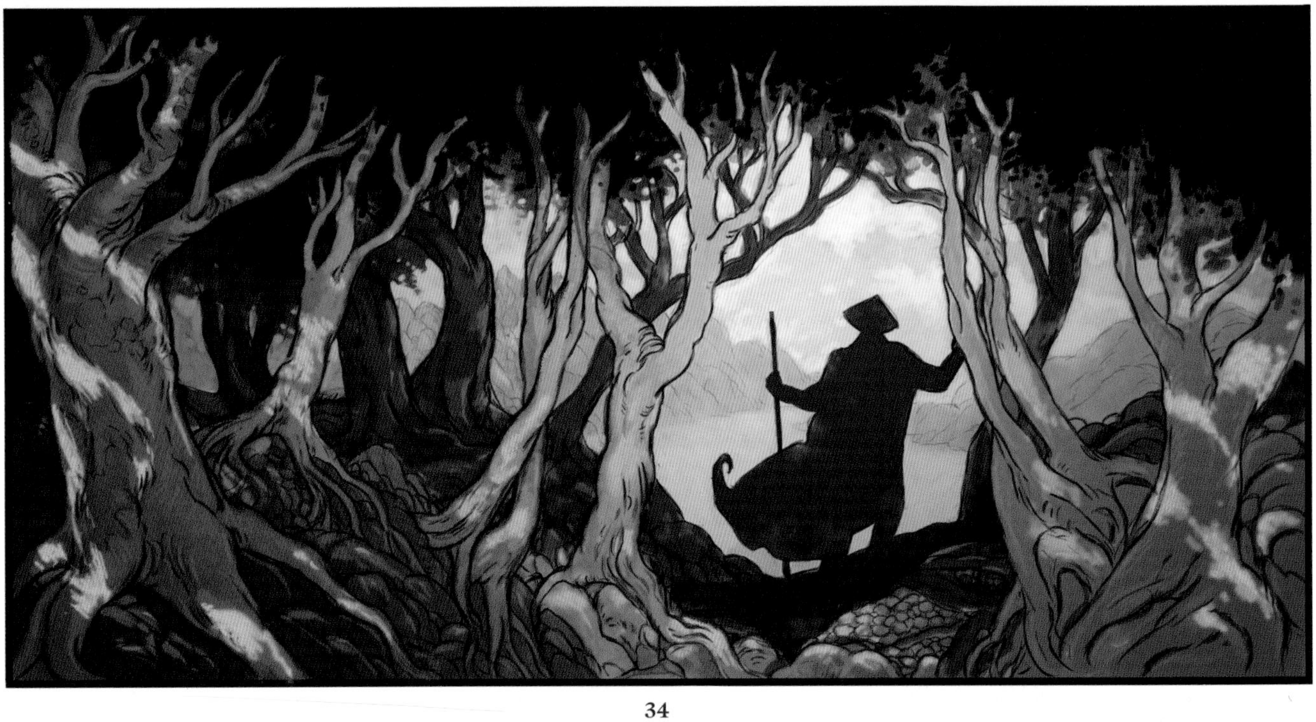

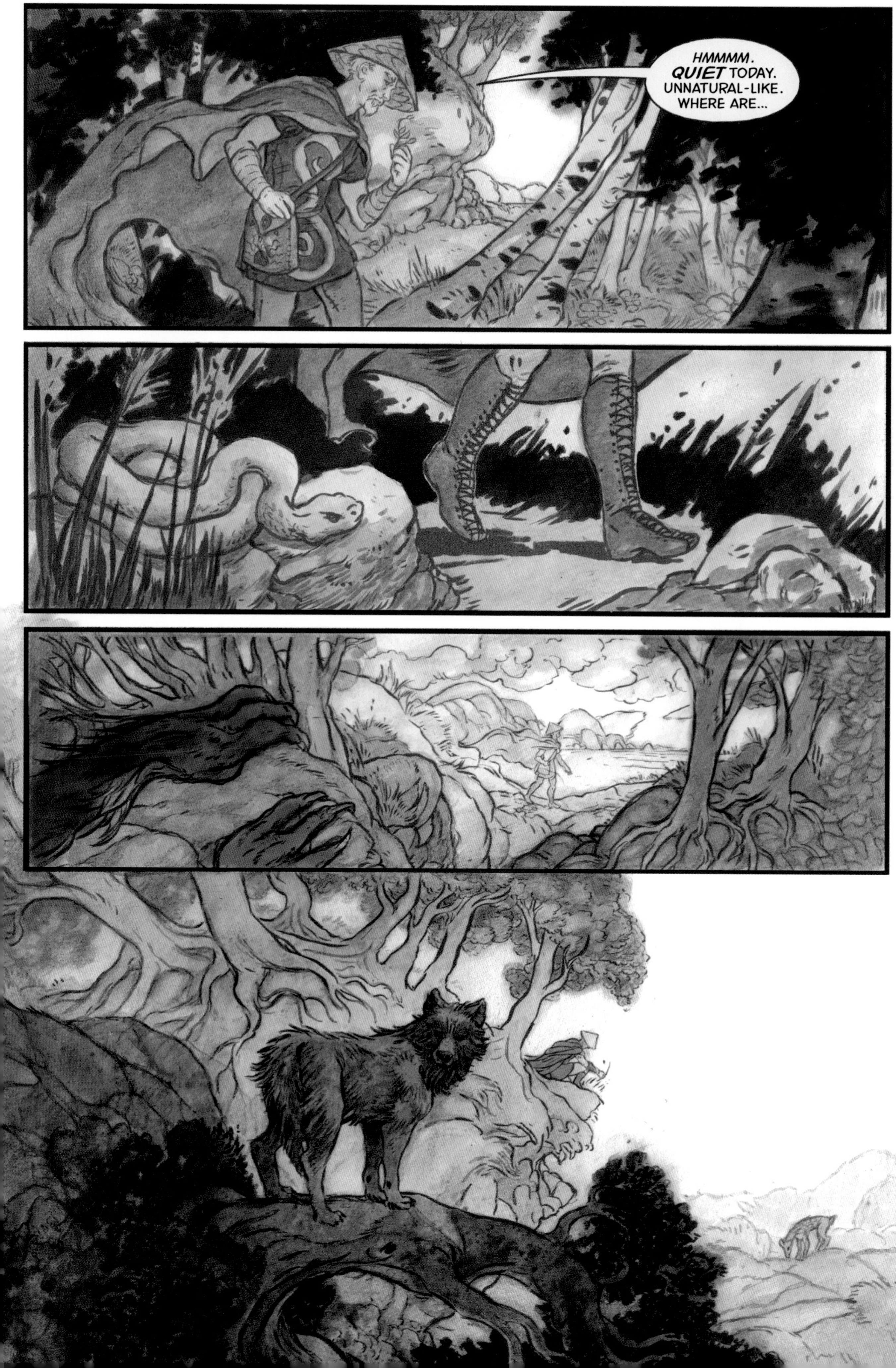
HMMMM. QUIET TODAY. UNNATURAL-LIKE. WHERE ARE...

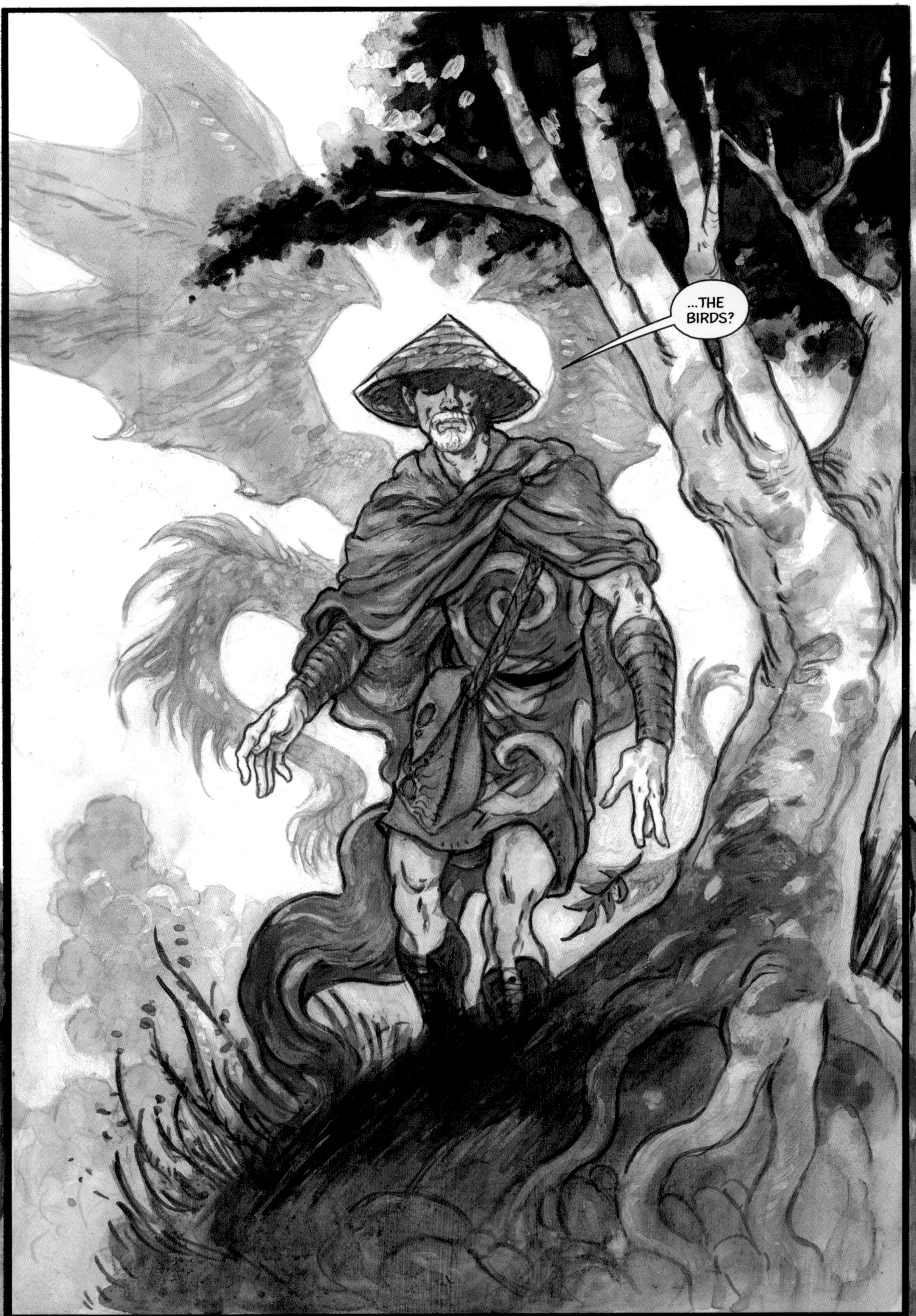
...THE BIRDS?

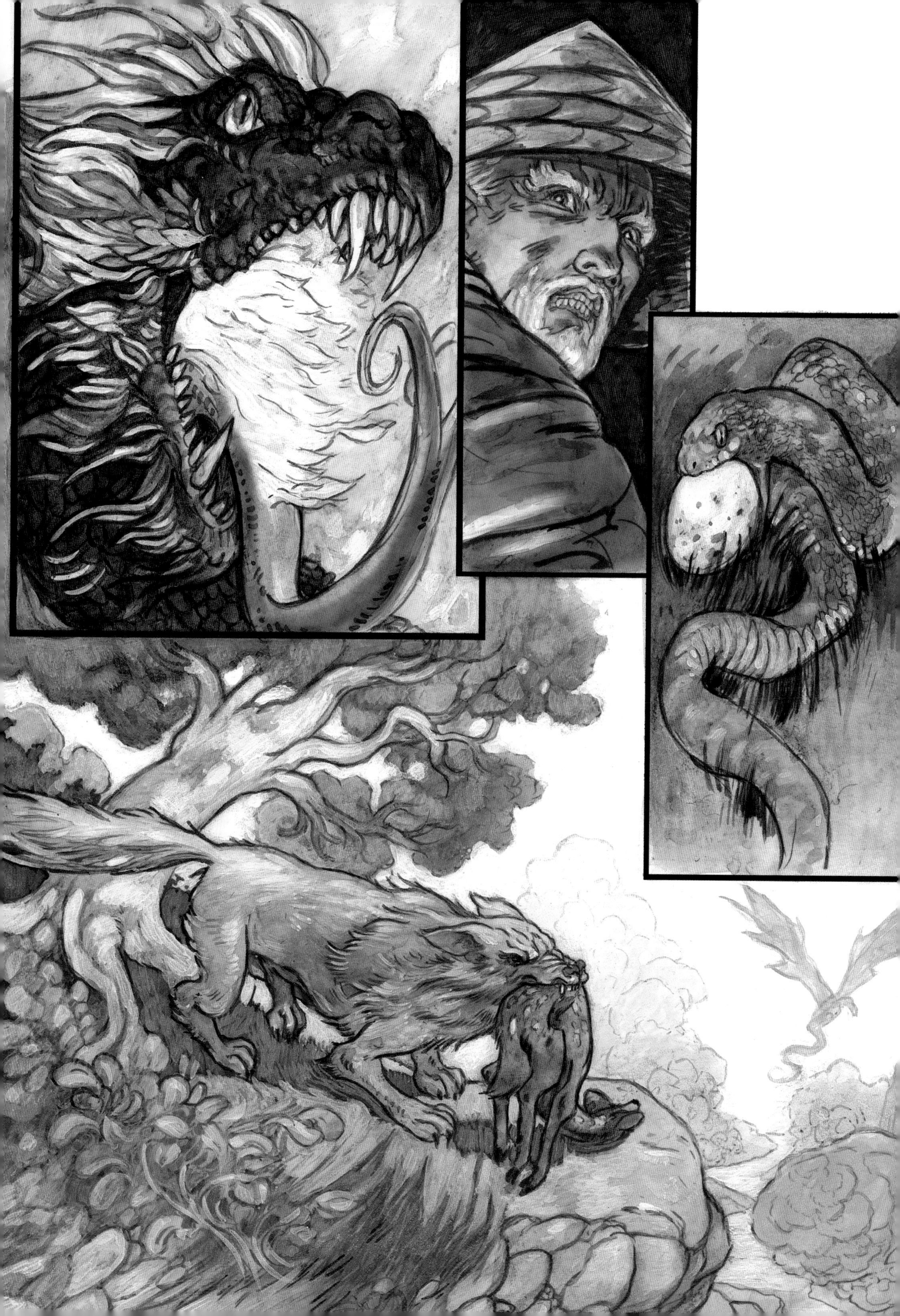

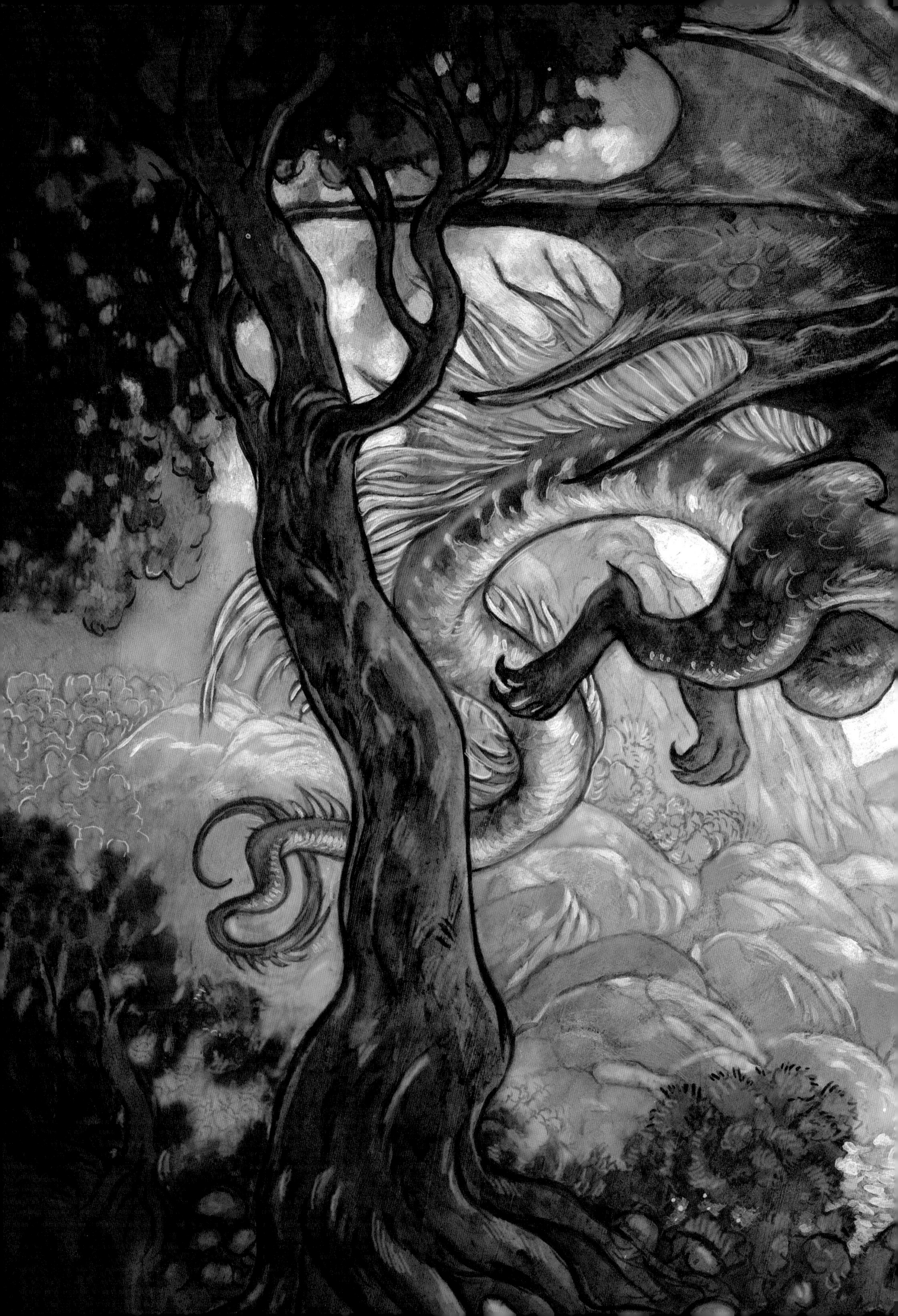

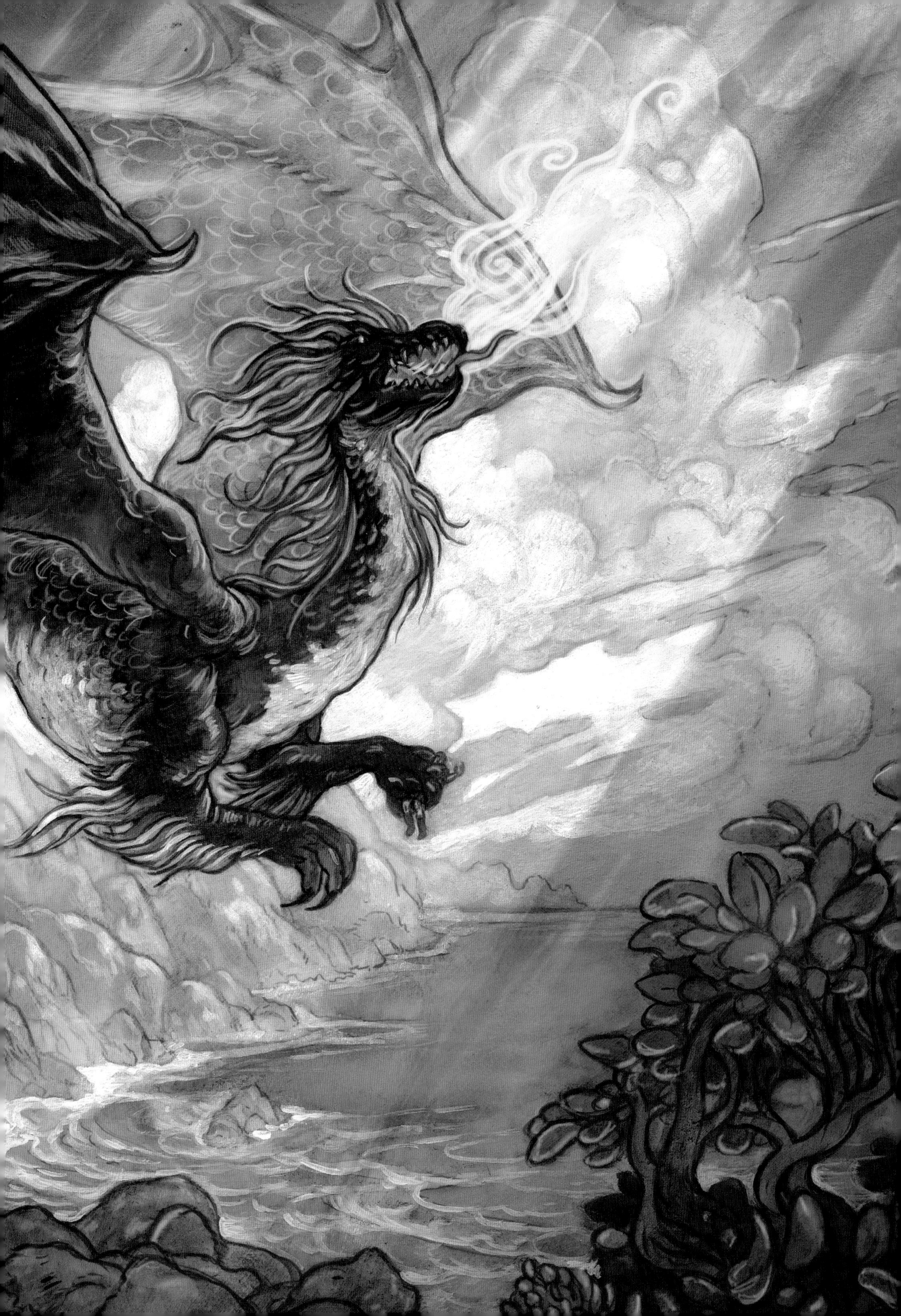

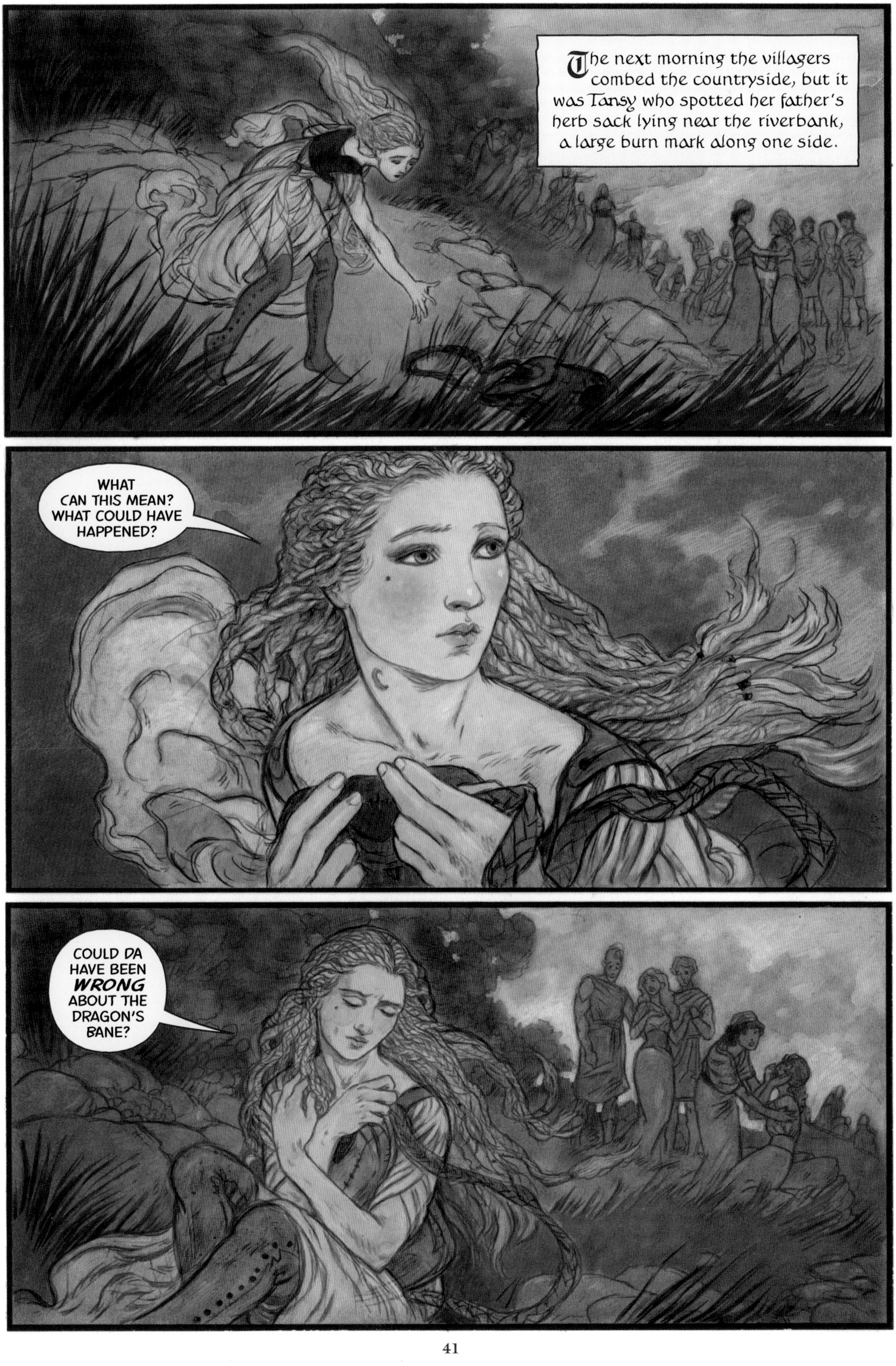
The next morning the villagers combed the countryside, but it was Tansy who spotted her father's herb sack lying near the riverbank, a large burn mark along one side.
WHAT CAN THIS MEAN? WHAT COULD HAVE HAPPENED?
COULD DA HAVE BEEN *WRONG* ABOUT THE DRAGON'S BANE?

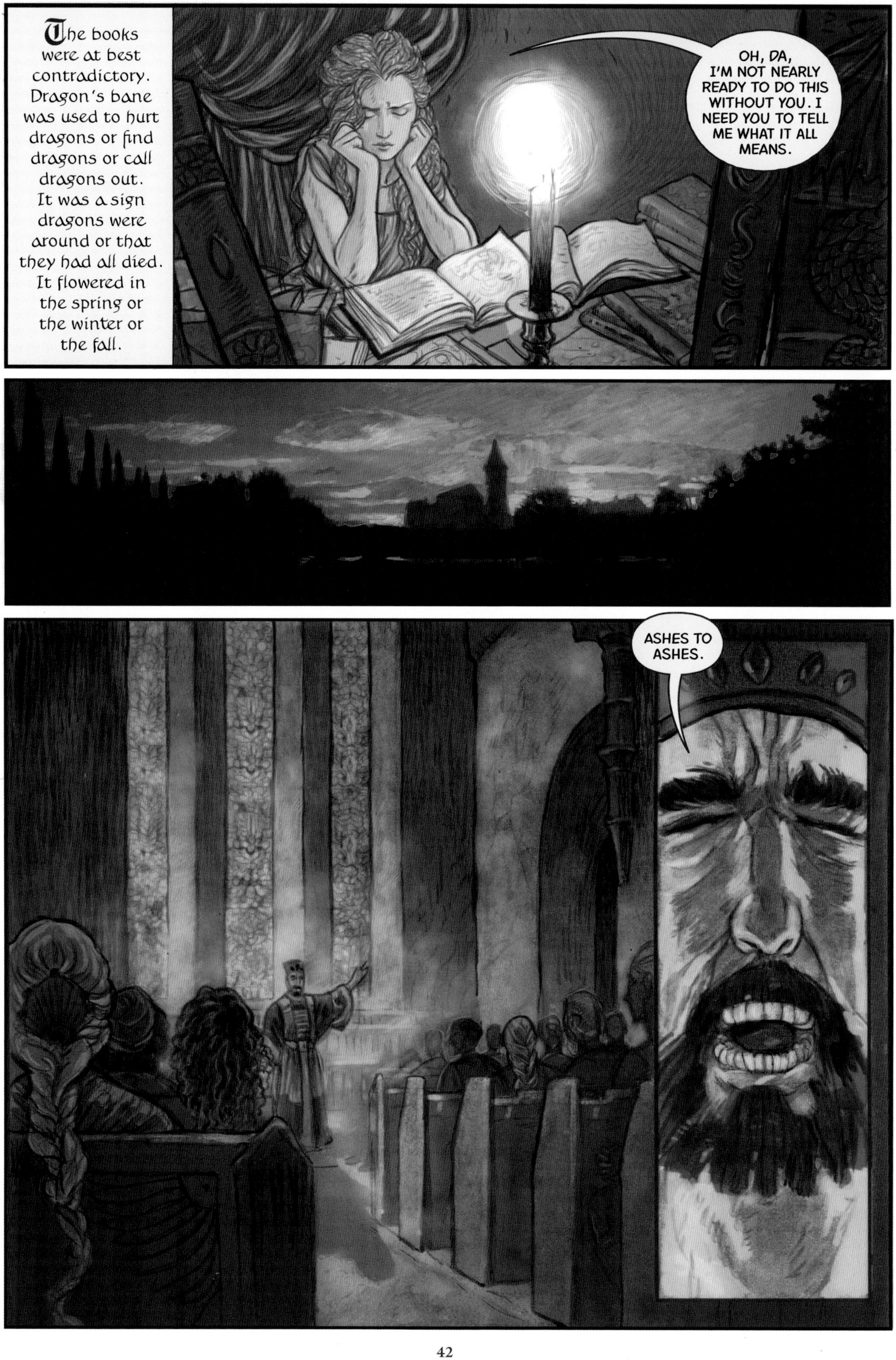
The books were at best contradictory. Dragon's bane was used to hurt dragons or find dragons or call dragons out. It was a sign dragons were around or that they had all died. It flowered in the spring or the winter or the fall.
OH, DA, I'M NOT NEARLY READY TO DO THIS WITHOUT YOU. I NEED YOU TO TELL ME WHAT IT ALL MEANS.
ASHES TO ASHES.

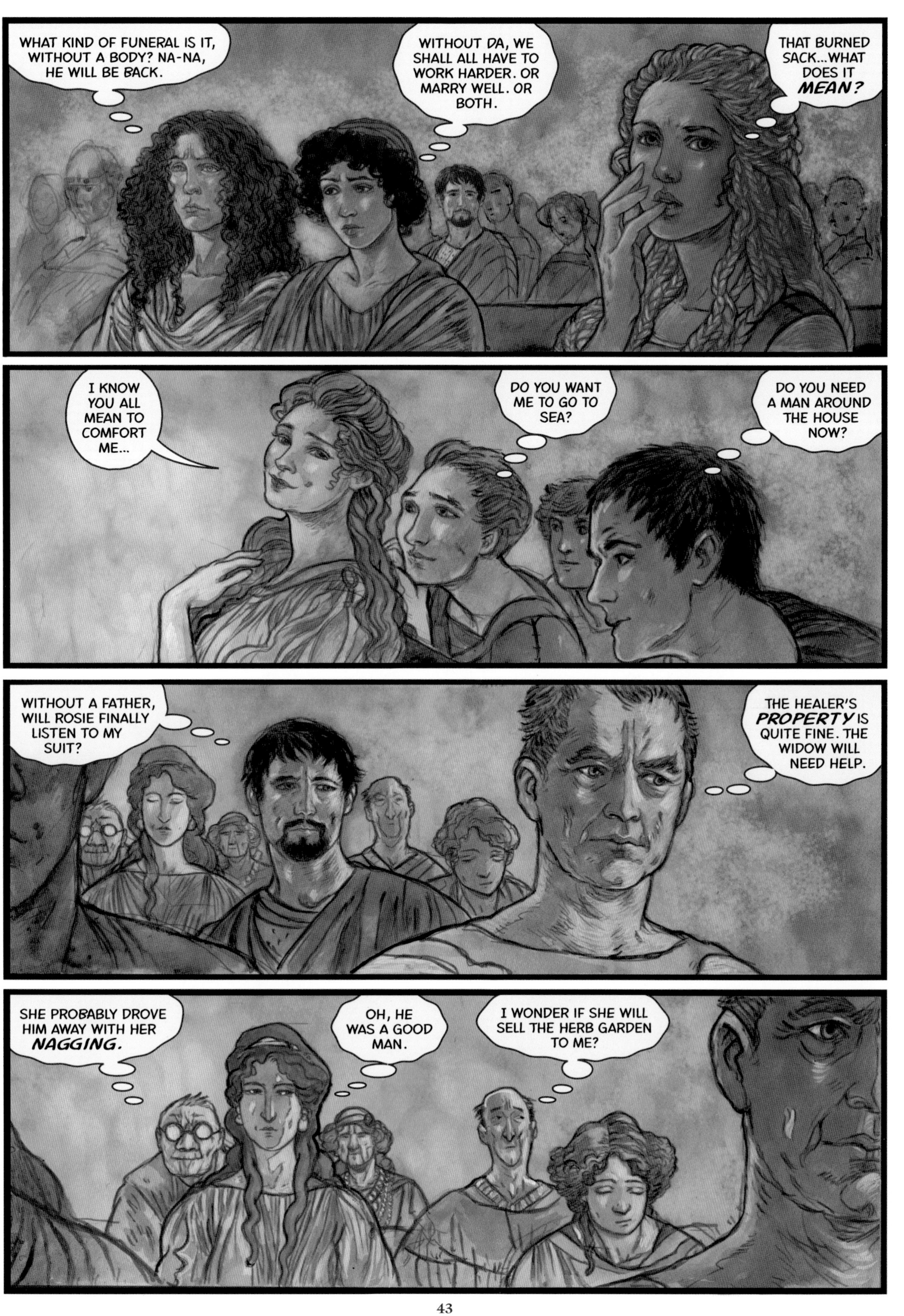
WHAT KIND OF FUNERAL IS IT, WITHOUT A BODY? NA-NA, HE WILL BE BACK.
WITHOUT DA, WE SHALL ALL HAVE TO WORK HARDER. OR MARRY WELL. OR BOTH.
THAT BURNED SACK...WHAT DOES IT *MEAN?*
I KNOW YOU ALL MEAN TO COMFORT ME...
DO YOU WANT ME TO GO TO SEA?
DO YOU NEED A MAN AROUND THE HOUSE NOW?
WITHOUT A FATHER, WILL ROSIE FINALLY LISTEN TO MY SUIT?
THE HEALER'S *PROPERTY* IS QUITE FINE. THE WIDOW WILL NEED HELP.
SHE PROBABLY DROVE HIM AWAY WITH HER *NAGGING.*
OH, HE WAS A GOOD MAN.
I WONDER IF SHE WILL SELL THE HERB GARDEN TO ME?

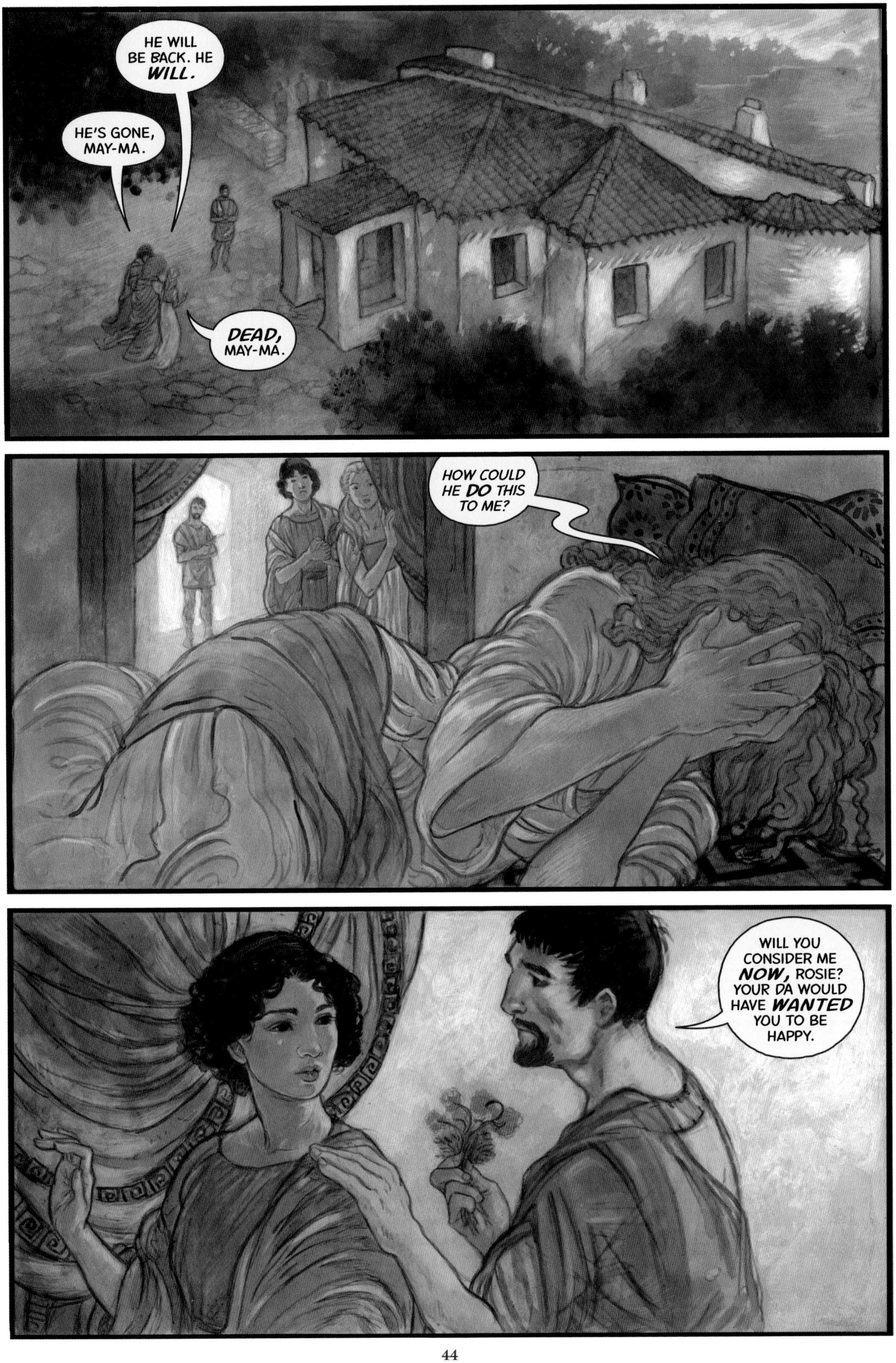
HE'S GONE, MAY-MA.
HE WILL BE BACK. HE WILL.
DEAD, MAY-MA.
HOW COULD HE DO THIS TO ME?
WILL YOU CONSIDER ME NOW, ROSIE? YOUR DA WOULD HAVE WANTED YOU TO BE HAPPY.

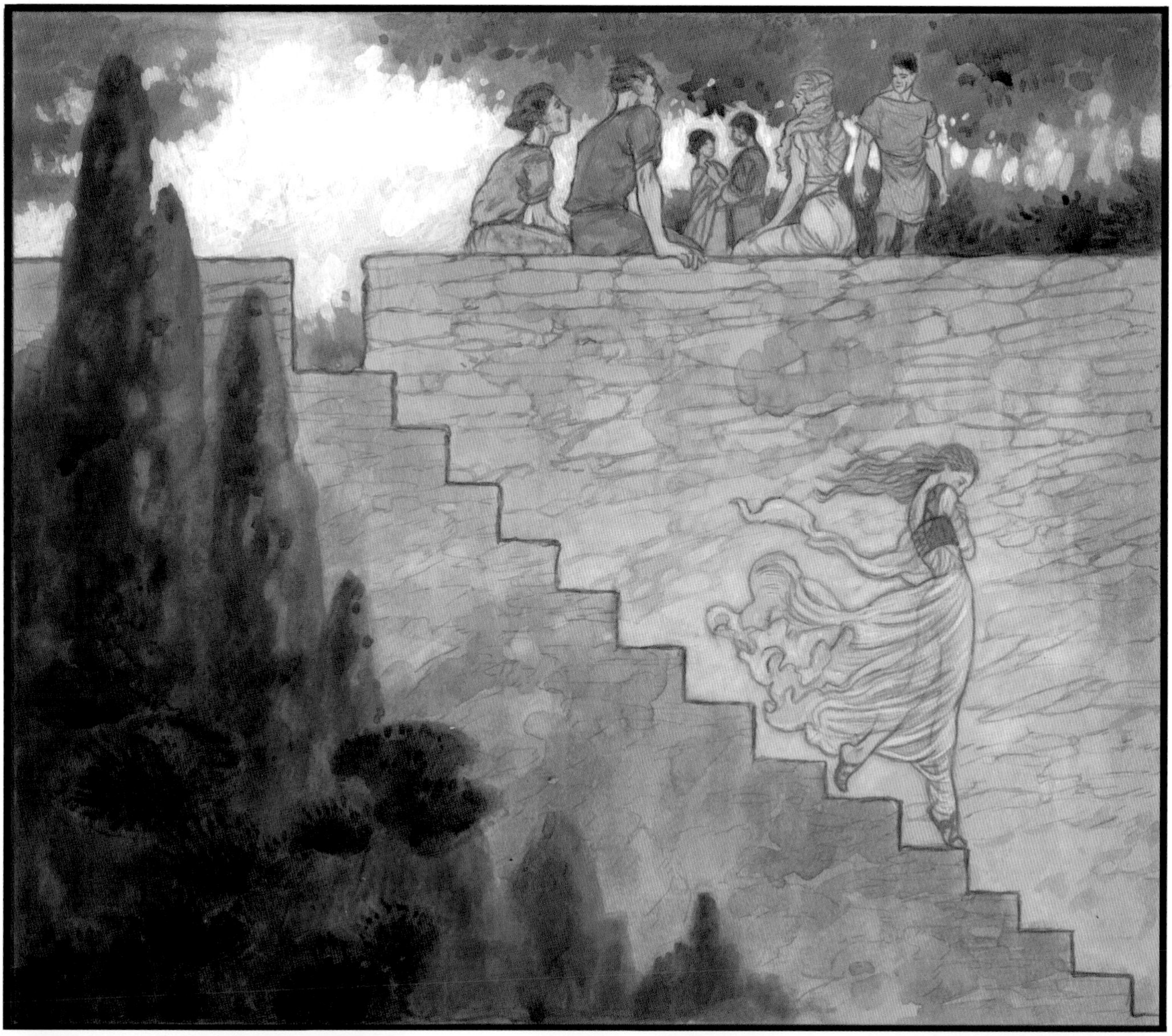

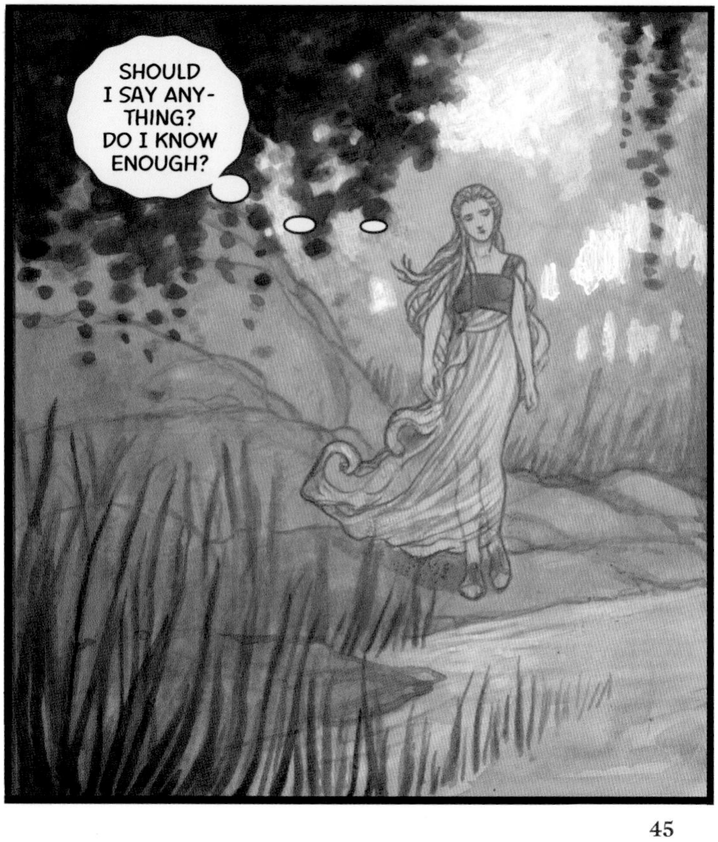
SHOULD I SAY ANY-THING? DO I KNOW ENOUGH?

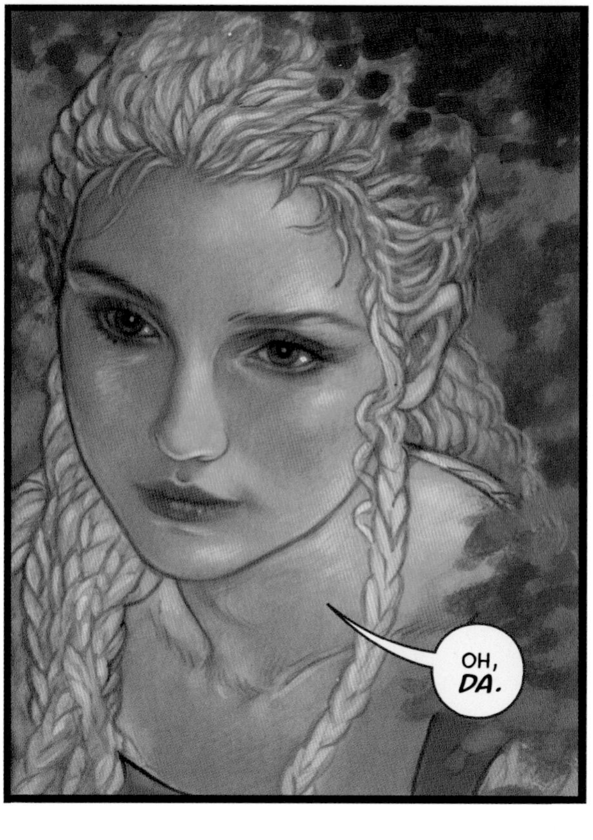
OH, *DA.*

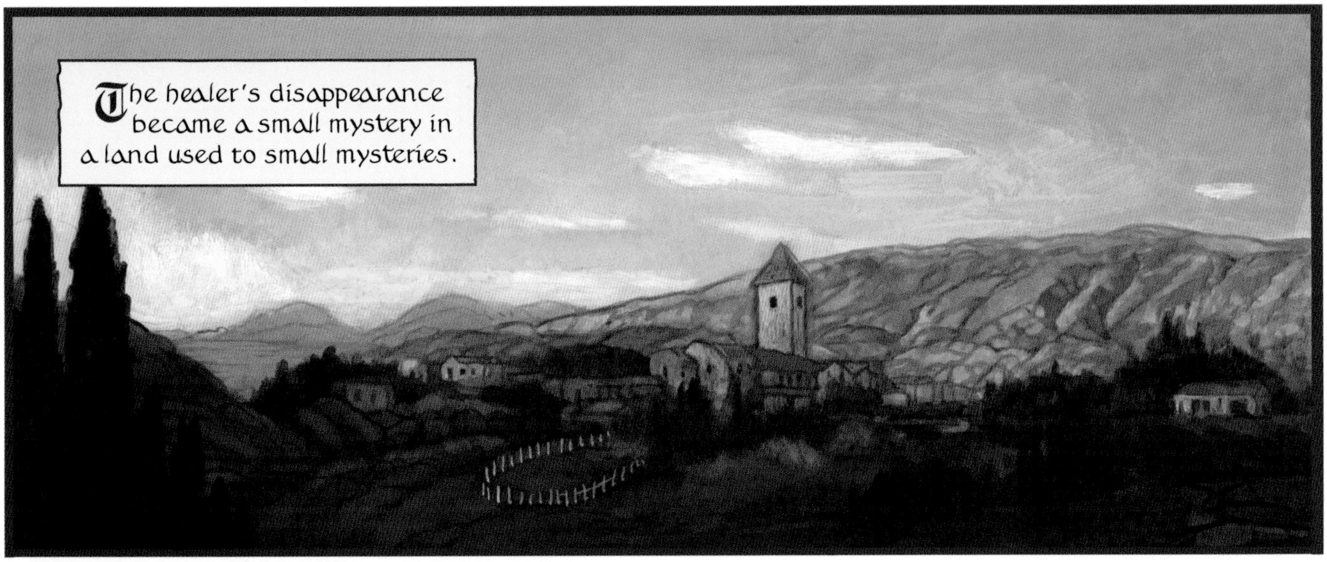
The healer's disappearance became a small mystery in a land used to small mysteries.

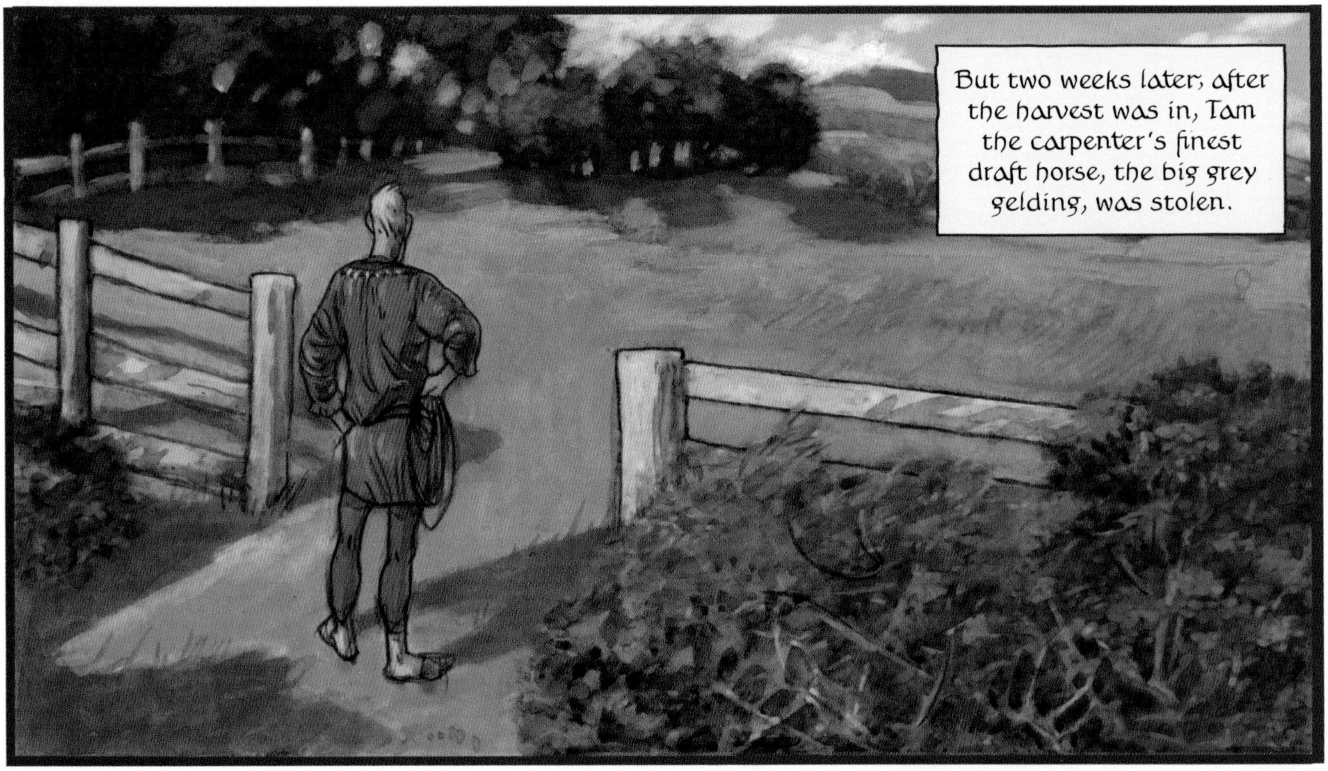
But two weeks later, after the harvest was in, Tam the carpenter's finest draft horse, the big grey gelding, was stolen.

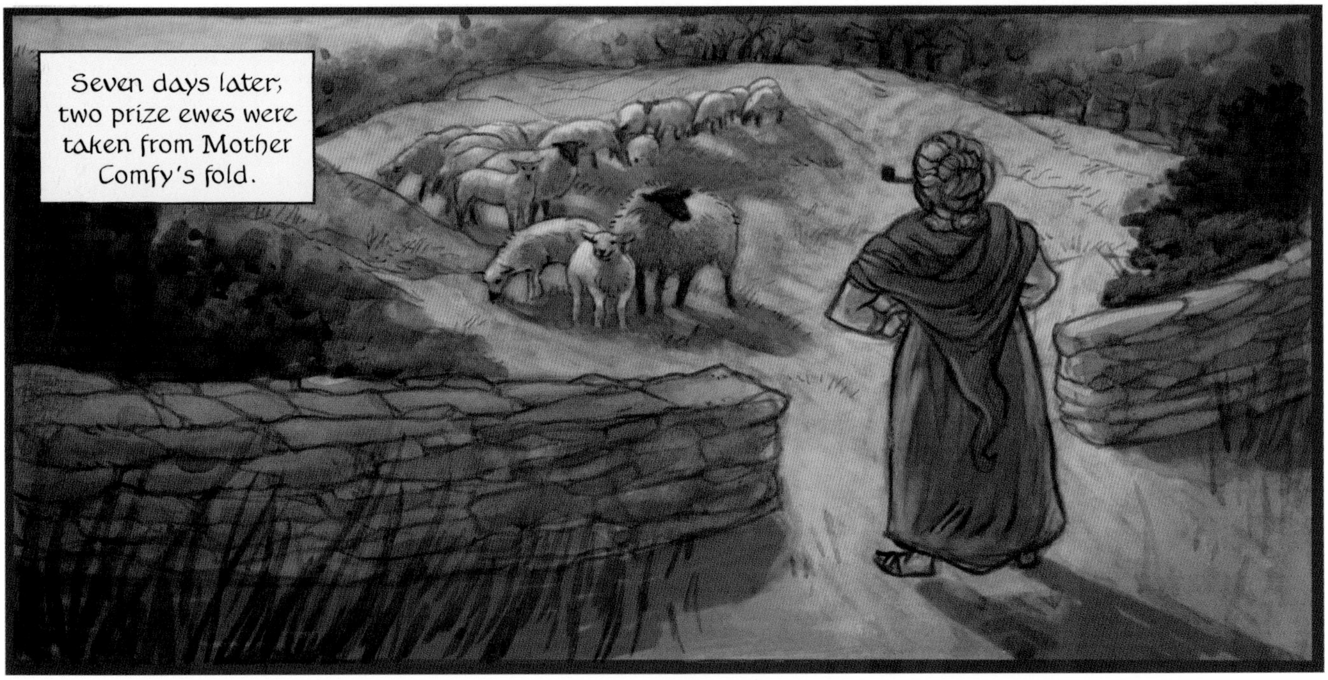
Seven days later, two prize ewes were taken from Mother Comfy's fold.

48

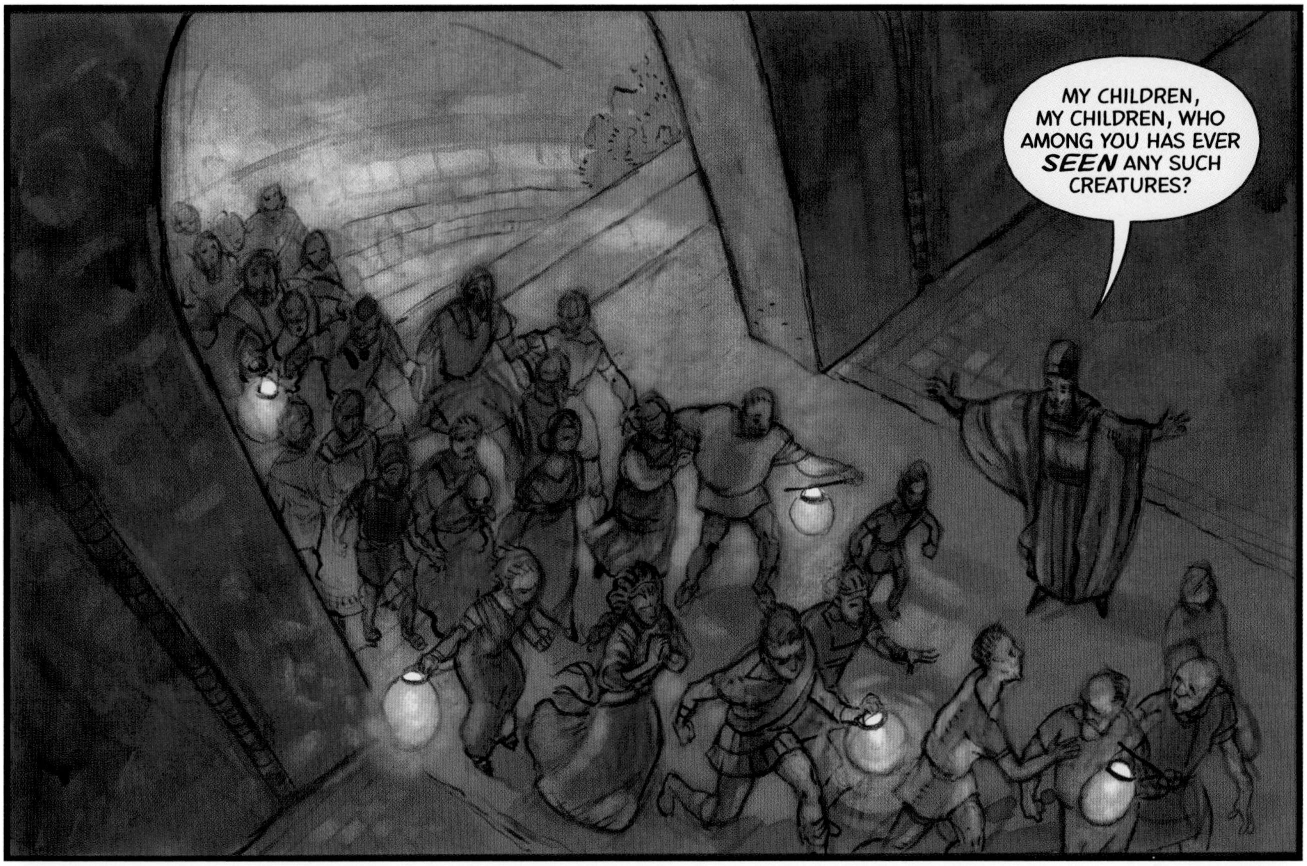
MY CHILDREN, MY CHILDREN, WHO AMONG YOU HAS EVER SEEN ANY SUCH CREATURES?

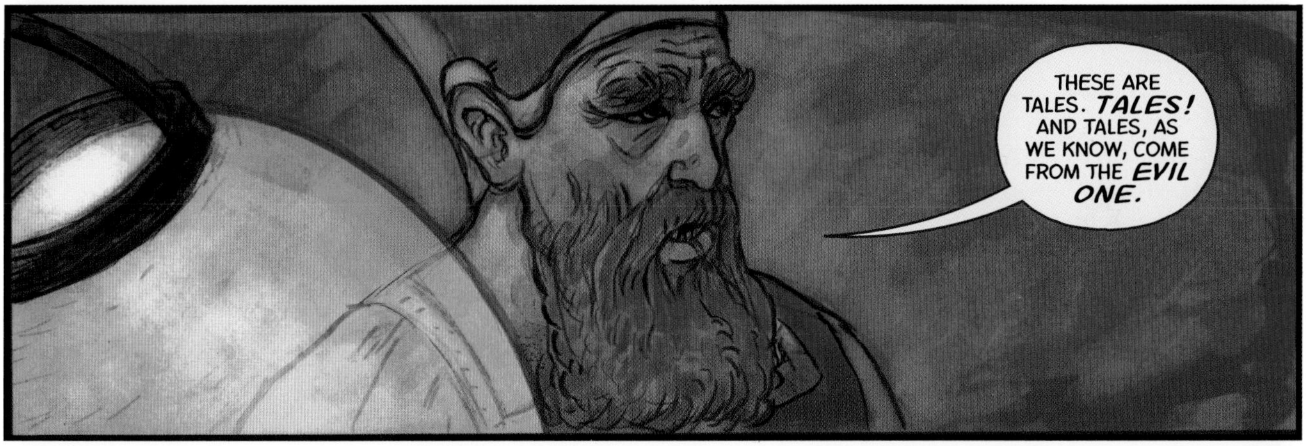
THESE ARE TALES. TALES! AND TALES, AS WE KNOW, COME FROM THE EVIL ONE.

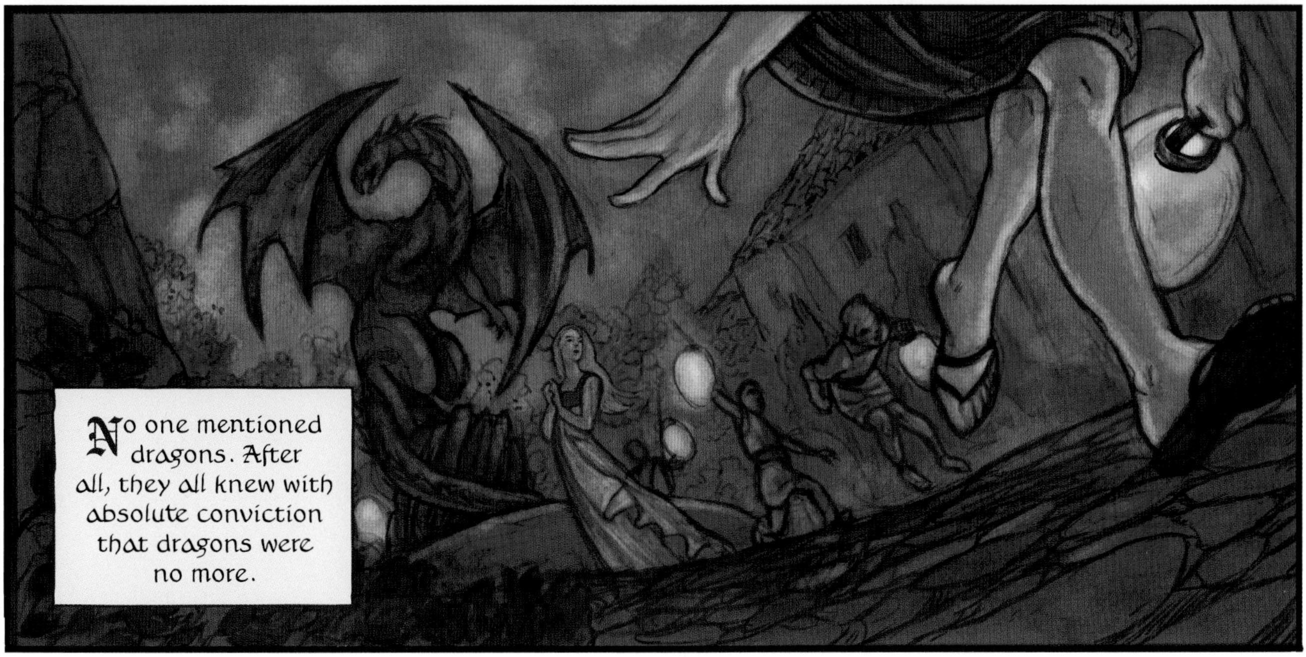
No one mentioned dragons. After all, they all knew with absolute conviction that dragons were no more.

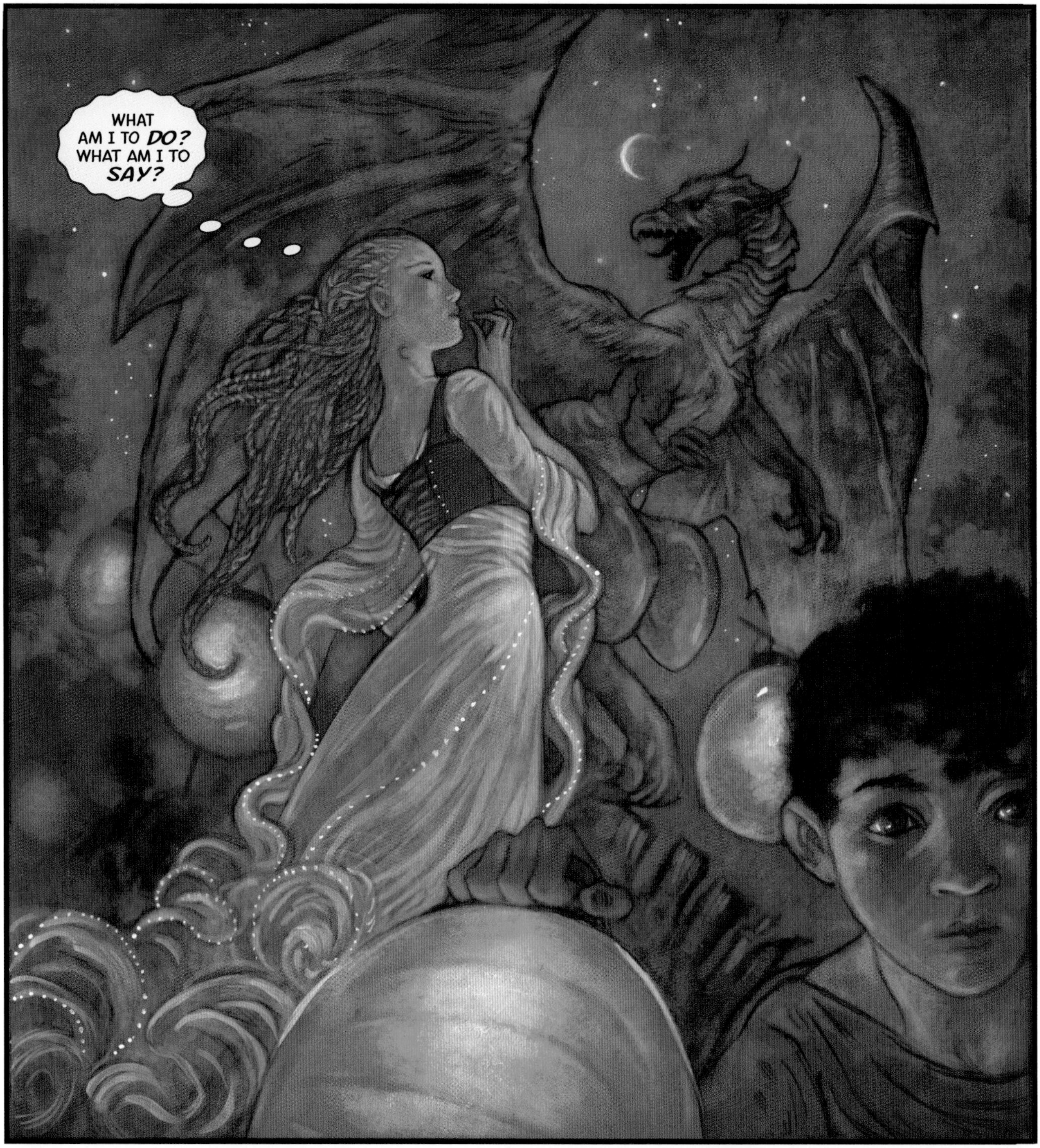
WHAT AM I TO DO? WHAT AM I TO SAY?

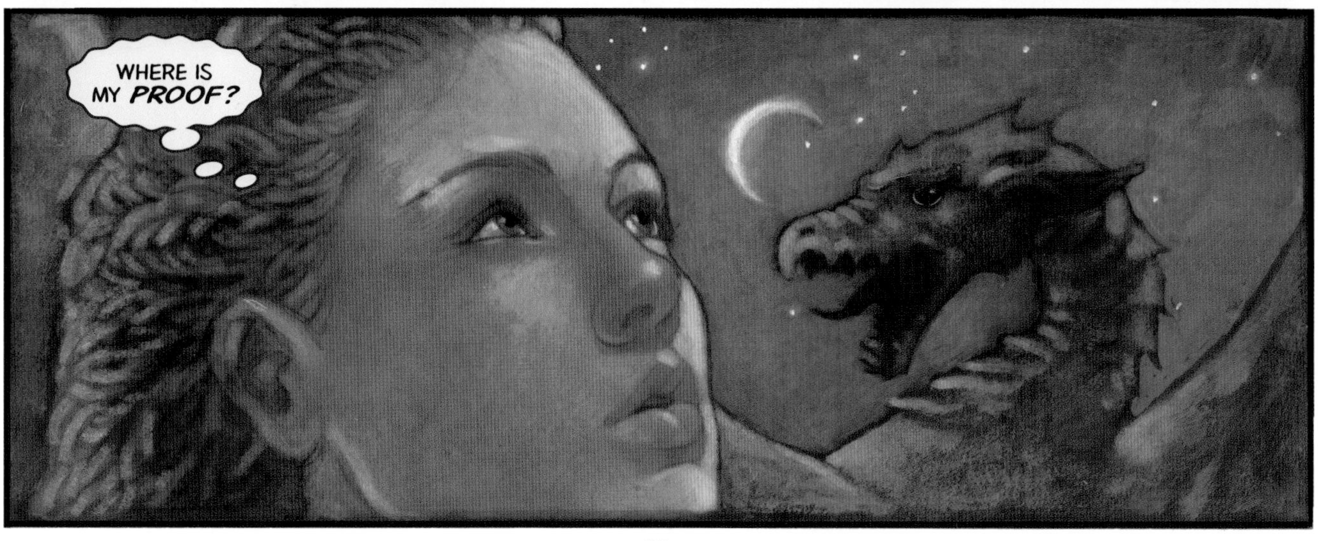
WHERE IS MY PROOF?

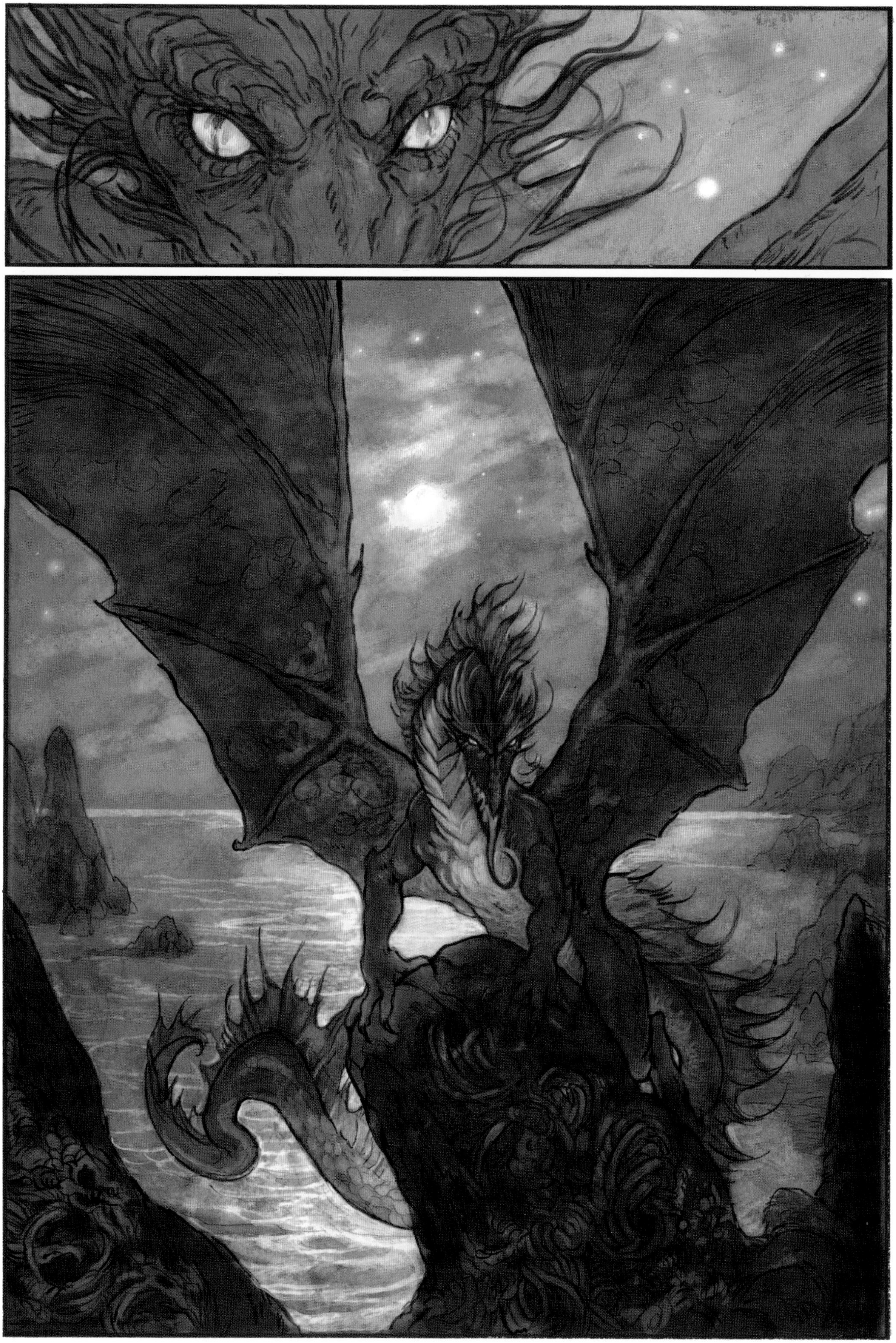

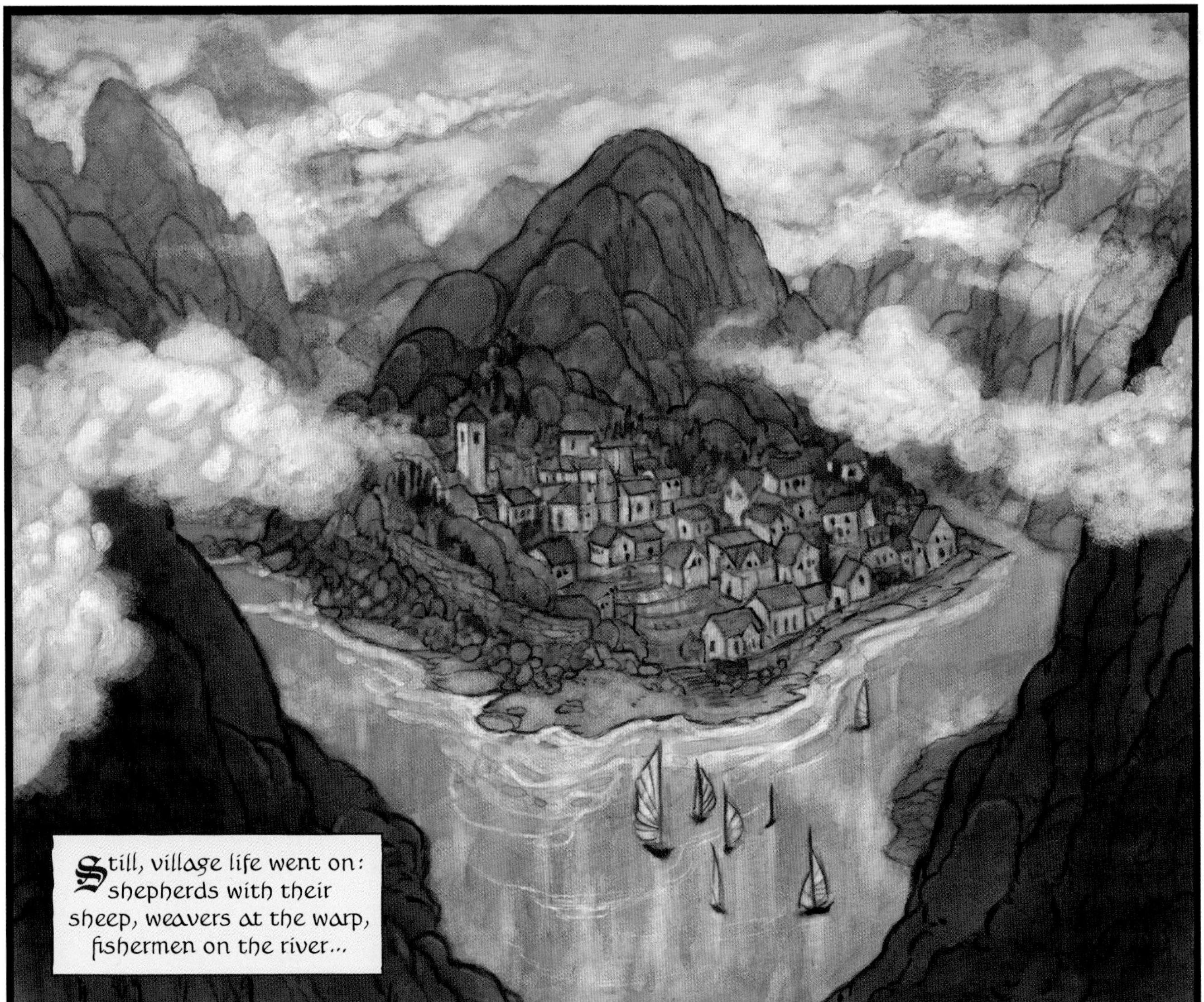
Still, village life went on: shepherds with their sheep, weavers at the warp, fishermen on the river...

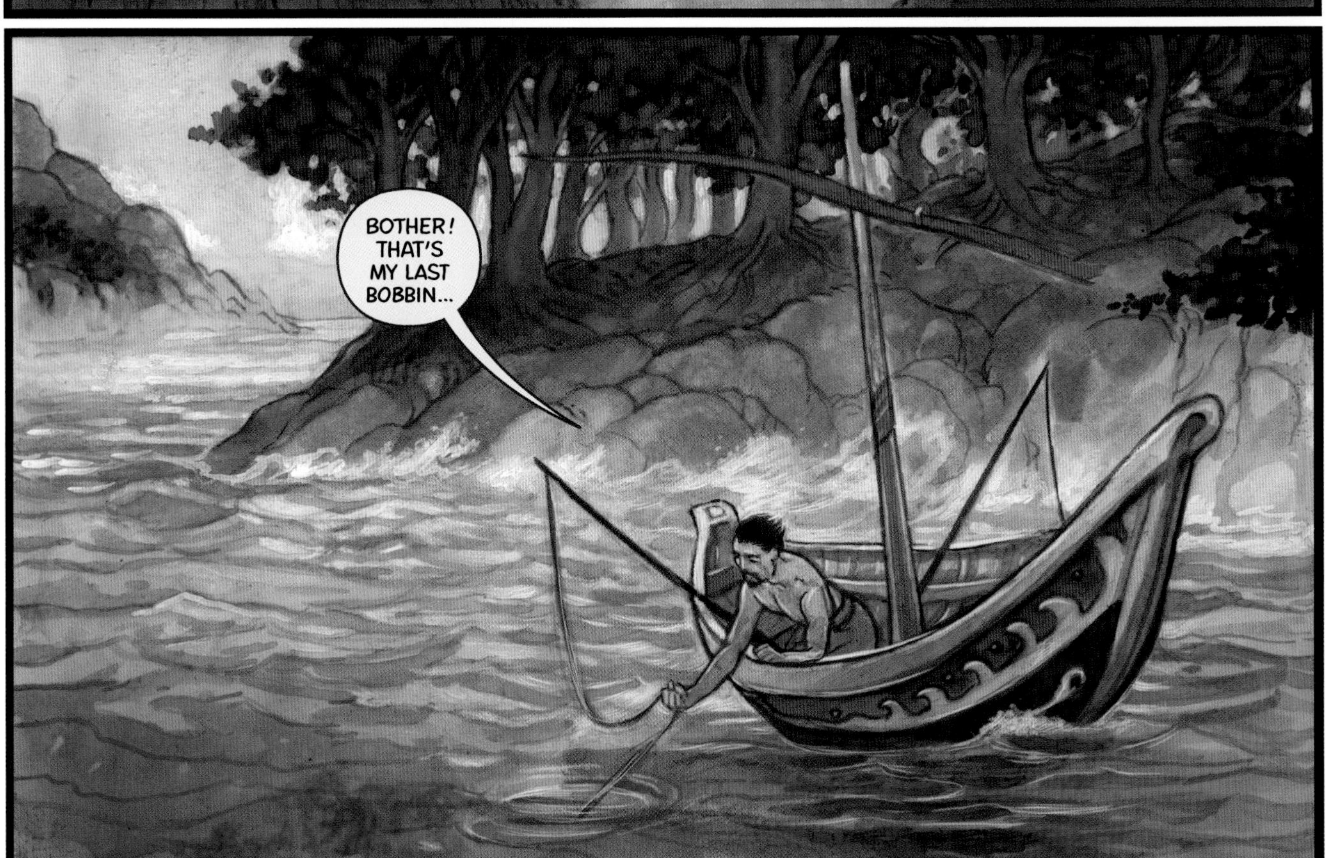
BOTHER! THAT'S MY LAST BOBBIN...

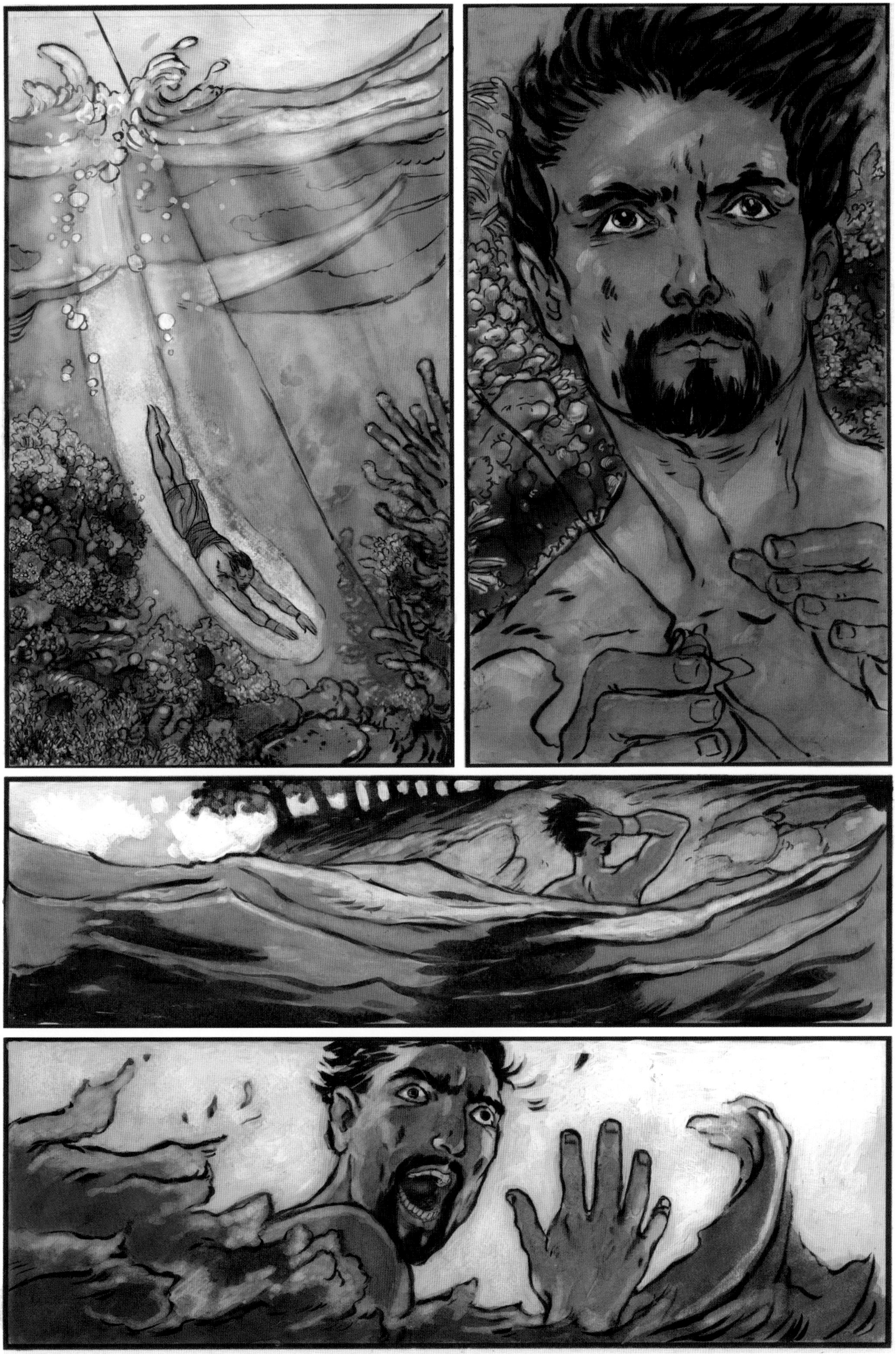

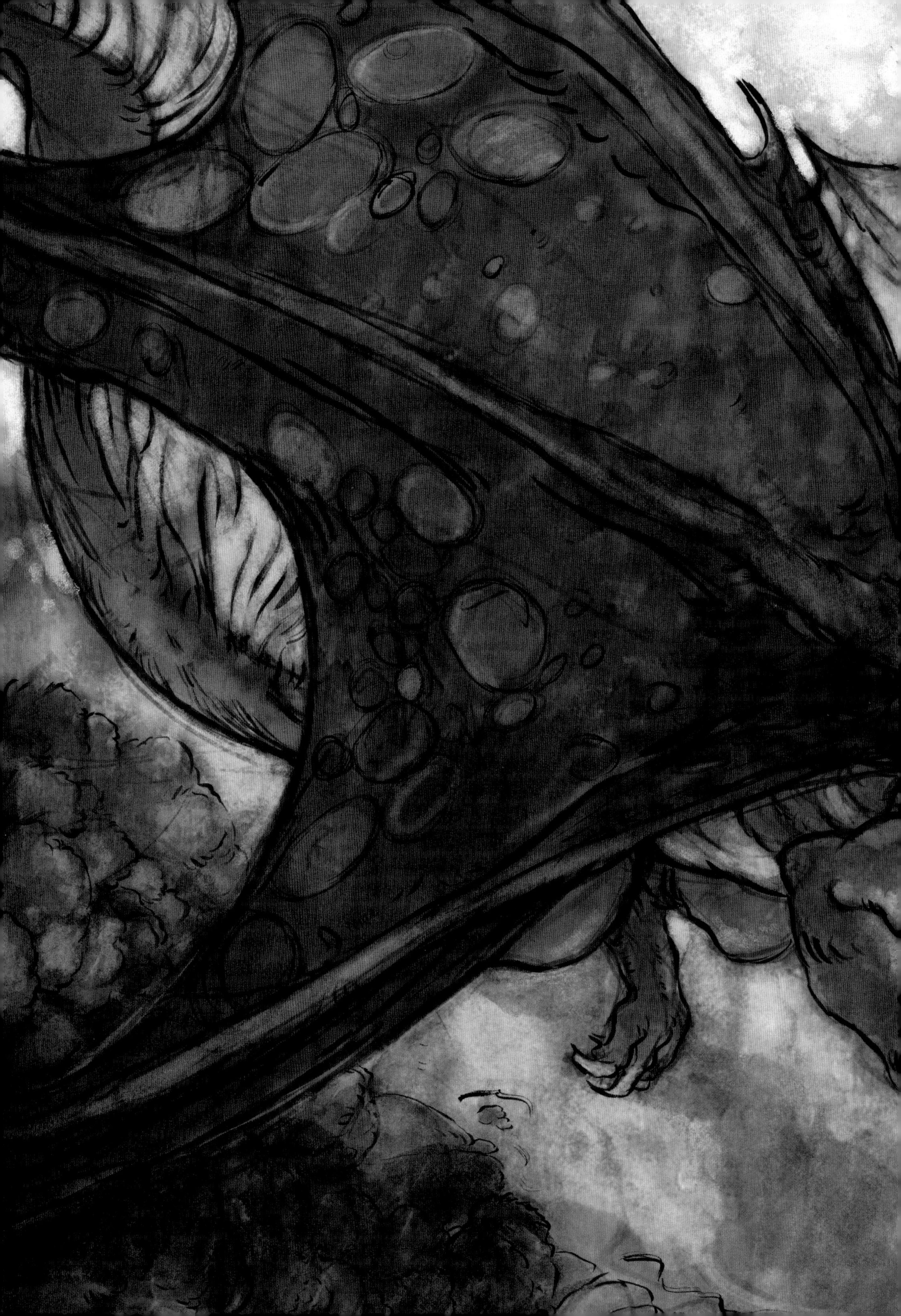

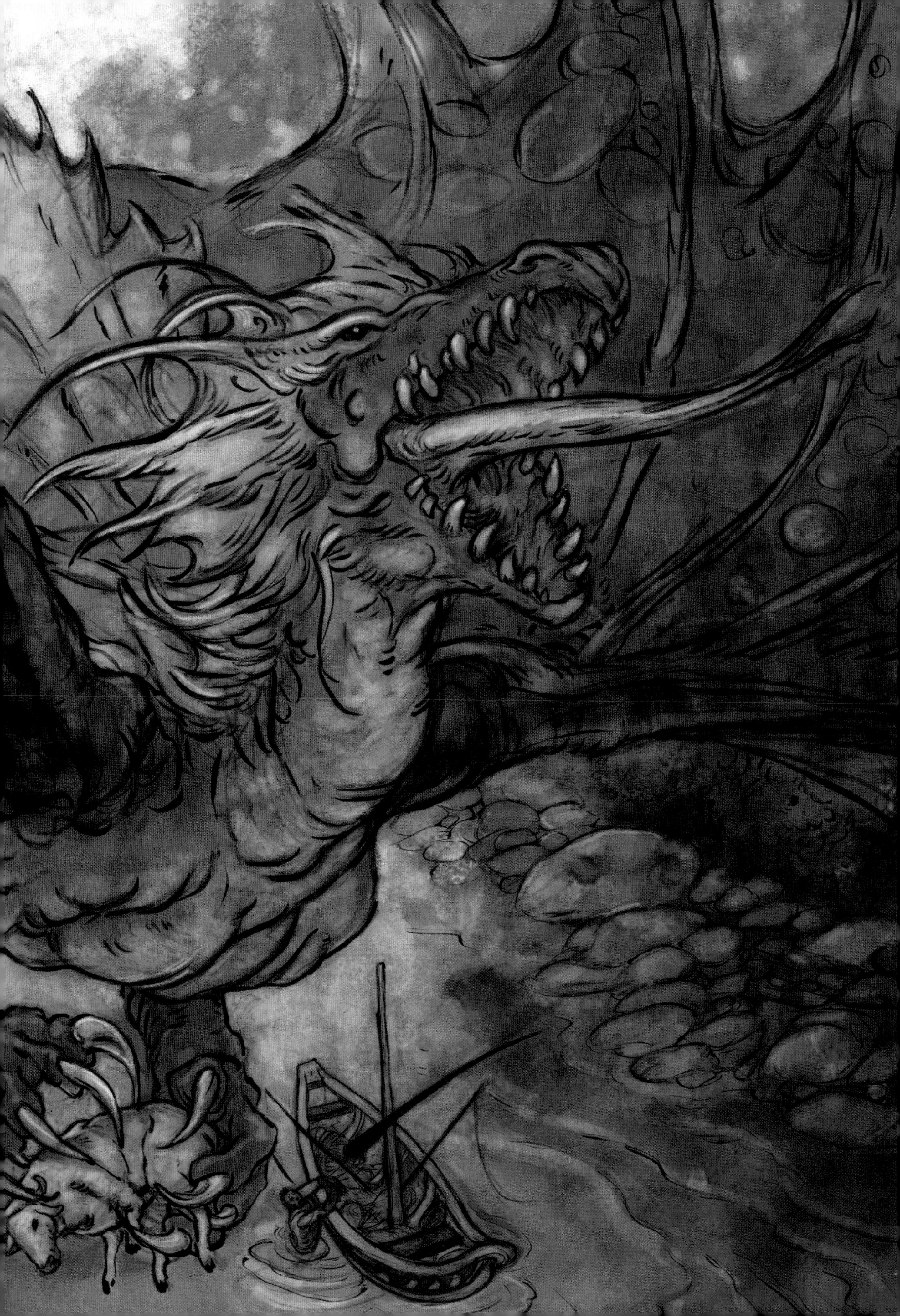

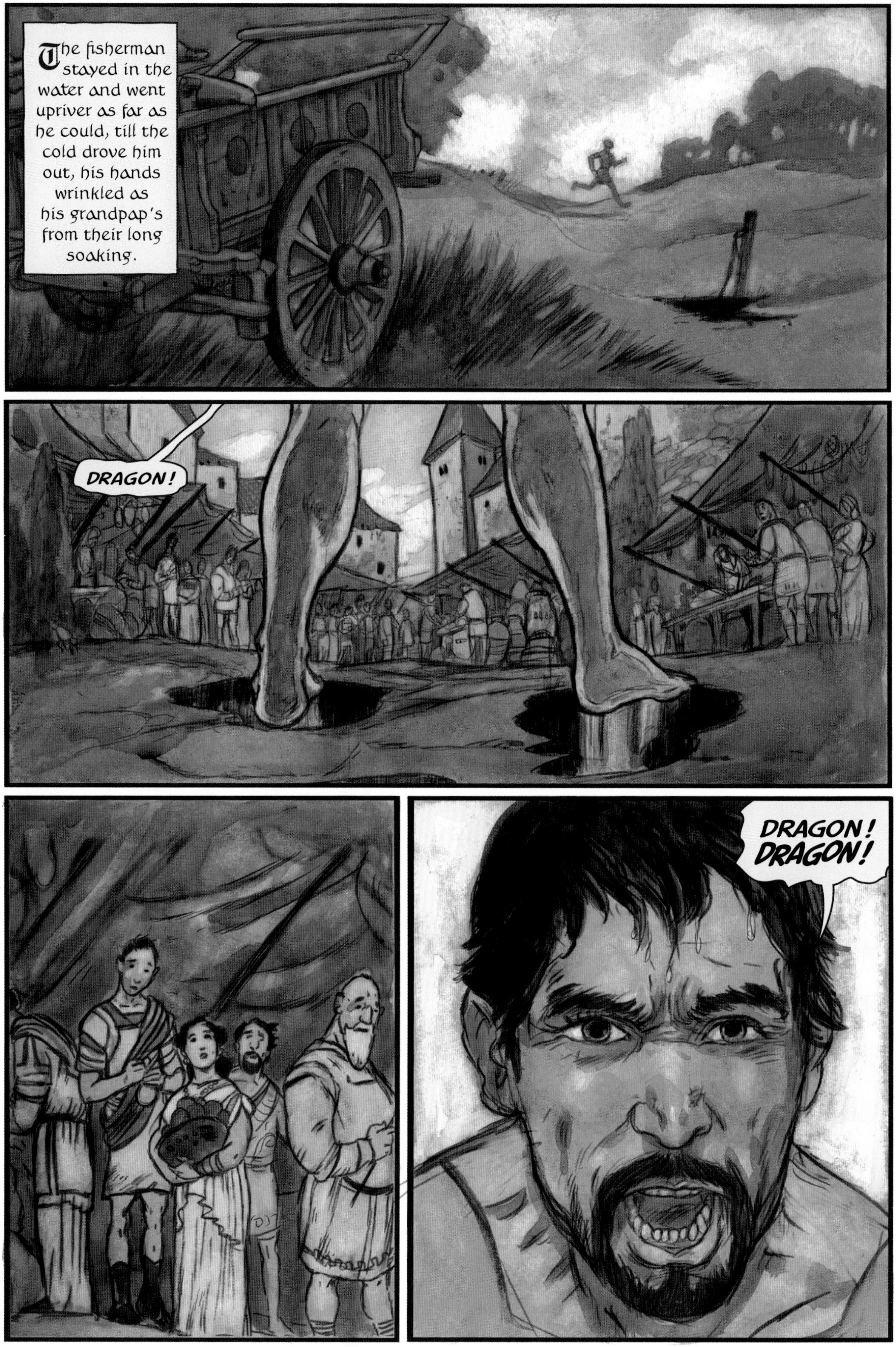
The fisherman stayed in the water and went upriver as far as he could, till the cold drove him out, his hands wrinkled as his grandpap's from their long soaking.
DRAGON!
DRAGON! DRAGON!

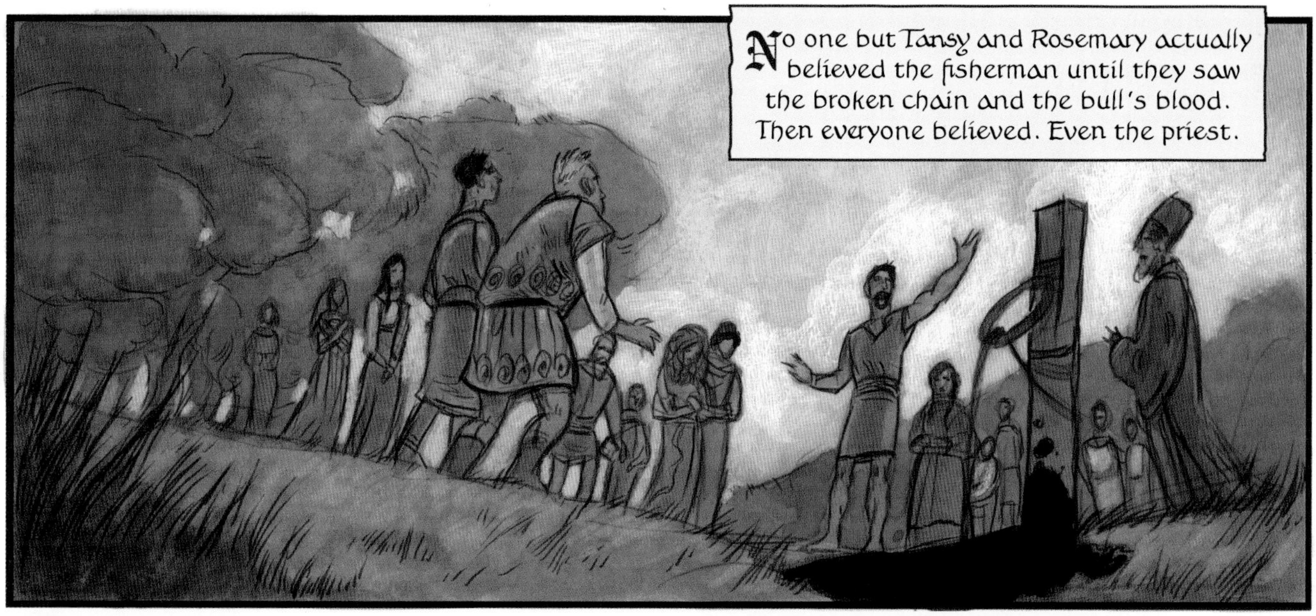
No one but Tansy and Rosemary actually believed the fisherman until they saw the broken chain and the bull's blood. Then everyone believed. Even the priest.

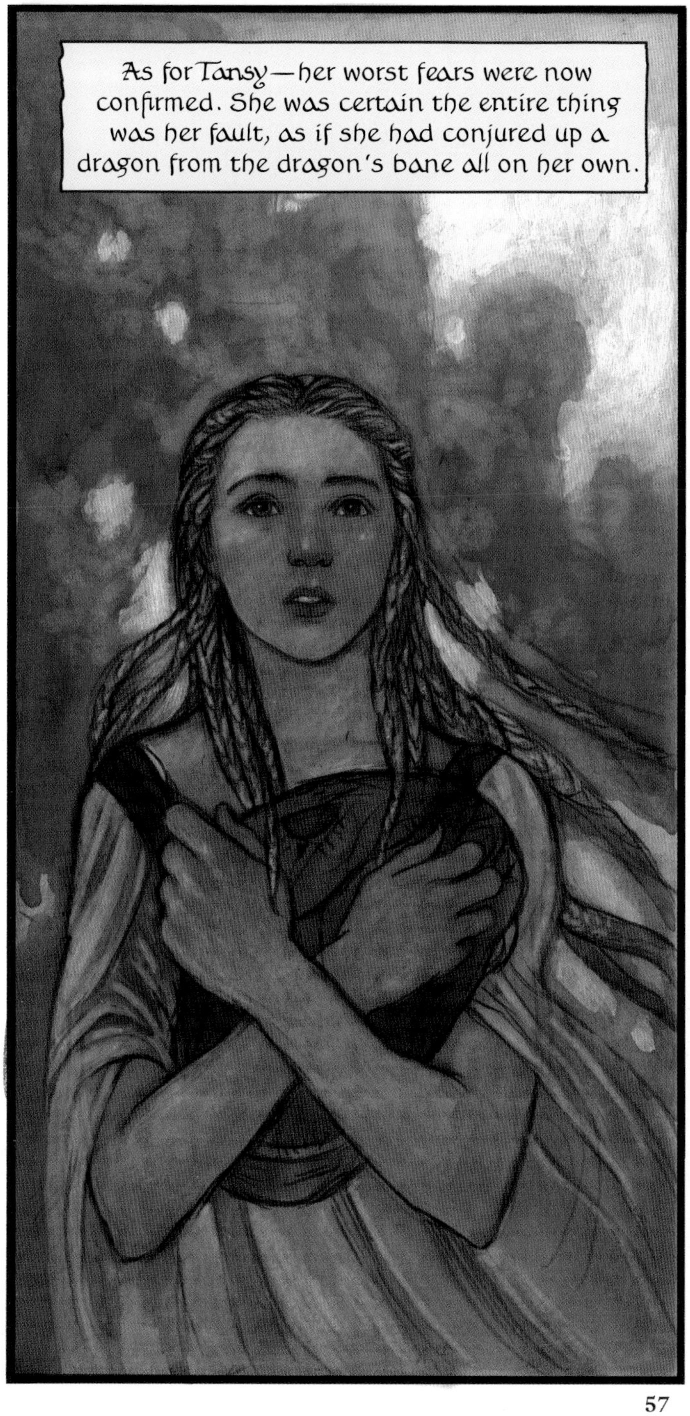
As for Tansy—her worst fears were now confirmed. She was certain the entire thing was her fault, as if she had conjured up a dragon from the dragon's bane all on her own.

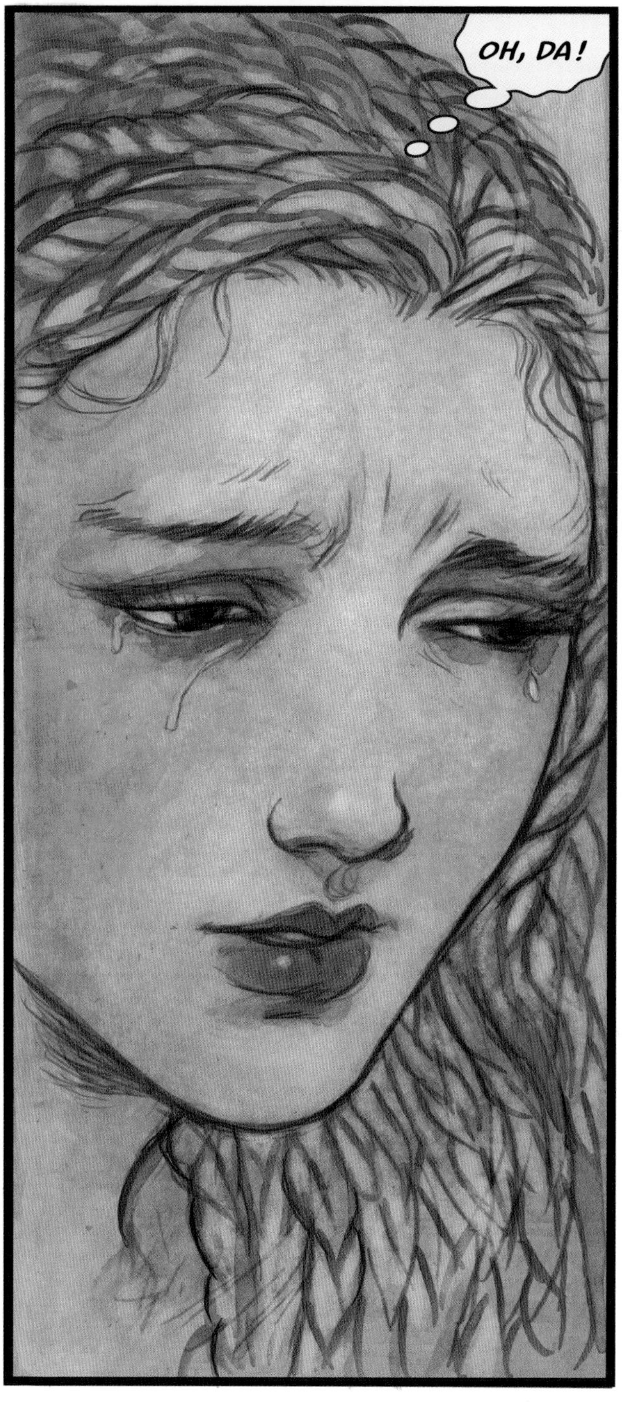
OH, DA!

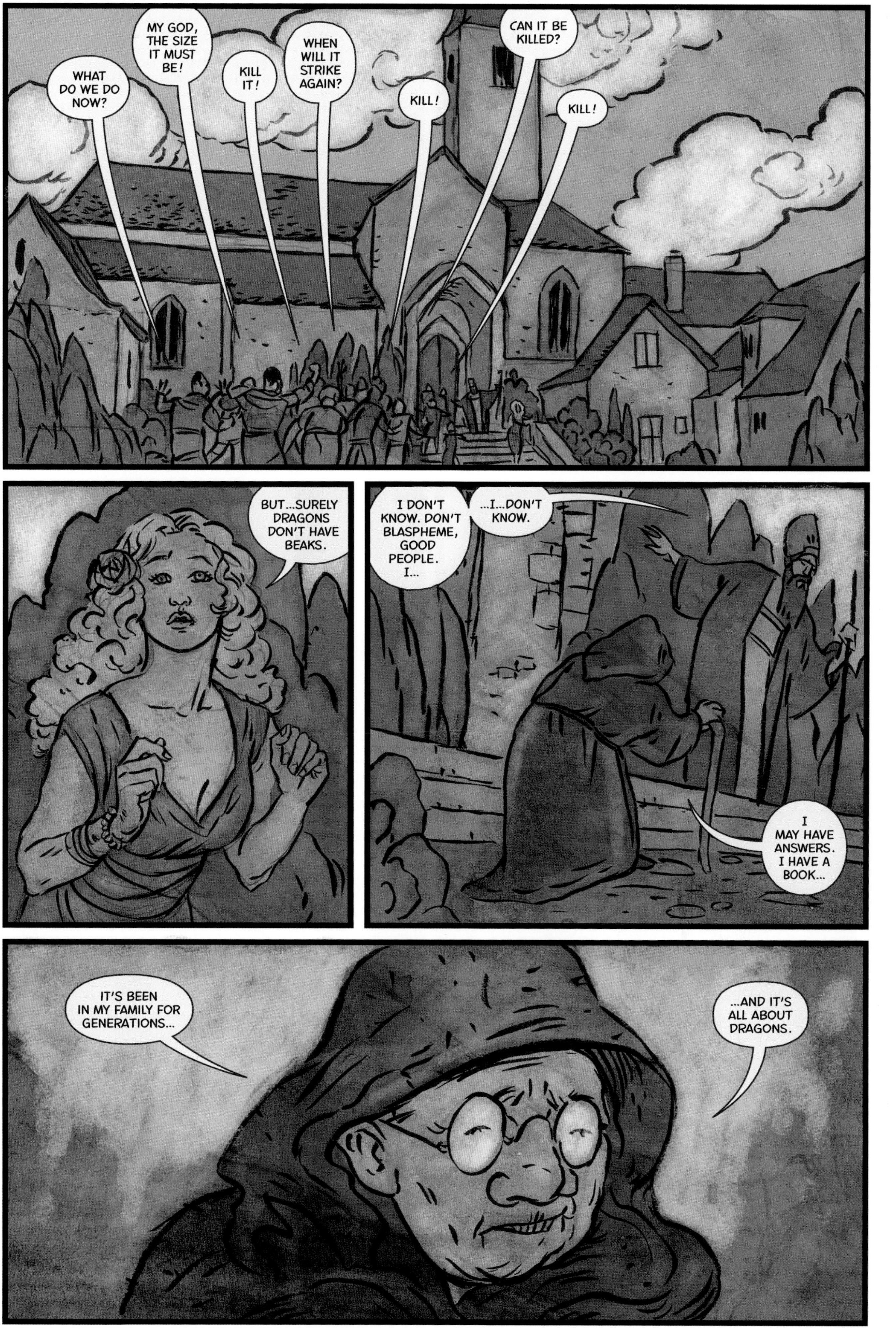
WHAT DO WE DO NOW?
MY GOD, THE SIZE IT MUST BE!
KILL IT!
WHEN WILL IT STRIKE AGAIN?
KILL!
CAN IT BE KILLED?
KILL!
BUT...SURELY DRAGONS DON'T HAVE BEAKS.
I DON'T KNOW. DON'T BLASPHEME, GOOD PEOPLE. I...
...I...DON'T KNOW.
I MAY HAVE ANSWERS. I HAVE A BOOK...
IT'S BEEN IN MY FAMILY FOR GENERATIONS...
...AND IT'S ALL ABOUT DRAGONS.

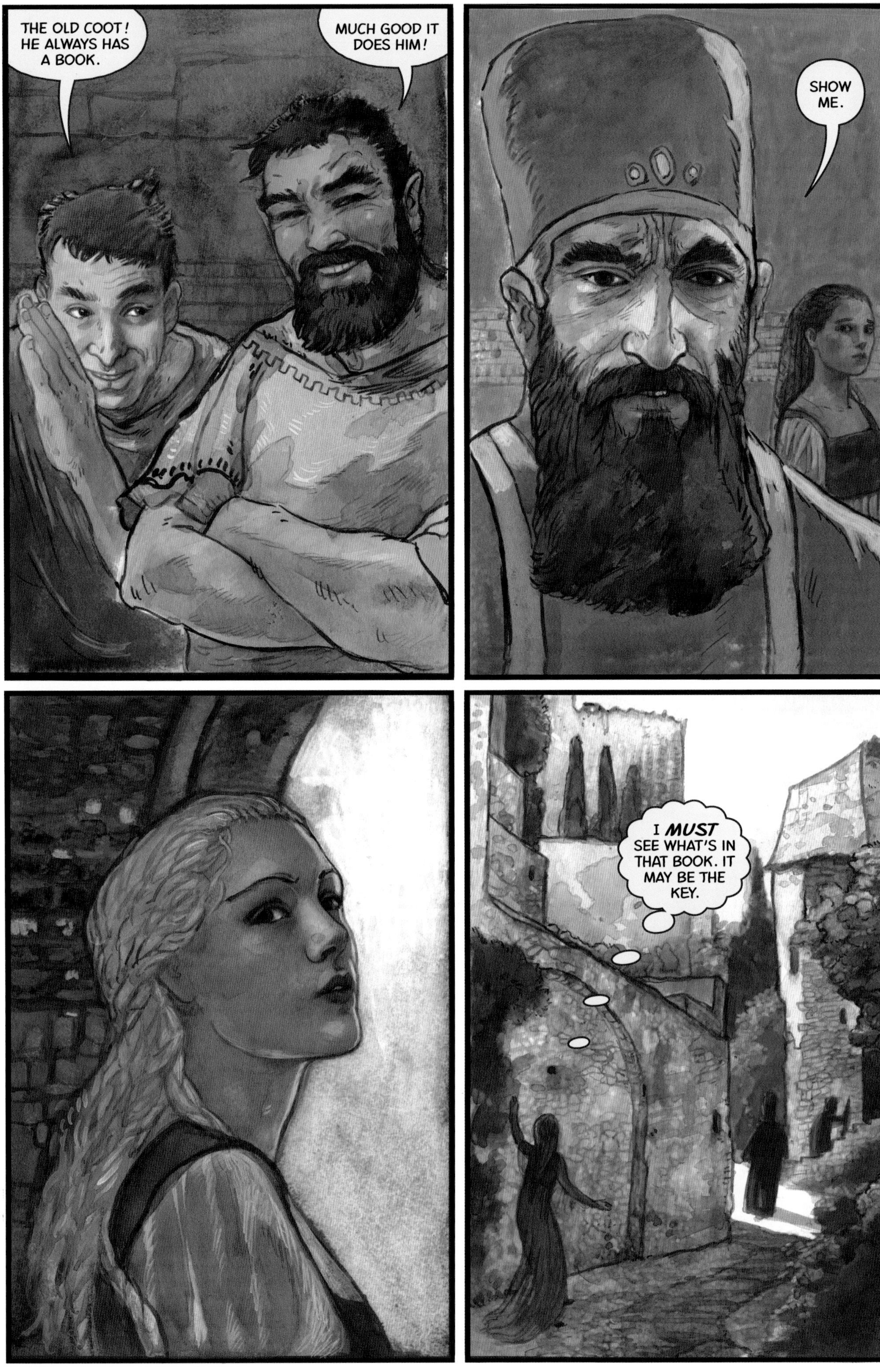
THE OLD COOT! HE ALWAYS HAS A BOOK.
MUCH GOOD IT DOES HIM!
SHOW ME.
I MUST SEE WHAT'S IN THAT BOOK. IT MAY BE THE KEY.

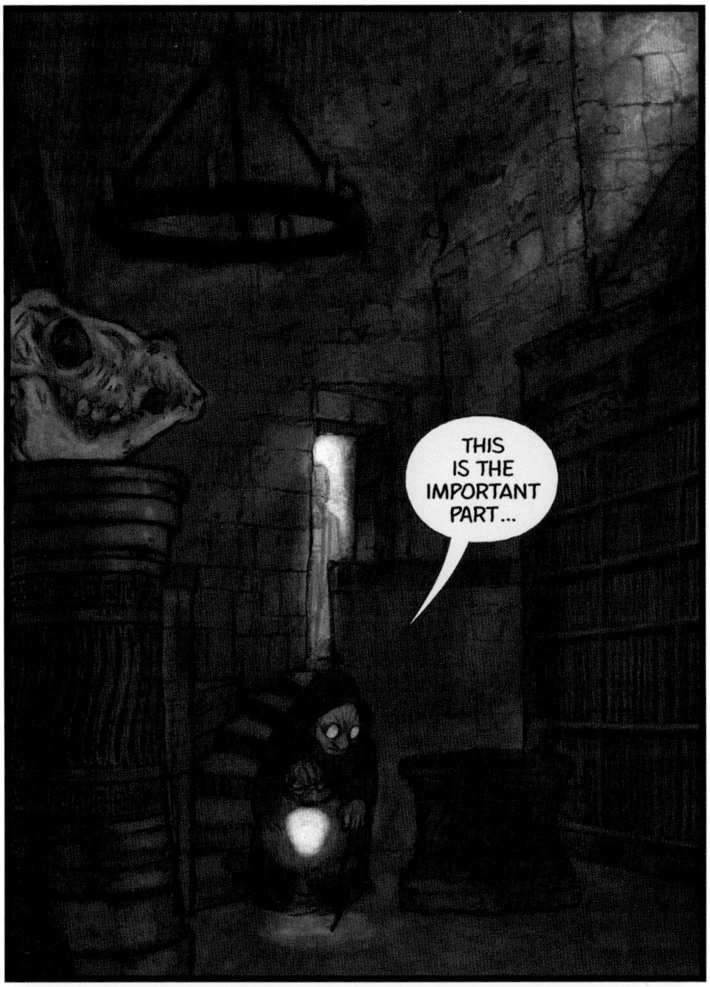
THIS IS THE IMPORTANT PART...
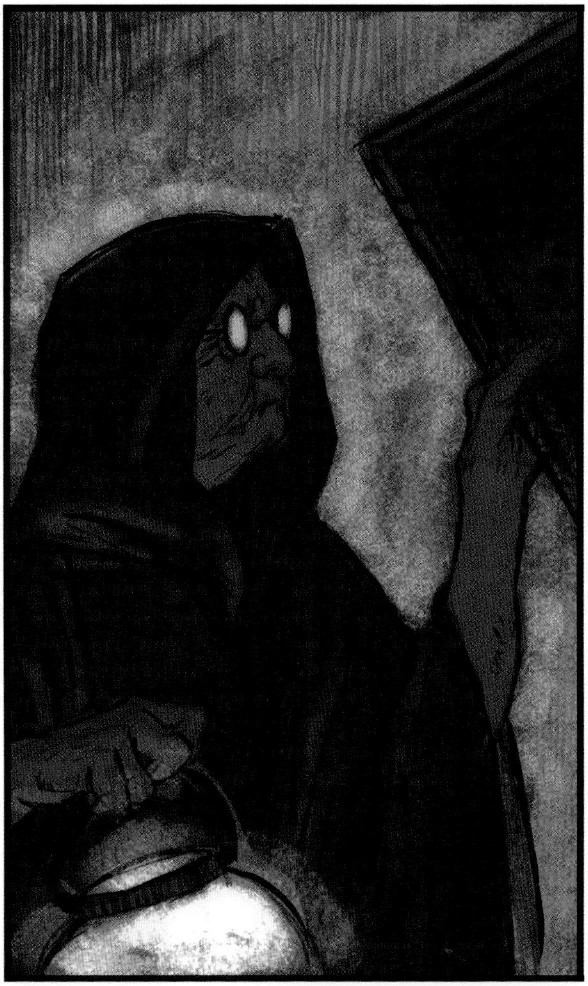
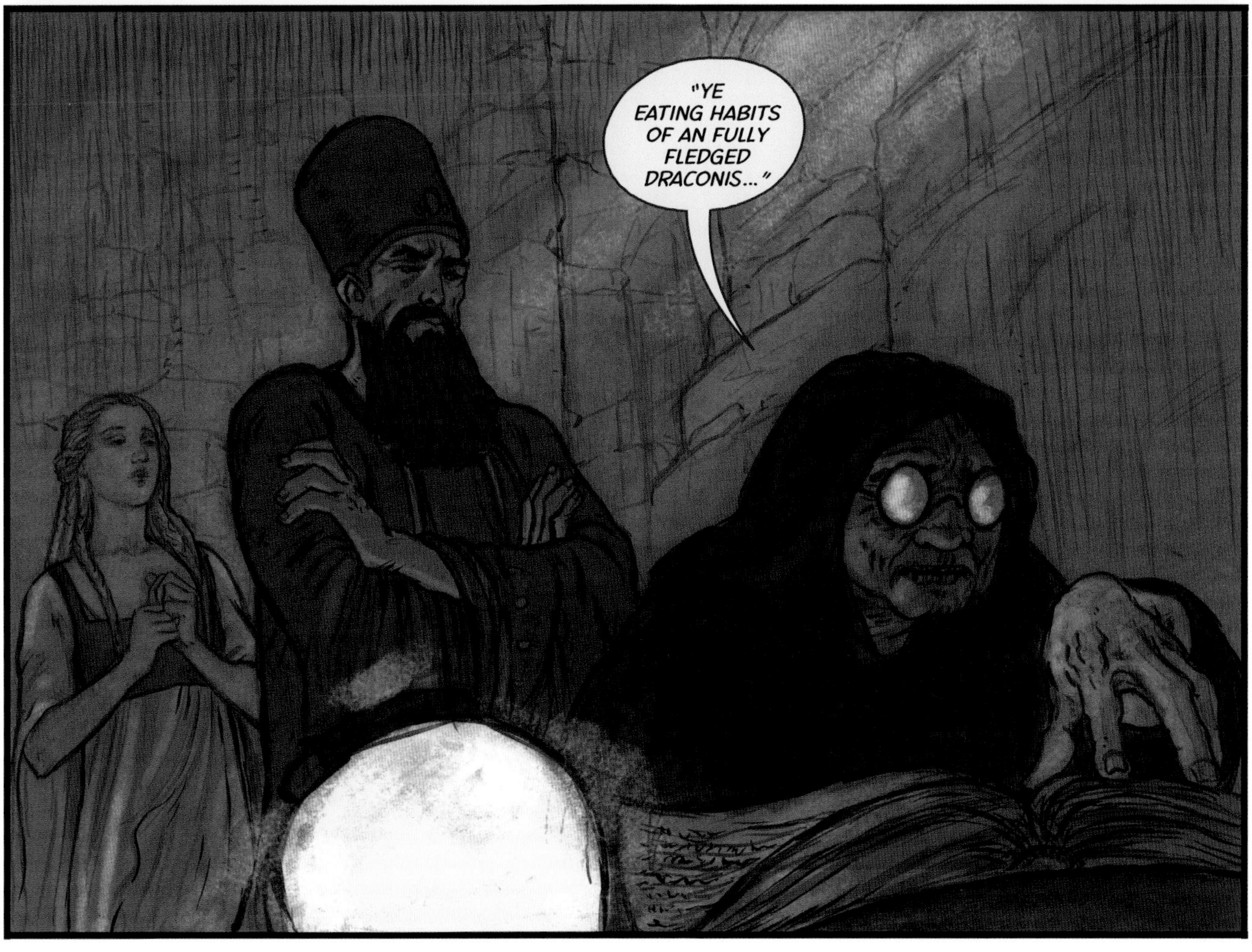
"YE EATING HABITS OF AN FULLY FLEDGED DRACONIS..."

A fully fledged draconis will suppe and digeste an infant in a daye, often supplementing the small meal with birds.

It will suppe and digeste a grown man or woman in five dayes, though if the man or woman be large and of a meaty composition, ye draconis may take an extra halfe daye before it needs to feed again...

...ste an ewe in...
...es an owle, th...
...been shorne.

...ppe and digeste a...
...es, a large heavy...

...full grown bull or bullock ye draconis will
...e and digeste in fourteen dayes, being logie
...rific for several dayes after first it eats

...dayes,
...ce if the

...lle horse in
...le horse in.

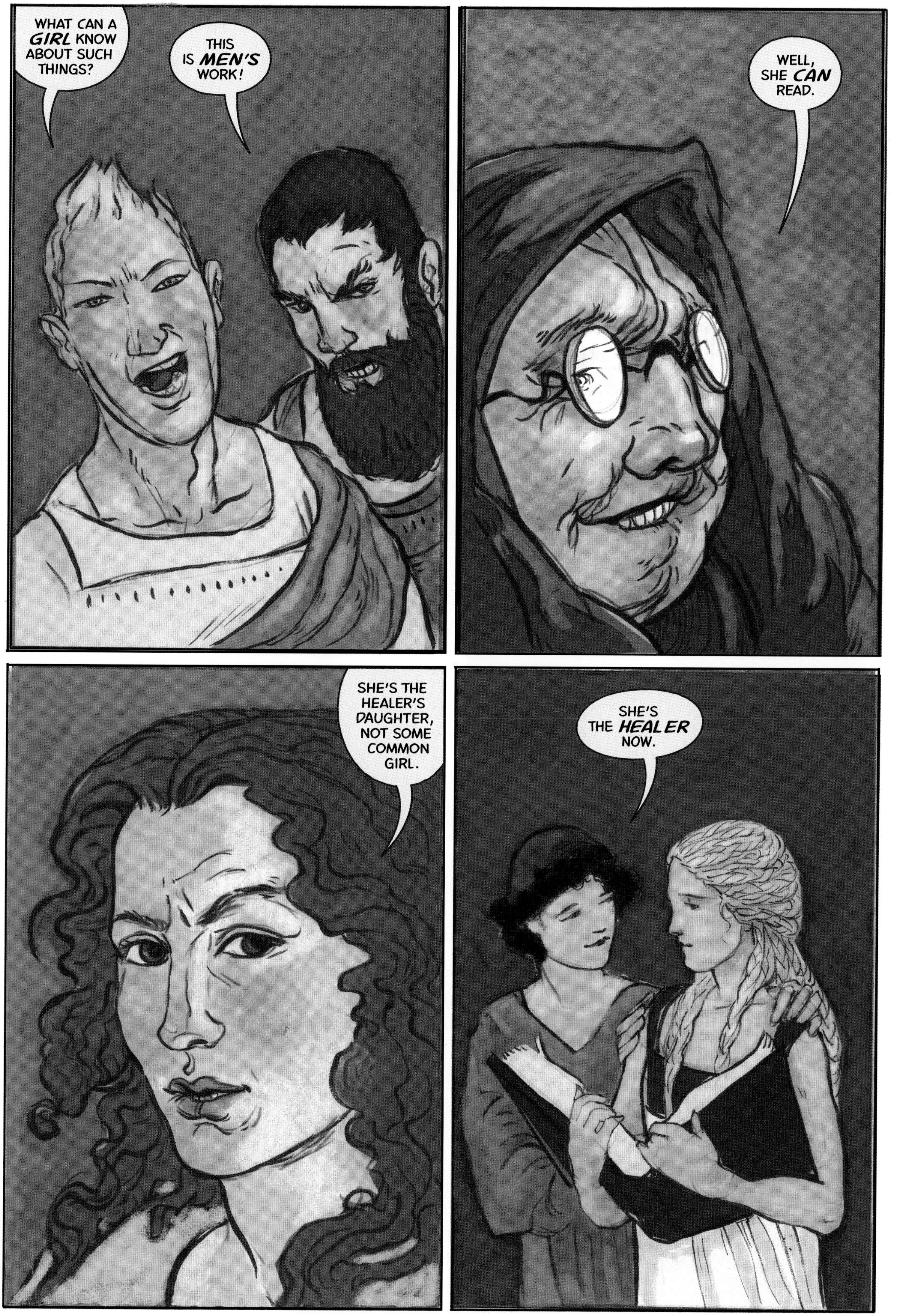
WHAT CAN A GIRL KNOW ABOUT SUCH THINGS?
THIS IS MEN'S WORK!
WELL, SHE CAN READ.
SHE'S THE HEALER'S DAUGHTER, NOT SOME COMMON GIRL.
SHE'S THE HEALER NOW.

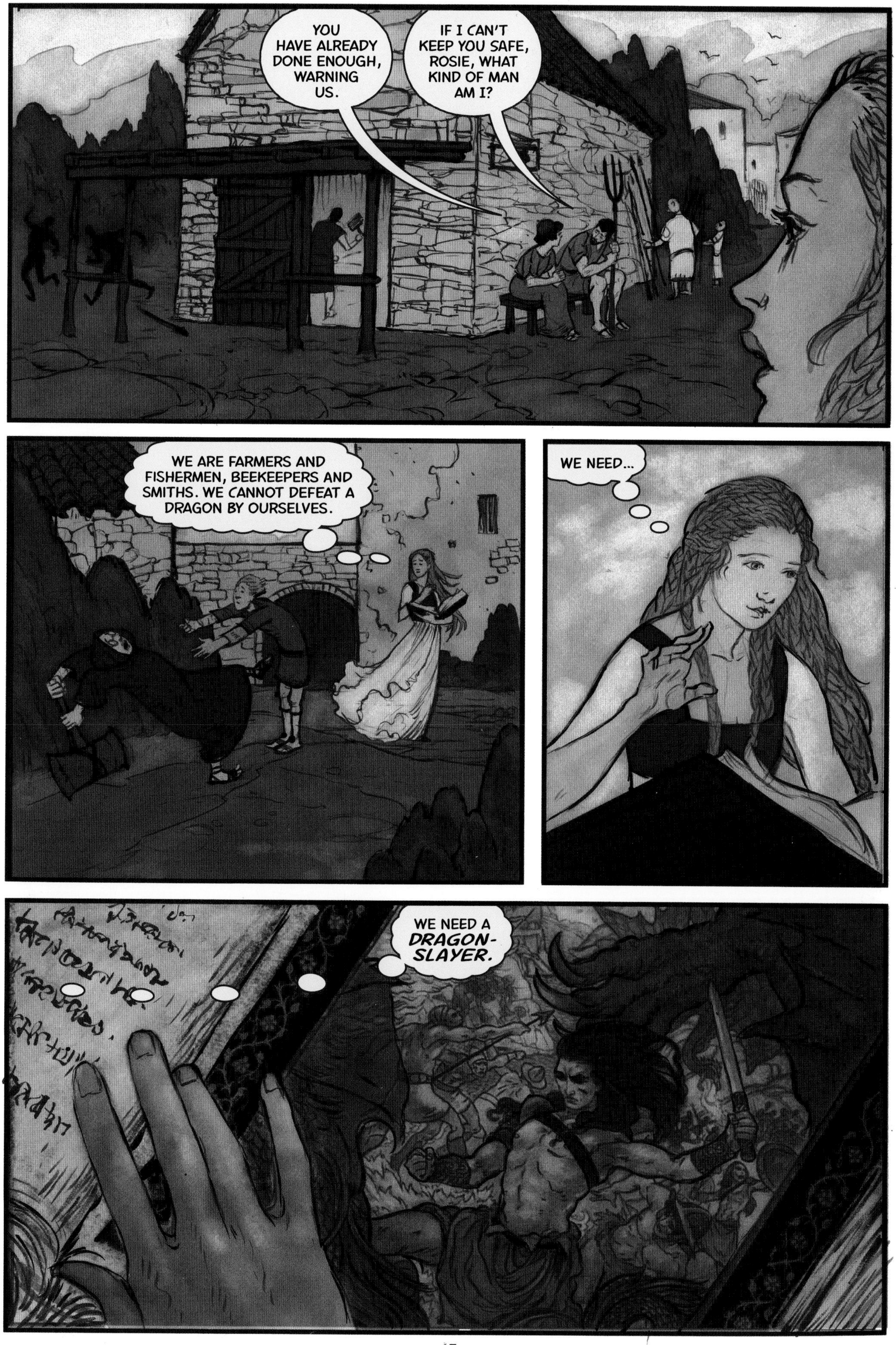
YOU HAVE ALREADY DONE ENOUGH, WARNING US.
IF I CAN'T KEEP YOU SAFE, ROSIE, WHAT KIND OF MAN AM I?
WE ARE FARMERS AND FISHERMEN, BEEKEEPERS AND SMITHS. WE CANNOT DEFEAT A DRAGON BY OURSELVES.
WE NEED...
WE NEED A *DRAGON-SLAYER.*

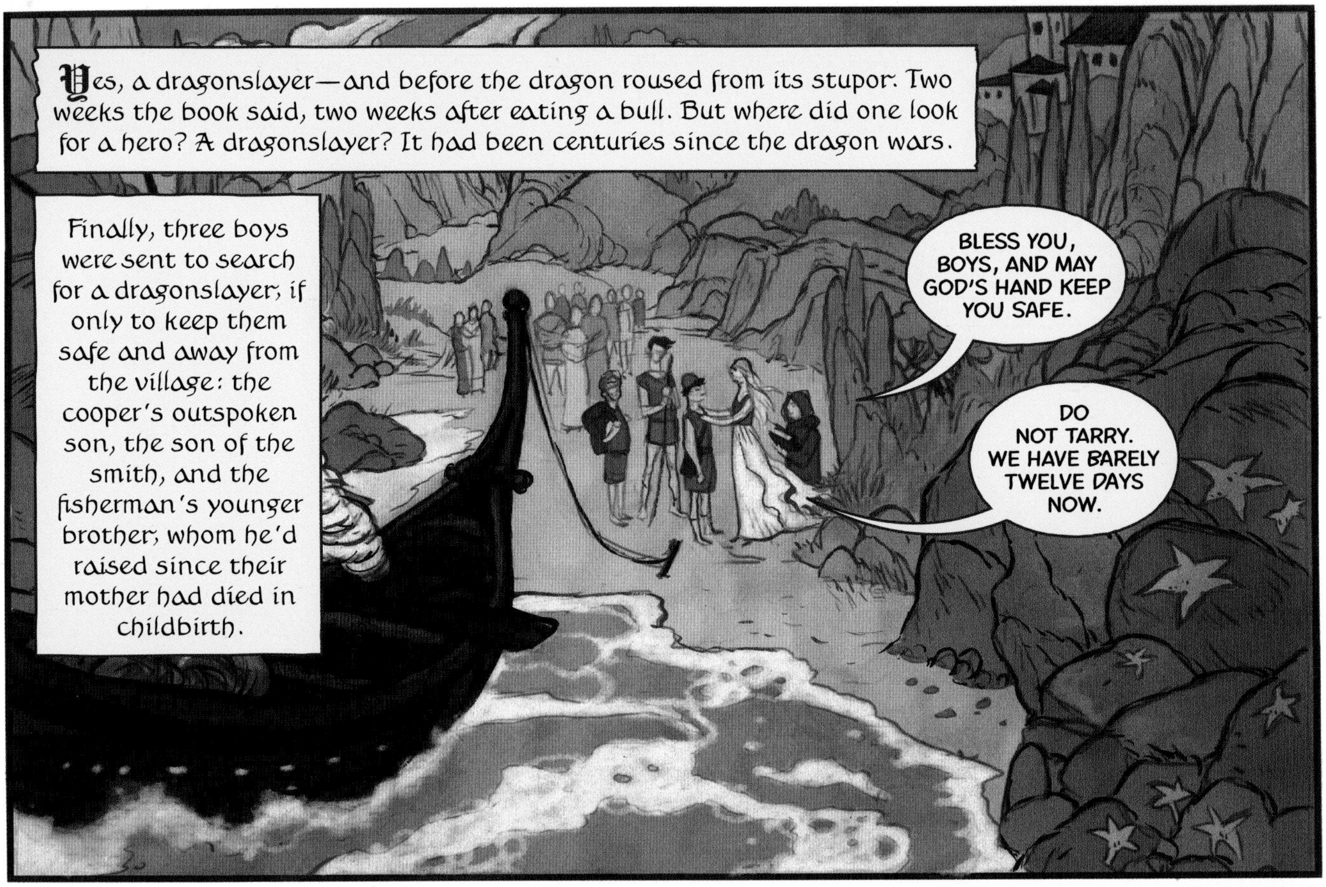
Yes, a dragonslayer—and before the dragon roused from its stupor. Two weeks the book said, two weeks after eating a bull. But where did one look for a hero? A dragonslayer? It had been centuries since the dragon wars.
Finally, three boys were sent to search for a dragonslayer, if only to keep them safe and away from the village: the cooper's outspoken son, the son of the smith, and the fisherman's younger brother, whom he'd raised since their mother had died in childbirth.
BLESS YOU, BOYS, AND MAY GOD'S HAND KEEP YOU SAFE.
DO NOT TARRY. WE HAVE BARELY TWELVE DAYS NOW.

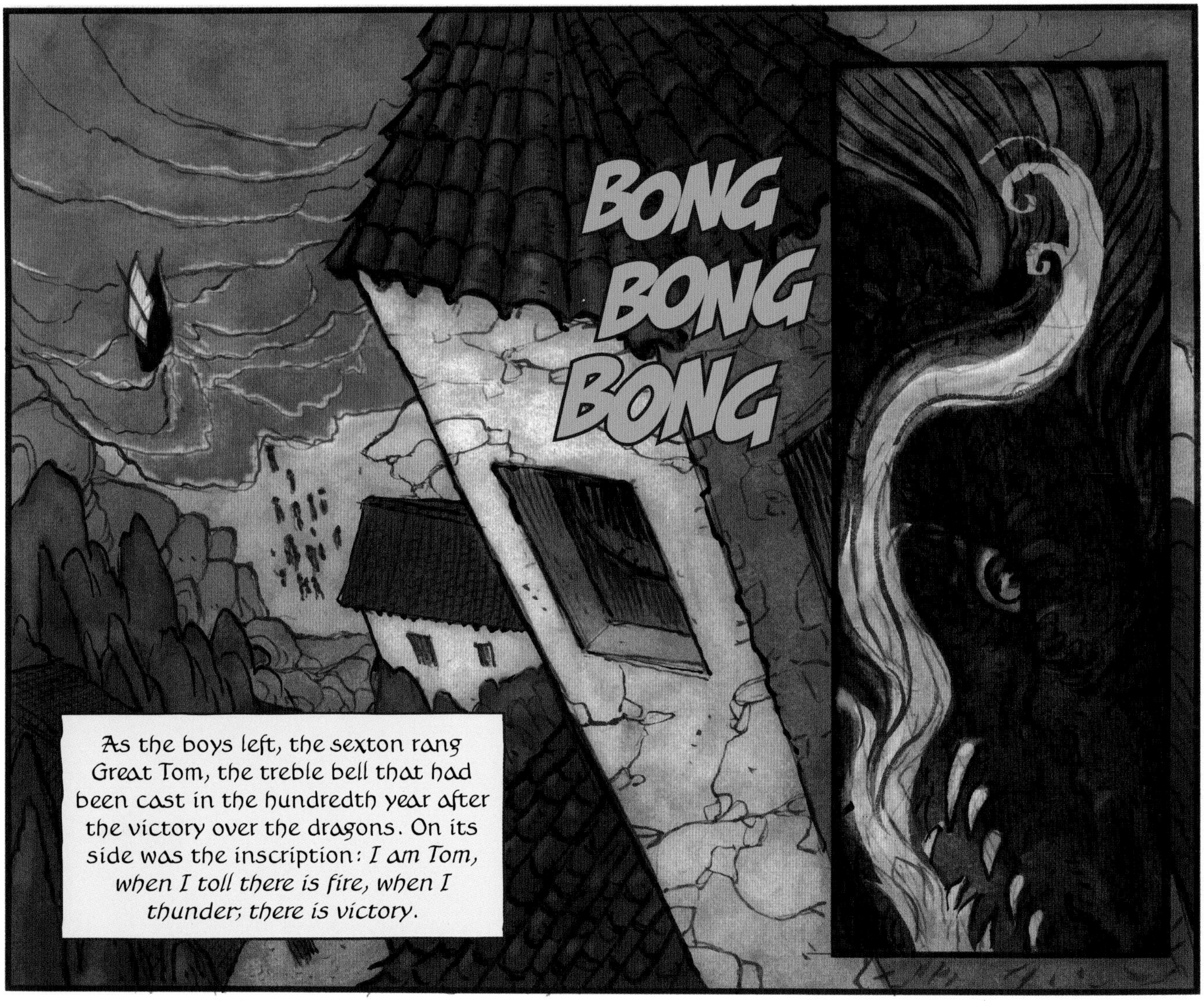
BONG
BONG
BONG
As the boys left, the sexton rang Great Tom, the treble bell that had been cast in the hundredth year after the victory over the dragons. On its side was the inscription: *I am Tom, when I toll there is fire, when I thunder, there is victory.*

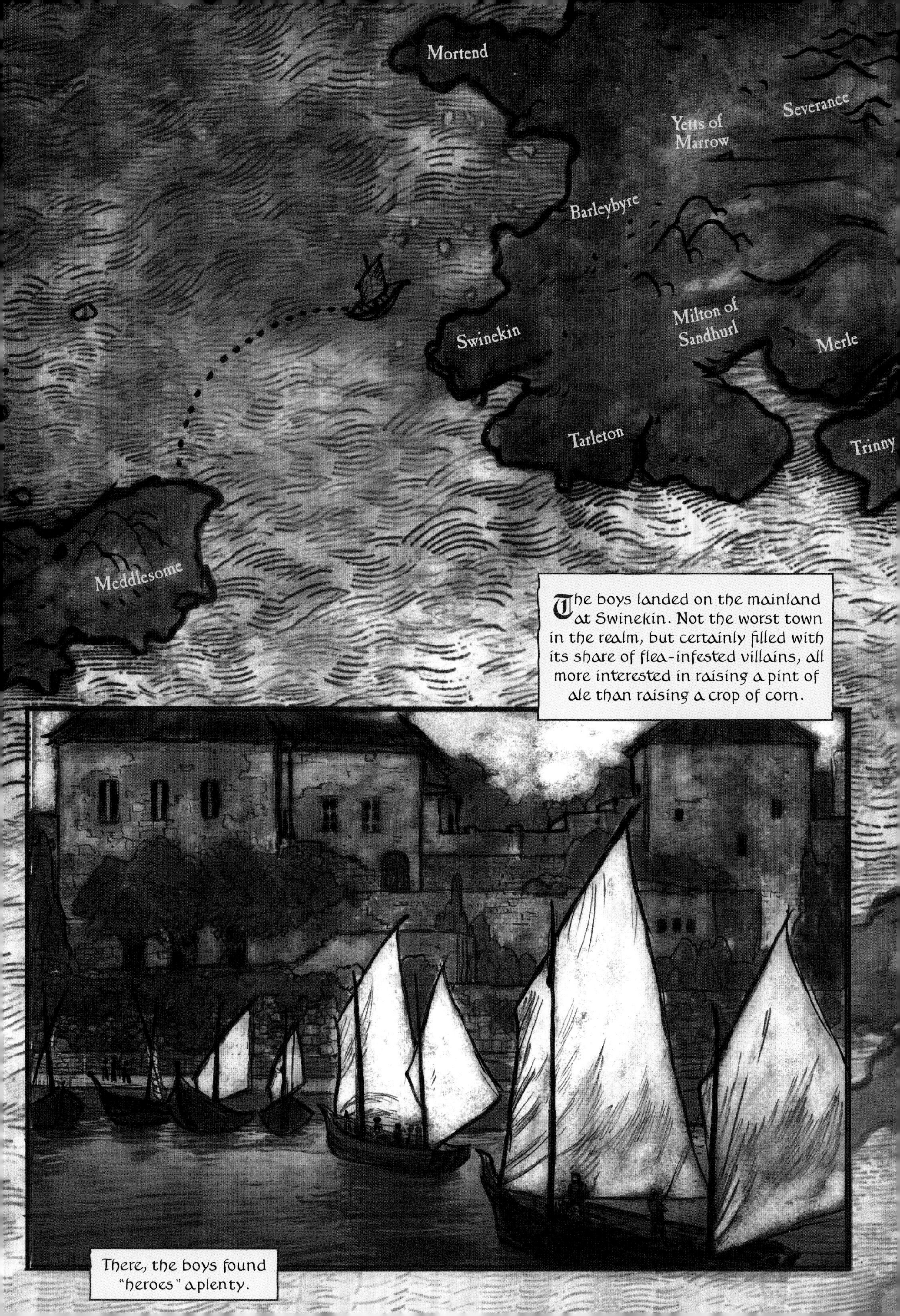

Mortend
Severance
Yetts of Marrow
Barleybyre
Swinekin
Milton of Sandhurl
Merle
Tarleton
Trinny
Meddlesome
The boys landed on the mainland at Swinekin. Not the worst town in the realm, but certainly filled with its share of flea-infested villains, all more interested in raising a pint of ale than raising a crop of corn.
There, the boys found "heroes" aplenty.

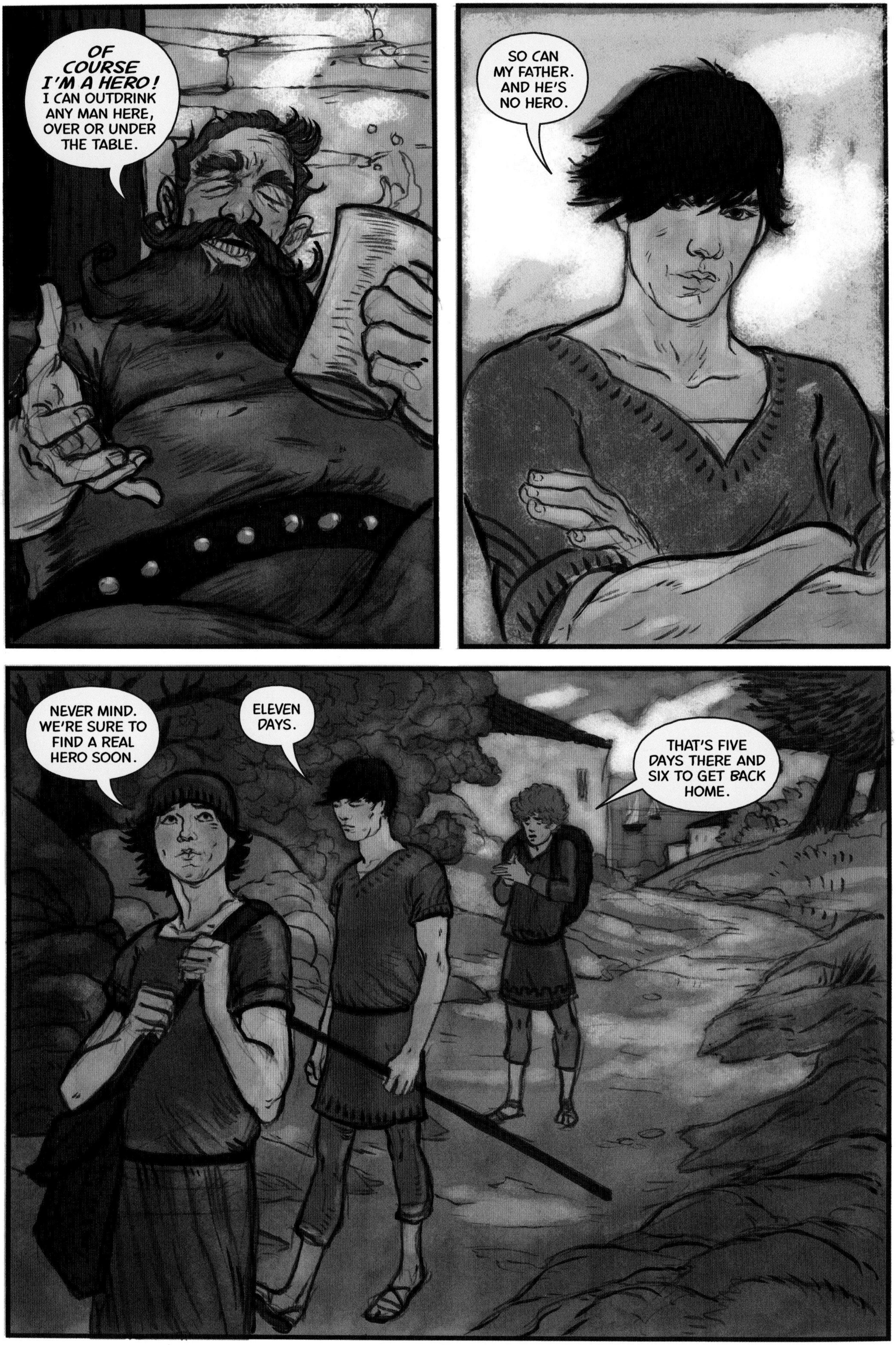

OF COURSE I'M A HERO! I CAN OUTDRINK ANY MAN HERE, OVER OR UNDER THE TABLE.
SO CAN MY FATHER. AND HE'S NO HERO.
NEVER MIND. WE'RE SURE TO FIND A REAL HERO SOON.
ELEVEN DAYS.
THAT'S FIVE DAYS THERE AND SIX TO GET BACK HOME.

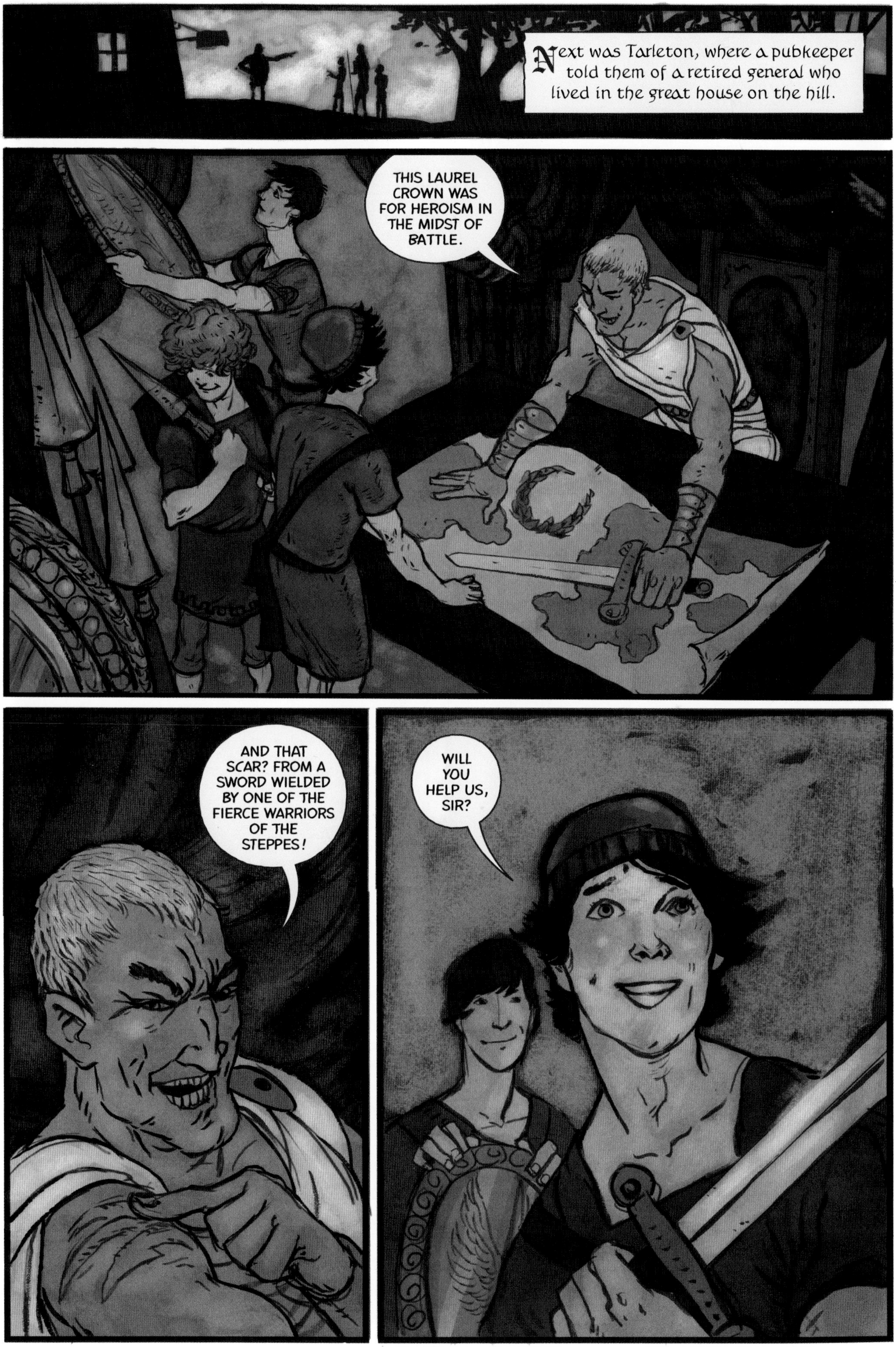
Next was Tarleton, where a pubkeeper told them of a retired general who lived in the great house on the hill.
THIS LAUREL CROWN WAS FOR HEROISM IN THE MIDST OF BATTLE.
AND THAT SCAR? FROM A SWORD WIELDED BY ONE OF THE FIERCE WARRIORS OF THE STEPPES!
WILL YOU HELP US, SIR?

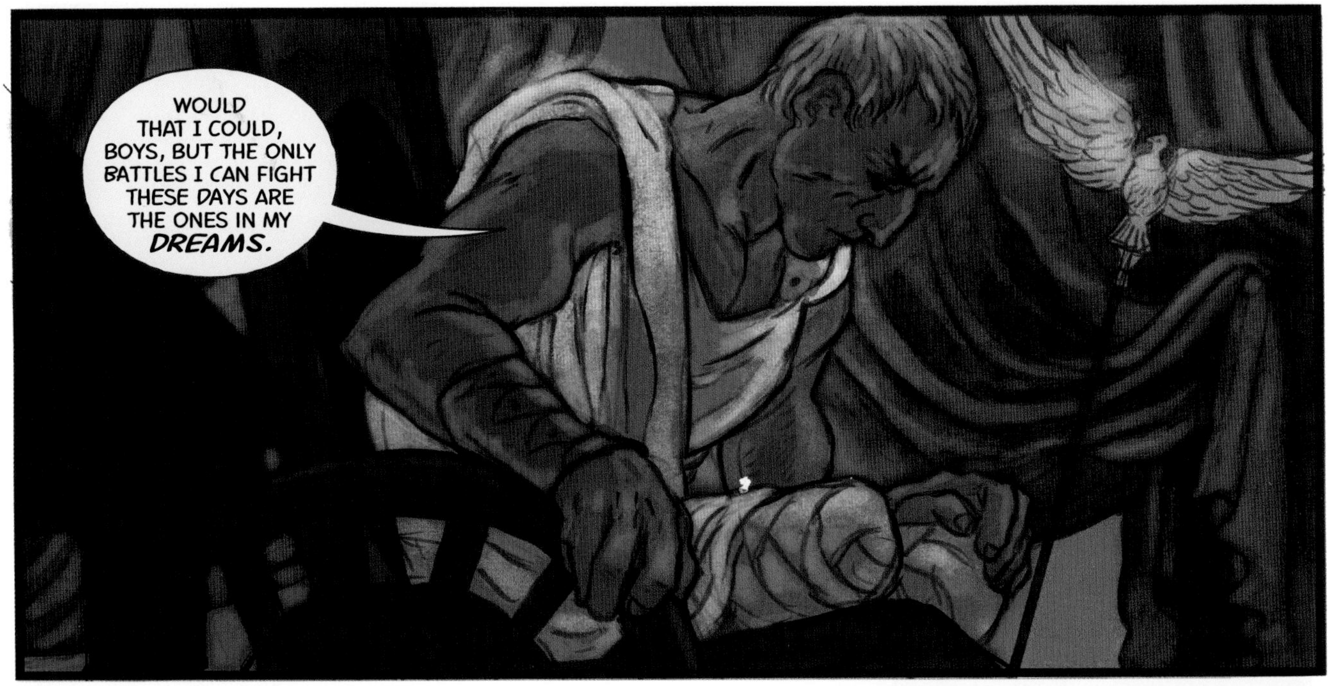
WOULD THAT I COULD, BOYS, BUT THE ONLY BATTLES I CAN FIGHT THESE DAYS ARE THE ONES IN MY *DREAMS.*

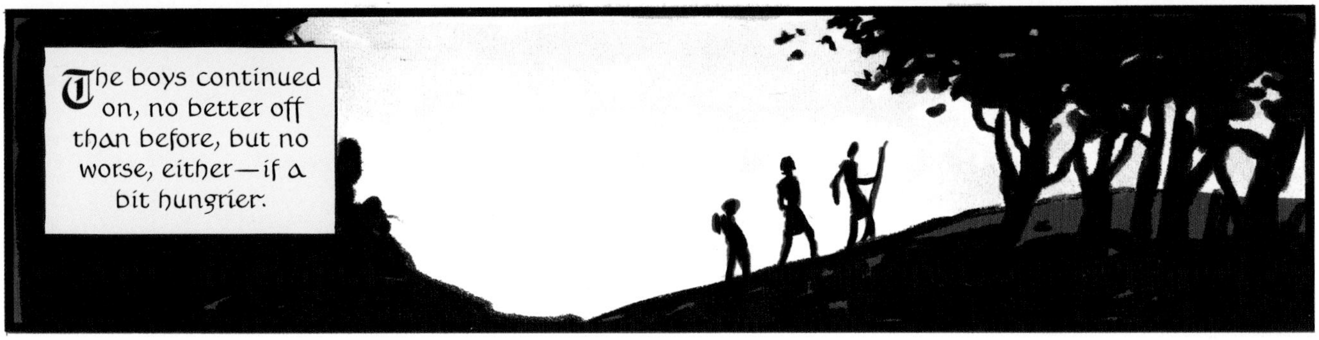
The boys continued on, no better off than before, but no worse, either—if a bit hungrier.

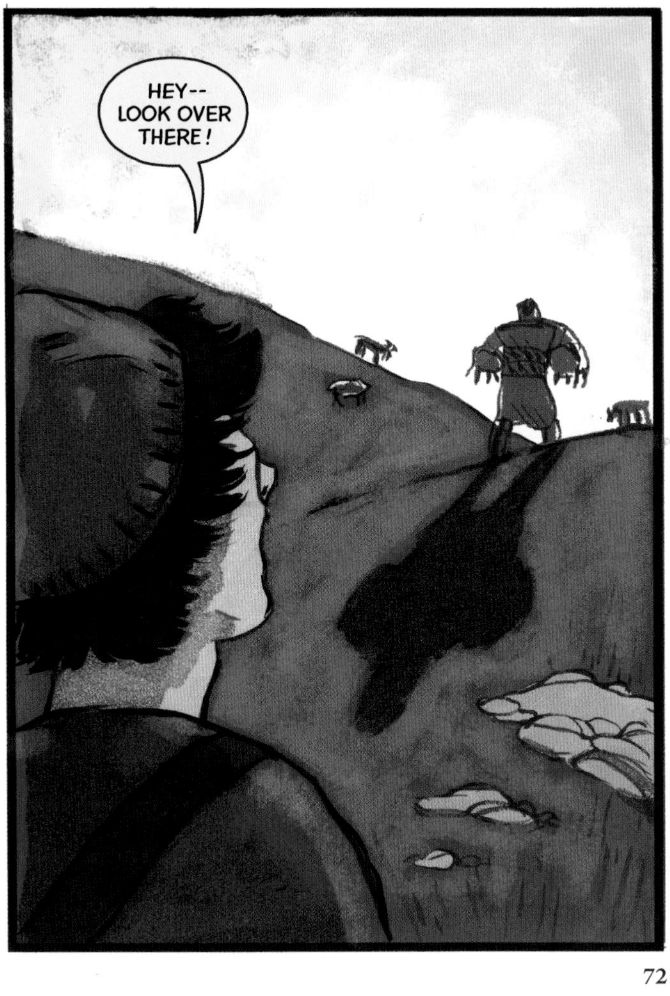
HEY-- LOOK OVER THERE!

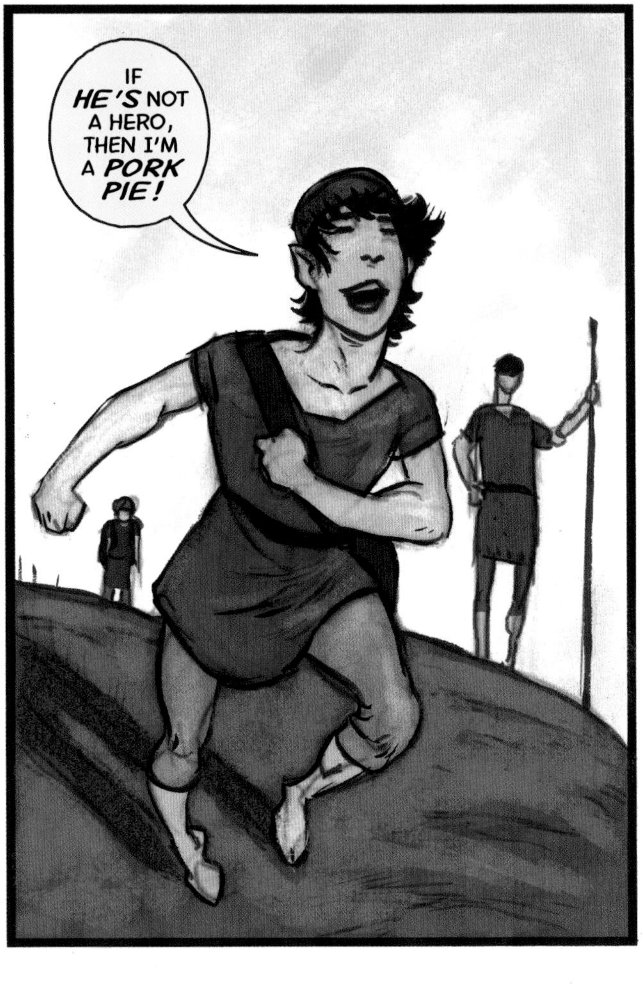
IF *HE'S* NOT A HERO, THEN I'M A *PORK PIE!*

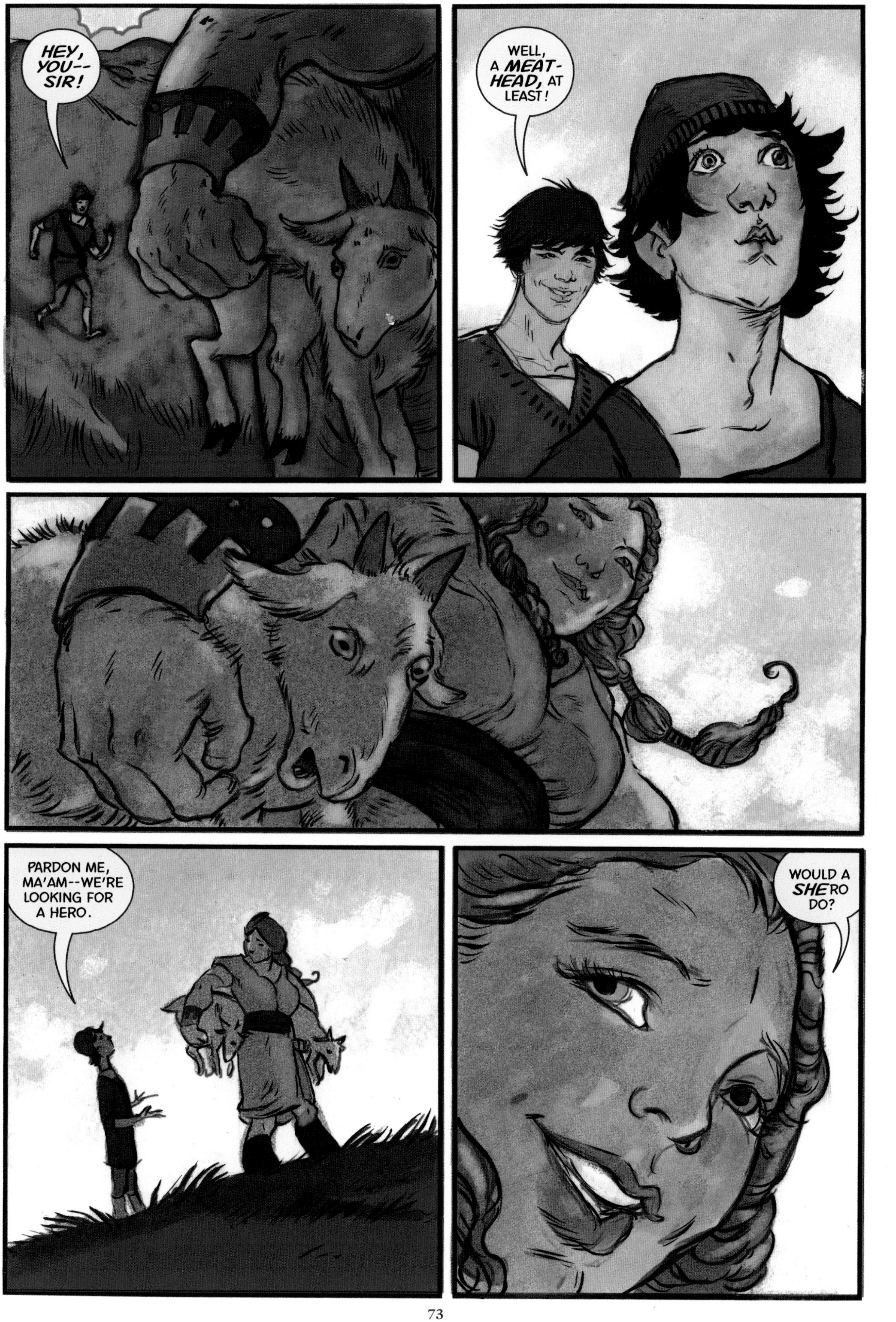
HEY, YOU--SIR!
WELL, A MEAT-HEAD, AT LEAST!
PARDON ME, MA'AM--WE'RE LOOKING FOR A HERO.
WOULD A SHERO DO?

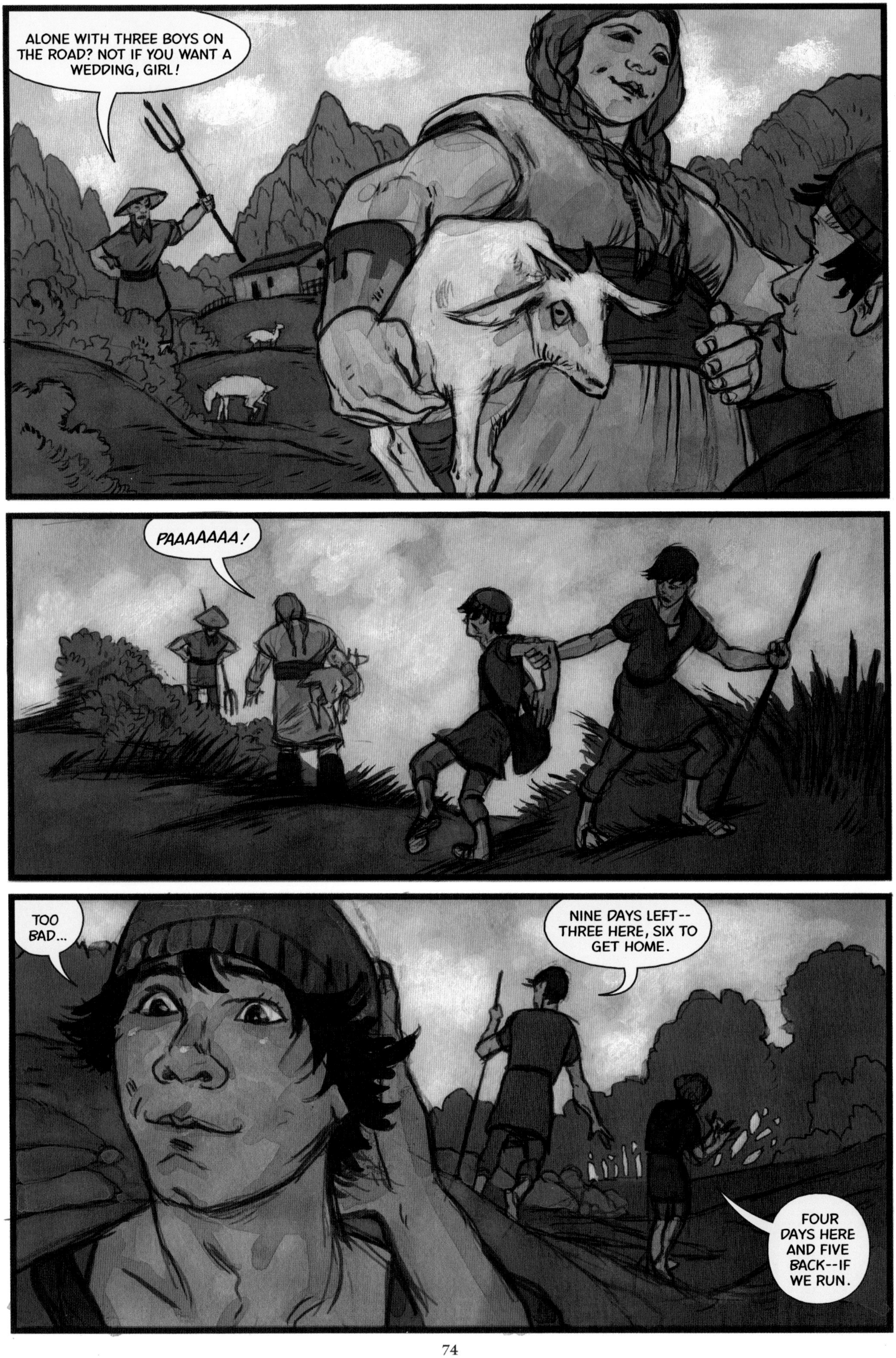
ALONE WITH THREE BOYS ON THE ROAD? NOT IF YOU WANT A WEDDING, GIRL!
PAAAAAAA!
TOO BAD...
NINE DAYS LEFT-- THREE HERE, SIX TO GET HOME.
FOUR DAYS HERE AND FIVE BACK--IF WE RUN.

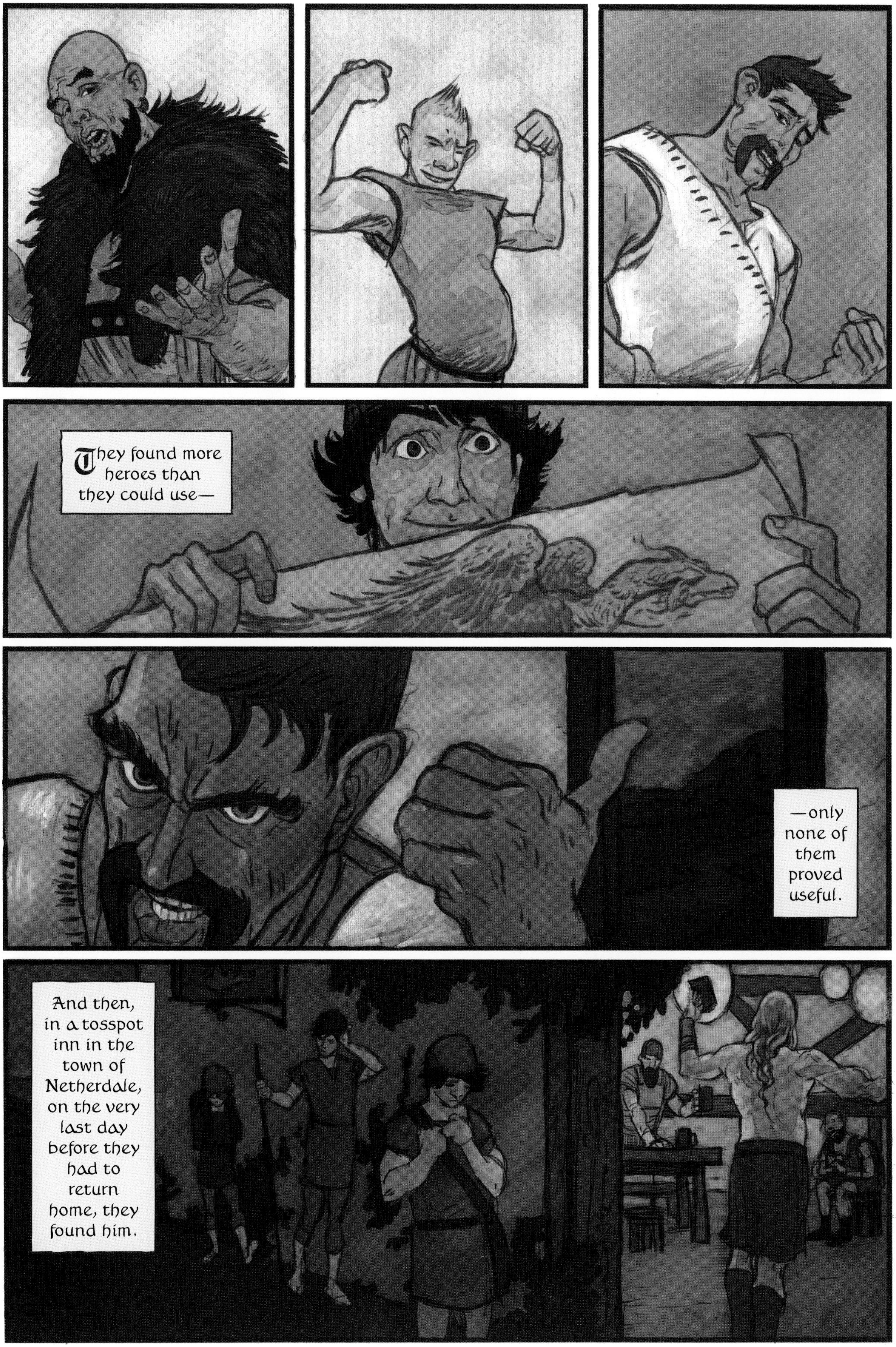
They found more heroes than they could use—
—only none of them proved useful.
And then, in a tosspot inn in the town of Netherdale, on the very last day before they had to return home, they found him.

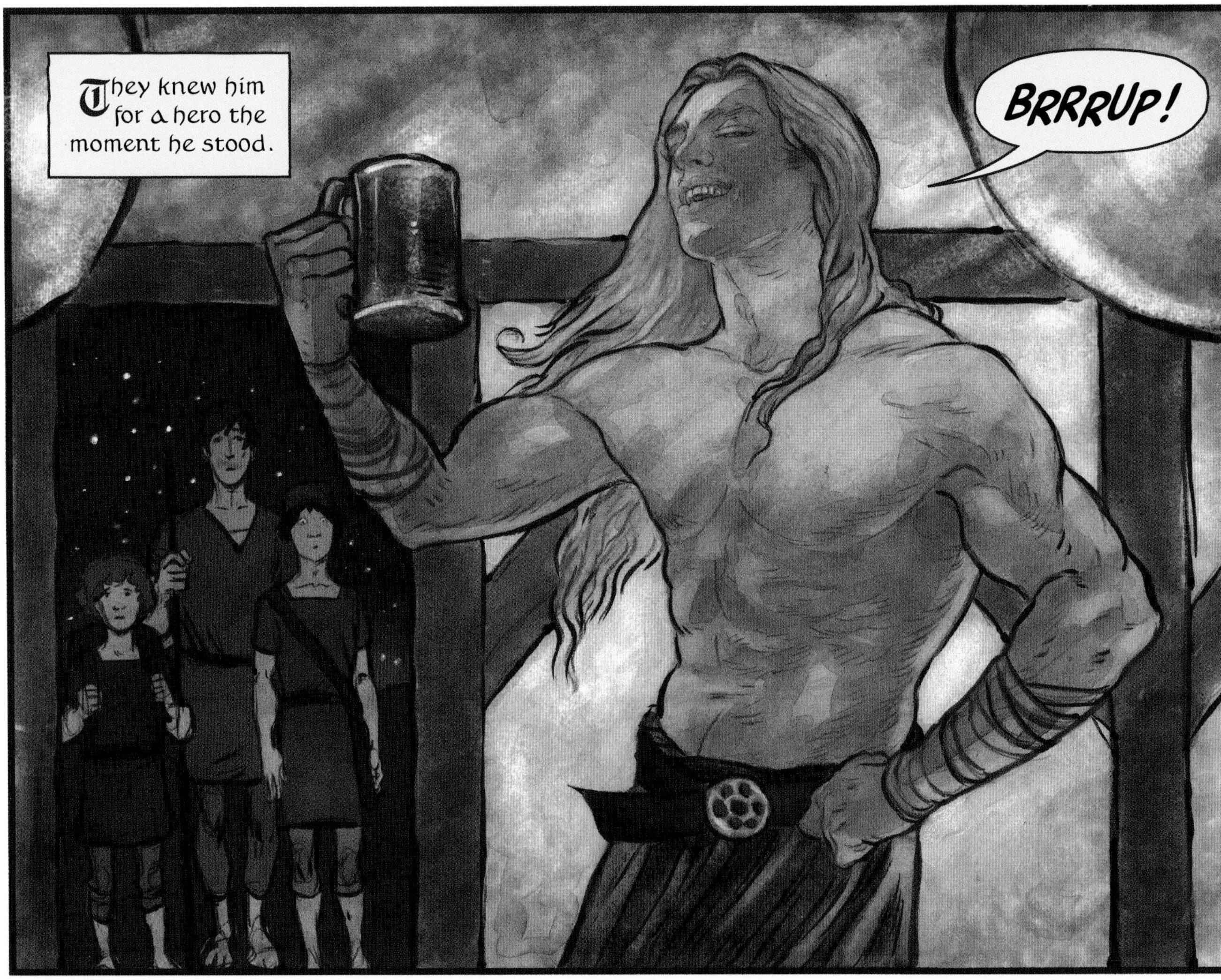
They knew him for a hero the moment he stood.
BRRRUP!

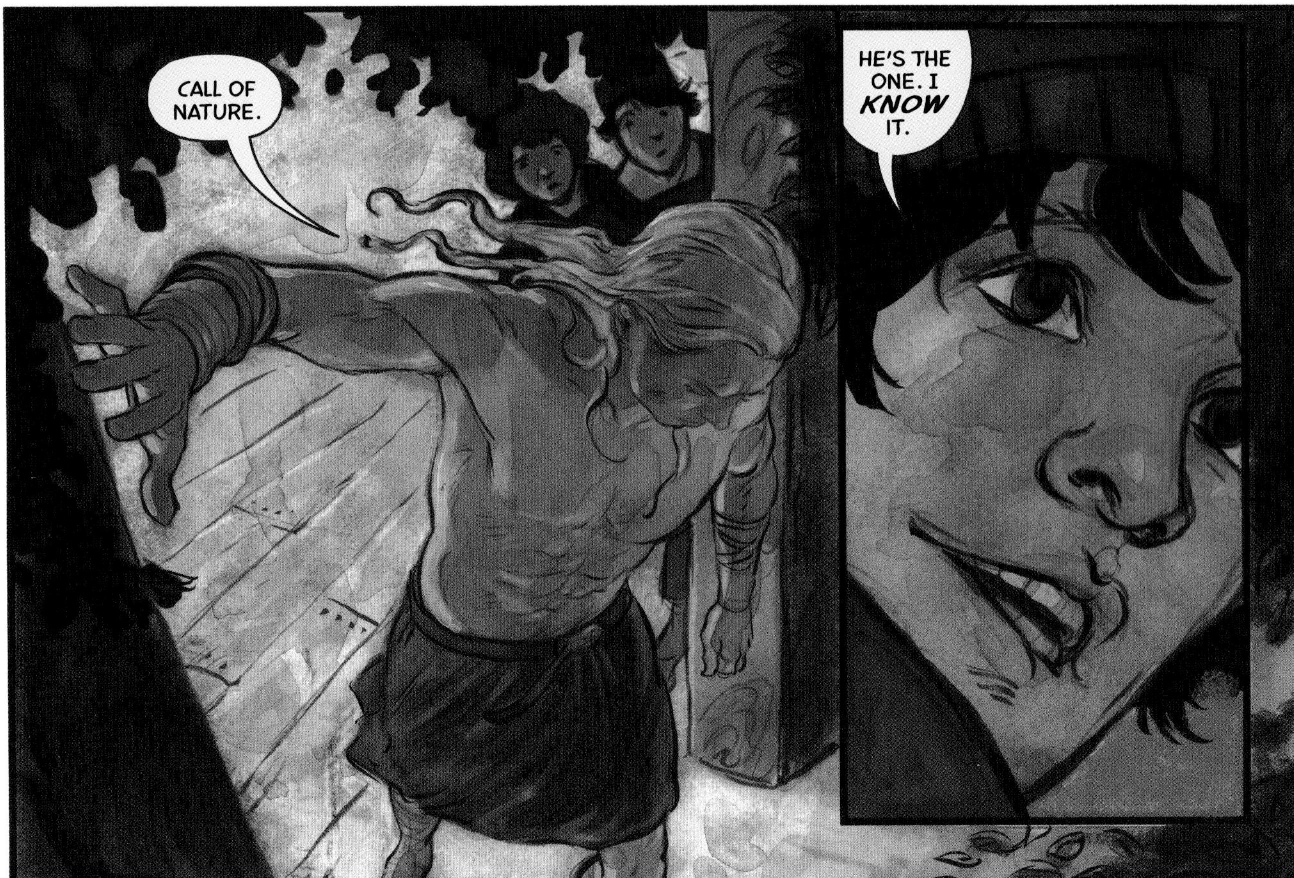
CALL OF NATURE.
HE'S THE ONE. I KNOW IT.

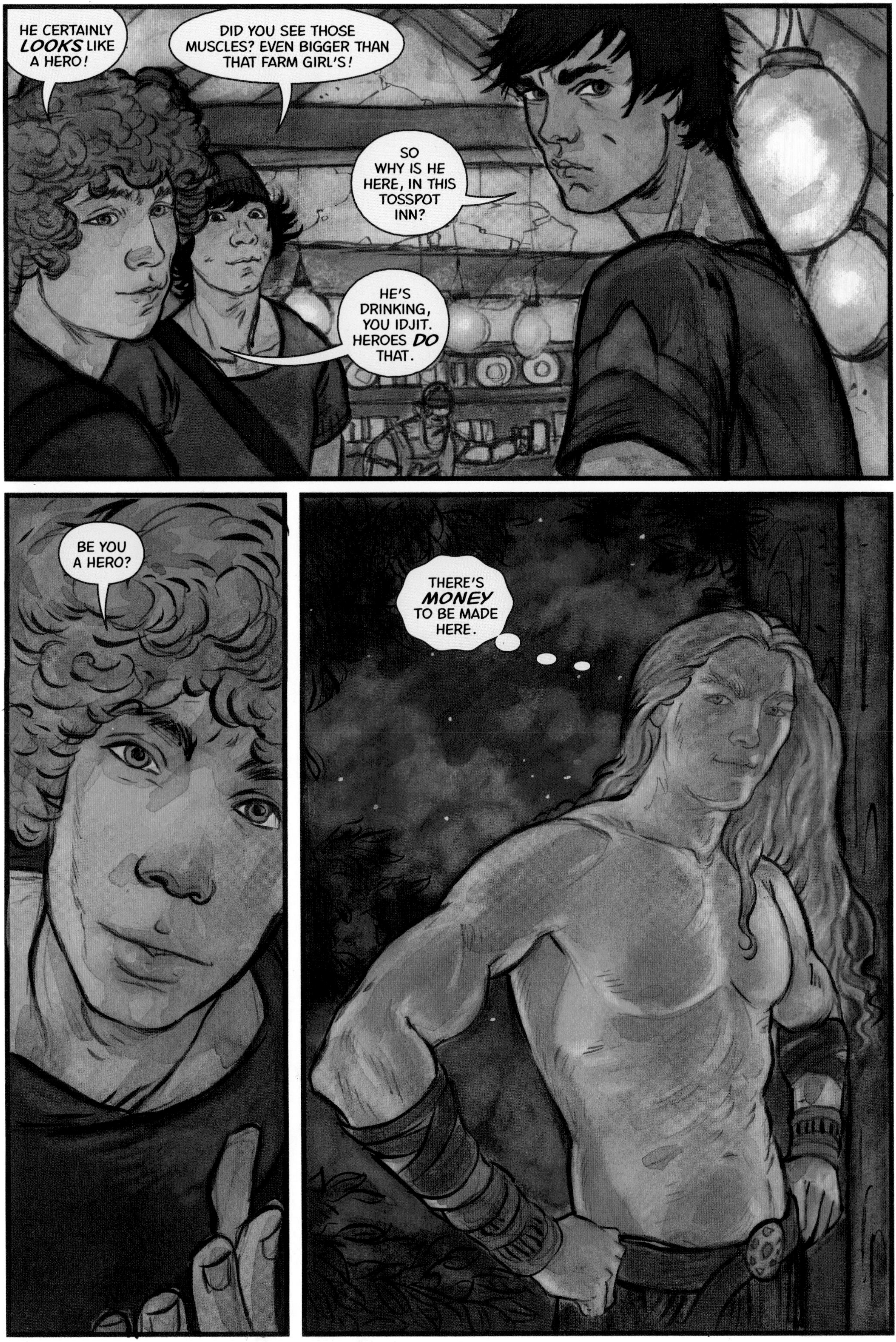
HE CERTAINLY LOOKS LIKE A HERO!
DID YOU SEE THOSE MUSCLES? EVEN BIGGER THAN THAT FARM GIRL'S!
SO WHY IS HE HERE, IN THIS TOSSPOT INN?
HE'S DRINKING, YOU IDJIT. HEROES DO THAT.
BE YOU A HERO?
THERE'S MONEY TO BE MADE HERE.

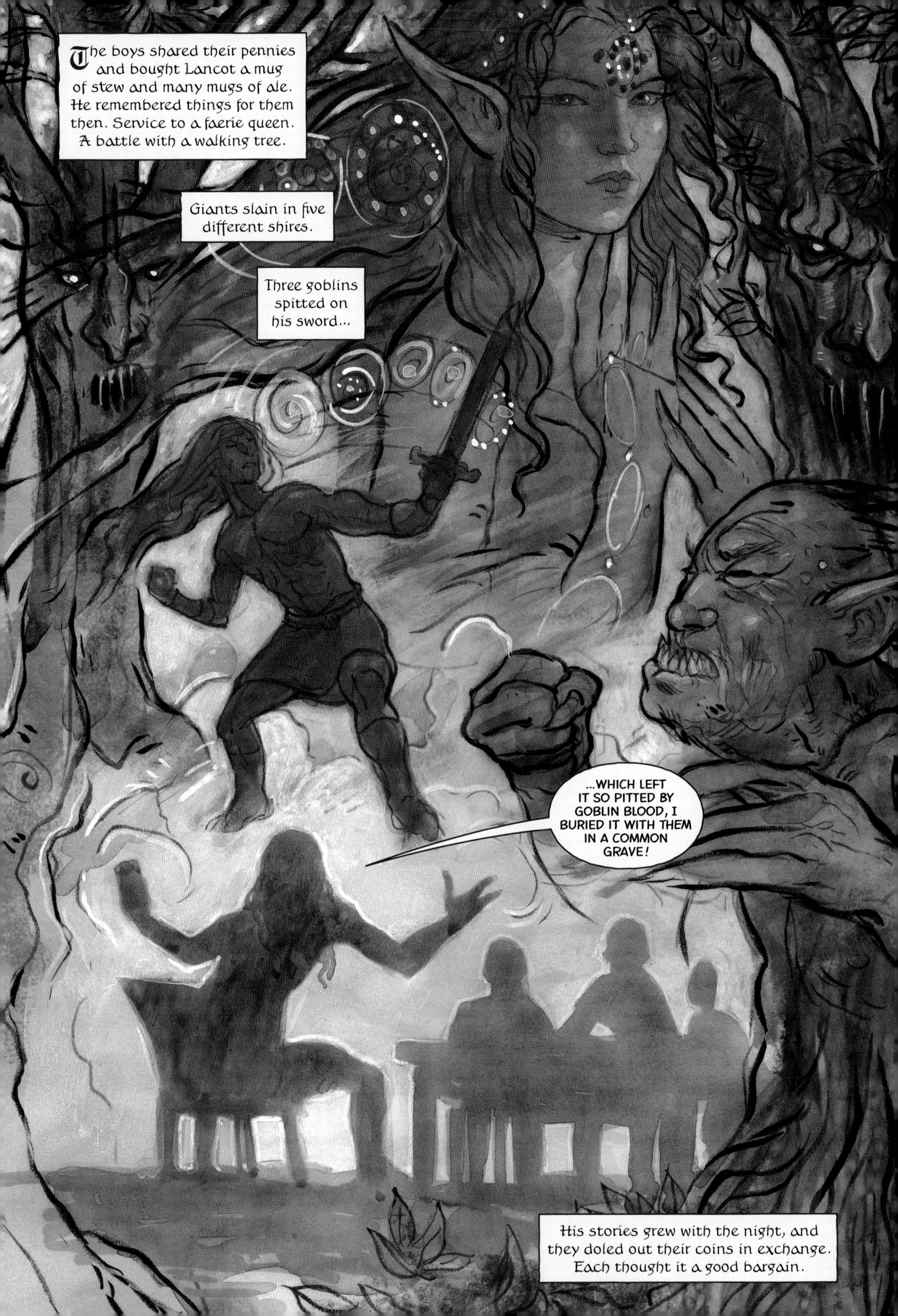
The boys shared their pennies and bought Lancot a mug of stew and many mugs of ale. He remembered things for them then. Service to a faerie queen. A battle with a walking tree.
Giants slain in five different shires.
Three goblins spitted on his sword...
...WHICH LEFT IT SO PITTED BY GOBLIN BLOOD, I BURIED IT WITH THEM IN A COMMON GRAVE!
His stories grew with the night, and they doled out their coins in exchange. Each thought it a good bargain.

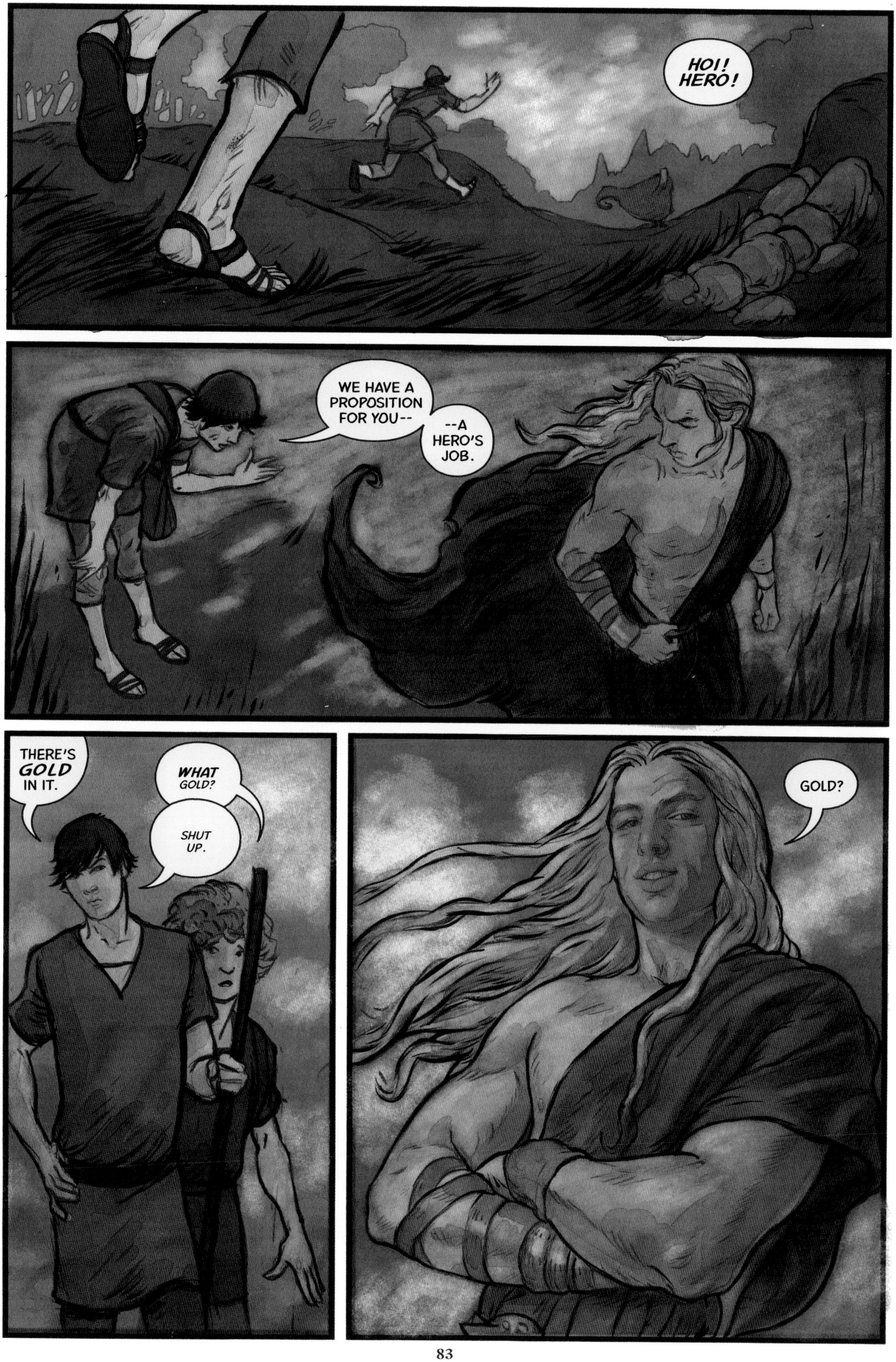
HOI! HERO!
WE HAVE A PROPOSITION FOR YOU--
--A HERO'S JOB.
THERE'S GOLD IN IT.
WHAT GOLD?
SHUT UP.
GOLD?

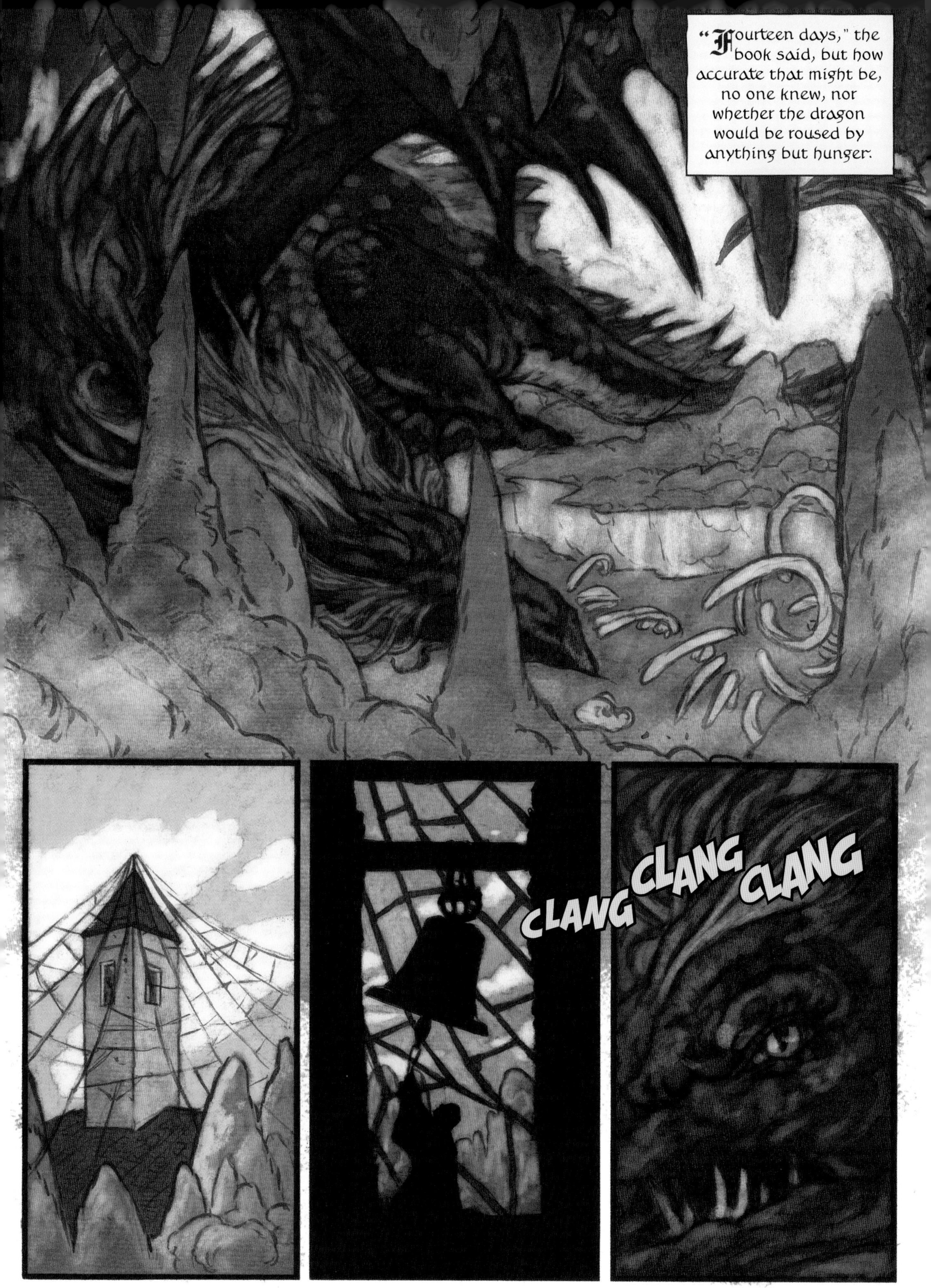
"Fourteen days," the book said, but how accurate that might be, no one knew, nor whether the dragon would be roused by anything but hunger.
CLANG
CLANG
CLANG

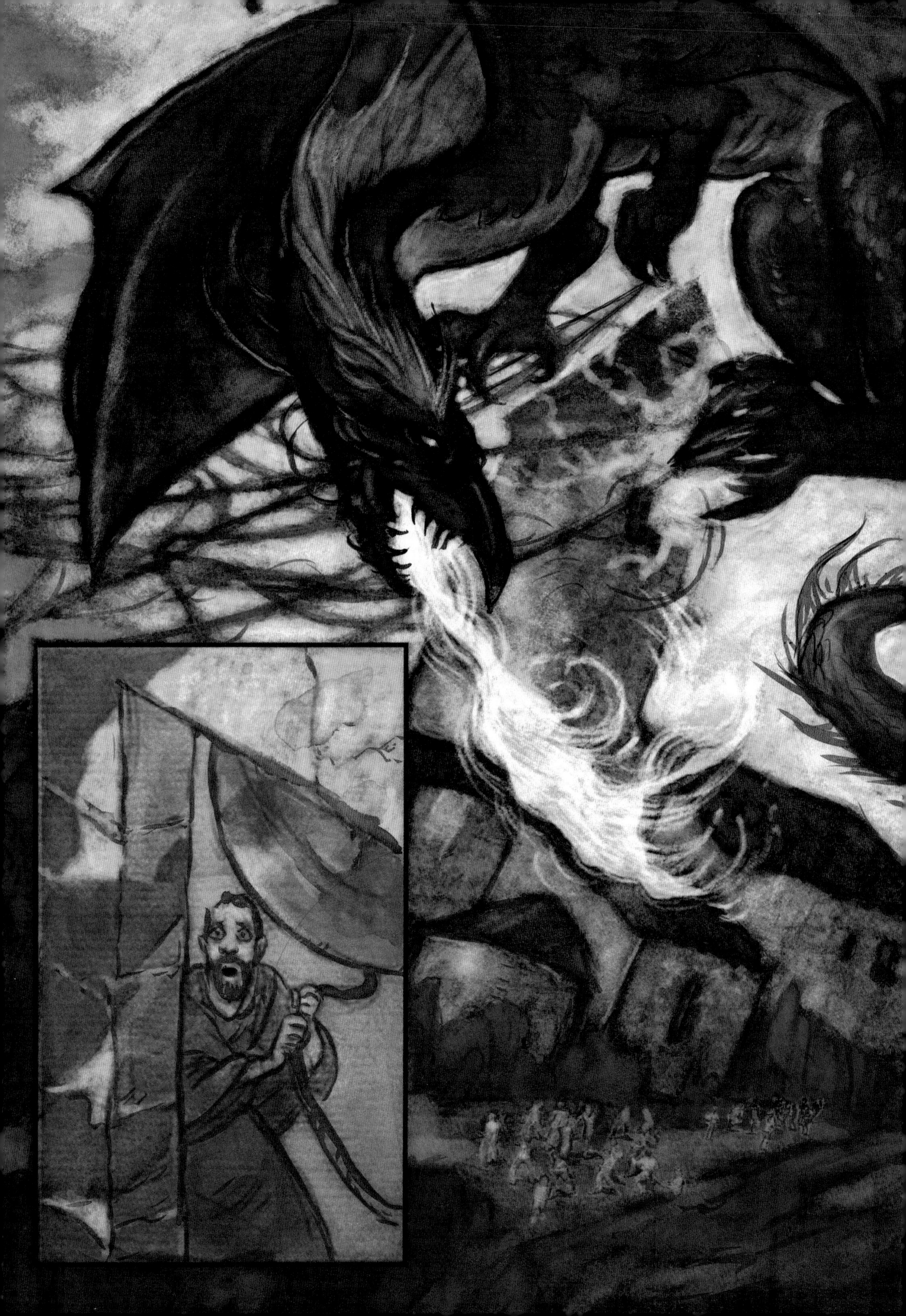

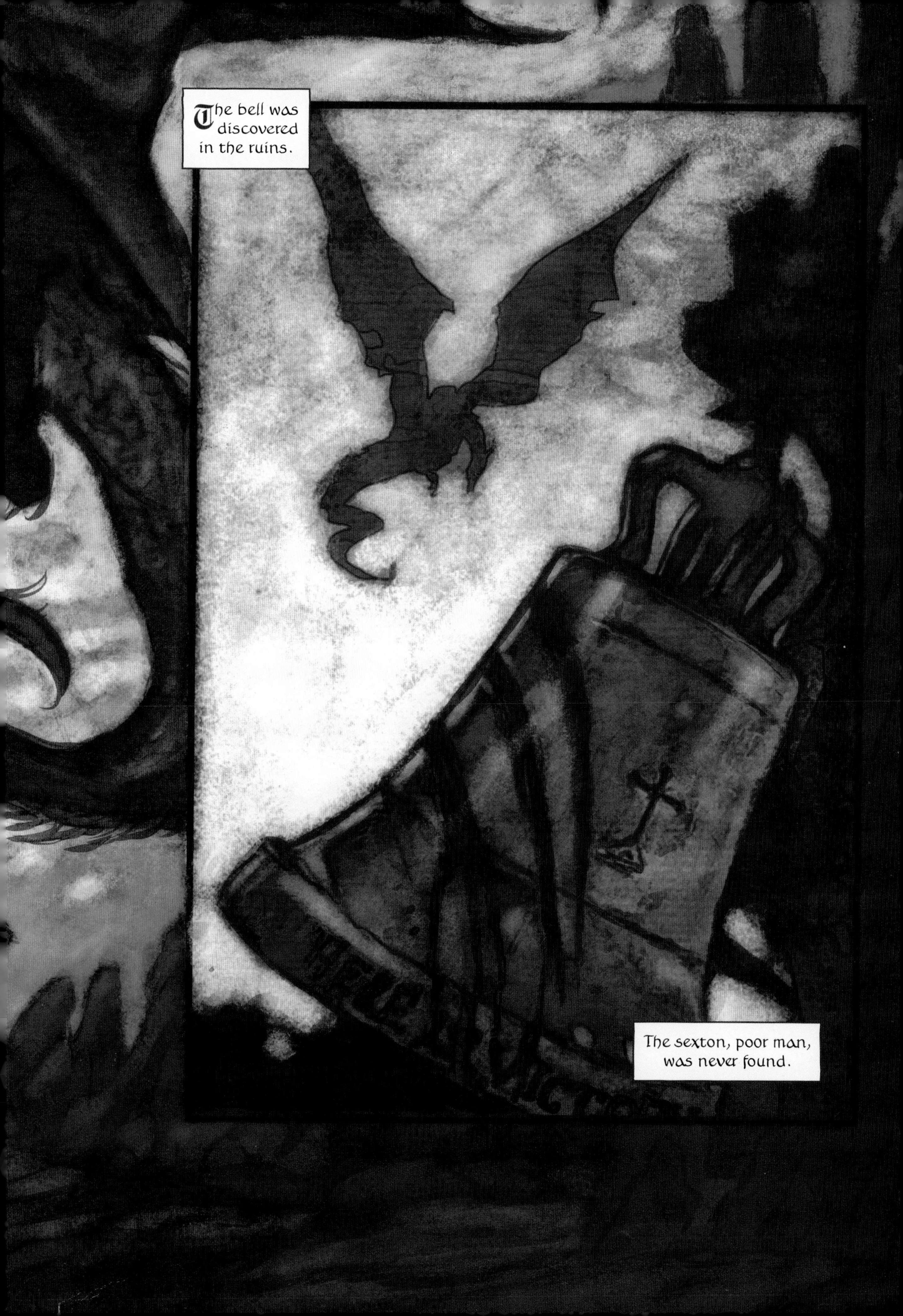
The bell was discovered in the ruins.
The sexton, poor man, was never found.

90

91

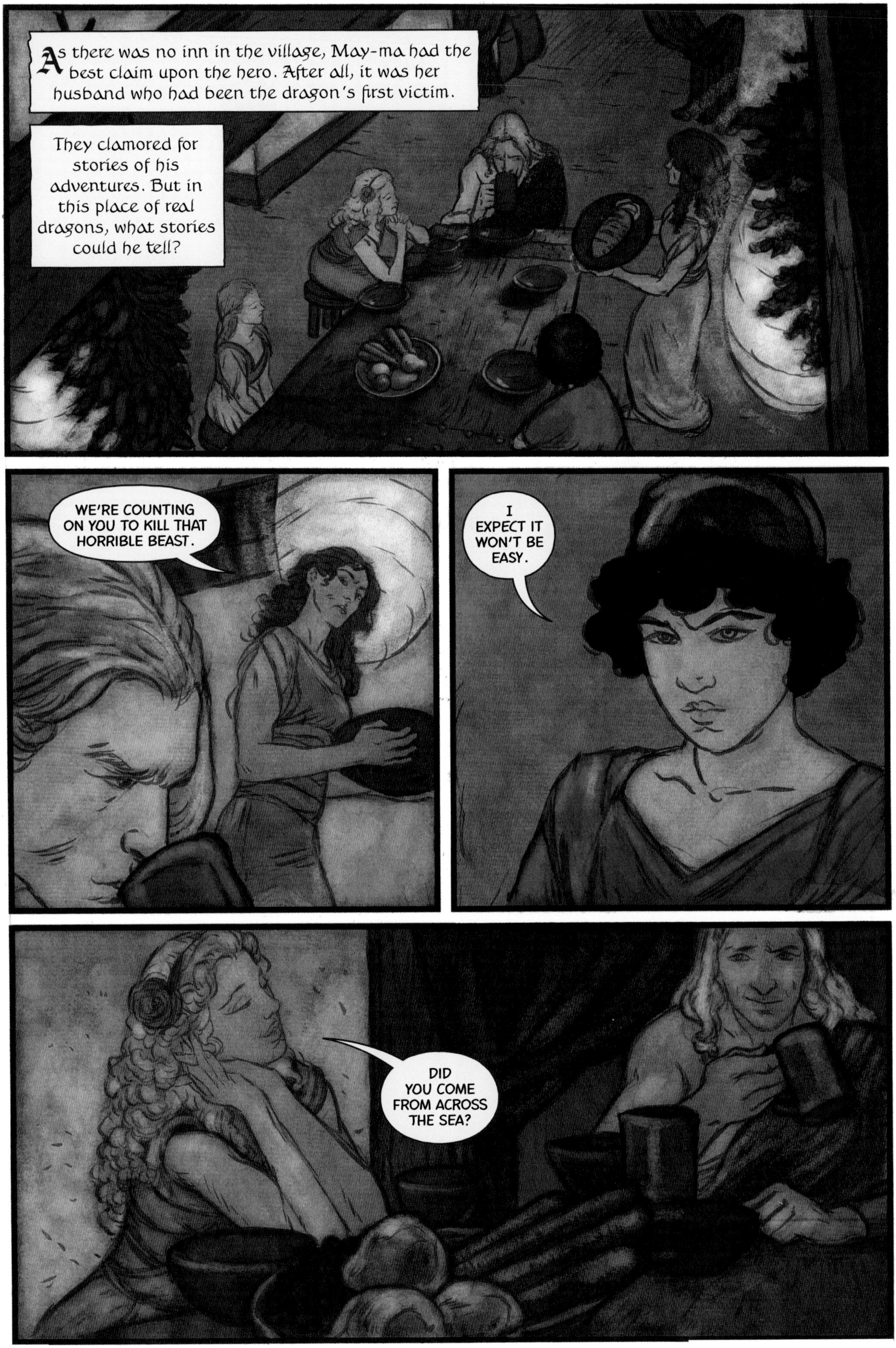
As there was no inn in the village, May-ma had the best claim upon the hero. After all, it was her husband who had been the dragon's first victim.
They clamored for stories of his adventures. But in this place of real dragons, what stories could he tell?
WE'RE COUNTING ON YOU TO KILL THAT HORRIBLE BEAST.
I EXPECT IT WON'T BE EASY.
DID YOU COME FROM ACROSS THE SEA?

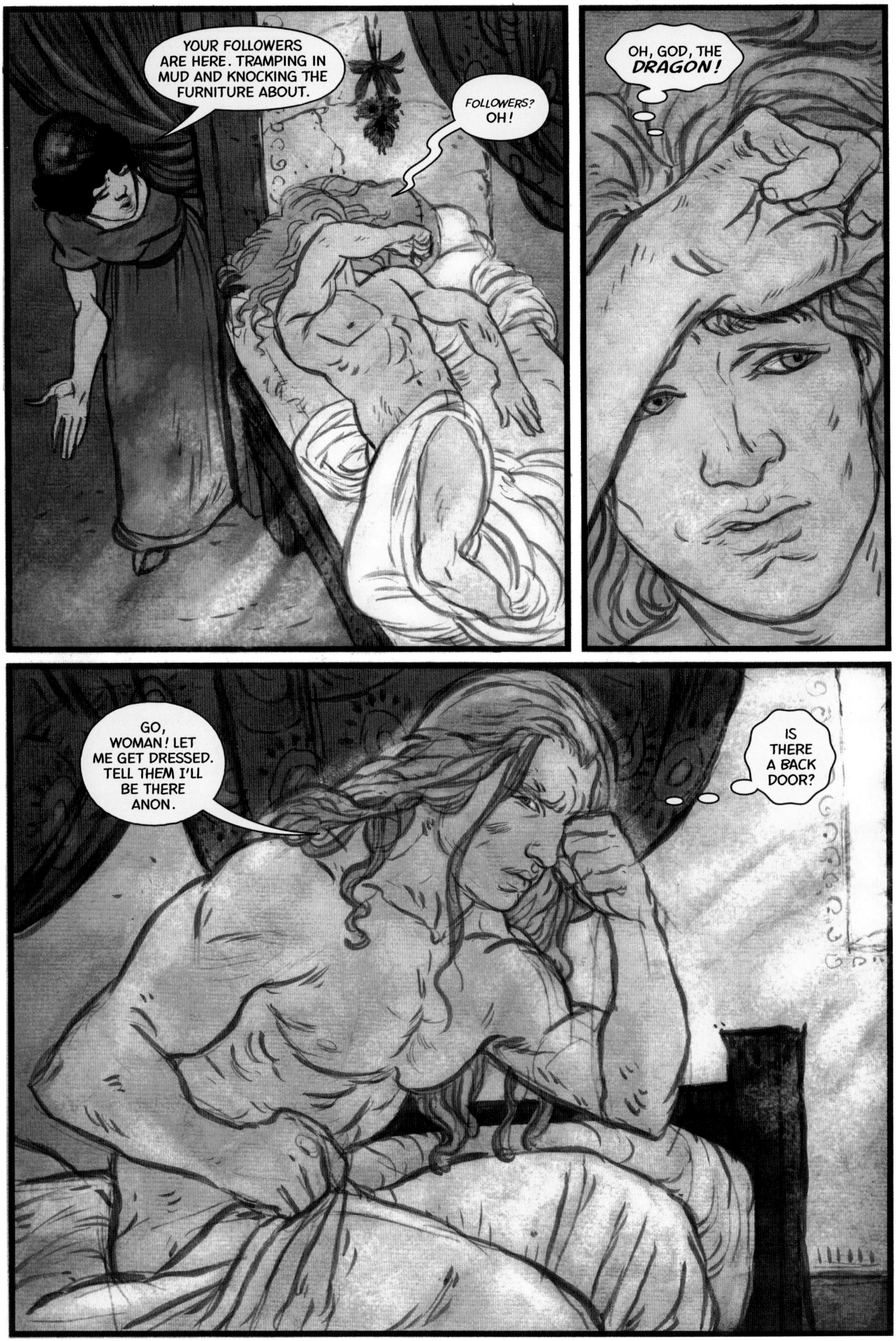
YOUR FOLLOWERS ARE HERE. TRAMPING IN MUD AND KNOCKING THE FURNITURE ABOUT.
FOLLOWERS? OH!
OH, GOD, THE *DRAGON!*
GO, WOMAN! LET ME GET DRESSED. TELL THEM I'LL BE THERE ANON.
IS THERE A BACK DOOR?

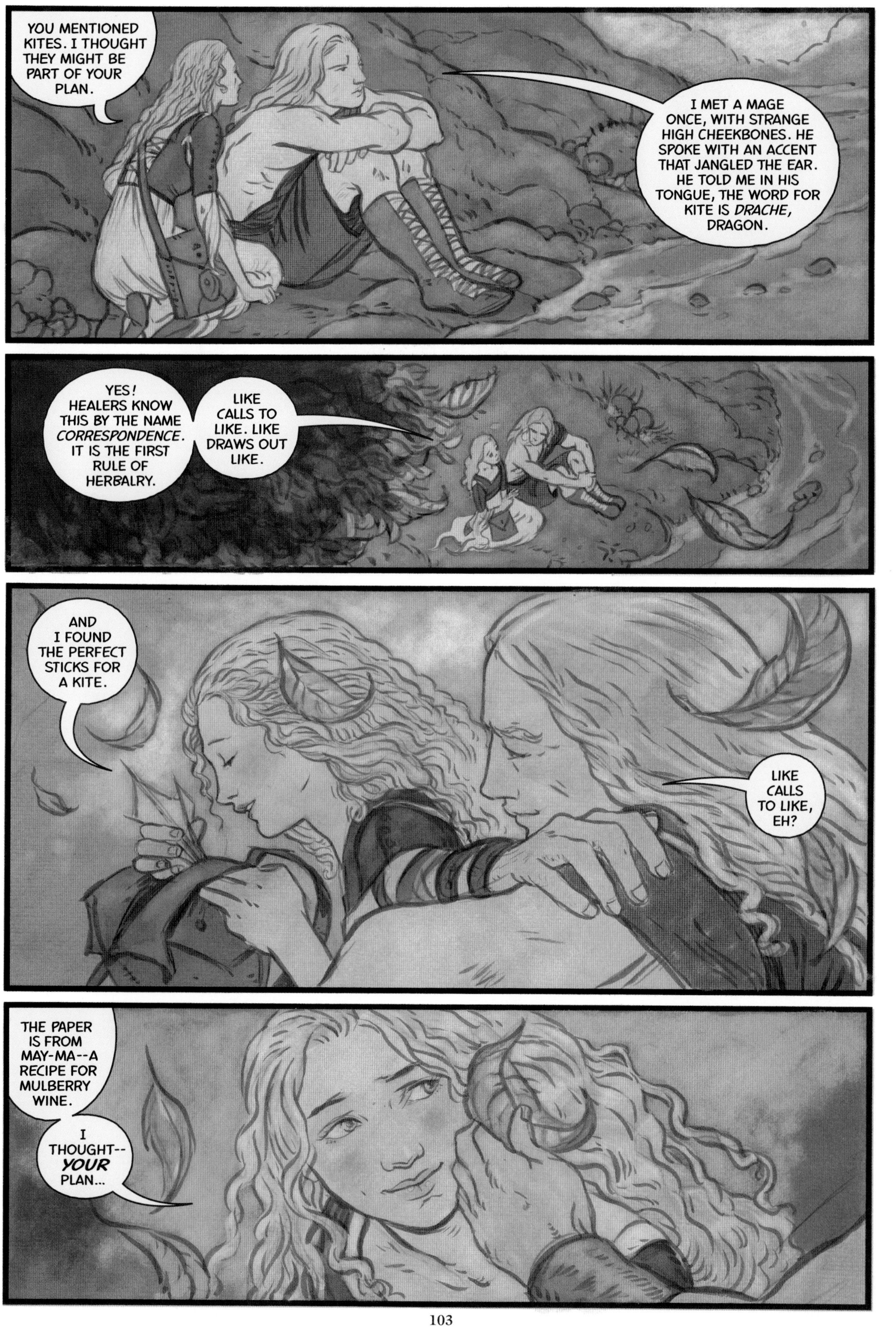
YOU MENTIONED KITES. I THOUGHT THEY MIGHT BE PART OF YOUR PLAN.
I MET A MAGE ONCE, WITH STRANGE HIGH CHEEKBONES. HE SPOKE WITH AN ACCENT THAT JANGLED THE EAR. HE TOLD ME IN HIS TONGUE, THE WORD FOR KITE IS *DRACHE*, DRAGON.
LIKE CALLS TO LIKE. LIKE DRAWS OUT LIKE.
YES! HEALERS KNOW THIS BY THE NAME *CORRESPONDENCE*. IT IS THE FIRST RULE OF HERBALRY.
AND I FOUND THE PERFECT STICKS FOR A KITE.
LIKE CALLS TO LIKE, EH?
THE PAPER IS FROM MAY-MA--A RECIPE FOR MULBERRY WINE.
I THOUGHT-- ***YOUR*** PLAN...

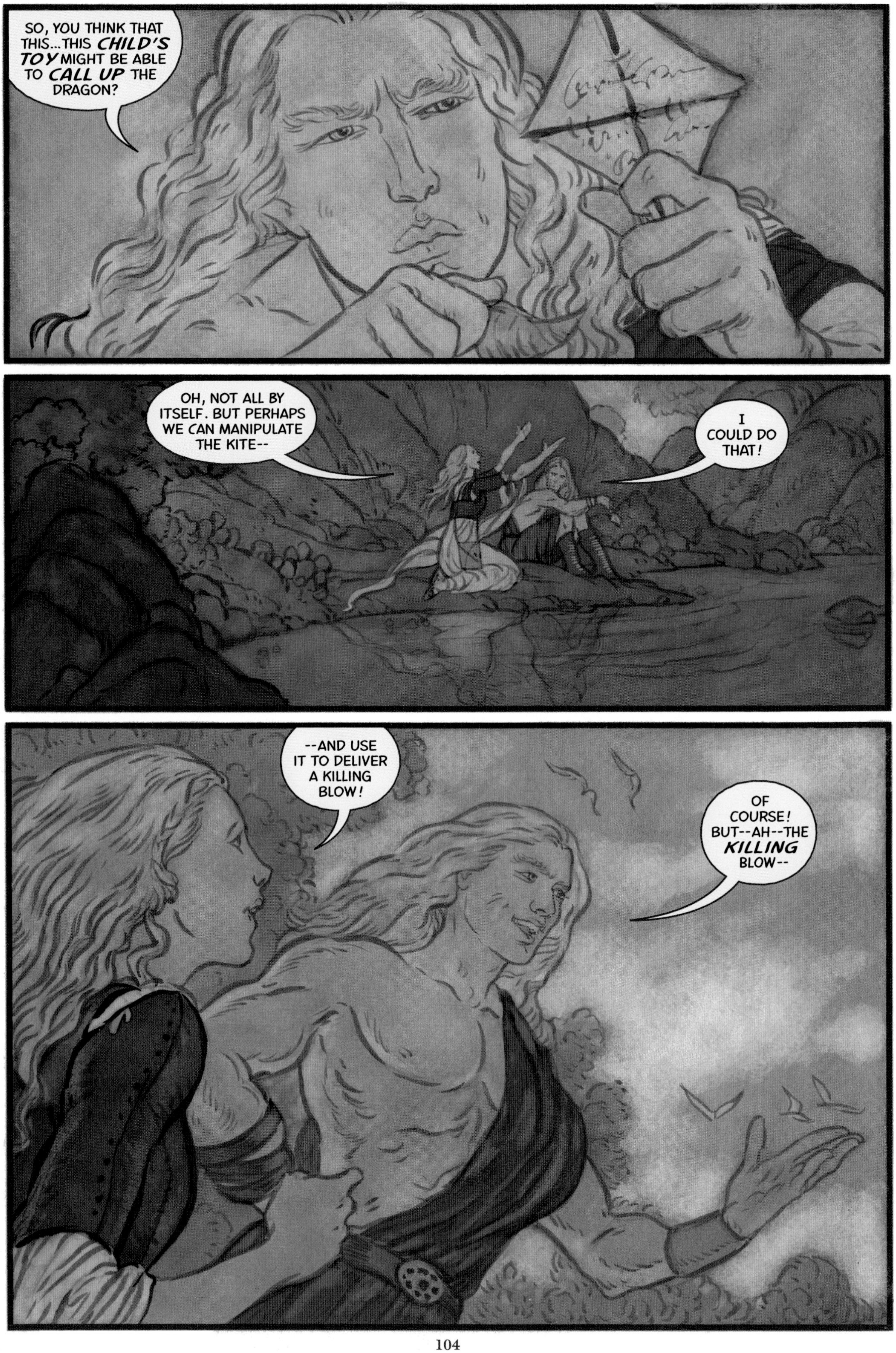
SO, YOU THINK THAT THIS...THIS CHILD'S TOY MIGHT BE ABLE TO CALL UP THE DRAGON?
OH, NOT ALL BY ITSELF. BUT PERHAPS WE CAN MANIPULATE THE KITE--
I COULD DO THAT!
--AND USE IT TO DELIVER A KILLING BLOW!
OF COURSE! BUT--AH--THE KILLING BLOW--

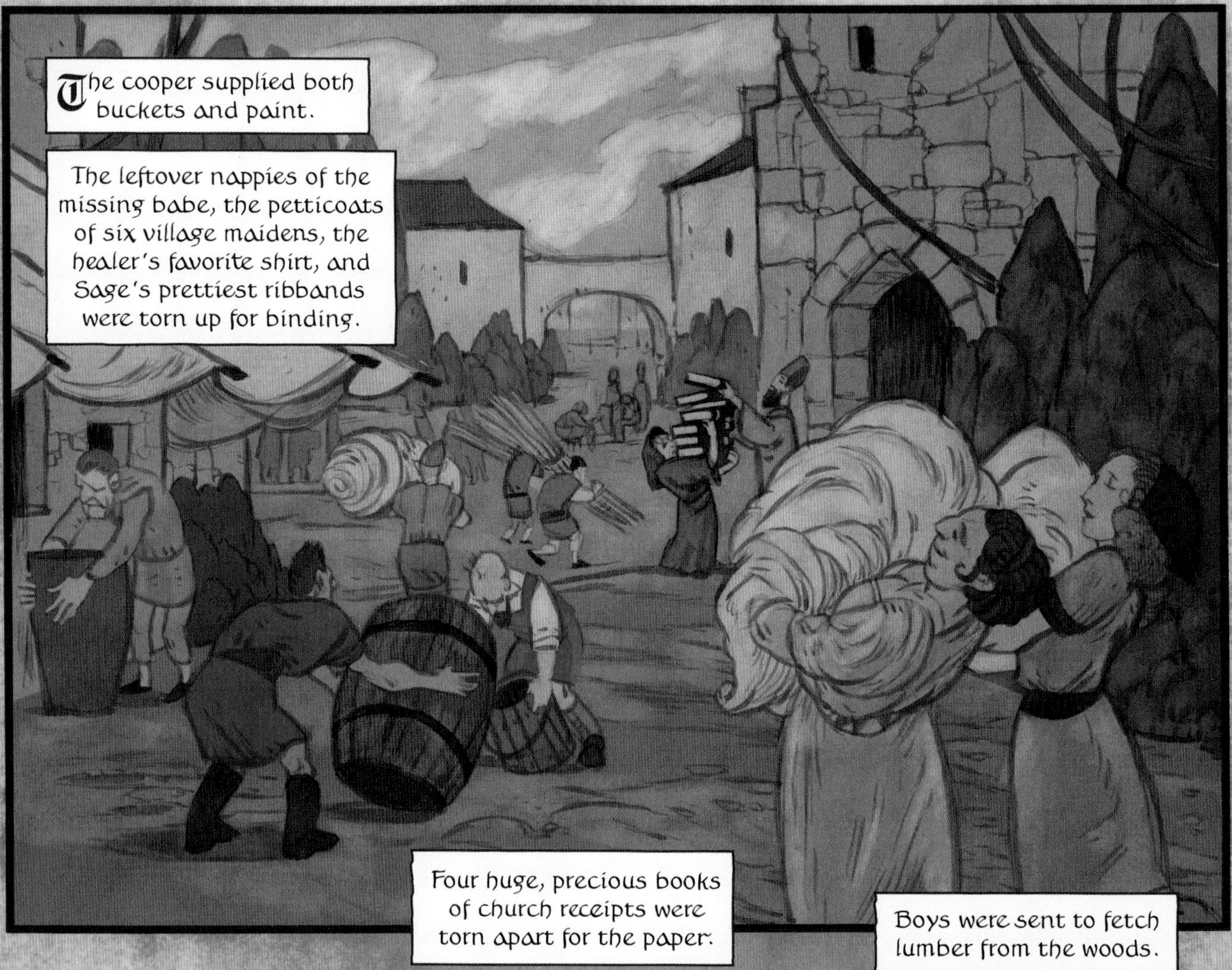
The cooper supplied both buckets and paint.
The leftover nappies of the missing babe, the petticoats of six village maidens, the healer's favorite shirt, and Sage's prettiest ribbands were torn up for binding.
Four huge, precious books of church receipts were torn apart for the paper.
Boys were sent to fetch lumber from the woods.

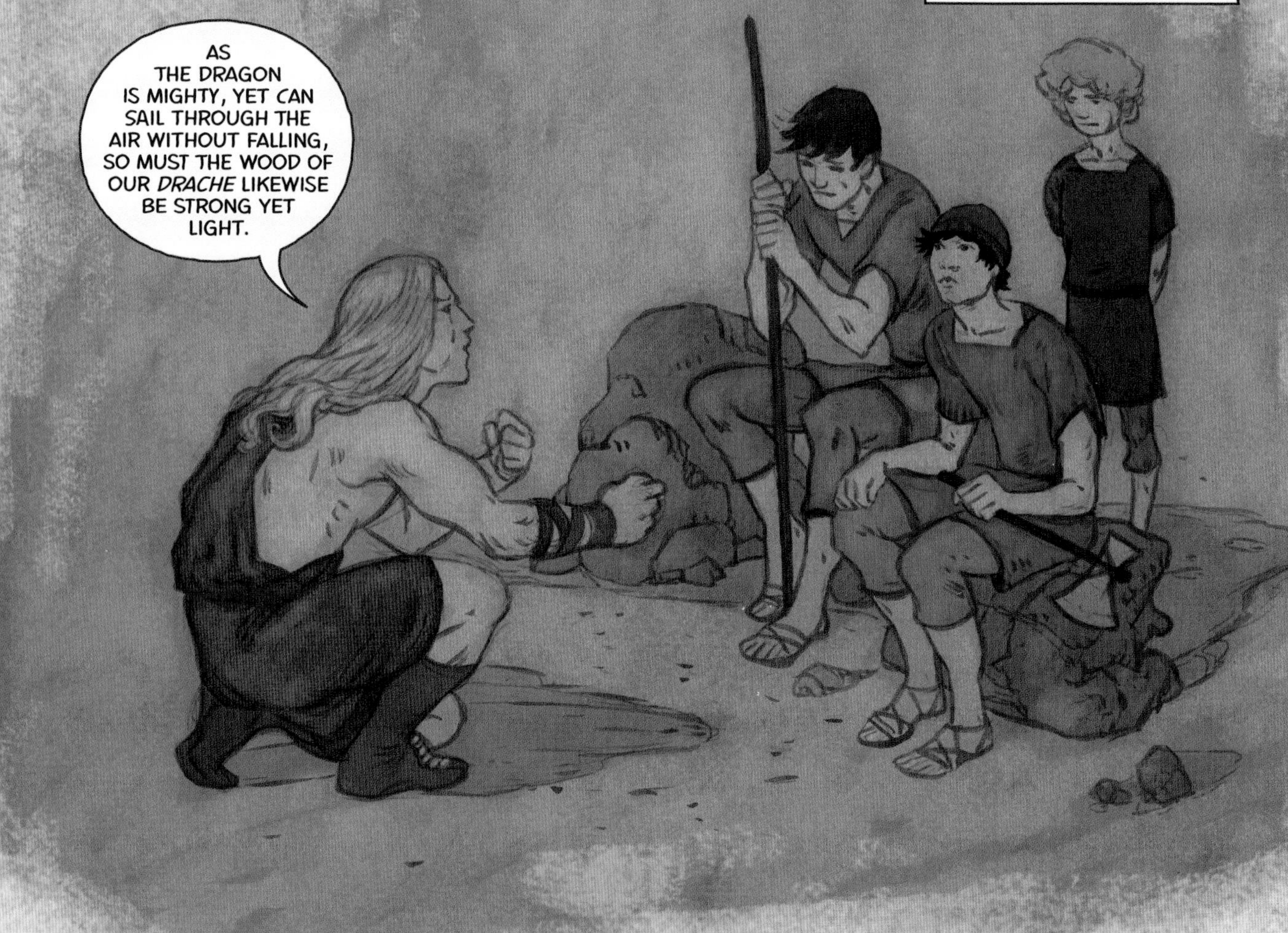
AS THE DRAGON IS MIGHTY, YET CAN SAIL THROUGH THE AIR WITHOUT FALLING, SO MUST THE WOOD OF OUR *DRACHE* LIKEWISE BE STRONG YET LIGHT.

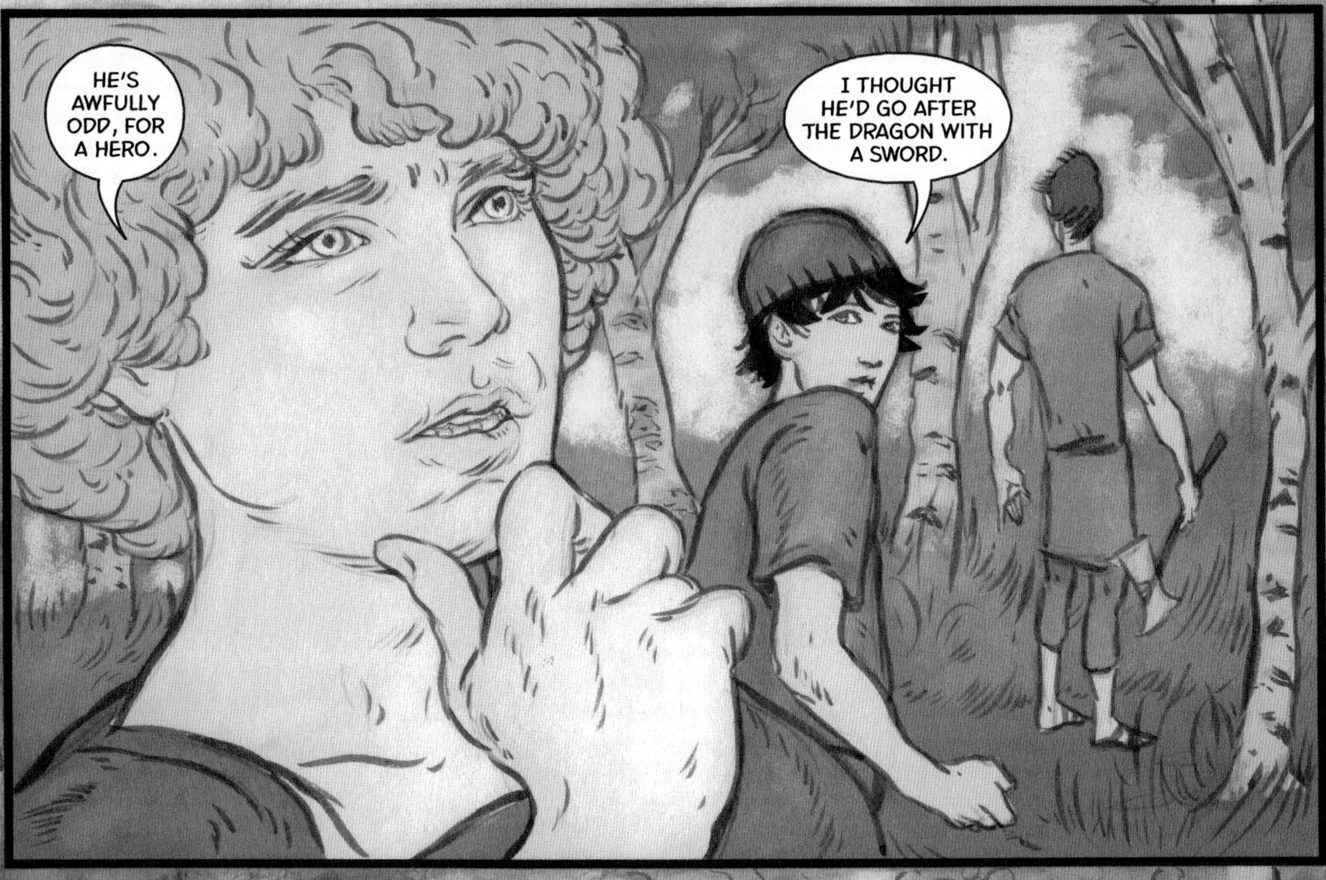
HE'S AWFULLY ODD, FOR A HERO.
I THOUGHT HE'D GO AFTER THE DRAGON WITH A SWORD.

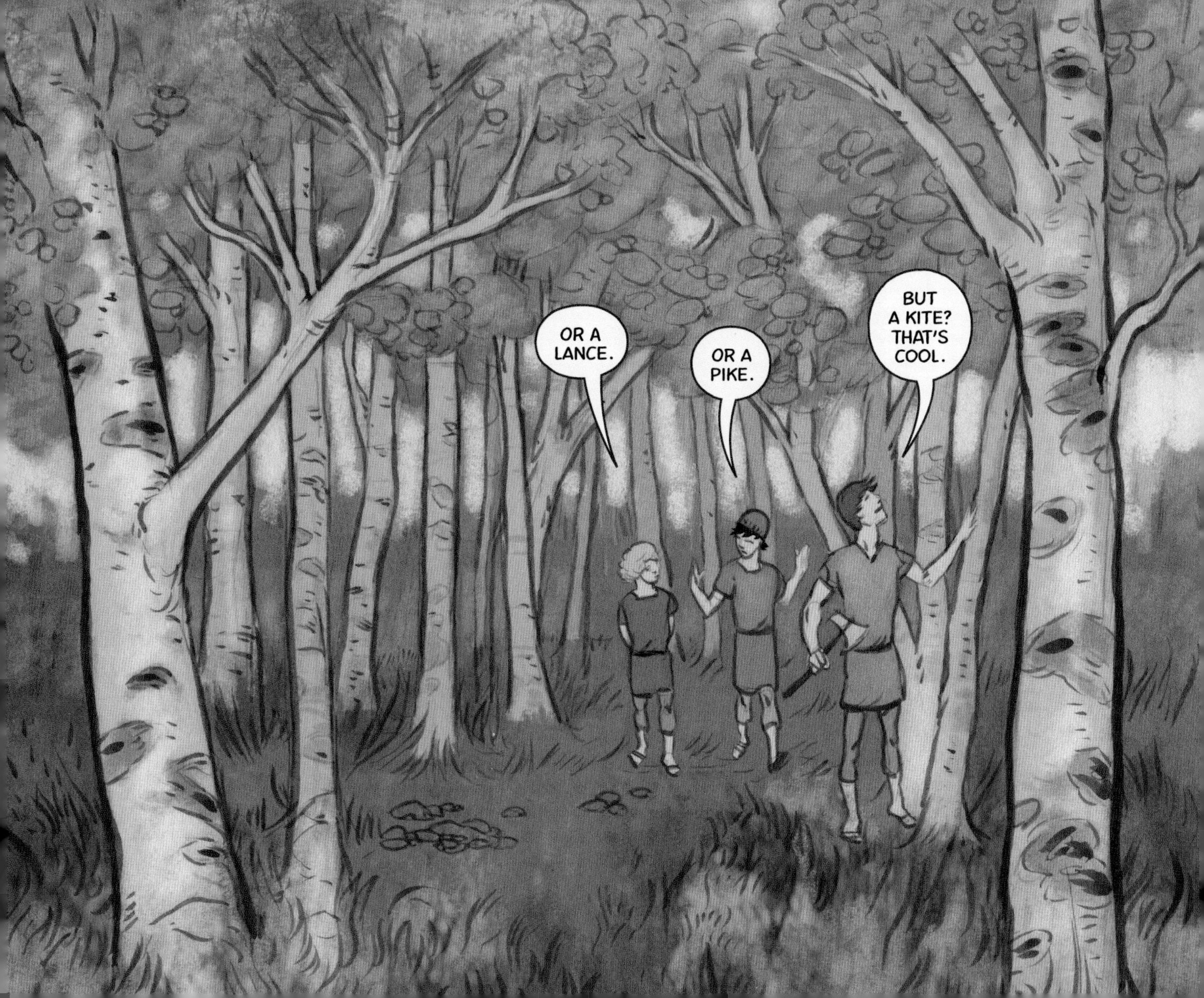
OR A LANCE.
OR A PIKE.
BUT A KITE? THAT'S COOL.

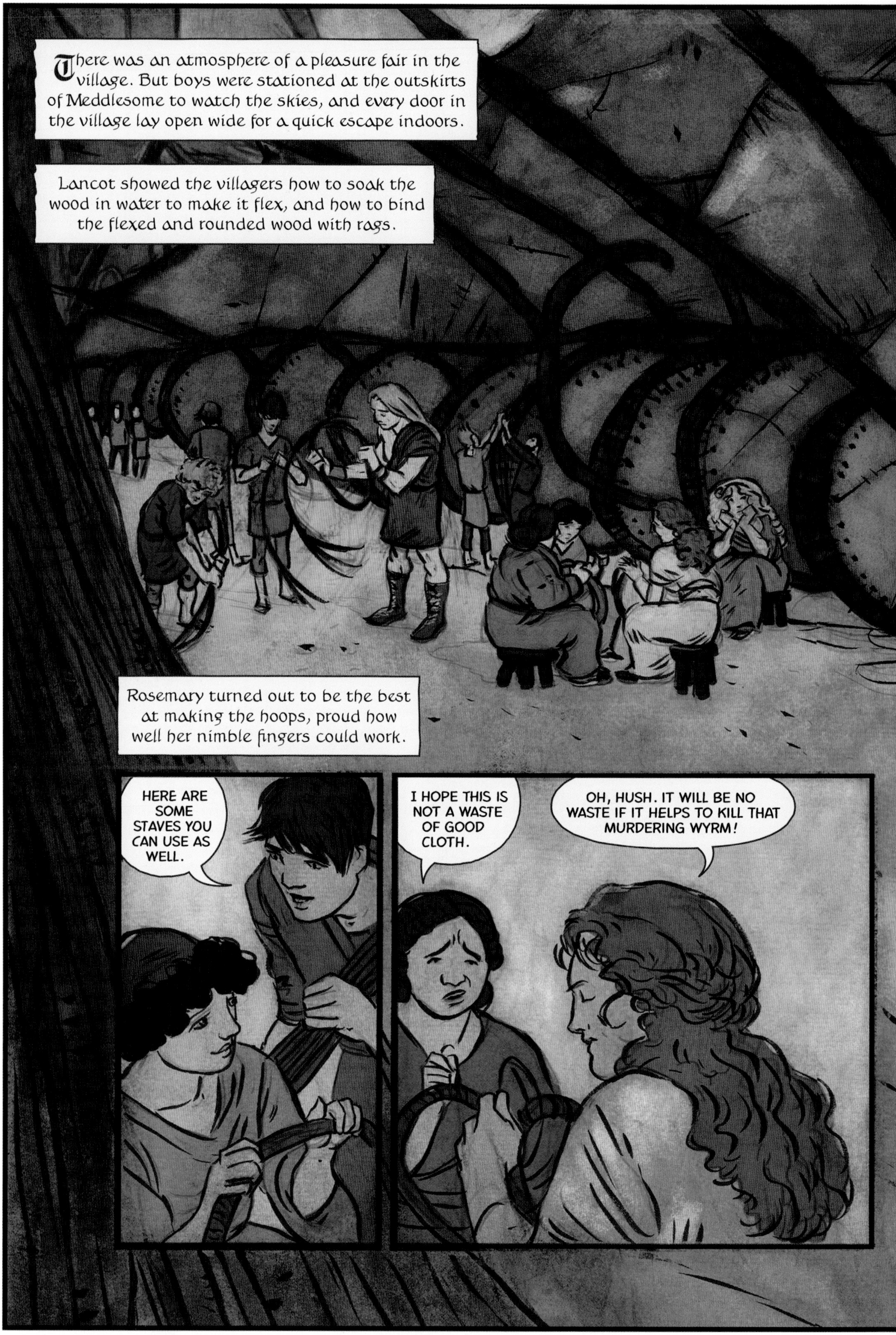
There was an atmosphere of a pleasure fair in the village. But boys were stationed at the outskirts of Meddlesome to watch the skies, and every door in the village lay open wide for a quick escape indoors.
Lancot showed the villagers how to soak the wood in water to make it flex, and how to bind the flexed and rounded wood with rags.
Rosemary turned out to be the best at making the hoops, proud how well her nimble fingers could work.
HERE ARE SOME STAVES YOU CAN USE AS WELL.
I HOPE THIS IS NOT A WASTE OF GOOD CLOTH.
OH, HUSH. IT WILL BE NO WASTE IF IT HELPS TO KILL THAT MURDERING WYRM!

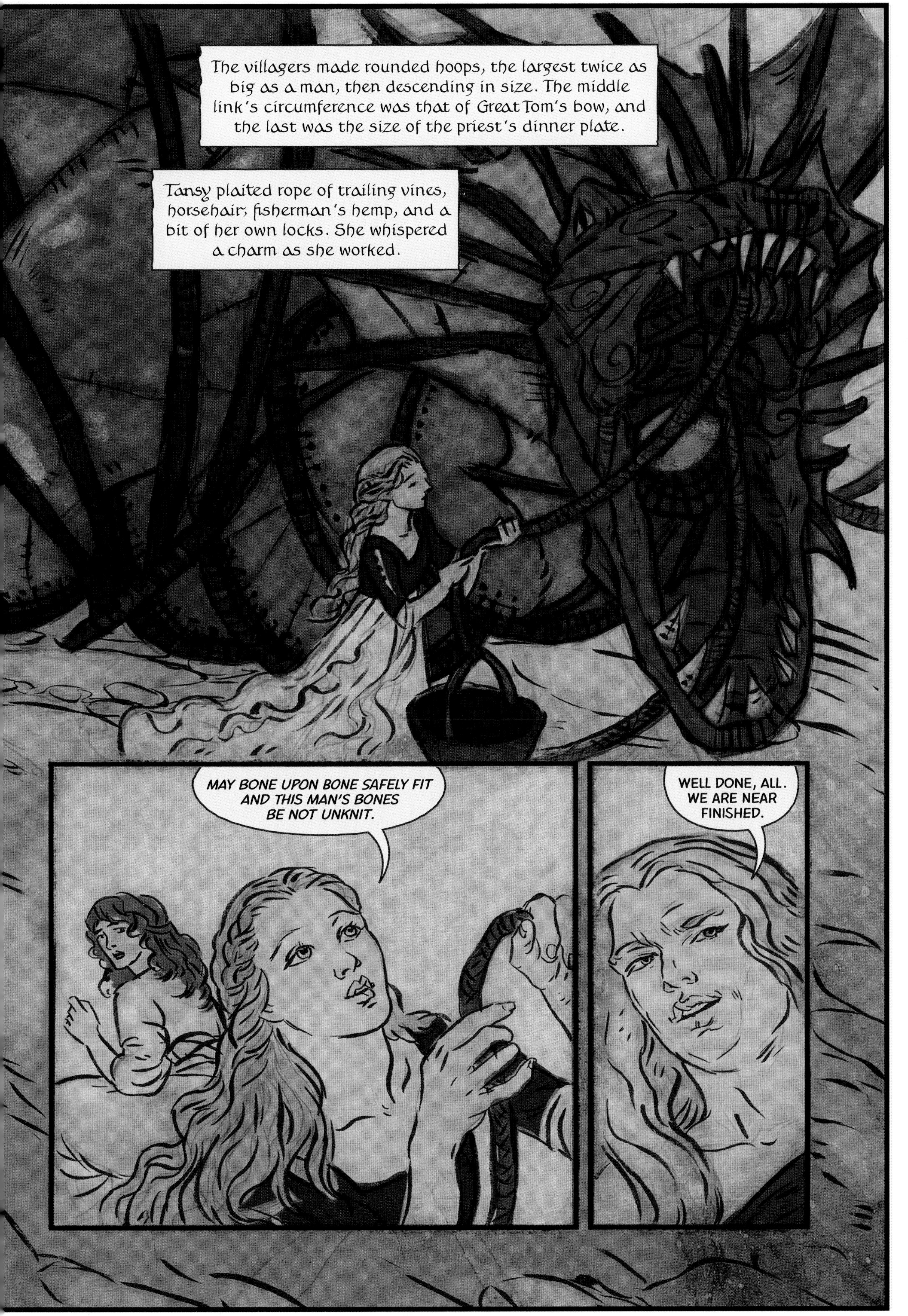
The villagers made rounded hoops, the largest twice as big as a man, then descending in size. The middle link's circumference was that of Great Tom's bow, and the last was the size of the priest's dinner plate.
Tansy plaited rope of trailing vines, horsehair, fisherman's hemp, and a bit of her own locks. She whispered a charm as she worked.
MAY BONE UPON BONE SAFELY FIT AND THIS MAN'S BONES BE NOT UNKNIT.
WELL DONE, ALL. WE ARE NEAR FINISHED.

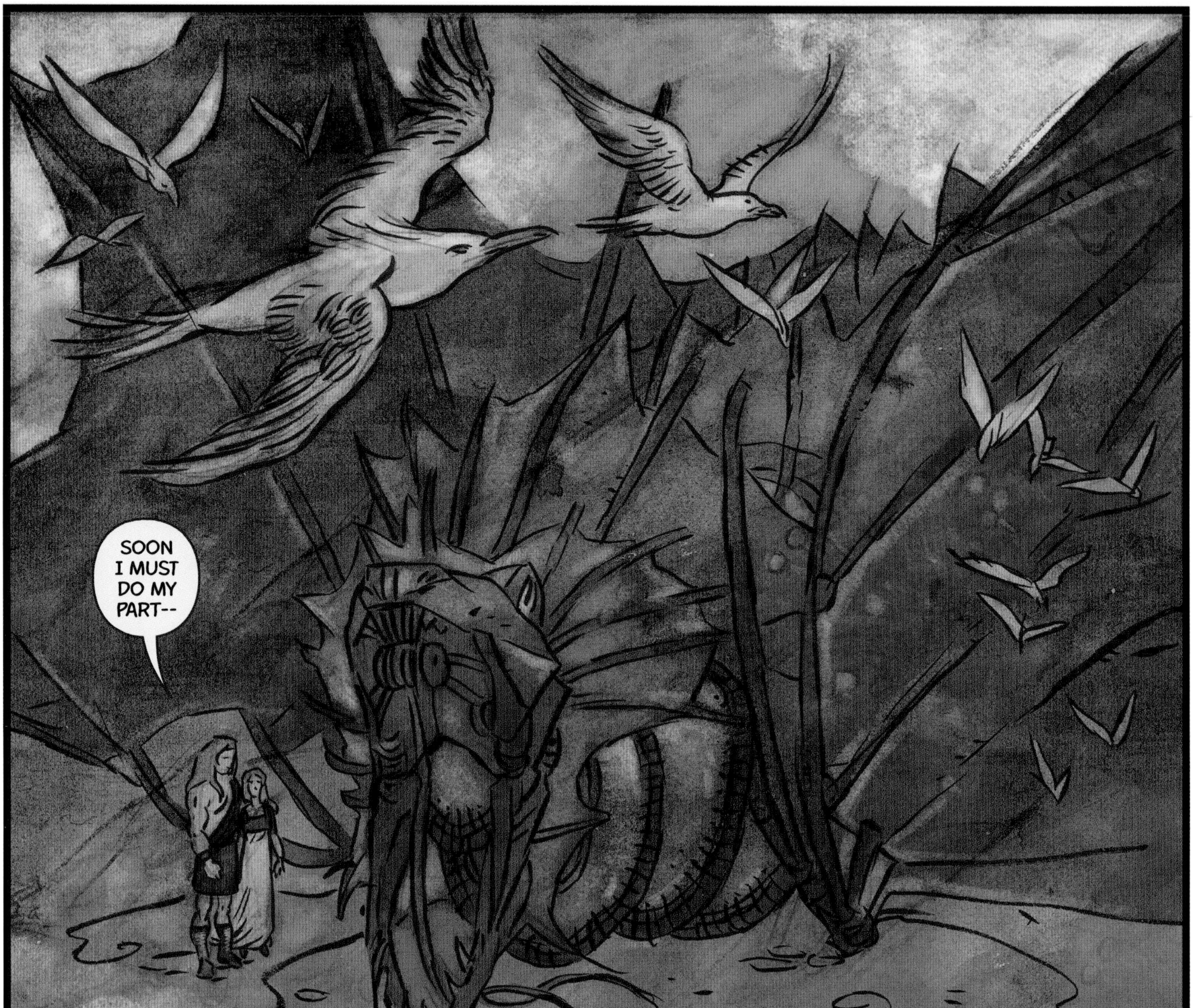
SOON I MUST DO MY PART--

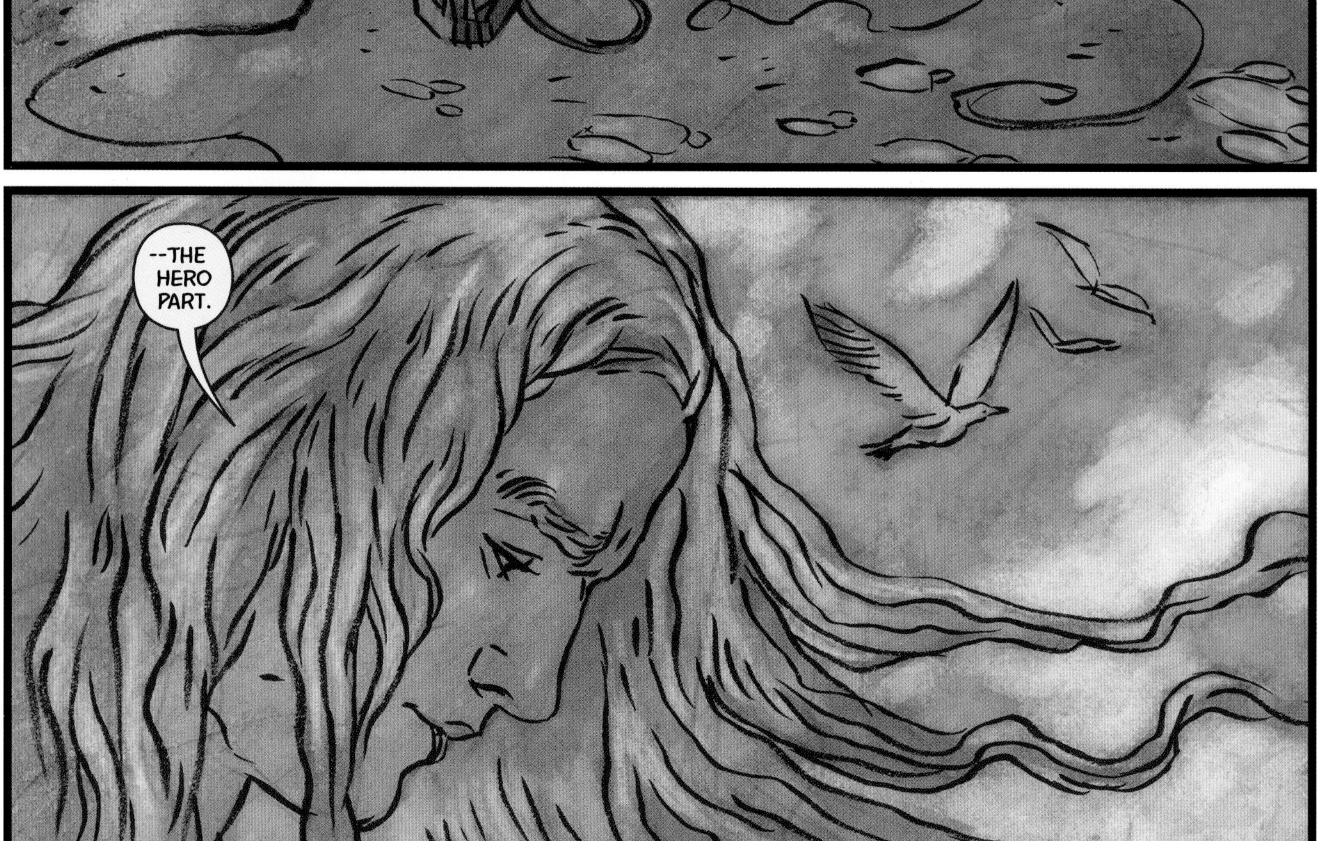
--THE HERO PART.

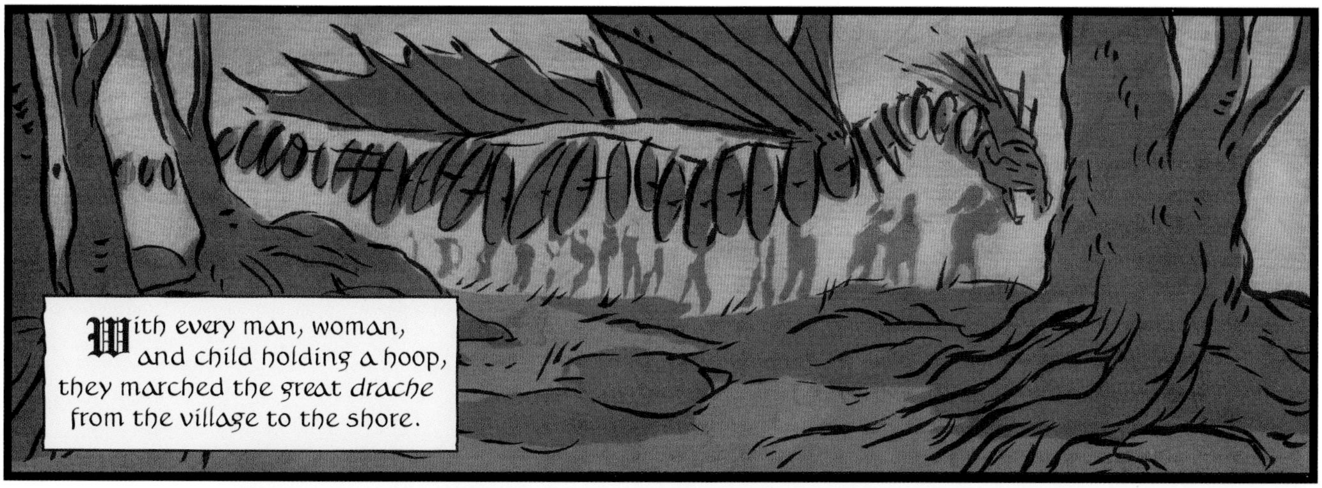
With every man, woman, and child holding a hoop, they marched the great *drache* from the village to the shore.

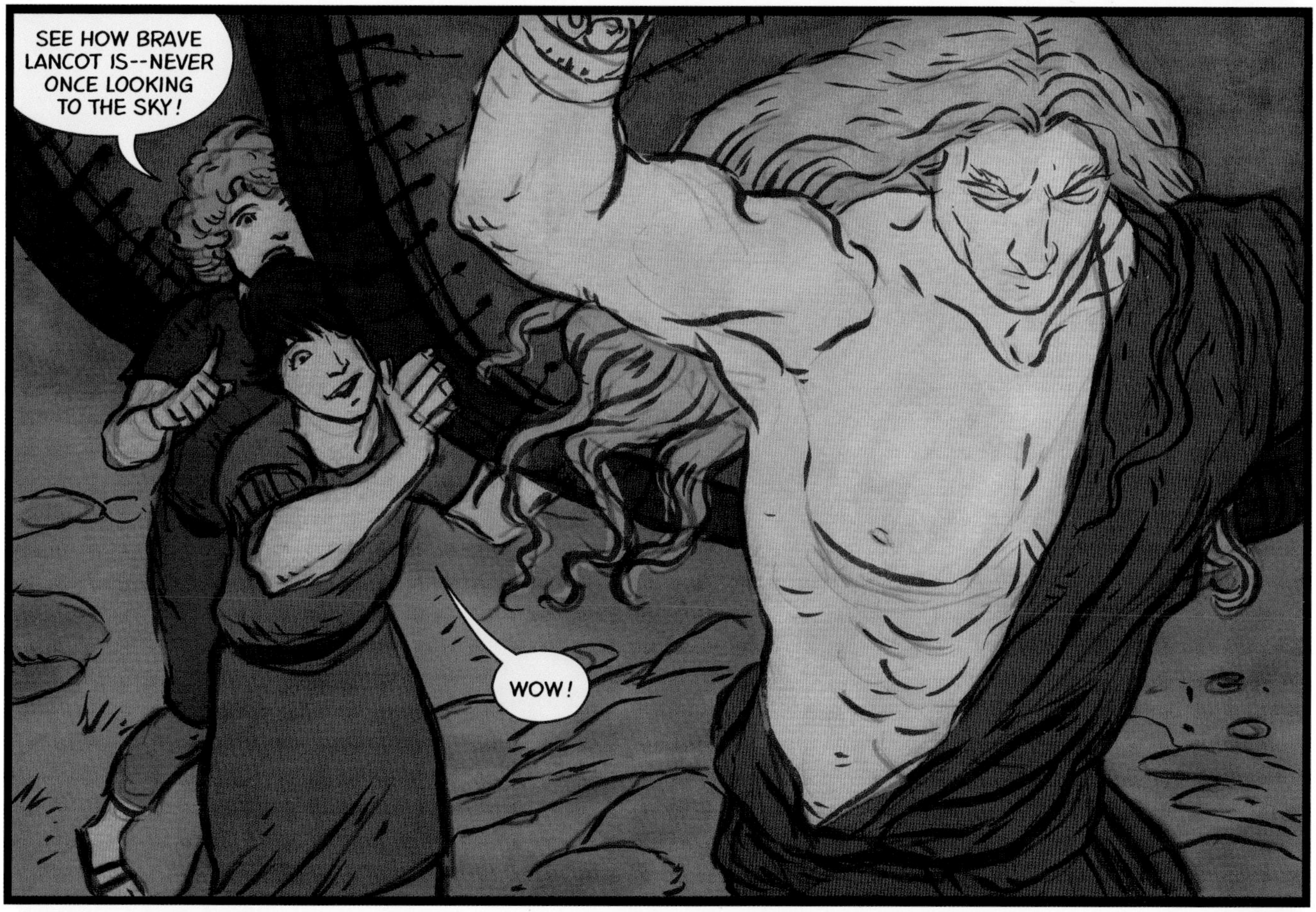
SEE HOW BRAVE LANCOT IS--NEVER ONCE LOOKING TO THE SKY!
WOW!

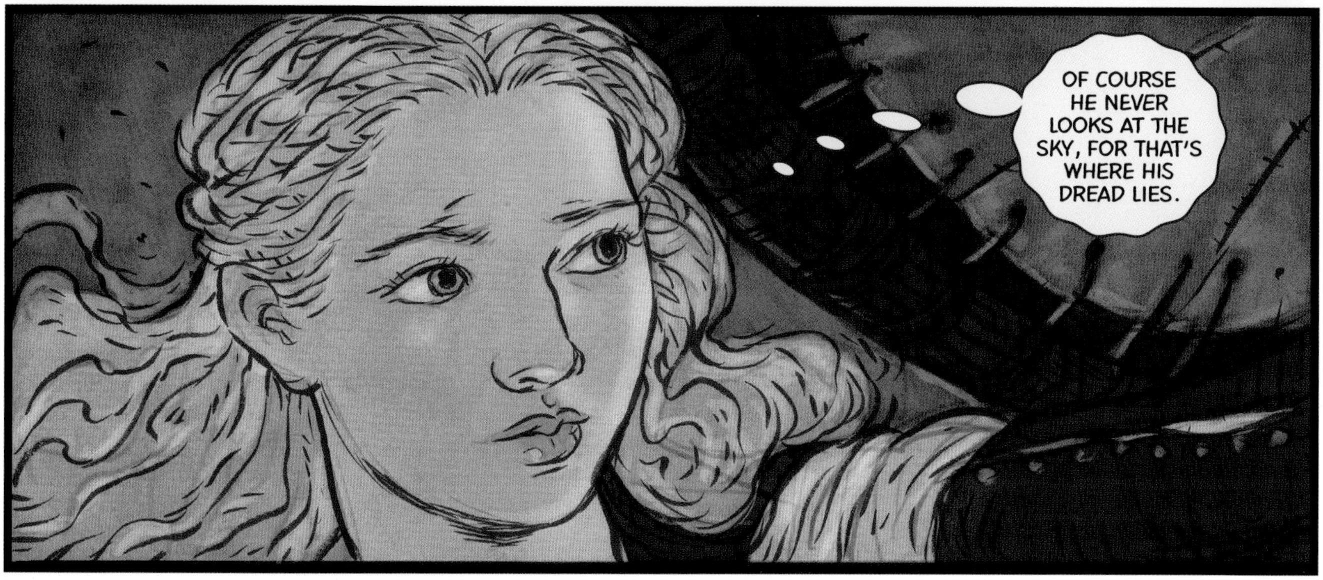
OF COURSE HE NEVER LOOKS AT THE SKY, FOR THAT'S WHERE HIS DREAD LIES.

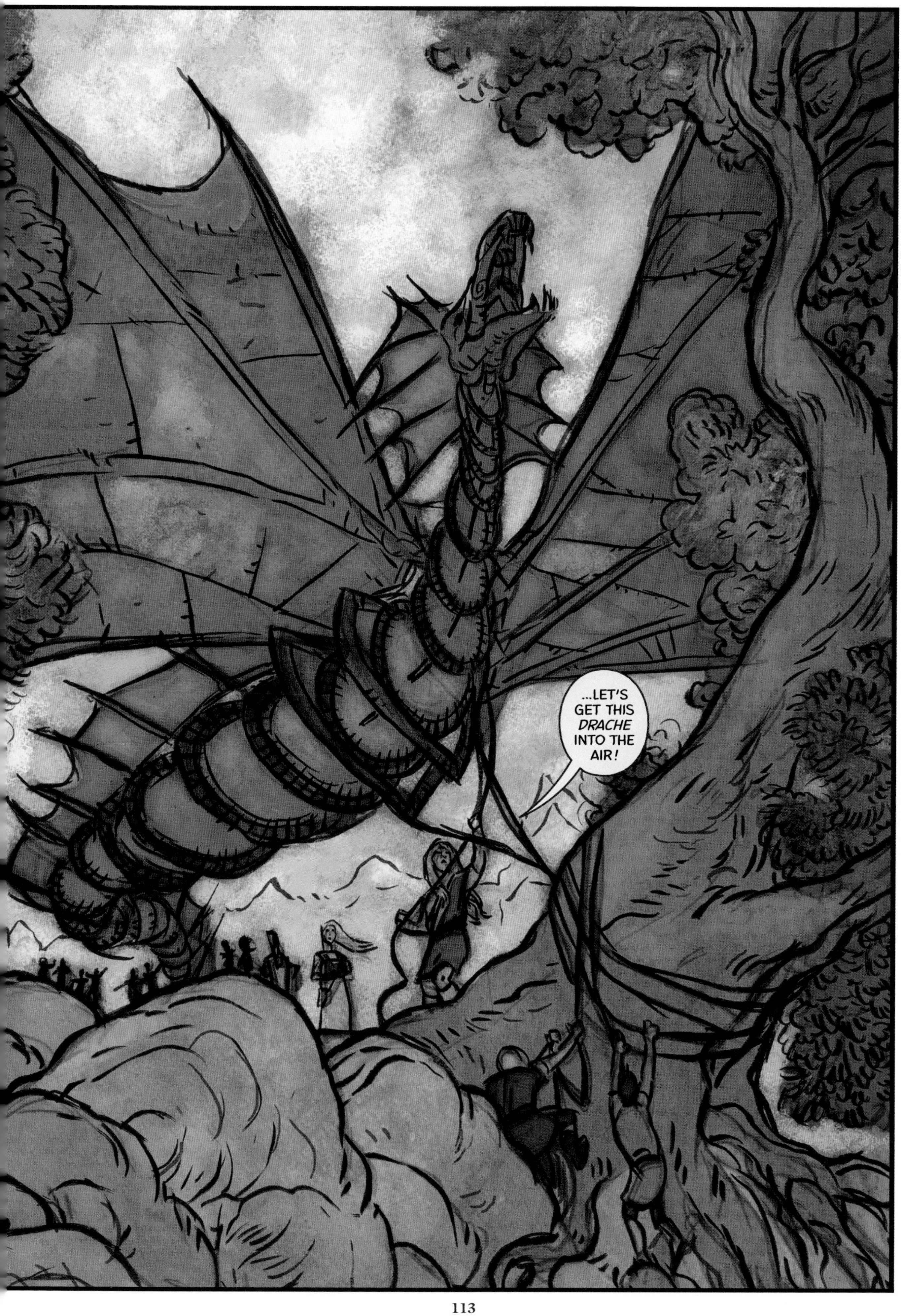
...LET'S GET THIS *DRACHE* INTO THE AIR!

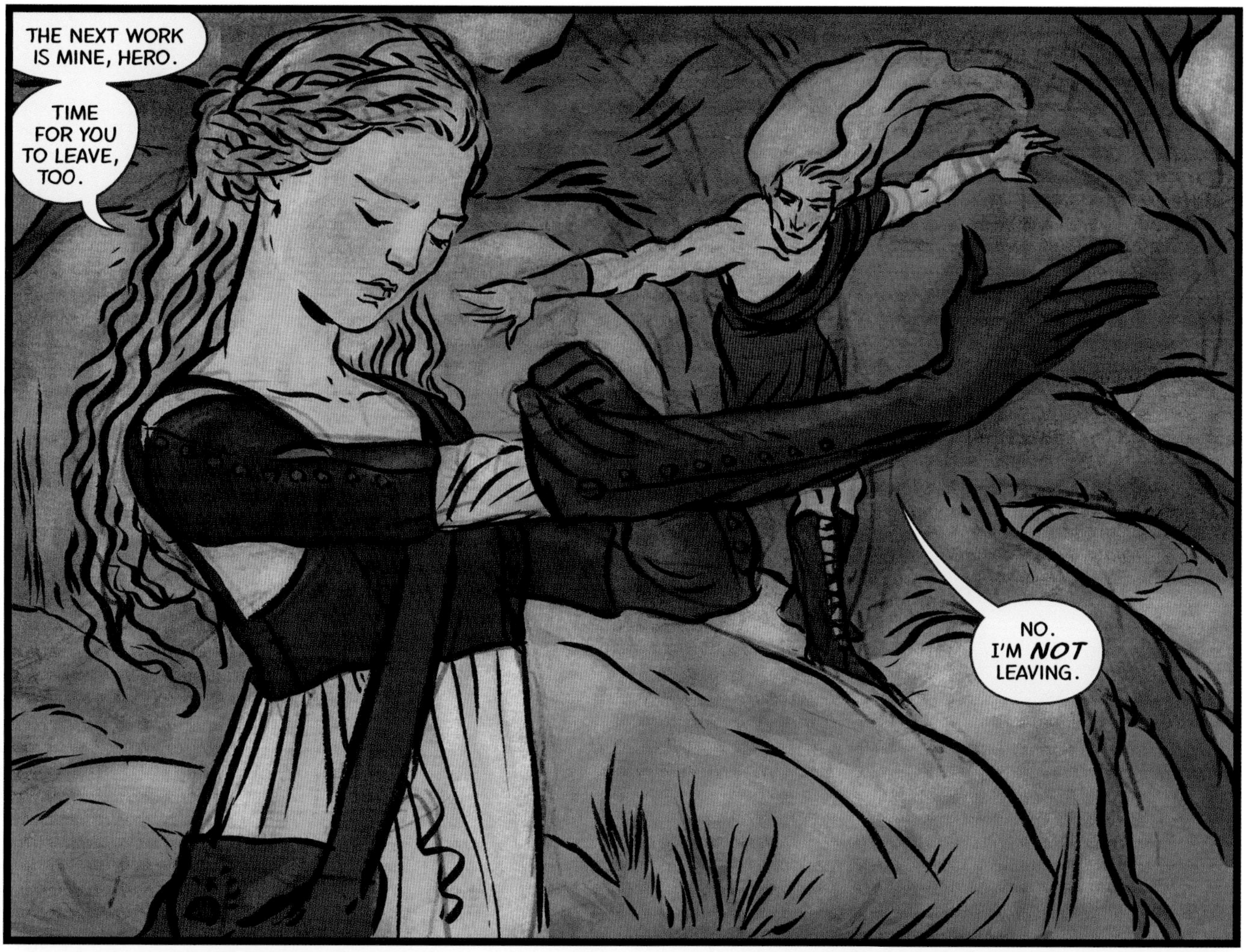
THE NEXT WORK IS MINE, HERO.
TIME FOR YOU TO LEAVE, TOO.
NO. I'M *NOT* LEAVING.

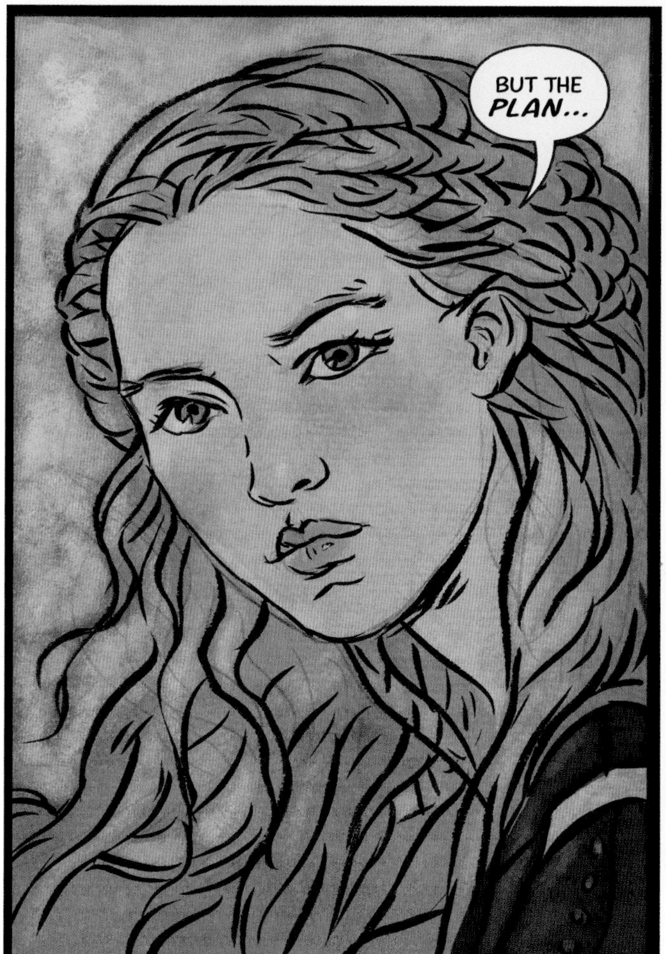
BUT THE *PLAN...*

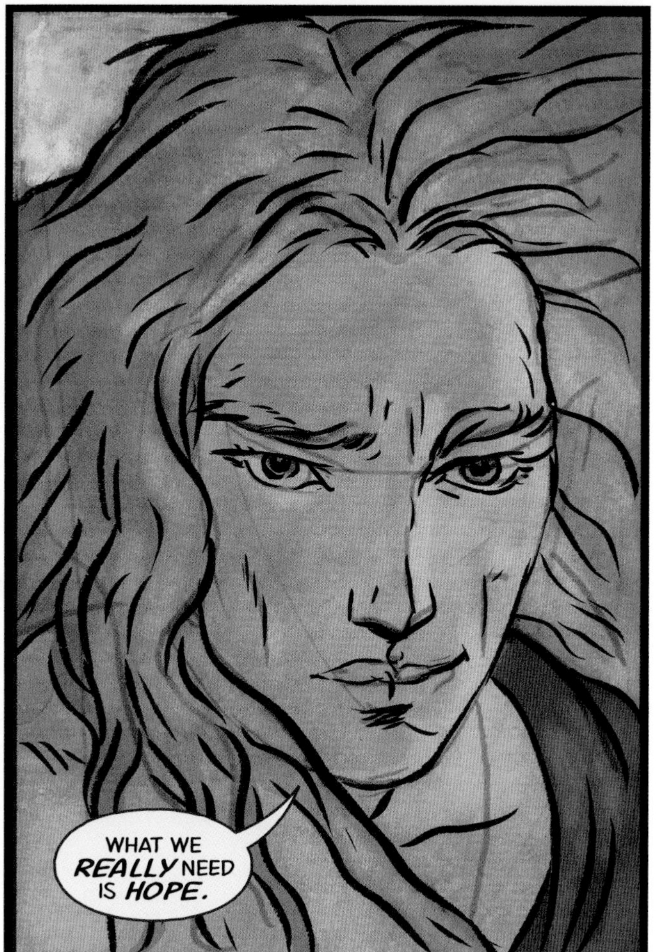
WHAT WE *REALLY* NEED IS *HOPE.*

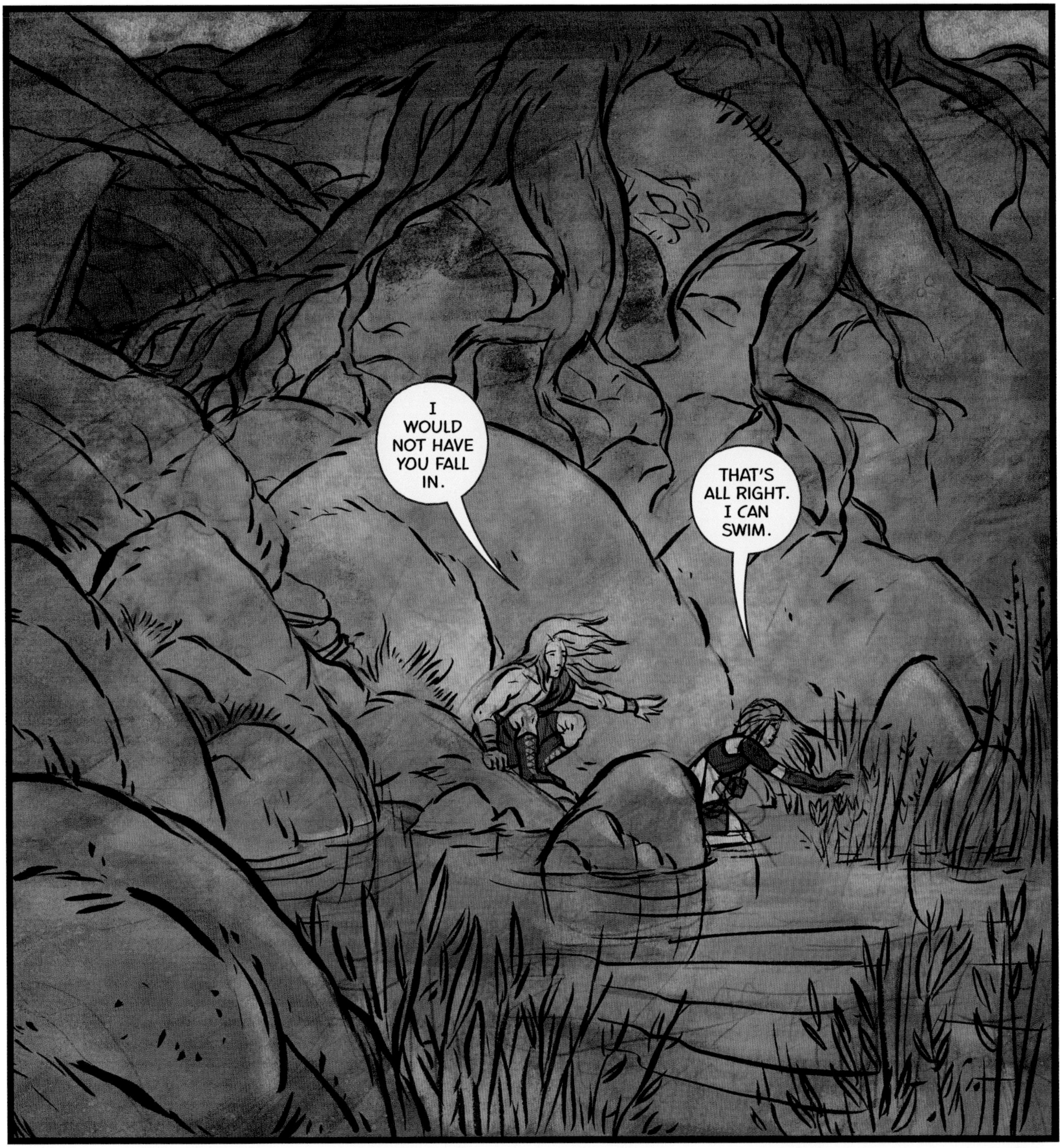
I WOULD NOT HAVE YOU FALL IN.
THAT'S ALL RIGHT. I CAN SWIM.

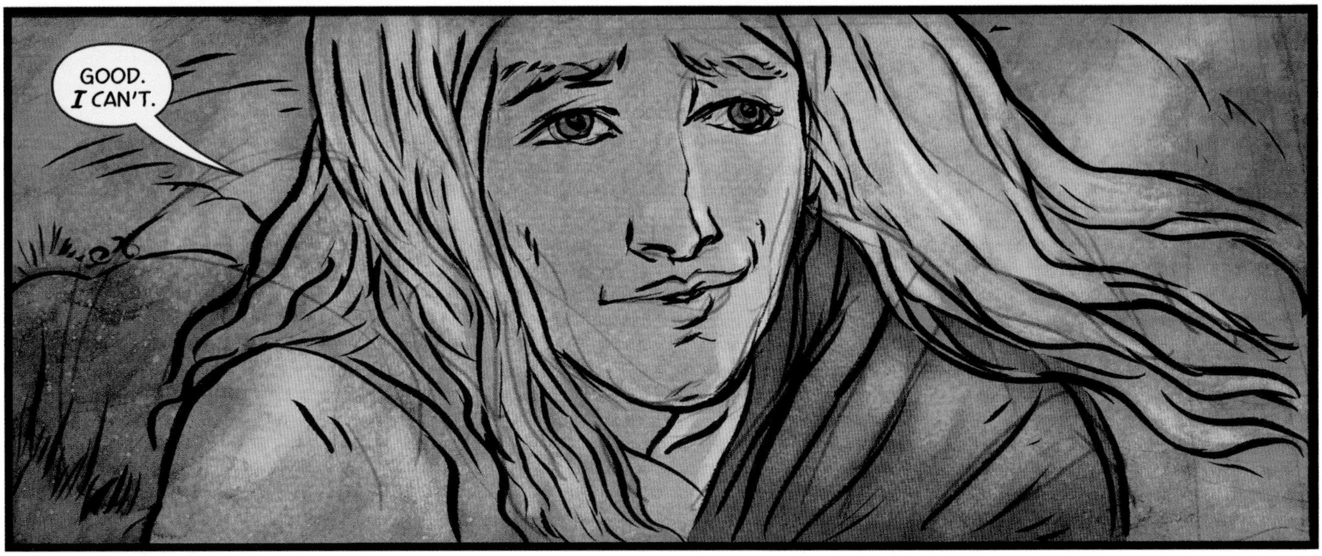
GOOD. *I* CAN'T.

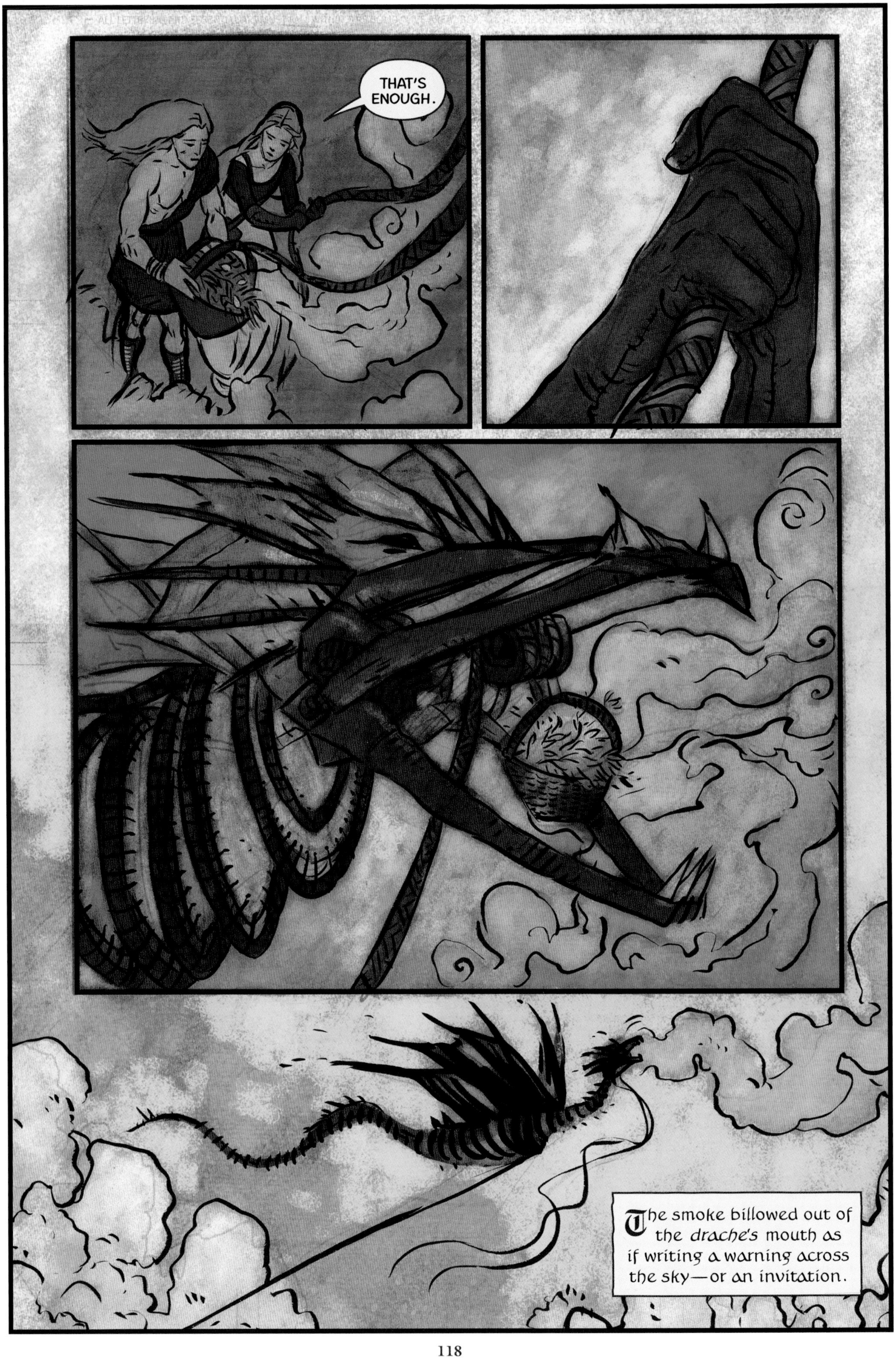
THAT'S ENOUGH.
The smoke billowed out of the *drache's* mouth as if writing a warning across the sky—or an invitation.

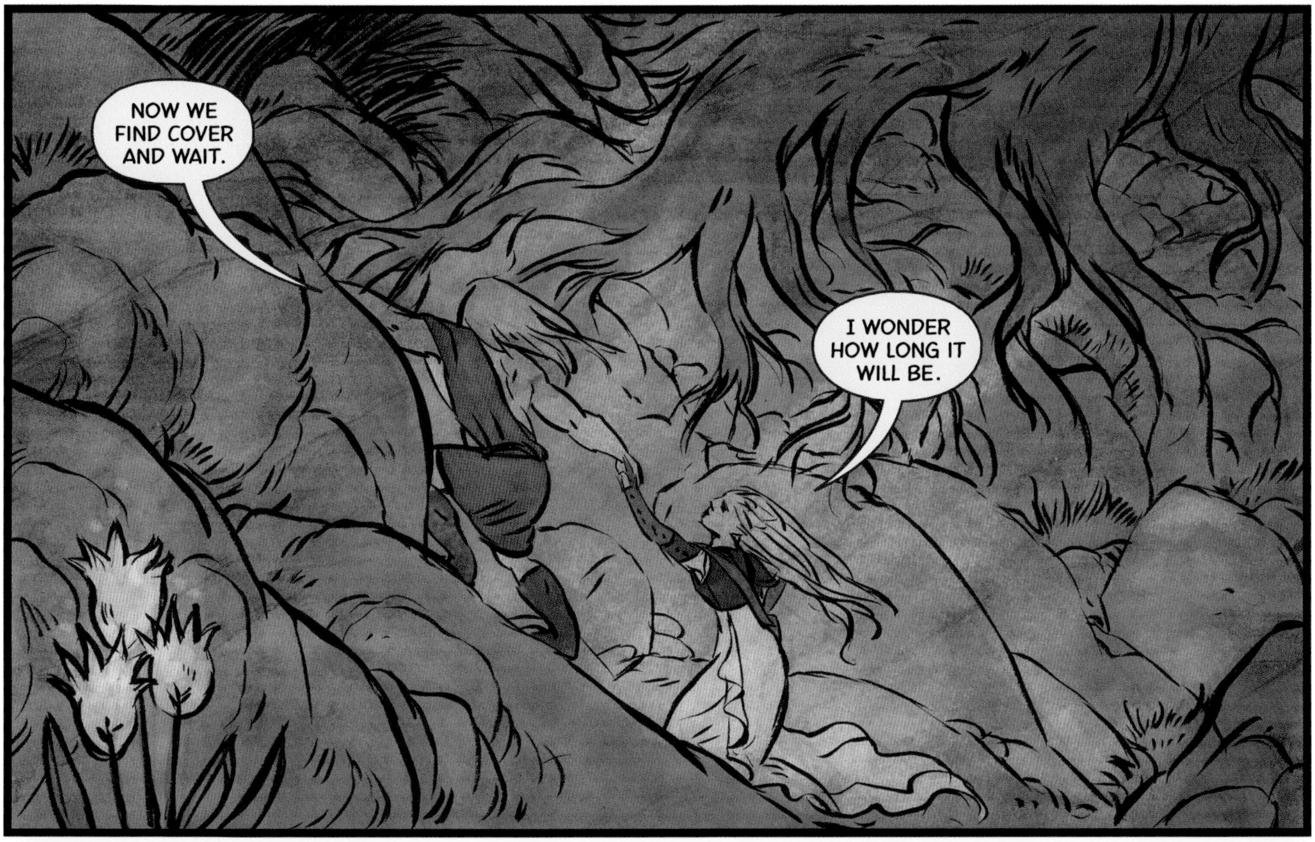
NOW WE FIND COVER AND WAIT.
I WONDER HOW LONG IT WILL BE.

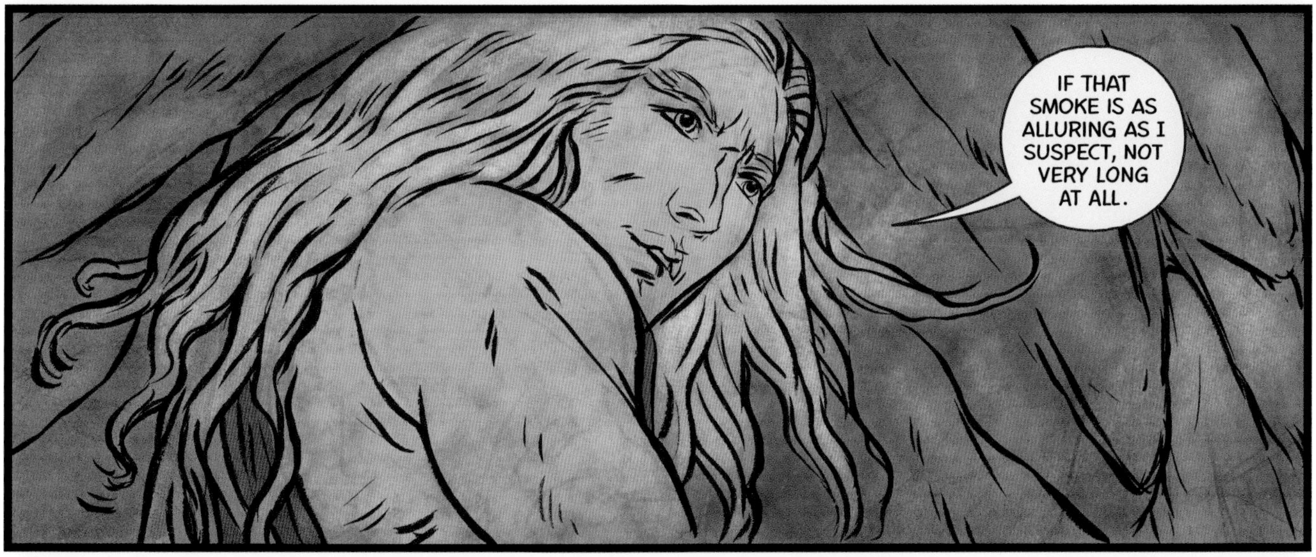
IF THAT SMOKE IS AS ALLURING AS I SUSPECT, NOT VERY LONG AT ALL.

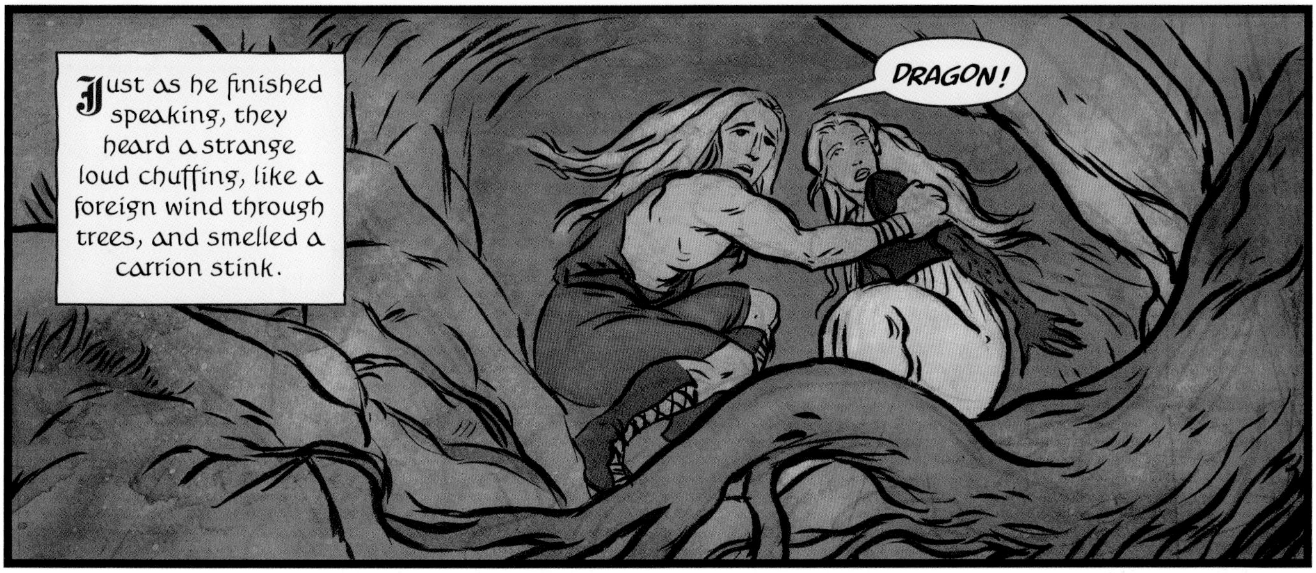
Just as he finished speaking, they heard a strange loud chuffing, like a foreign wind through trees, and smelled a carrion stink.
DRAGON!

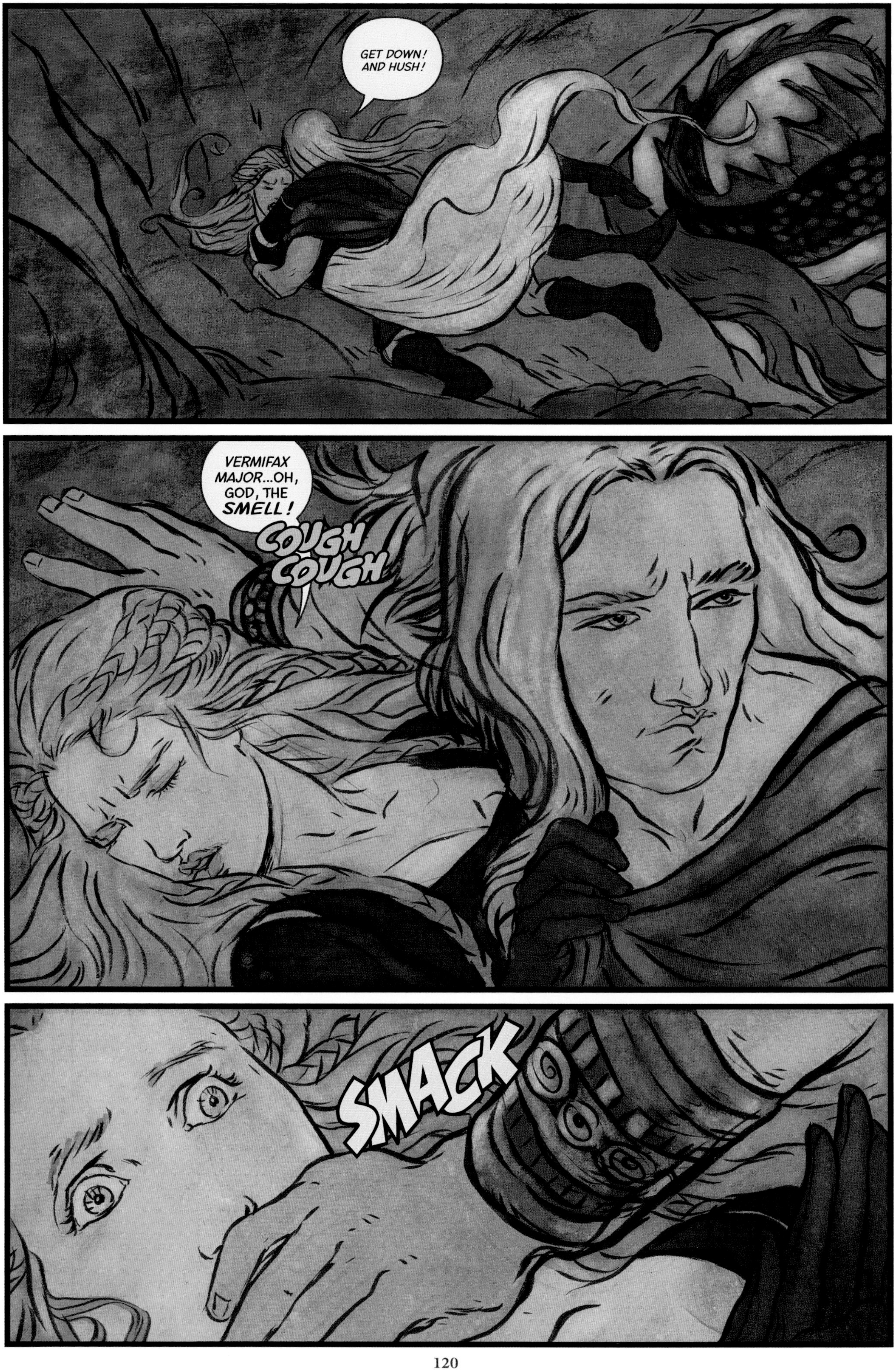
GET DOWN! AND HUSH!
VERMIFAX MAJOR...OH, GOD, THE SMELL!
COUGH COUGH
SMACK

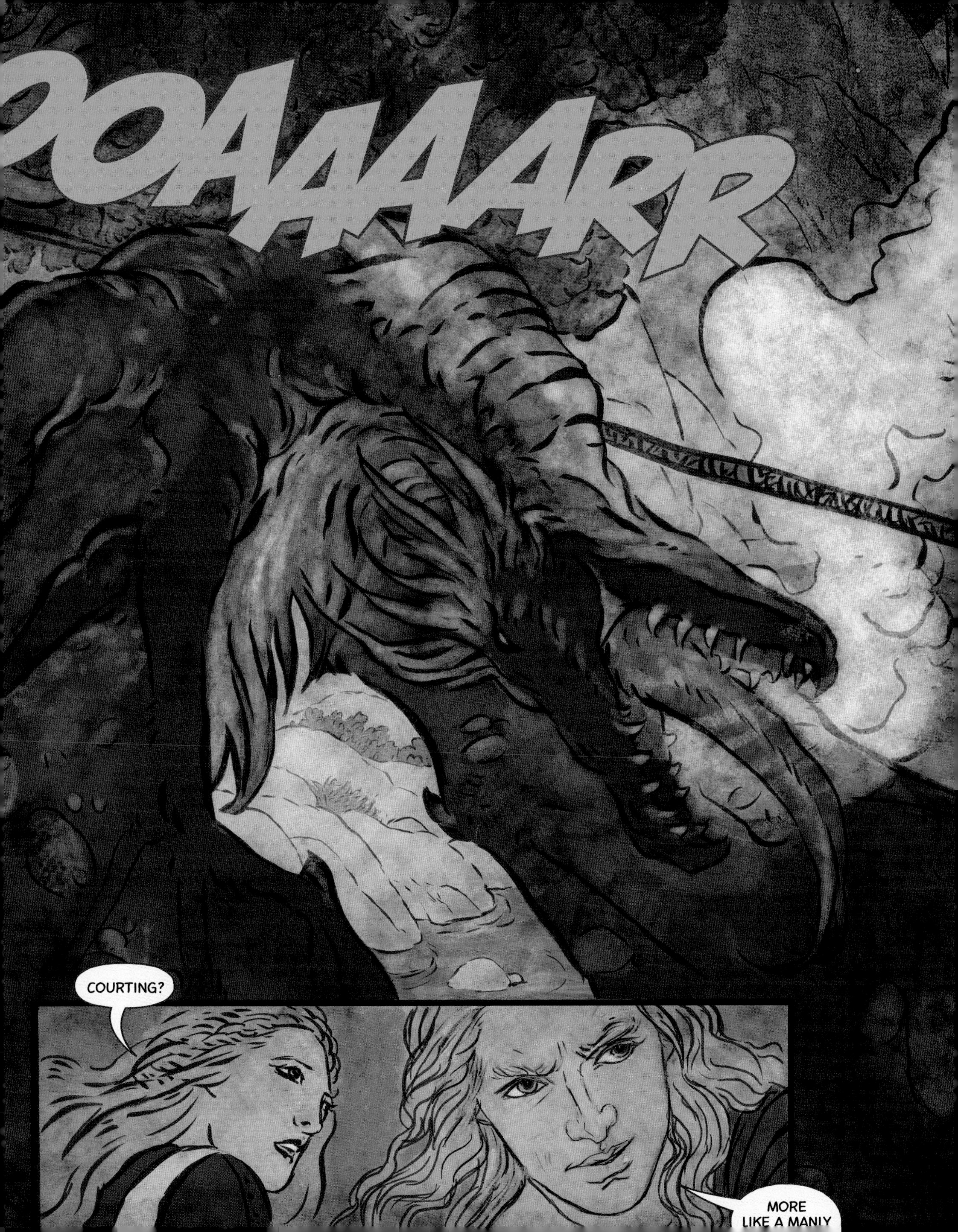
OOAAAARR
COURTING?
MORE LIKE A MANLY

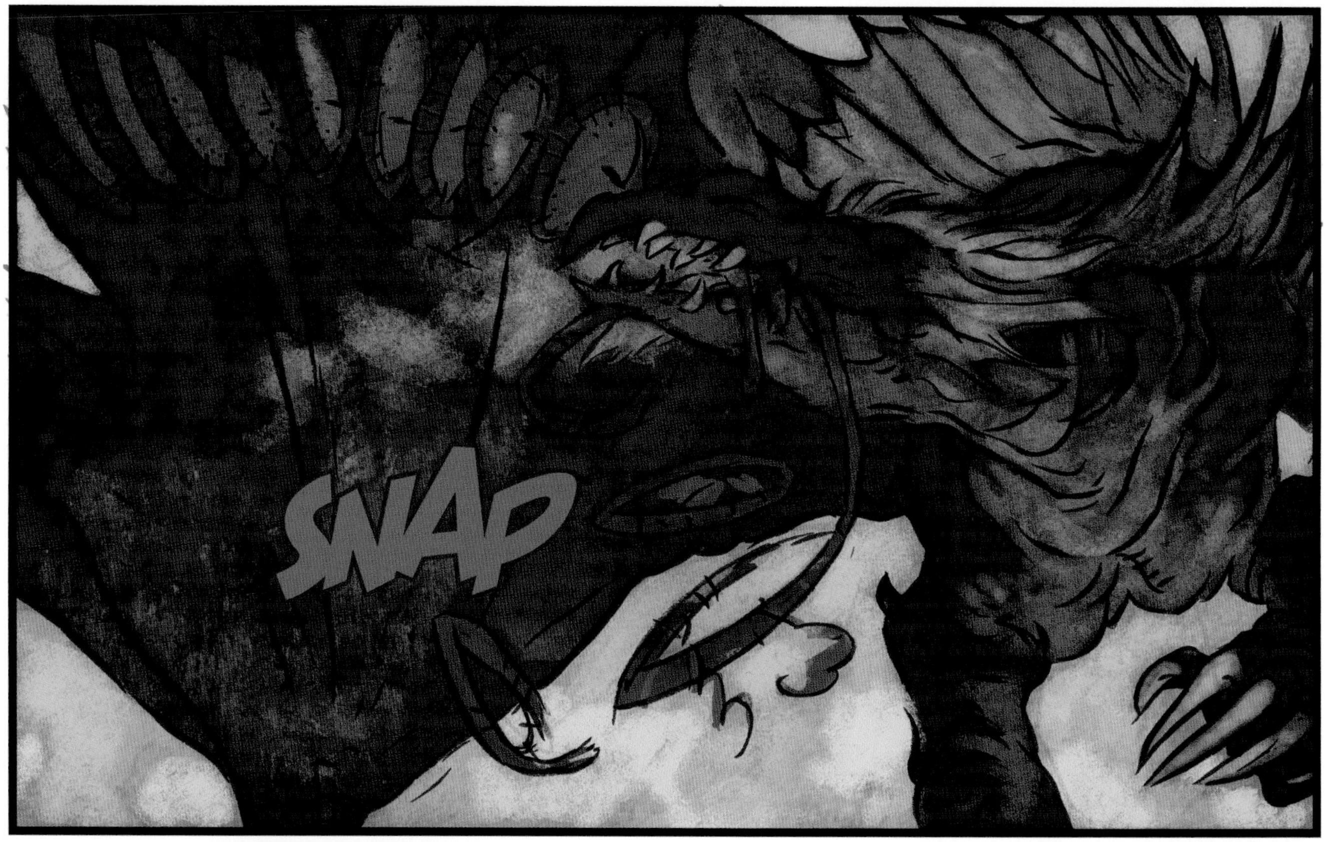
SNAP

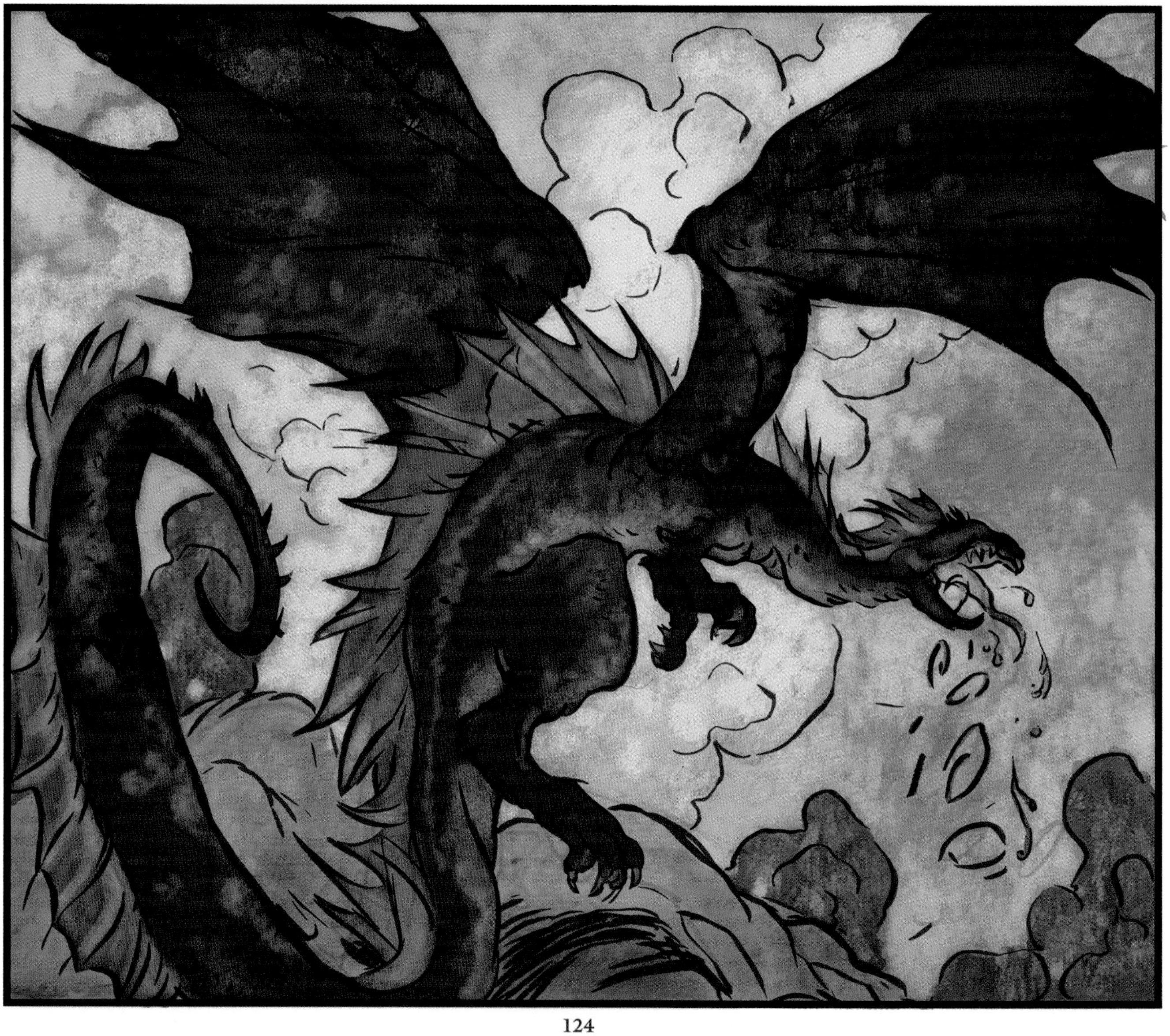

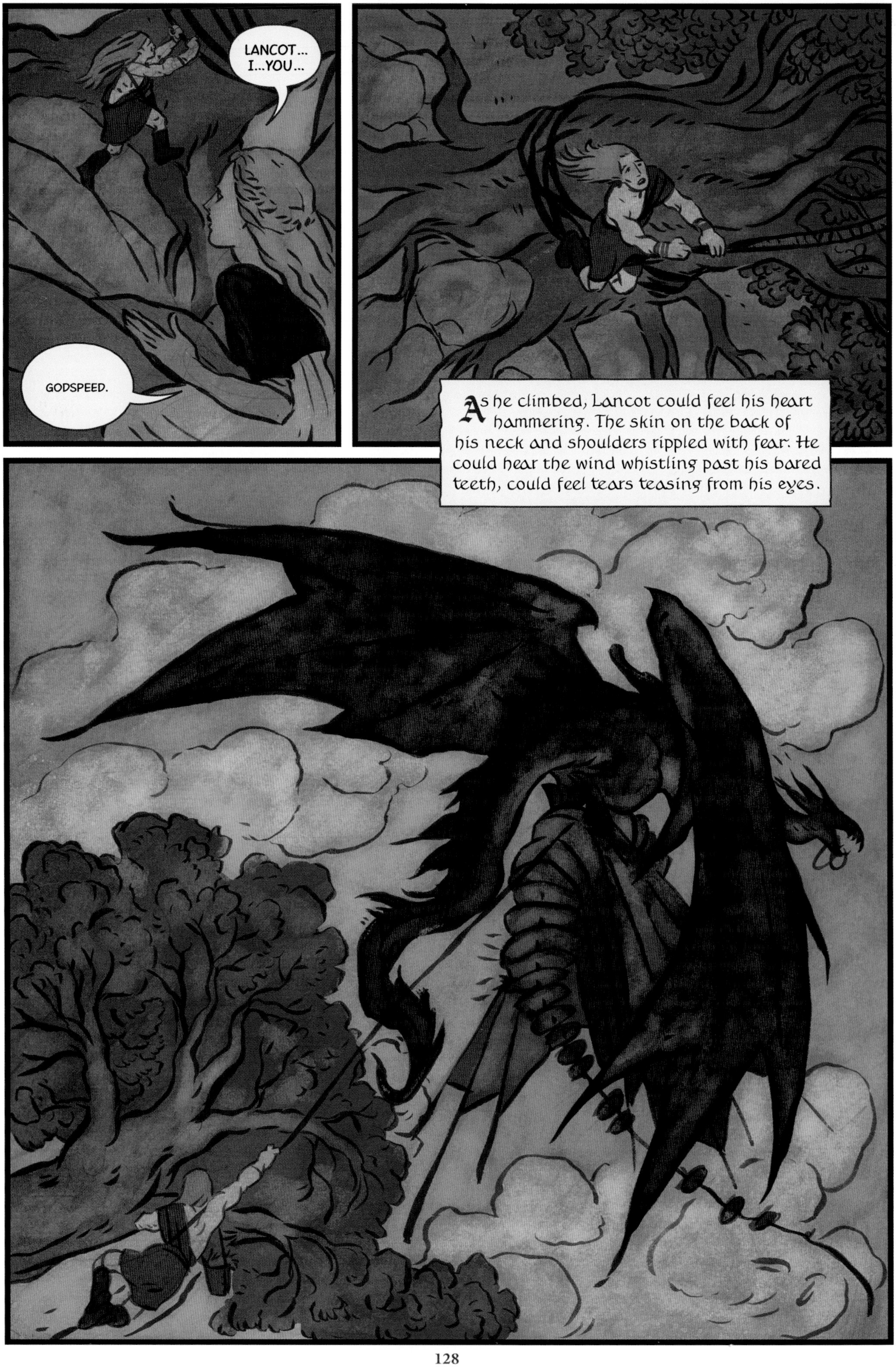
LANCOT... I...YOU...
GODSPEED.
As he climbed, Lancot could feel his heart hammering. The skin on the back of his neck and shoulders rippled with fear. He could hear the wind whistling past his bared teeth, could feel tears teasing from his eyes.

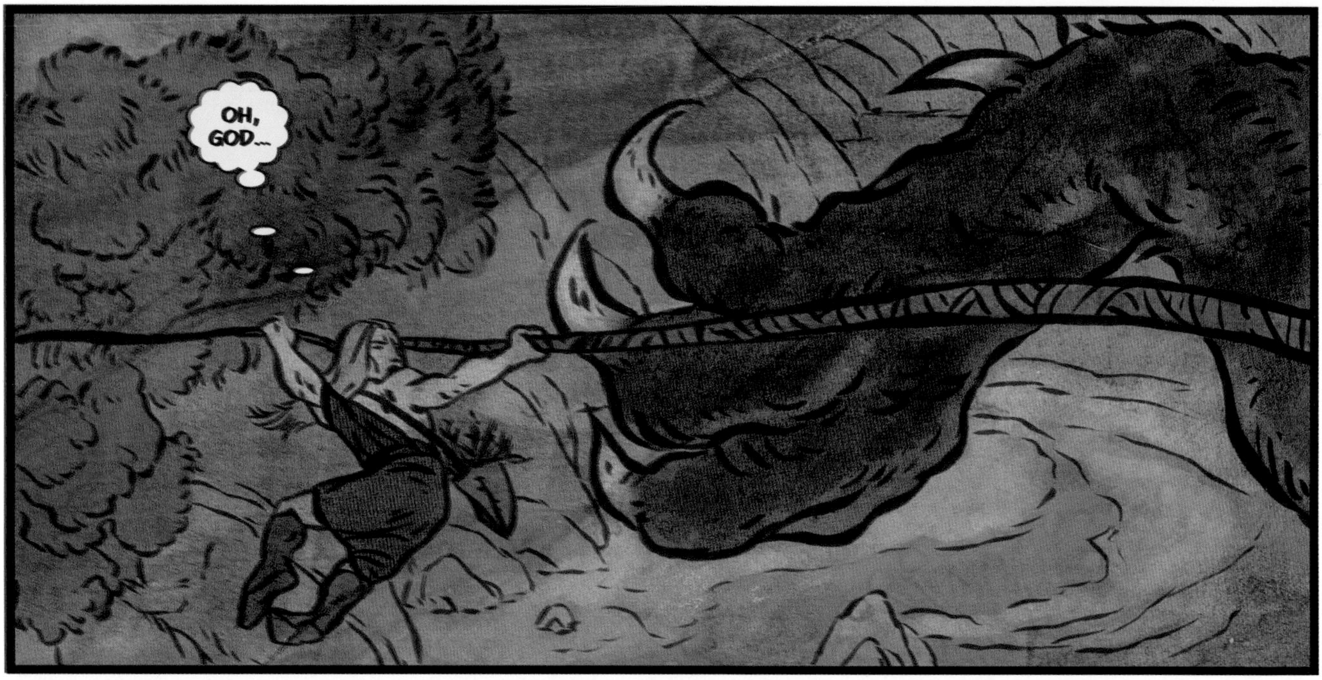
OH, GOD...

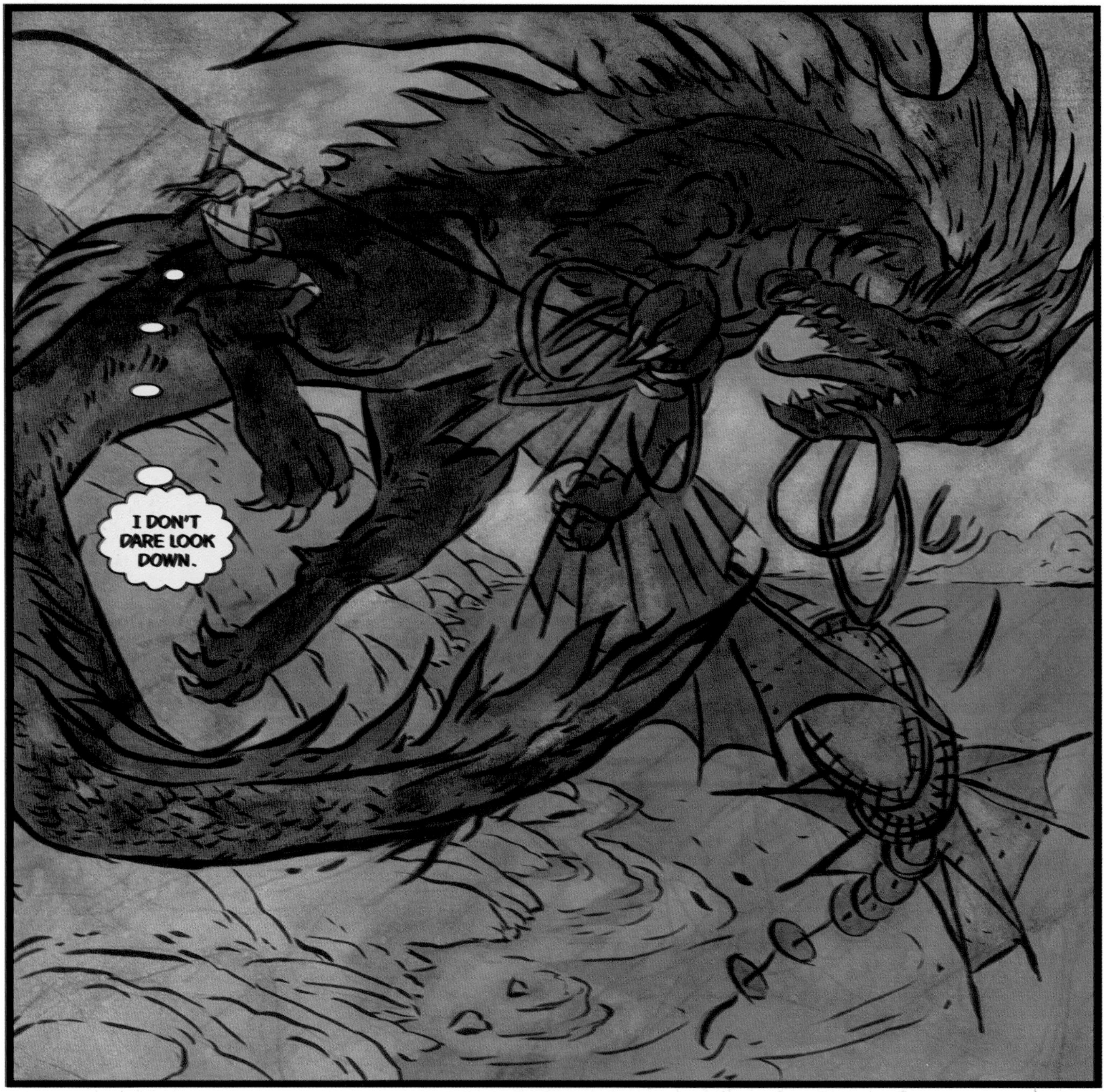
I DON'T DARE LOOK DOWN.

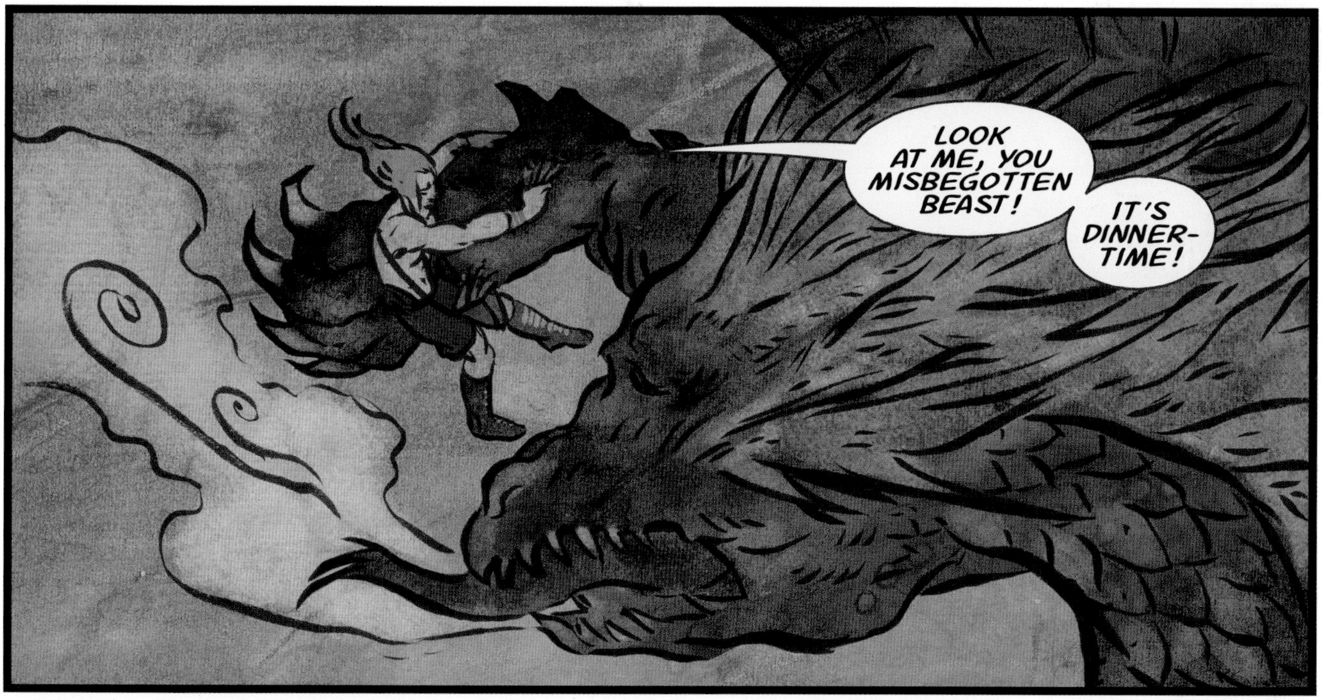
LOOK AT ME, YOU MISBEGOTTEN BEAST!
IT'S DINNER-TIME!

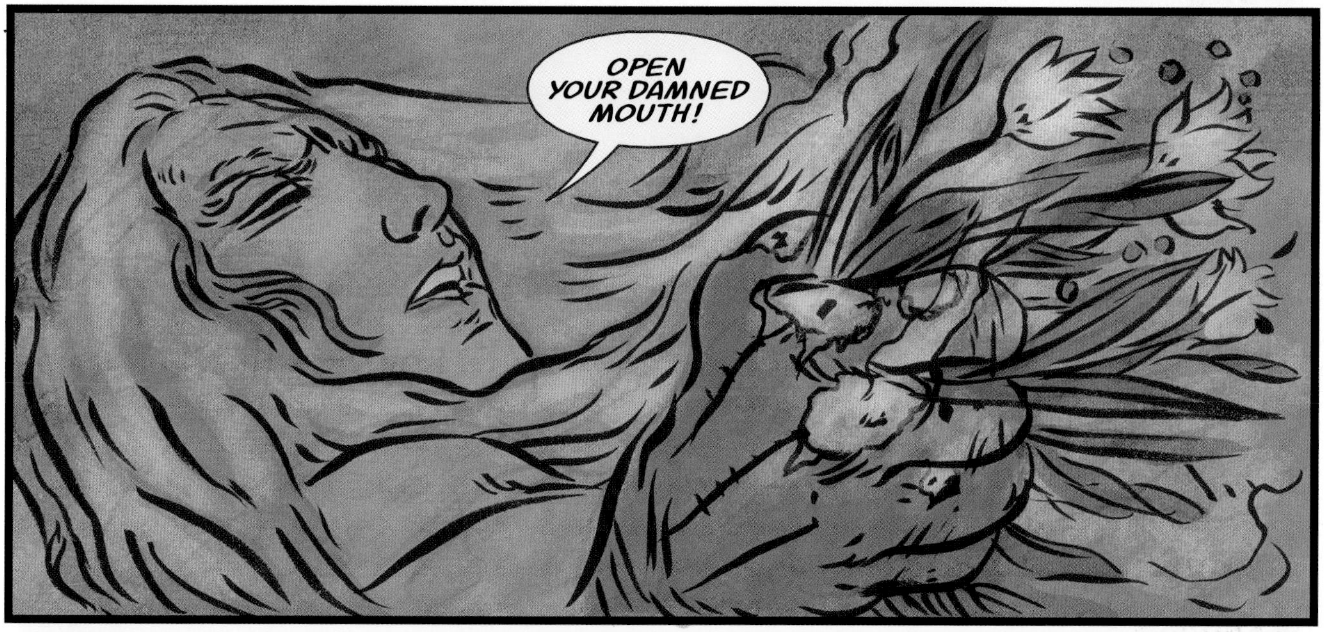
OPEN YOUR DAMNED MOUTH!

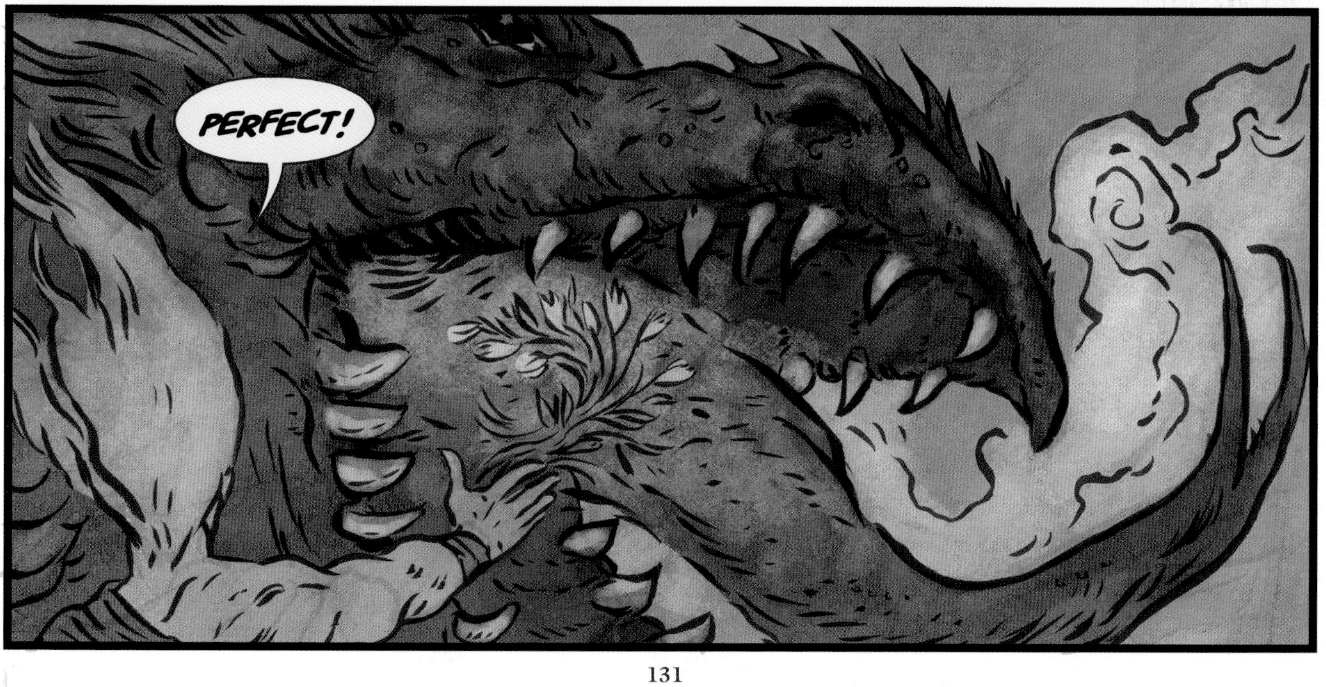
PERFECT!

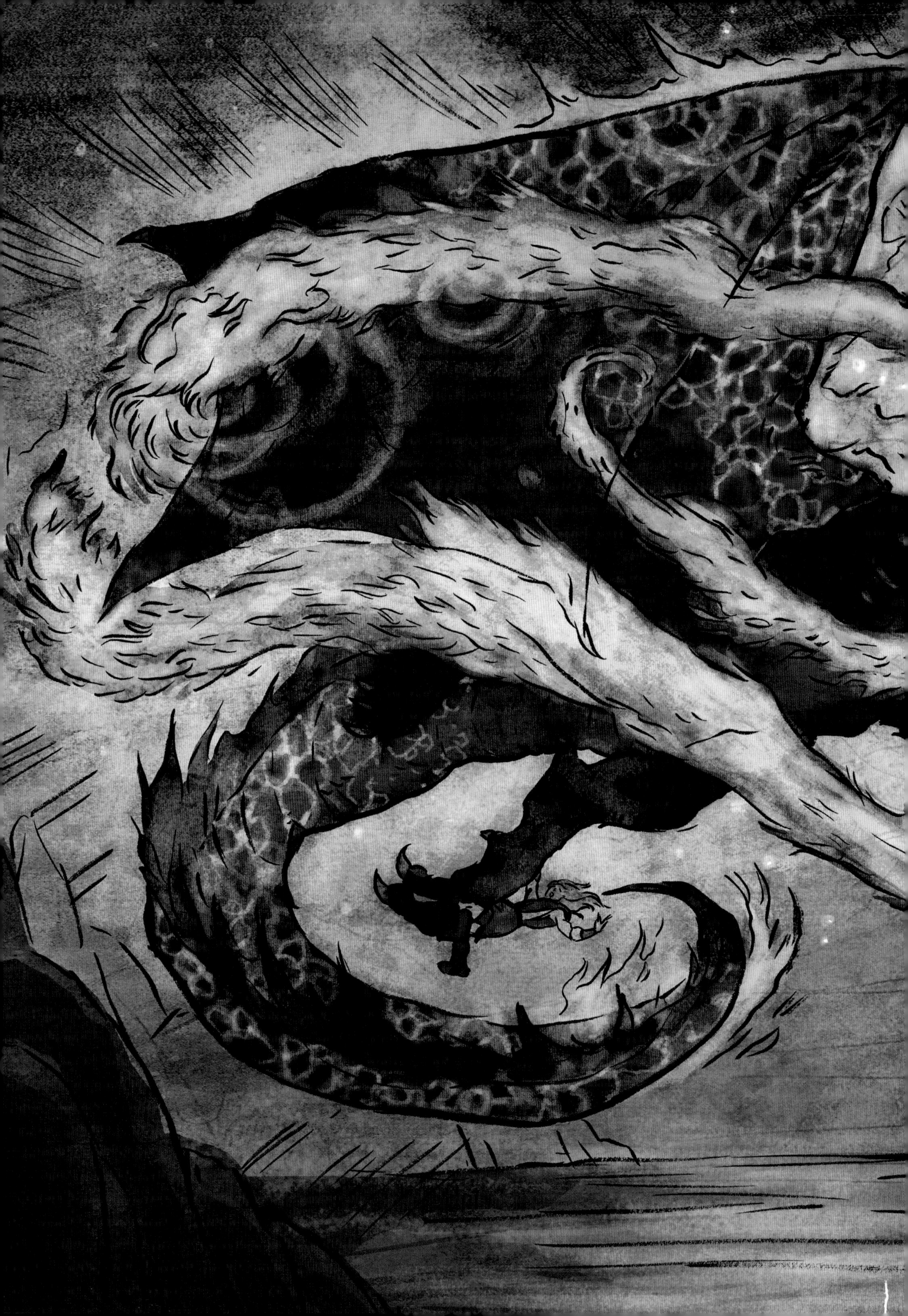

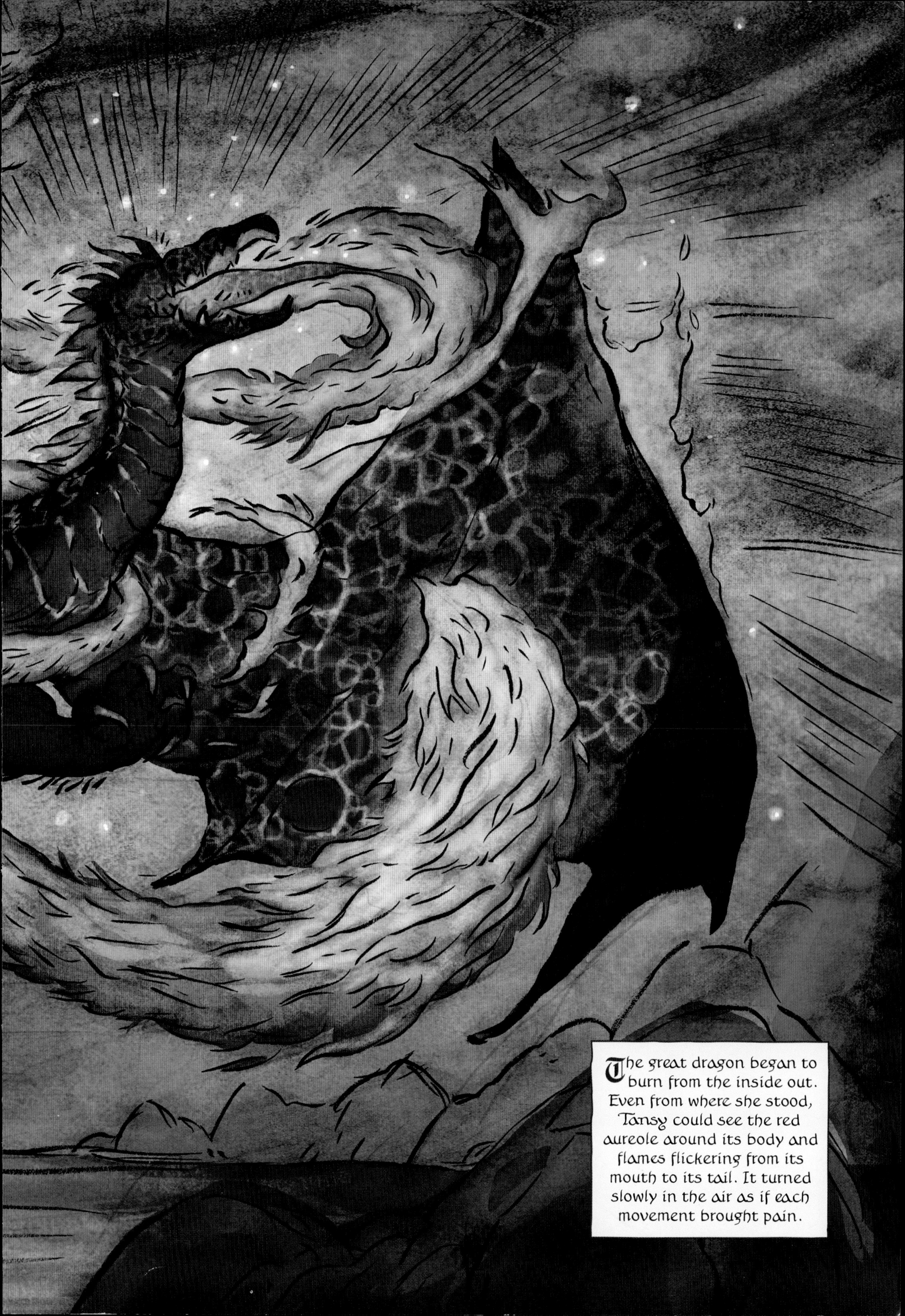
The great dragon began to burn from the inside out. Even from where she stood, Tansy could see the red aureole around its body and flames flickering from its mouth to its tail. It turned slowly in the air as if each movement brought pain.

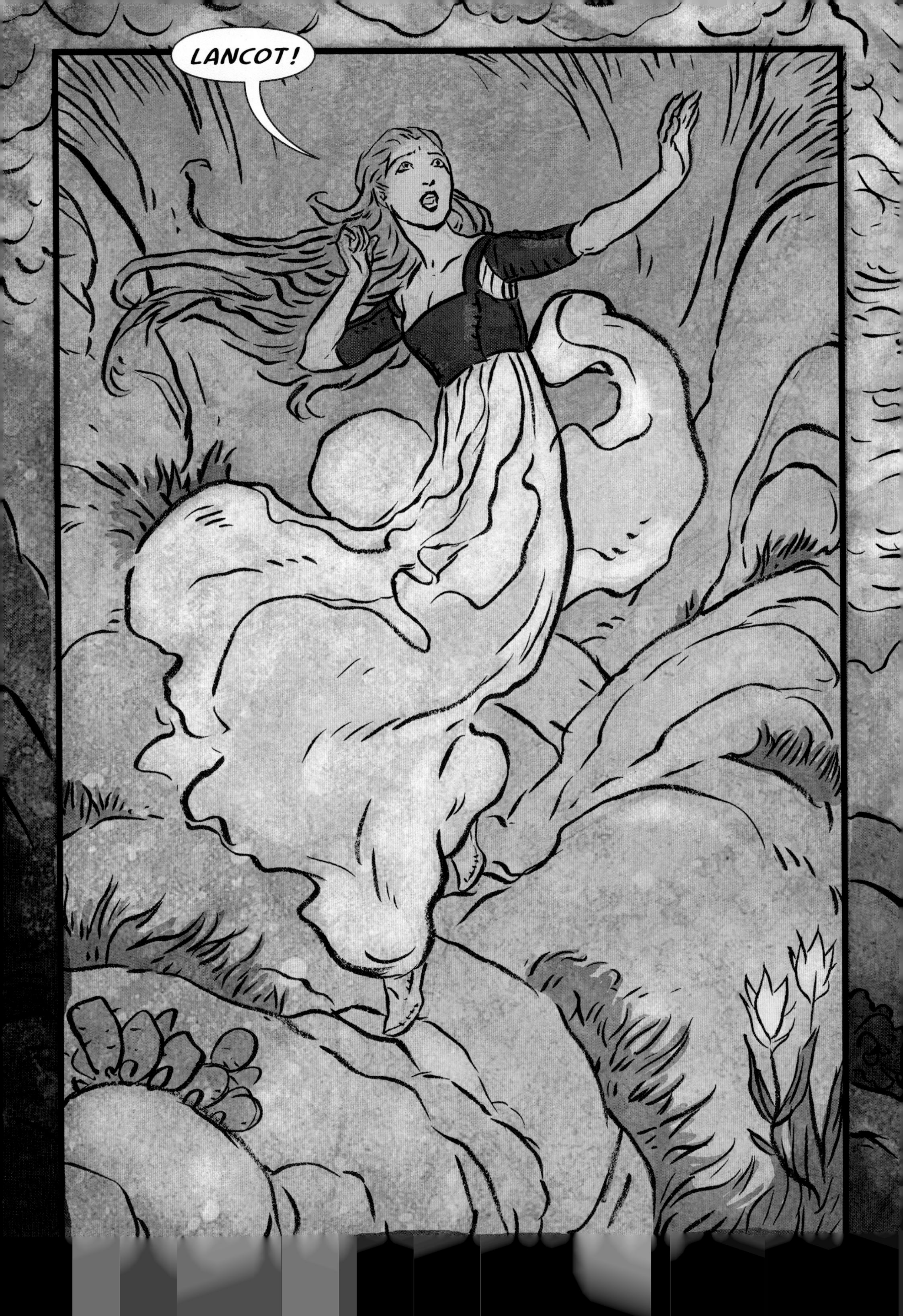
LANCOT!

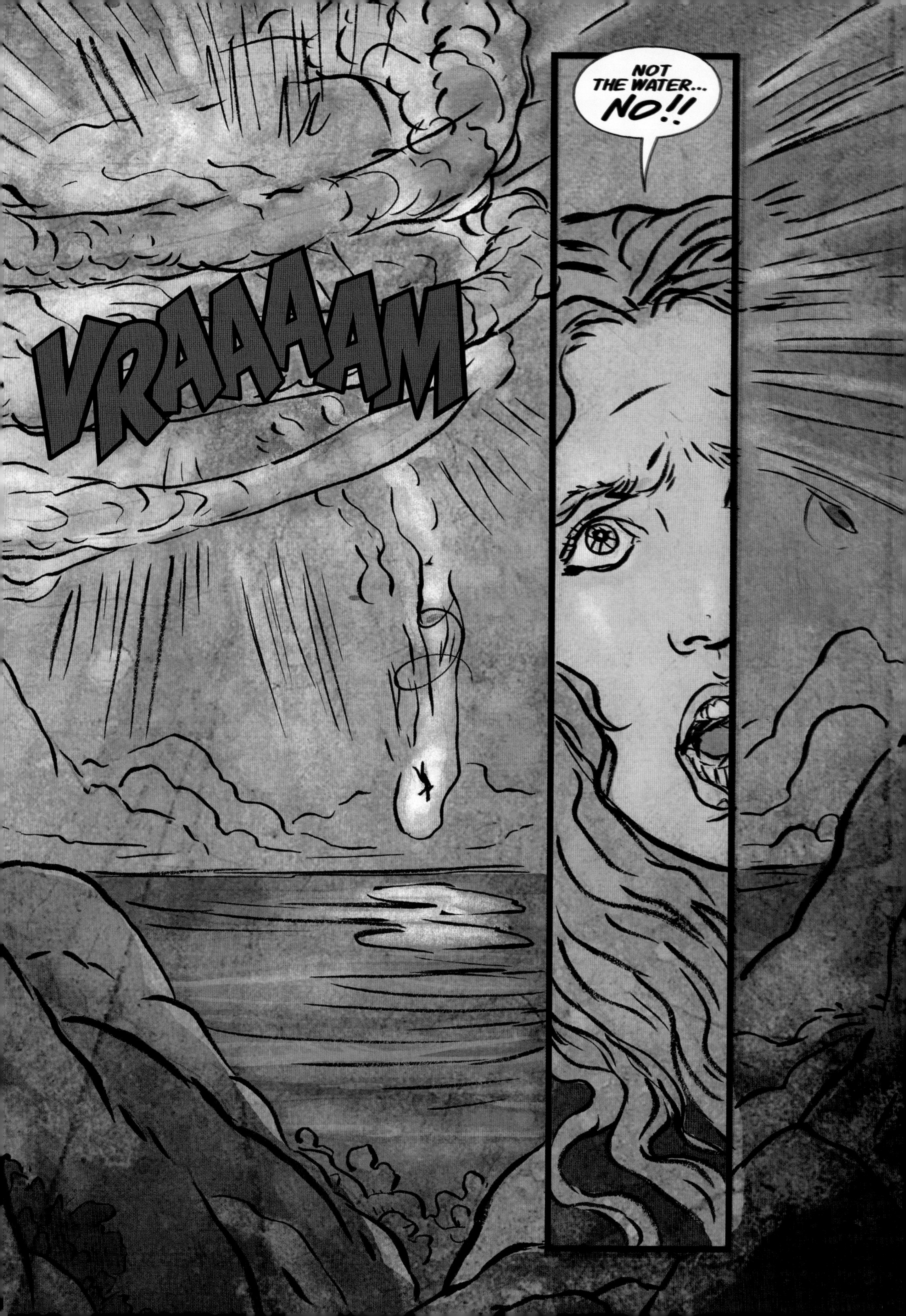
VRAAAAAM
NOT THE WATER... NO!!

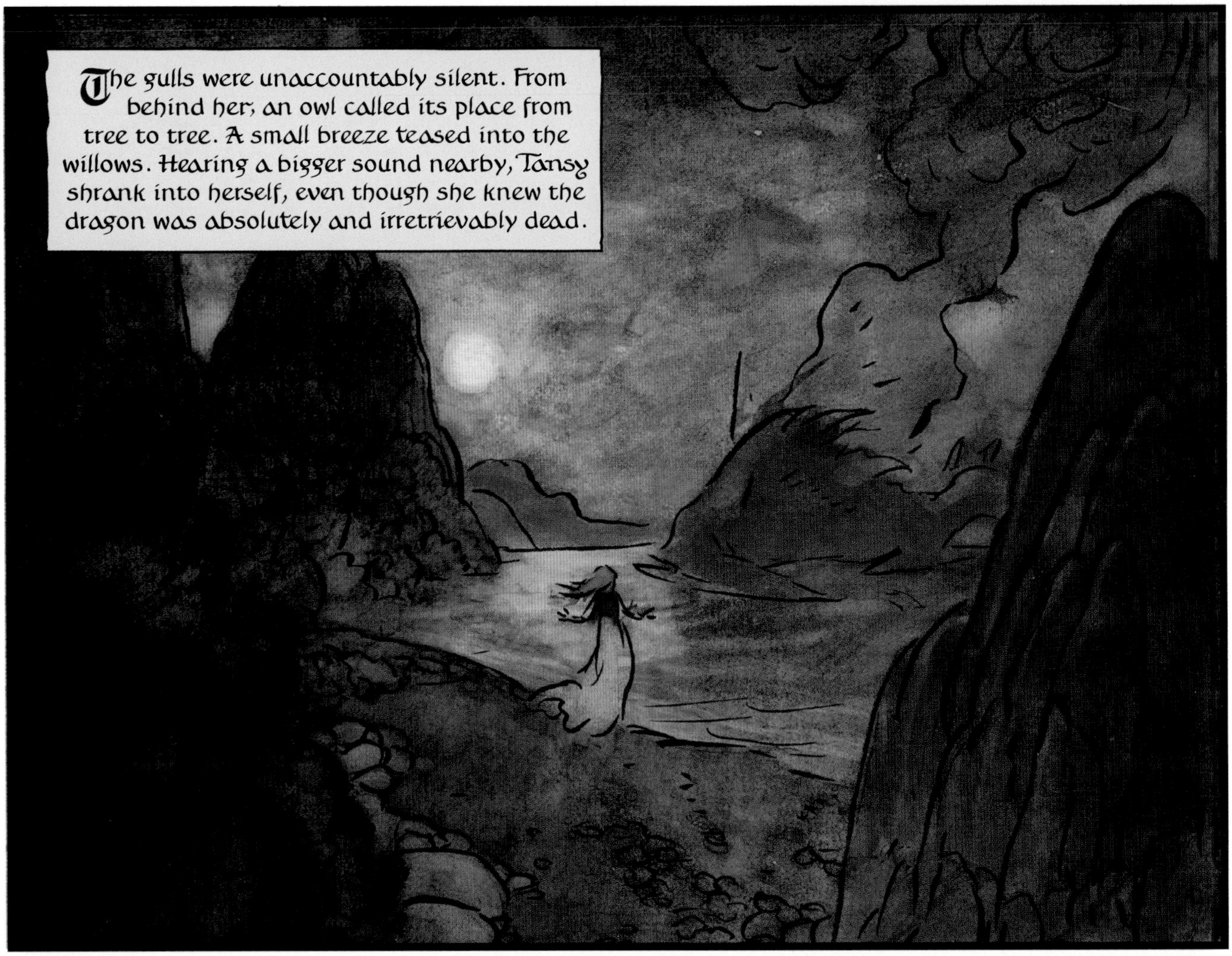
The gulls were unaccountably silent. From behind her, an owl called its place from tree to tree. A small breeze teased into the willows. Hearing a bigger sound nearby, Tansy shrank into herself, even though she knew the dragon was absolutely and irretrievably dead.

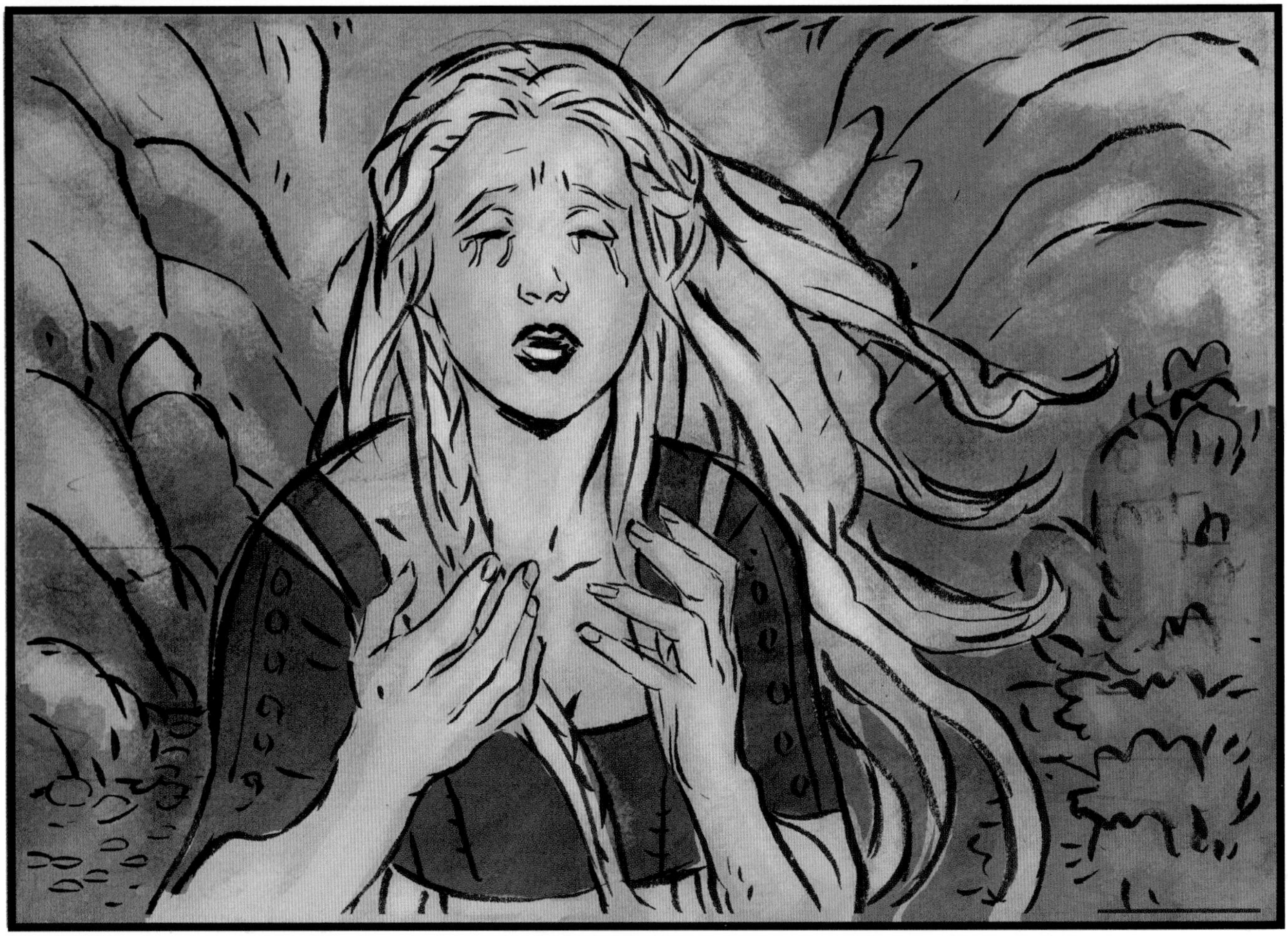

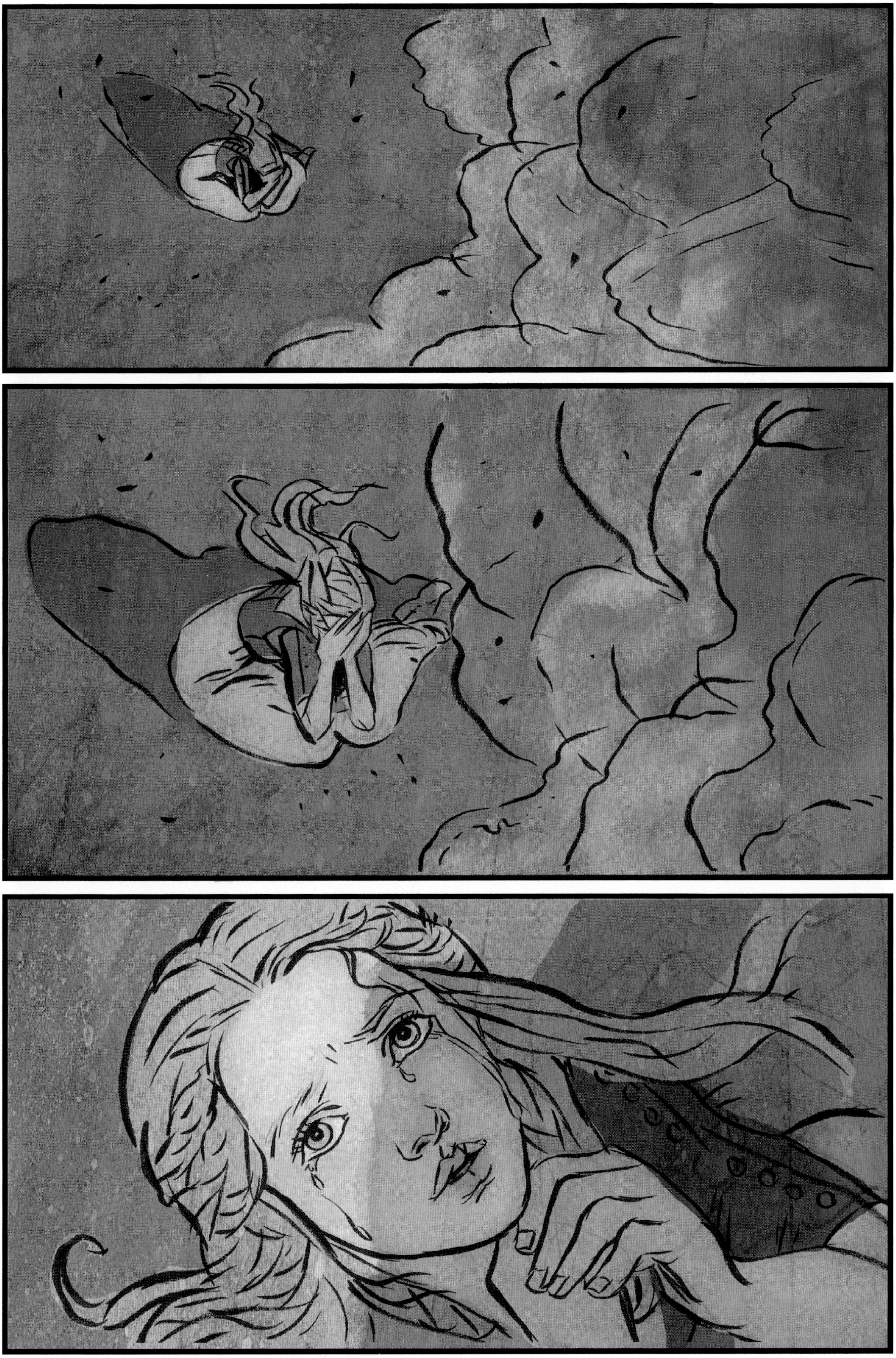

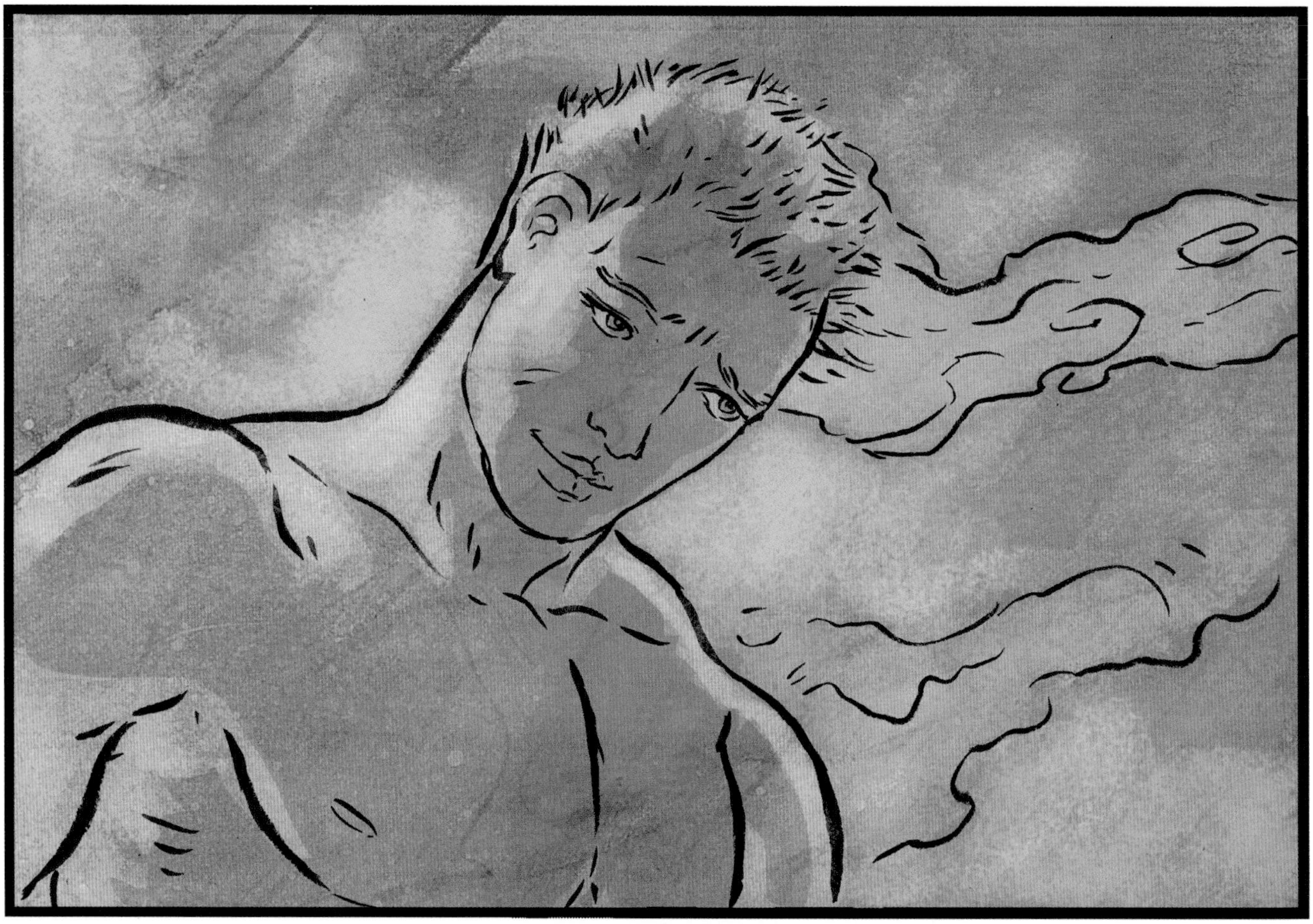

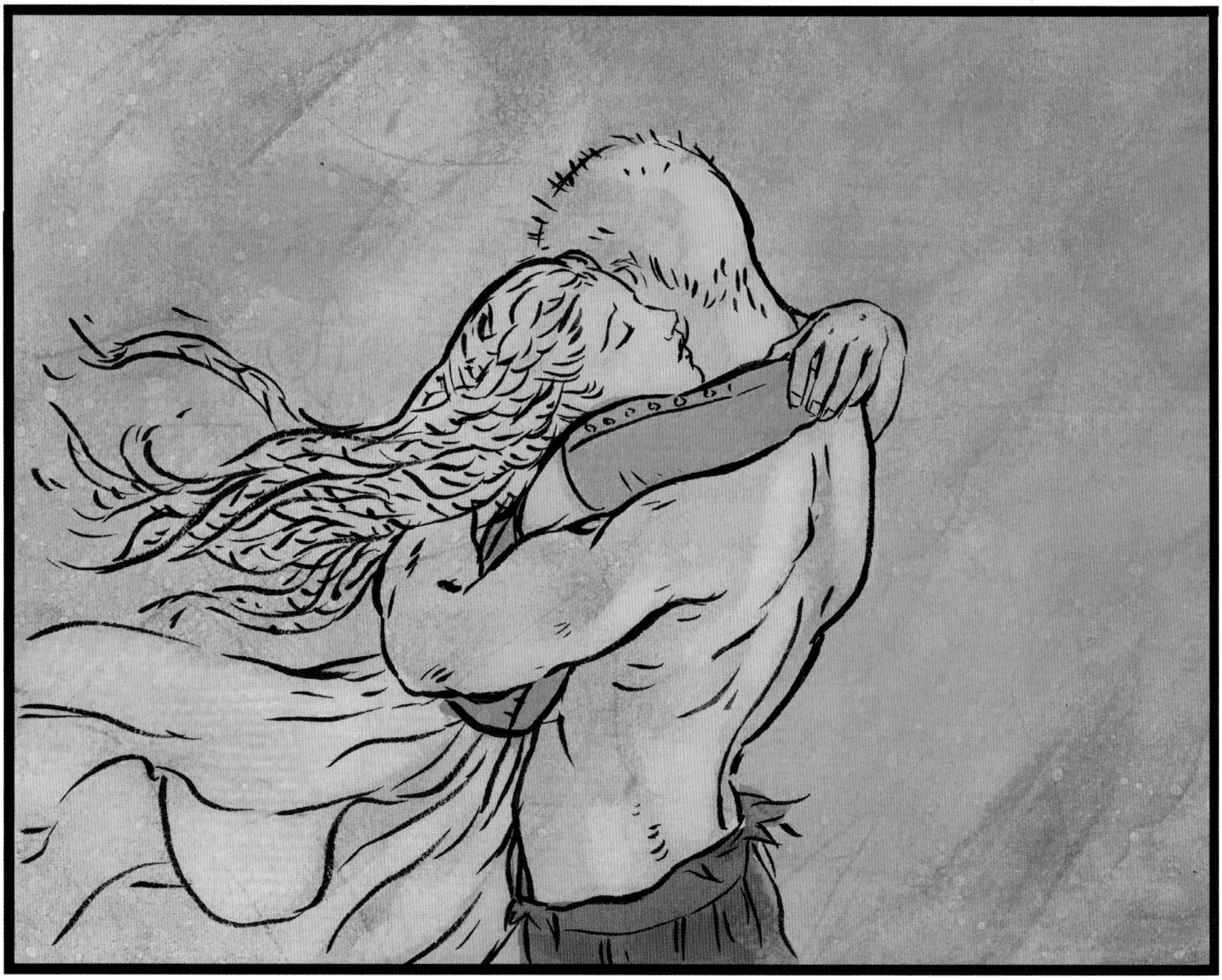

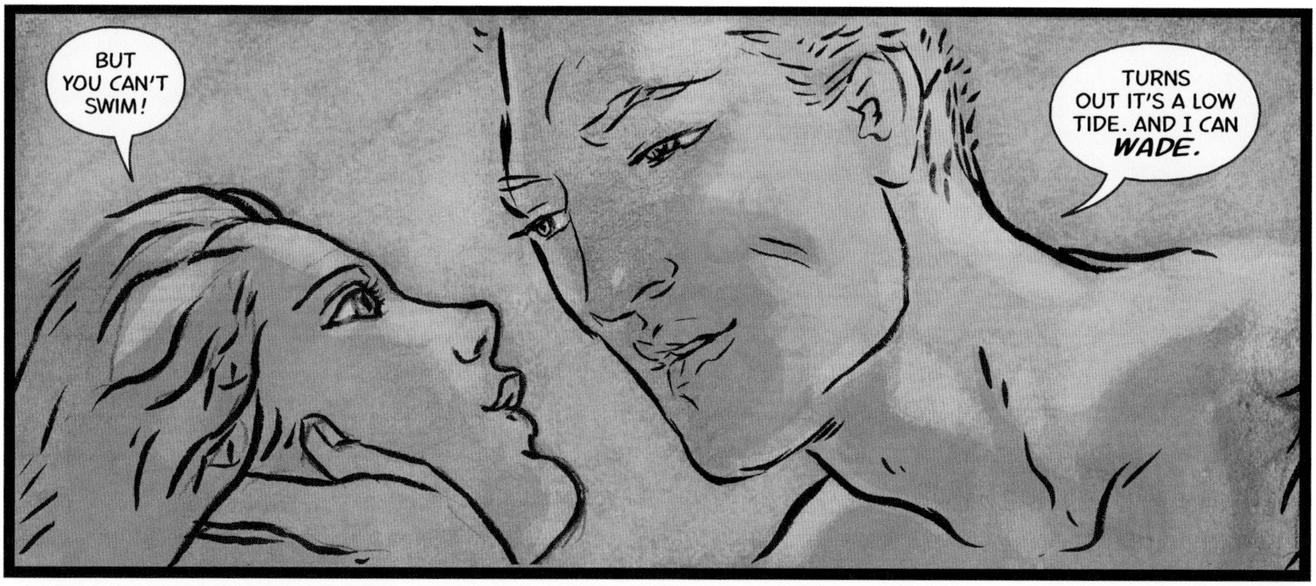
BUT YOU CAN'T SWIM!
TURNS OUT IT'S A LOW TIDE. AND I CAN *WADE.*

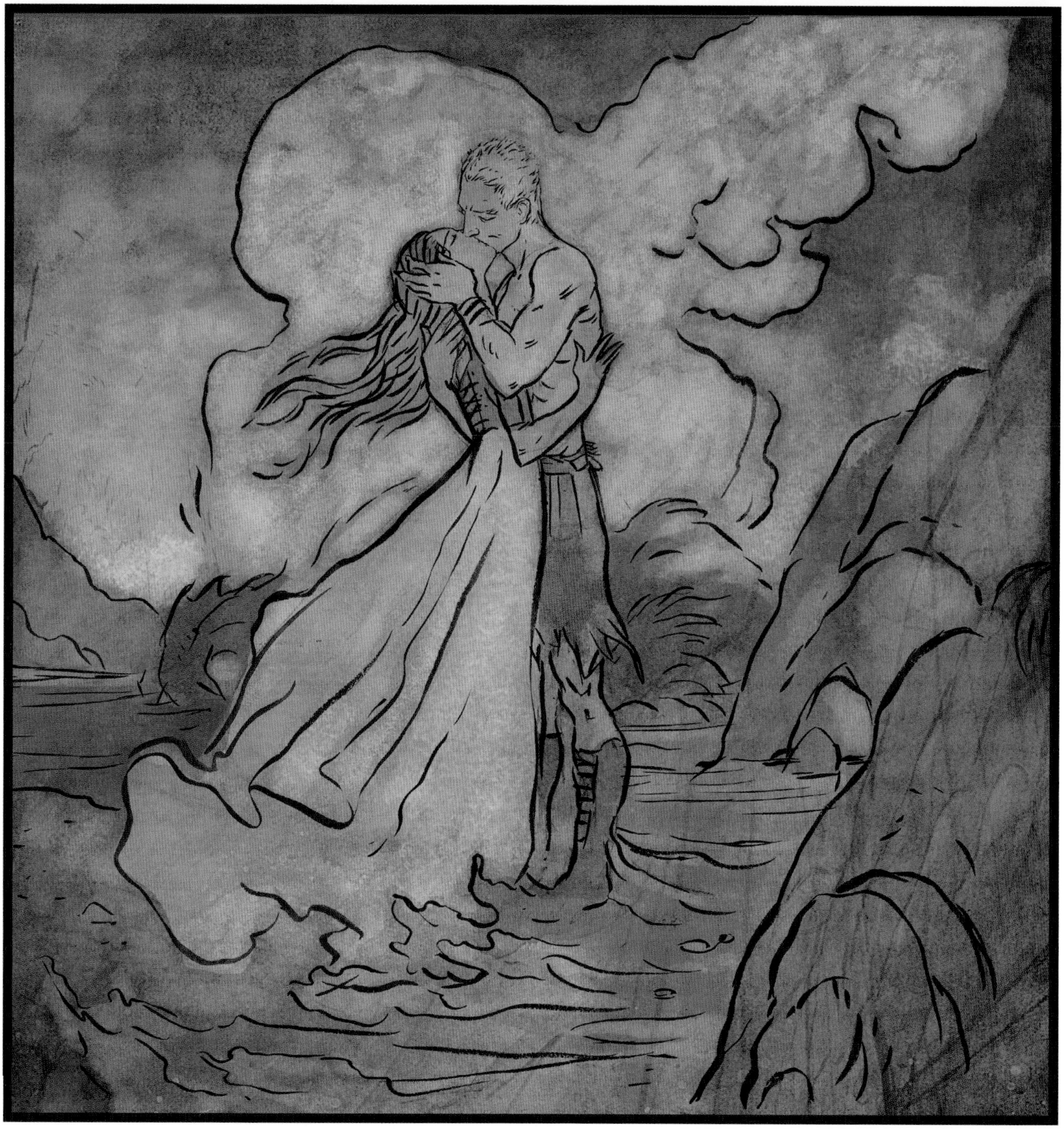

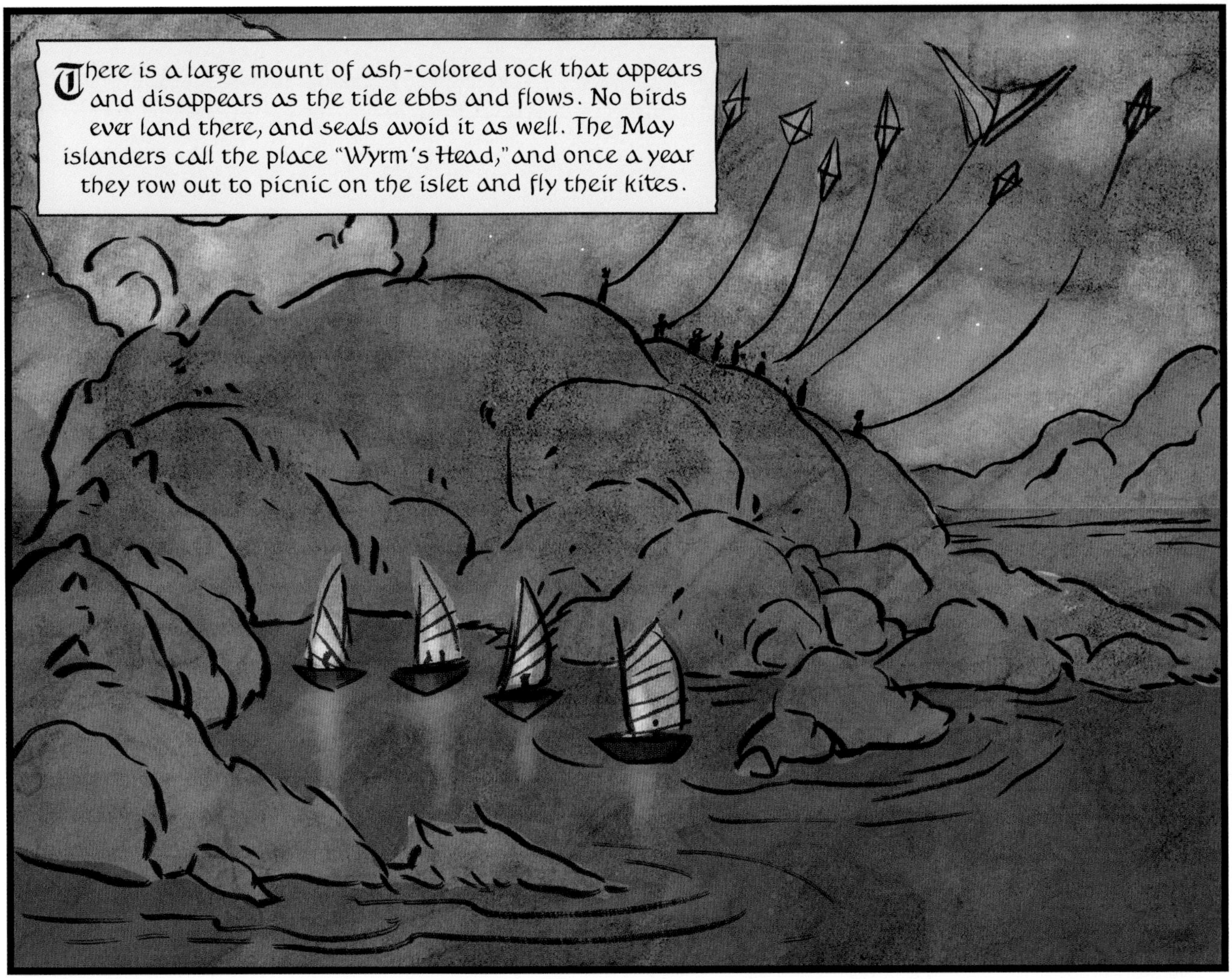
There is a large mount of ash-colored rock that appears and disappears as the tide ebbs and flows. No birds ever land there, and seals avoid it as well. The May islanders call the place "Wyrm's Head," and once a year they row out to picnic on the islet and fly their kites.

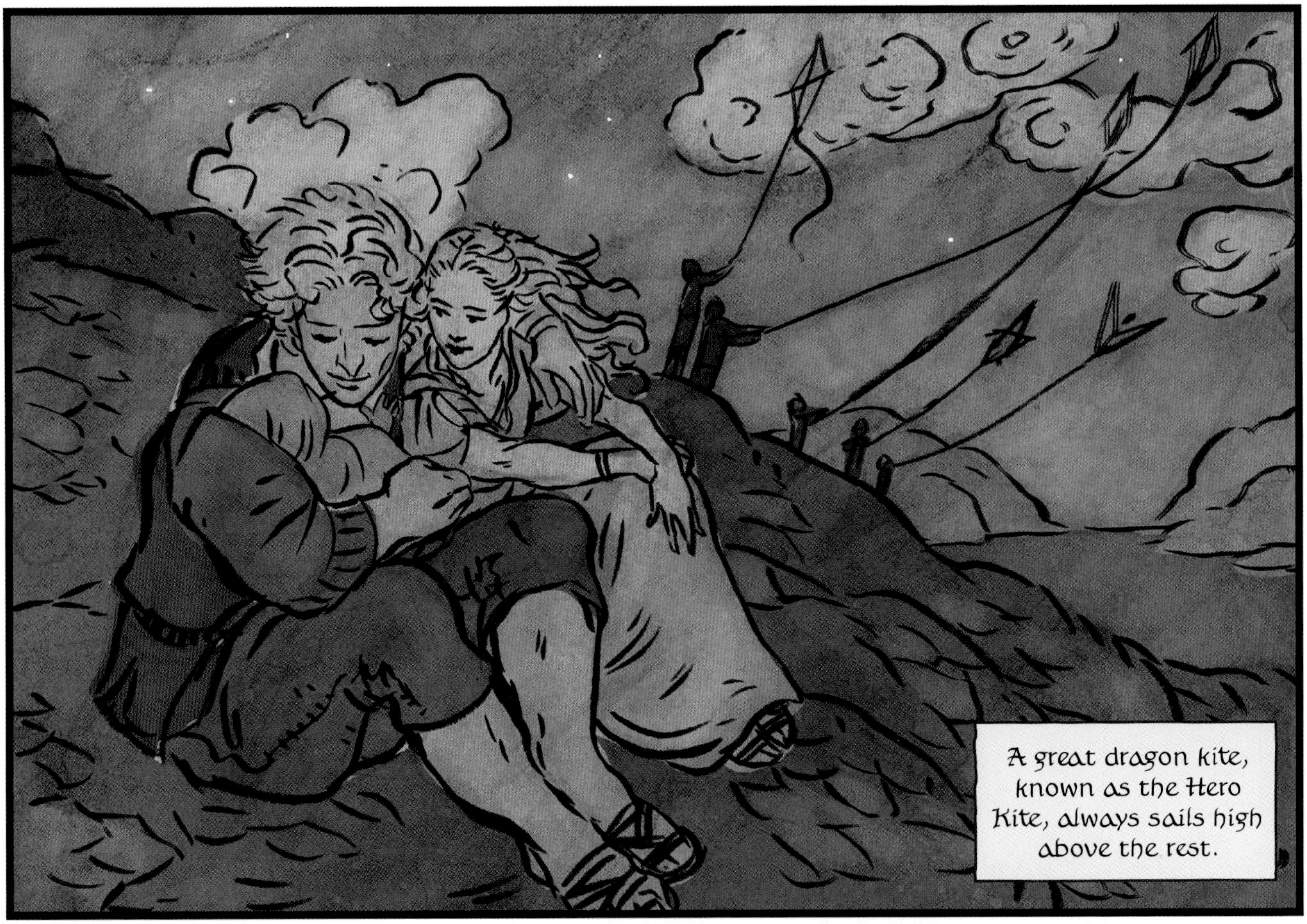
A great dragon kite, known as the Hero Kite, always sails high above the rest.

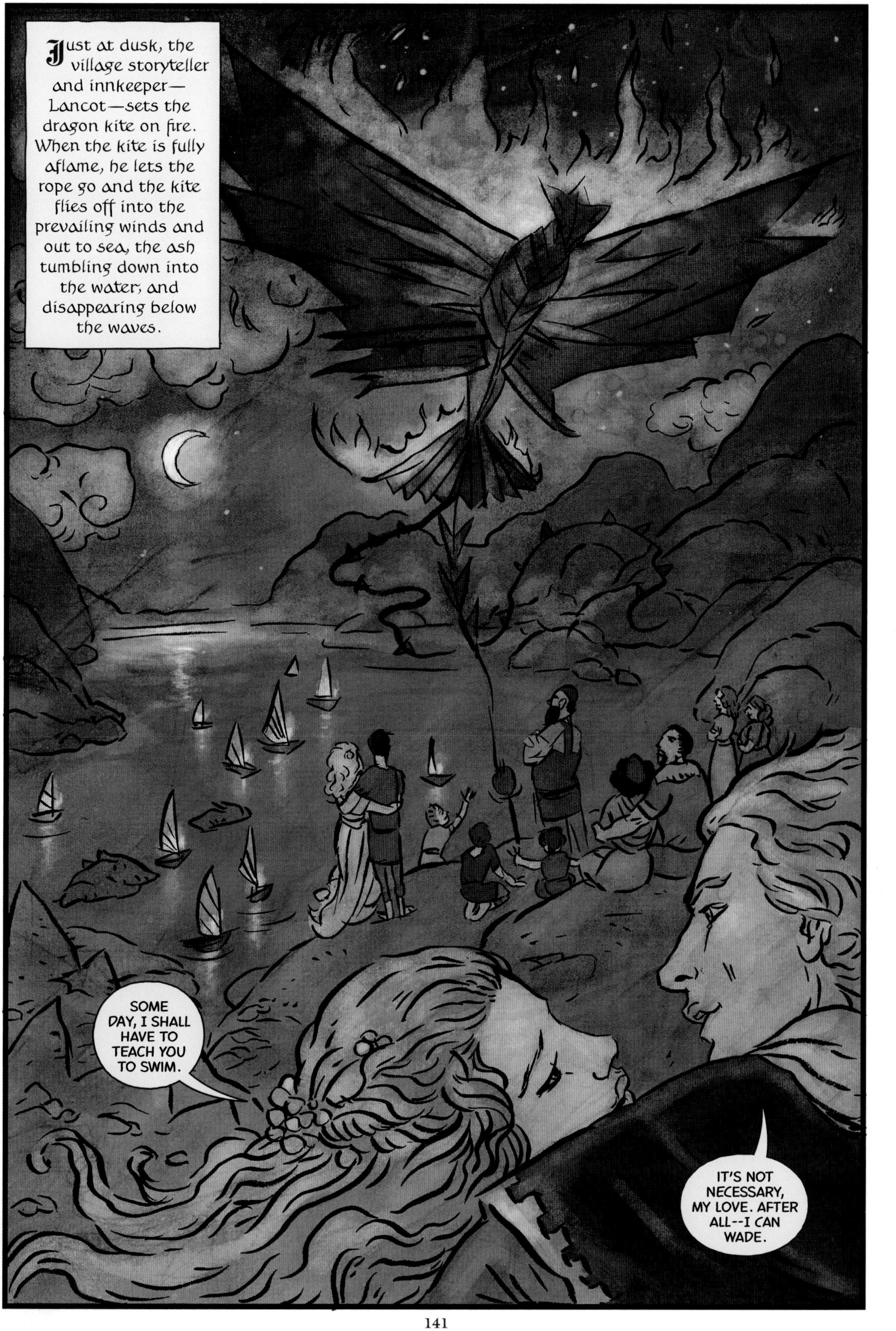
Just at dusk, the village storyteller and innkeeper—Lancot—sets the dragon kite on fire. When the kite is fully aflame, he lets the rope go and the kite flies off into the prevailing winds and out to sea, the ash tumbling down into the water, and disappearing below the waves.
SOME DAY, I SHALL HAVE TO TEACH YOU TO SWIM.
IT'S NOT NECESSARY, MY LOVE. AFTER ALL--I CAN WADE.

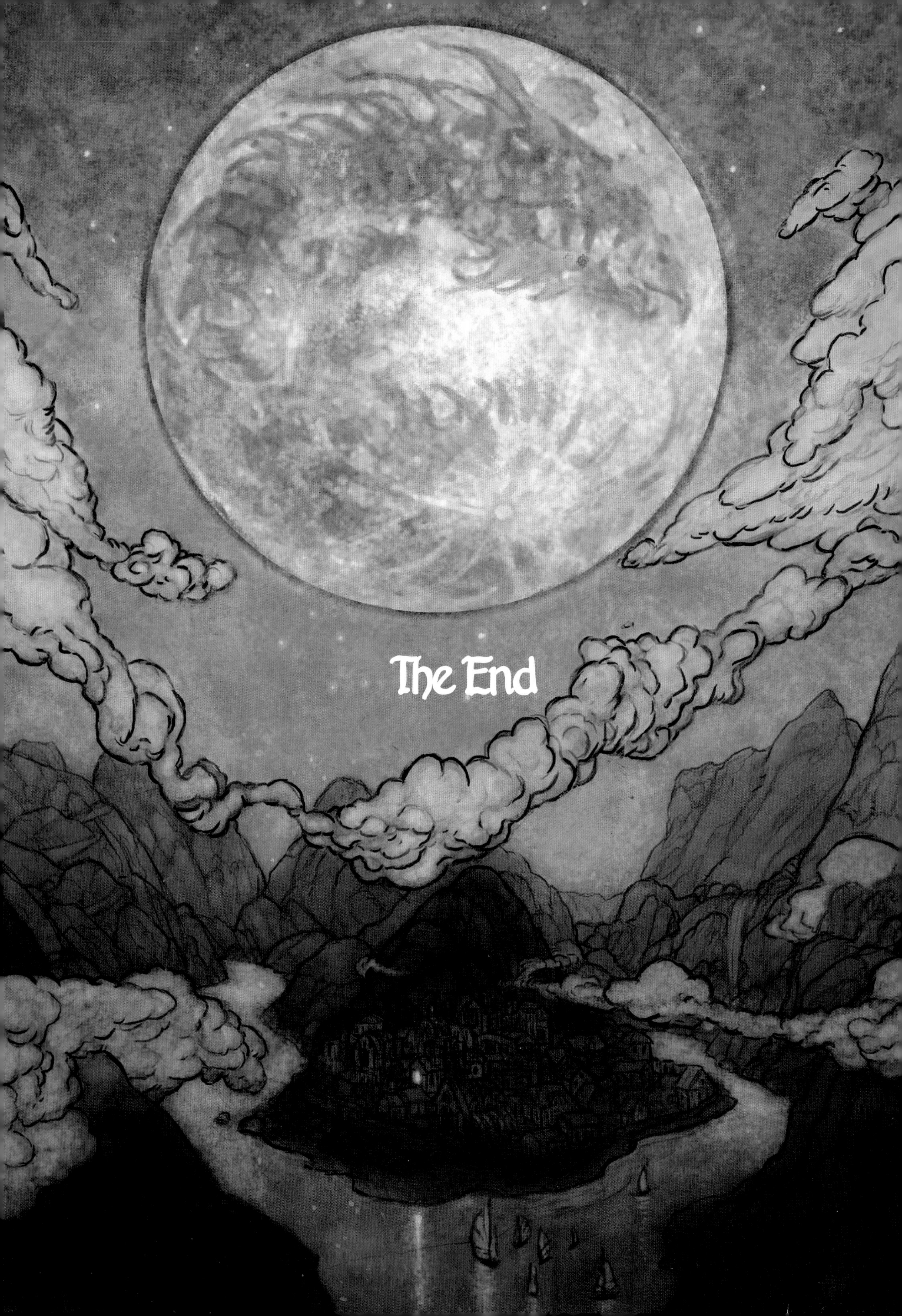
The End

Also from Dark Horse Books

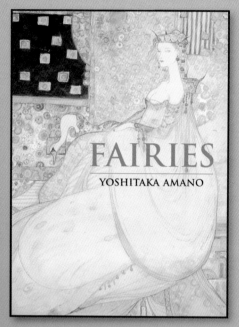

FAIRIES
YOSHITAKA AMANO

FAIRIES
Yoshitaka Amano
978-1-59582-062-4 $24.99

FEMINA
&
FAUNA
The Art of
CAMILLA
d'ERRICO
ASHLEY WOOD

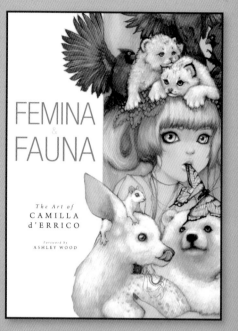

FEMINA AND FAUNA:
THE ART OF CAMILLA D'ERRICO
Camilla d'Errico
978-1-59582-583-4 $22.99

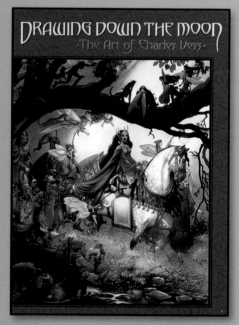

DRAWING DOWN THE MOON
·The Art of Charles Vess·

DRAWING DOWN THE MOON:
THE ART OF CHARLES VESS
Charles Vess
978-1-59307-813-3 $39.99

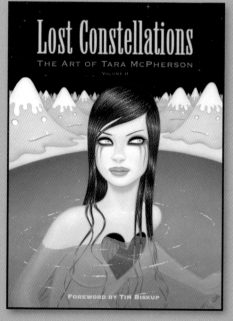

Lost Constellations
THE ART OF TARA McPHERSON
FOREWORD BY TIM BISKUP

LOST CONSTELLATIONS:
THE ART OF TARA MCPHERSON
Tara McPherson
978-1-59582-222-2 $22.99

Also from Dark Horse Books

CLOVER OMNIBUS EDITION
Story and Art by CLAMP

Clover is a gorgeous epic from Japan's *shoujo*-artist supergroup CLAMP! In a baroque, retro-tech future, Kazuhiko is a young black-ops agent pulled out of retirement to escort Sue, a mysterious waif, a military top secret, and the most dangerous person in the world.

ISBN 978-1-59582-196-6 $19.99

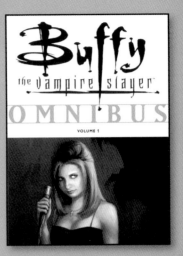

BUFFY THE VAMPIRE SLAYER OMNIBUS VOLUME 1
Written by Joss Whedon, Christopher Golden, Paul Lee, and others
Art by Paul Lee, Eric Powell, Cliff Richards, and others

The smash TV hit *Buffy the Vampire Slayer* has led to over a decade of comics at Dark Horse. This omnibus series is the ultimate compilation of the *Buffy* comics Dark Horse has published, and runs along the TV series' timeline. The definitive comics collection of all things *Buffy* starts here.

ISBN 978-1-59307-784-6 $24.99

FINDER: VOICE
Story and Art by Carla Speed McNeil

Carla Speed McNeil's Eisner Award–winning series comes to Dark Horse. In a society defined by its intricate network of clans, Rachel Grosvenor has grown up an outcast, straddling worlds. Now, her quest for admission to a highly exclusive clan sends Rachel spiraling into the dark underbelly of Anvard and a paradox that holds the key to her future: *How do you find a Finder?*

ISBN 978-1-59582-651-0 $19.99

HARLEQUIN VALENTINE
Written by Neil Gaiman
Art by John Bolton

This hardcover retelling of the *Commedia dell'arte* legend of hopeless, fawning love updates the relationship of buffoonish Harlequin and his sensible, oblivious Columbine. Consumed with love, the impulsive clown gives his heart freely, only to see it dragged about town, with a charming surprise to bend the tale in a modern direction.

ISBN 978-1-56971-620-5 $12.99

AVAILABLE AT YOUR LOCAL COMICS SHOP OR BOOKSTORE

To find a comics shop in your area, call 1-888-266-4226. For more information or to order direct, visit DarkHorse.com or call 1-800-862-0052 • Mon.–Fri. 9 a.m. to 5 p.m. Pacific Time. Prices and availability subject to change without notice.

DARK HORSE BOOKS

DarkHorse.com